HOW TO
KILL A
GUY
IN
TEN
DATES

HOW TO KILL A GUY IN TEN DATES

A Novel

Shailee Thompson

G

GALLERY BOOKS

New York   Amsterdam/Antwerp   London
Toronto   Sydney/Melbourne   New Delhi

G

Gallery Books
An Imprint of Simon & Schuster, LLC
1230 Avenue of the Americas
New York, NY 10020

Copyright © 2026 by Eeliahs Pty Ltd

Map by Tonia Composto

First Gallery Books trade paperback edition February 2026

GALLERY BOOKS and colophon are registered trademarks of Simon & Schuster, LLC

For information about special discounts for bulk purchases, please contact Simon & Schuster Special Sales at 1-866-506-1949 or business@simonandschuster.com.

The Simon & Schuster Speakers Bureau can bring authors to your live event. For more information or to book an event, contact the Simon & Schuster Speakers Bureau at 1-866-248-3049 or visit our website at www.simonspeakers.com.

Interior design by Hope Herr-Cardillo

Manufactured in the United States of America

10 9 8 7 6 5 4 3 2 1

Library of Congress Control Number: 2025946380

ISBN 978-1-6682-0671-3
ISBN 978-1-6682-0672-0 (ebook)

Let's stay in touch! Scan here to get book recommendations, exclusive offers, and more delivered to your inbox.

For the Leading Ladies and the Final Girls.
Have you guys met? I think you'll be the best of friends.

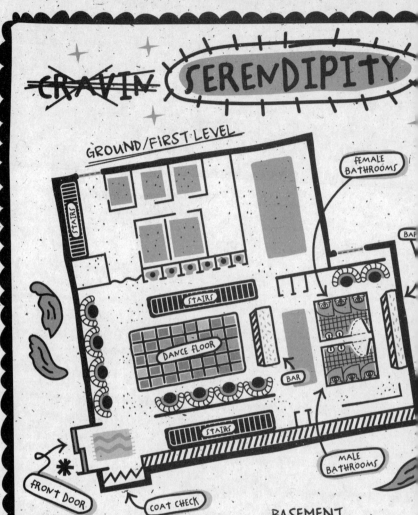

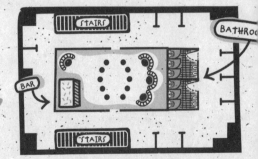

HOW TO SURVIVE A
SLASHER

1. DON'T HAVE SEX

2. ALWAYS HIDE FOR LONGER THAN
   YOU THINK YOU SHOULD

3. FIND A WEAPON

4. TURN ON THE LIGHT

5. DON'T SPLIT UP

6. WATCH YOUR BACK

7. DON'T RUN UP THE STAIRS

8. DON'T SAY "I'LL BE RIGHT BACK"

9. SOBRIETY EQUALS SURVIVAL

10. DOWN DOESN'T MEAN DEAD—
    DOUBLE TAP

CHAPTER 1

"I suppose I think about murder more than anyone really should. I am constantly amazed by its sheer power to alter and define our lives."

—Not *The Holiday*

All's Fair in Love and Gore: The Intersection of Romantic Comedies and Slasher Films in the Late Twentieth and Early Twenty-First Centuries

While slasher and rom-com films may draw harsher criticism than other genres, the sociocultural impact of these types of films cannot be understated. There's a reason they both have a pull at the box office. A reason why, despite the turbulent swing of audience taste and film trends over the years, for every *Halloween* that's been produced, there's been a Julia Roberts–fronted "will they/won't they" to match (see appendix 1).

From a behavioral standpoint it could be argued that slashers and rom-coms maintain their permanency within the cinema landscape by the way their predictable outcomes appeal to basic instinctual human needs. Coincidentally (or perhaps not), the textbook endings within each genre align with consecutive stages of Maslow's hierarchy of needs: slashers—safety and security; rom-coms—love and belonging (see appendix 2). Put simply, these films give us something we all inherently want: a life to live and a reason to live it.

However, the inherent structural similarities between these two ostensibly opposed genres suggest far wider applications could be obtained from not just their individual study but a complementary investigation. A more in-depth consideration of these films reveals that they follow an analogous format, one that contains certain rules. If the protagonists follow those rules, they win. In slashers, they live. In rom-coms, they find love. If they don't follow the rules, they lose. For slashers, that means getting decapitated in some gruesome, yet satisfying, way (often while topless). For a rom-com, losing leads to crying in the rain outside an unrequited love's house, doomed to be alone and sexless forever. Either of these scenarios could apply to countless classics within the slasher and rom-com repertoire of the late twentieth century. While these films are dismissed in some circles for an apparent lack of depth and a heavy reliance on tropes, audiences continue to come back for more.

Consider this dissertation a genealogical study of slashers and rom-coms; distant cousins stuck in the same generational cycle. Influenced and precast by their predecessors. Destined to repeat the tropes and clichés of their pa—

"I just don't see what point you're trying to make here, Jamie." Laurie lifts her gaze from the computer screen, russet-brown eyes squinting over to where I'm perched on the breakfast bar in my garlic bread–patterned blanket hoodie. I've been watching her read the introduction of my dissertation like I'm Norman Bates, but instead of observing her through a peephole it's from behind the lenses of my blue light glasses.

"I think you need to choose one," she adds.

I squint back at her.

"Choose one what?"

There's a slight pull in my gut that tells me I know what she's going to suggest, but then my soft little heart assures me that she's my friend—my best friend ever since we met in our Intro to Cinema Studies tutorial at NYU during the first semester of our freshman year. And she wouldn't be so cruel and thoughtless and just plain fucking *wron*—

"Slasher *or* rom-com."

The offended, strangled scream that escapes my mouth wouldn't be out of place in Snyder's *Dawn of the Dead* remake. Considering how many hours of sleep I missed to work on that opening page, I could double as an undead extra, too.

"That's the whole *point* of my research, Laurie!"

"I just don't think they go together."

"I'm not saying they *go* together. I'm saying their intrinsic purpose within the collective discipline of film and their formulaic structures are the *same*."

At least that was how I sold the idea—verbatim—to my adviser.

She turns her eyes back to the screen, tilts her head.

"I don't see it."

"Of course you wouldn't," I growl, pointing an almond-shaped, beige gel-tipped nail at her. I got them done yesterday, and I hope they help prove my point. "Because you're an uninspired, documentary-loving, elitist piece of shit."

She turns in her chair and points a longer, pointier, fully natural red nail back at me. She had them done this morning, and their effect cannot be denied.

"I am *not* elitist."

She doesn't argue about the other parts. We've been friends for too long, lived together in an apartment so small every bowel movement, orgasm, and opinion has been shared, willingly or unwillingly.

This is just a normal Tuesday afternoon.

"*Laurieeeee*," I whine, dropping my head into my fleece-covered lap. The heatless curling ribbon I've wrapped my blond hair into jostles around my ears as I brace my feet against the bar stool to avoid toppling over. I don't want to add injury to her insult.

I've been slaving away on the groundwork of my dissertation for a year. My first draft is due in a month, and she doesn't get it. Granted, Laurie's deepest desire is to spend her years making films that document aspects of *real life*. She has no interest in grand romantic gestures or gratuitous violence. Her film preferences extend to an in-depth expository of the daily lives of nomadic sheep farmers and, I don't know . . . paint drying?

"I like the title!" she says, and that's probably the closest I'll get to consolation. Laurie's not really a demonstrative person. Last year, when my parents called to tell me Cujo, the King Charles spaniel we'd had since I was twelve, had died at the tragically young age of fourteen, she gave me a firm handshake. Surprisingly, it did make me feel better.

"*All's Fair in Love and Gore: The Intersection of Romantic Comedies and Slasher Films in the Late Twentieth and Early Twenty-First Centuries* really speaks to the elitist piece of shit in me."

"Well, if they're handing out PhDs based on titles, I—"

"Baby girl," she says like a warning, and it takes everything in me to keep my lips fashioned in a pout when she uses the pet name we have for each other. We adopted it after I made her watch *365 Days* as payback for having to sit through the nomadic sheep farmer documentary. Attempts at making Stockholm syndrome sexy aside, what started off as a sardonic joke has evolved into an enduring term of endearment. It's the closest thing I'll get to overt affection from a woman whose general demeanor could rival the impenetrable surface of Crystal Lake at the end of *Friday the 13th*.

"You need a break."

"I need to *write*."

"You're ahead of your Gantt Chart."

She points to where it lies to the side of my laptop, as if I haven't memorized each little row of achievement like I memorized Kat's speech in *10 Things I Hate About You*.

"Exactly!" I say. "I have all my research, my outline, my *title*. I *know* what I want to say, I should just be able to write it."

"Well maybe, as an 'elitist piece of shit,' *I'm* not the right person to be reading it." With that she scoots out of the chair and heads for the refrigerator, making a wide berth around the counter when I fling my foot out at her. She opens the fridge and inserts her head into the top shelf as she asks, "When do you see Jordan?"

Romero. My adviser. Not related to the Father of the Zombie Film, but certainly wishes he was.

"Friday."

"Then this seems like a fantastic concern to raise in that conversation." Her voice sounds tinny in the confines of the fridge, and I have half a mind to swivel around, place my bare foot on her bony ass, and Spartan-kick her into a container of leftover chow mein for being so logical.

It's not that I don't believe in my work. I do.

I could talk about slashers and rom-coms for *hours*. Longer.

If the makers of *Saw* need an inventive form of torture for a new installment, just stick me in a dirty bathroom with a chained morally ambiguous gentleman and he'd end up cutting his own leg off to escape one of my lectures on how Nora Ephron was a visionary.

I *know* I know what I'm talking about. But *what if?* creeps in as easily as a masked killer at a summer camp. My brain forgets I'm perfectly capable of writing about a topic I have spent the majority of my adult life (and even before) studying and researching and unpacking.

Laurie's right, though. There's no point dwelling on a problem that has no hope of being solved until I can engage in some academic repartee with my adviser. She knows she's right, too, but I don't want her to get a big head.

"Stop being smart," I mutter at her sweatpant-covered ass.

"Stop being dramatic," echoes from the refrigerator.

I heave the most dramatic of dramatic sighs, then grin when she backs out of the fridge with a can of passion fruit sparkling water, holding it to her heart and widening her eyes. The pout is a nice touch, too. It's the last one, and because I'm not an elitist piece of shit I let her have it.

"What time do we have to be there tonight?" I ask as Laurie takes the sacred last can to the couch and turns on the TV, switching it from Netflix to the news. Yeah, she still *watches* the news. I think it's a guilty pleasure, the closest thing to fiction she'll view willingly.

"Cocktail hour begins at seven. Dates start at eight. So be ready by . . . six thir— No, six fifteen? Google Maps predicts it could take anywhere from thirty to forty minutes to get to the bar from Bed-Stuy."

"You and Google Maps," I muse, jumping off the counter and sliding into the seat in front of my laptop. "If it were a person, we wouldn't even need to go tonight." With a few taps of the keys, I save and close the apparently pointless beginning pages of my dissertation, pulling the screen down in time to see Laurie lift a middle finger in my direction.

"This is as much for you as it is for me," she calls over her shoulder, keeping her focus squarely on the newscaster who fills the frame of our TV. "Consider this your allotted 'popping the thesis bubble and reconnecting with the real world' time for the week. You can't spend every hour with masked murderers and men who get all starry-eyed every time a girl trips in a nice dress."

I mean, I *could* spend every hour doing that, but she's got a point. And I've already paid for the ticket. We're going speed dating. It's not our first singles event. After a particularly heinous nonstarter situationship a few months ago, Laurie went down a Google rabbit hole incited by her own dating app fatigue. She loves a statistic more than I love a well-executed jump scare, and when the numbers showed that *a lot* of people in our generation were as fed up with swiping as her ("Seventy-eight percent of users, Jamie!"), I accepted her proposal to attend at least one in-person social event a month. It was an easy decision, since I'm vehemently against apps (it seems more likely you'll get murdered rather than find love through Tinder these days). And while speed dating definitely has a kind of dated, nineties feel to it, I've had fun at the other events we've gone to in the past. They've never led to actual dates—especially not after we went to a film trivia night, and I got a little too passionate during the horror category—but I like the idea of a real-life meet-cute. I like the idea of locking eyes with someone and thinking: *Oh, it's* you. I like it a lot.

I just haven't seen it outside of the movies yet.

The newscaster changes their angle upon the completion of the weather report and the inset image flips to a story about a pretty woman around our age who was found with her throat slit.

I don't even blink. It's not the first time this has happened this year. The banner slowly crawling across the screen with the words "Brooklyn Serial Killer" is evidence enough of that. There's been four murders in about as many months, and now Casey Langenkamp is number five. The photos pulled from her social media depict a sweet-faced twentysomething who wouldn't look out of place on a poster with Glen Powell. She fits the usual victim profile that incites fervid, yet fleeting, public interest: blond, petite, pretty, loved by all, and of course she lit up the room when she walked in.

All the classic markers of someone who is destined to be murdered and discarded like the rose petals that have been found surrounding each of the bodies. There's a clip of a stern-looking woman—the lower third at the bottom of the screen identifies her as a police captain—confirming that the police believe the murders are connected, and then the report closes with the newscaster encouraging women to:

- Be vigilant when out and about.
- Ensure you share your location with someone you trust.
- Avoid dark, isolated, or obstructed areas if walking alone.

And my favorite:

- *Trust your instincts.*

Because, duh, if you're a woman and you happen to find yourself in a situation where you end up murdered, you really do have to consider the part that *you* played in getting to that point. Things like murder don't just happen to women. It's because your *instincts* were off. As if every woman's intuition isn't a finely tuned divining rod for identifying danger. The reality is you can't avoid that danger if someone really wants to manhandle you into its path.

The reporter allows a moment of grim eye contact with the camera before, with a head tilt and lip quirk, they move on to some "good news" segment to counteract the brutal murder coverage. It's a stark change of tone. One accepted and extended by Laurie when she bends her head over the couch, a pensive look on her pretty little face as she asks, "So, what are you wearing tonight?"

CHAPTER 2

"I came here tonight because when you realize you want to spend the rest of your life killing somebody, you want the rest of your life to start as soon as possible."

—Not *When Harry Met Sally*

After a montage-worthy rotation of outfits, and two breakdowns that end with Laurie and me agreeing the fashion industry is a sick, twisted terror on society, I end up wearing the first dress I tried on. It's my favorite: *Pretty Woman* red with sheer rose petal–like sleeves and a square neckline that—teamed with a well-fitted underwire bra—makes my boobs look absolutely fantastic. When I did a little twirl in front of the only full-length mirror in our apartment before we left, it flared out above my knees in a way that rivals *Dirty Dancing*.

Of course, it might turn out to be too dressy for an event whose dress code consisted of a bullet point list for the men and a vague "cocktail attire" command for the women. Of course, I bought it on sale, and even then, cursed its existence each time my credit card bill turned up for the next few months. Of course, it's the first week of November and the coat I have to wear completely dampens the effect of the dress. But that doesn't matter. Because it makes me feel confident and sexy and like I can hold my own through one hundred minutes of anonymous dating—even if that little self-doubting voice was the one that made me take it off the first time.

If watching rom-coms has taught me anything, it's that you don't dim yourself for fear of shining too bright. You wear the dress, you sing out loud, you take the leap. And if watching slashers has taught me anything, it's that you take chances whenever you can. Run out the door, grab the knife, double tap the killer in the head with a sawed-off shotgun. That's why I do my makeup like a Hitchcock lead and pretend it wasn't a fluke when my hair falls over my shoulders in bouncy honey-blond curls after I release it from the clutches of the curling ribbon. Even if tonight is a bust, Laurie and I will walk off arm in arm in the direction of the nearest gyros purveyor, giggling like we're freshman in college again as we detail the highs and lows of our round-robin dating experience.

New York traffic decides to play nice, but as we make our way across Brooklyn, I wonder if my meticulous roommate has typed in the wrong address. The route becomes familiar in that hazy déjà vu kind of way, and when I look at Laurie, I catch her eyes narrowing in recognition as we get closer and closer to our destination.

When she steps out of the Uber before me, looking stunning in a black, slippery silk jumpsuit that moonlights as a vest and wide-legged pantsuit, she props her fists on her hips, turning her head to survey the street.

"Huh . . ." she says as I slide myself off the leather seat and step onto the sidewalk carefully. The cocktail attire dress code knocked out any chance of wearing comfortable shoes, thus Laurie and I are both wearing heels that were designed for sitting rather than walking.

"We've been here before," she says confidently, and it draws my attention away from watching our Uber take off down the street. The taillights look like two glowing eyes retreating into the darkness and the visibility of our surroundings becomes highly dependent on the dim light of the streetlamps that curve up and over where we idle on the sidewalk. A brief invasive thought of how they look like the metal claws of Freddy Krueger's gloves crosses my mind before I fully focus on the building in front of us.

"Really?" I ask. "I think we'd remember a singles thing at a club."

The other events we've been to have been in art studios, bars, restaurants: warmly lit, open plan, first-floor spaces with large windows so you can gaze out at the street if your date is boring. But the building in front of us looks like it used to be a warehouse or something. It looms large over the dark, empty street. The neighboring clubs are closed, in stasis until Friday, and while this whole street would've been bustling on the weekend, right now, on a Tuesday night, it just looks like a ghost town.

"No, I mean, I feel like I just stepped back in time."

I squint at the two heavy metal doors—one open, one closed—in front of us. The sign above them, a romantic tangle of glowing blue letters that spell out "Serendipity," is the only one that's lit on the whole street. I'd remember a name like that. Cocking my head to the side, I consider the double doors. There *is* something about them that rings a bell, though.

"It *is* familiar in that fuzzy 'this place is the reason I don't drink Kamikazes anymore' kind of way," I say, and that is the prompt Laurie needs. She clicks her fingers rapidly at the sign as if the name is on the tip of her tongue, before pointing and exclaiming, "Cravin'!"

I'm almost knocked over by a wave of memories flooding in at the name of an earlier iteration of the club. Very fuzzy memories. Memories of strong drinks, bad kisses, glass crunching under shoes, and deep and meaningful conversations with strangers in the bathroom.

"Cravinnnnnnn'!" I reply like it's a call and response. We haven't been here in years, but this was *the* place when we were twenty-one. For a few months, at least. Back before we lived together. Before I started my master's and Laurie got her first of many internships, and weekends became less about going out and more about discussing whether pursuing careers in the arts and academia were reasonable life choices.

"I wonder if it still looks the same inside," she muses.

"Surely not."

The thing that was such a draw about Cravin' was all the spaces. Not "space." *Spaces.* The building must have been converted from a factory—one with offices and maybe even lodging for workers—because across the three levels of the club, there were hallways that led to dead ends, rooms with love seats, alcoves with booths, and a whole range of other kinds of hidey-holes. Aside from the huge, open space of the dance floor, the rest of the building—the perimeter of the club on the ground level, the bar in the basement, and the mezzanine on the top level—was like a mouse maze. It was the highlight of a drunk girl's night and the best way to avoid the attentions of a guy who refused to take a hint—or find a covert spot to hook up with a guy who was able to take a very different kind of hint.

"Let's go check it out." Laurie grins at me, grabbing the sleeve of my coat and pulling me toward the entrance. Once we make it inside, I realize the cool blue signage above the doors was a ruse because the interior of Serendipity is red.

Like, *Suspiria* red. *Carrie* red. The iconic river of blood spewing out of an elevator in Stanley Kubrick's seminal masterpiece *The Shining* red.

Cravin' was all black and brushed metal and slick minimalist design.

Serendipity looks like the set designer of *Moulin Rouge!* took LSD and cleaned out every velvet and gas lamp supplier in the state.

The coat check is still in the same place and a fist pops up from beneath the counter like a hand out of a grave as we step into the entrance. There's a white charging cord trapped between the clenched fingers, an exclamation of "Fucking *finally*," and then a head appears. A triumphant smile stretches across the face of a woman a few years younger than us before she catches sight of Laurie and me on the other side of the counter.

"Oh, sorry." She flushes, holding the charging cord to her chest like the precious treasure it is. "I've been looking for this for an hour. Somehow our normal cleaning crew was canceled this morning, and whatever last-minute contractors they were able to get in have messed everything up. I can't find *anything*." She untangles the cable before plugging it into the iPad in front of her. "Sorry again. Are you here for our speed date tonight?"

"Yeah, we are," I answer. "Jamie Prescott and Laurie Hamilton."

"IDs?"

She gives them a passing glance when we offer them, more preoccupied with finding our names on her screen and quickly ticking them off with a tap of her finger.

"I just have to check that you know you've booked our hetero event for the twenty-five to thirty-five age bracket. We have a queer speed date, same age bracket, taking place *next* Tuesday. I know the site can be confusing, some people just see the age bracket—"

"Tragically, we are both straight," Laurie says drily, and I can't help but snort.

The woman's pinched face softens in amusement. "Can't relate. Though all the men who have come through so far seem nice. Normal."

Whatever *that* means.

"Let's get you checked in before you go downstairs."

She takes our coats, our phones, our handbags, and Laurie's smartwatch. This was what attracted Laurie to this event in the first place.

Apparently, taking away our devices and belongings encourages more robust conversation by removing the temptation to glance at your notifications, or dig around in your purse, avoiding eye contact. It seems like overkill, but I'm capable of a digital detox for a couple of hours. I watch our phones go into marked bags with the same number as our coats before they're placed into a lockbox, the coat check attendant detailing the particulars of our night as she bullies our coats onto hangers and carries them to a rack at the back of the room.

Ten men, ten women, ten minutes per date and just a handful of rules:

- No digital devices.
- Don't discuss your day job ("a person is more than their profession").
- Keep it light and polite.
- Move on when the bell rings.

It's easy enough to remember, and as an academic and former teacher's pet, I can follow a rule like my life depends on it.

"The ladies will have cocktail hour downstairs in the basement bar, while the gentlemen have been directed up to the mezzanine bar. Your host, Marion, will be available for any questions before the men are escorted down to meet you. As you know, your drinks are included in the ticket price, so please drink responsibly." The harried tone of her voice and the distant look in her eyes tells me these instructions are part of her muscle memory, but I don't hold it against her when she adds, a little wearily, "This is the first time we've hosted an event here and we're a little understaffed. Our security guy is running late, so until he gets here, let Marion or one of the bartenders know if you feel uncomfortable at any time."

With that warning, she gestures to the long, thin staircase that runs up along the wall to the mezzanine and down to the basement. It's just wide enough to allow guys ample opportunities to grab on to a female waist to "get past" on their journey up or down a level, and there's another set on the other side of the club. Each set of stairs makes the shape of a giant arrow, the one closest to us pointing to the front of the building—and the only exit I remember in this three-floor adult playground—while the other is a point in the opposite direction.

I glance toward the entry to the dance floor, and of course it's empty, but when I lift my gaze to the mezzanine, I see movement. It's just far away enough, and the lighting dim enough, that I can make out the silhouettes of tonight's bachelors as they socialize in front of the bar. They circle around up there, looking down at the open space like it's a gladiator ring and the entertainment is going to burst onto the floor and draw blood for their amusement.

"Let's go," Laurie says as I'm staring into the darkness, giving me a swift tap on the butt that sends me in the direction of the staircase. I hand her my coat check ticket to keep safe in the pocket of her jumpsuit, glancing back up at the mezzanine just before we dip below ground level. It's then I catch a glimpse of a shadow leaning against the railing, the dark shape of a head dipped in our direction. It's a blink-and-miss moment, but as I walk down the stairs, the bottom of my shoes sticking to the thin coat of dried alcohol that coats the steps like varnish, a prickle breaks out across the back of my neck. The shiver is followed by a brief clench in my stomach, an anxious pulse I'm used to experiencing at the beginning of these phone-free events, when my brain wants to flick through all the bad scenarios of how tonight could play out in some misguided attempt at self-preservation. I choose to ignore it as I follow Laurie down to the basement level.

After all . . . What's the worst that could happen?

CHAPTER 3

*"This is the type of girl he wants to murder! This is what I
need to become to be slaughtered!"*

—Not *Legally Blonde*

$\mathcal{T}$alk about overkill.

If I thought the first level of the club was bathed in red, it's
nothing compared to the basement beneath it. It's like we've walked
into a bloody beating heart from the way the flickering electric can-
dles within the gas lamps glow against the velvet curtains. They make
the walls look like they're pulsing. The booths on the right side give
the room an atrium-like curve, and to our left—favoring a longer,
more ventricle-like shape—is the bar. A lone bartender lifts his head
in greeting when we walk in, in the middle of pouring a drink for a
woman who has her back to us. Ten tables are set up in the middle
of the room, evenly spaced around a small dance floor. The seating
arrangement is like two parentheses, leaving a mingling space in the
middle where five other women are holding drinks and chatting.

Laurie and I make a beeline for the bar, but before we can get too
close to any kind of social lubricant, a voice behind us brings me to a halt.

"Ladies!"

A woman in her fifties with a dark bob and even darker eyes pushes off the booth closest to the door, clipboard in one hand and a practiced smile on her face.

"Welcome to our event. I'm Marion, your host for this evening. May I have your names?"

When we provide them, she refers to the list on her clipboard and nods like we've given the appropriate secret password. She flips the list over the top of the clipboard and turns it toward me, revealing a sheet of blank Hello, My Name Is stickers. Most of them are missing, and when I glance over at the other women, I spy the red-and-white tags marring their carefully coordinated outfits.

"If you could just write your names on a sticker and place it somewhere visible, we can get your night started!" Marion says in an upbeat tone, and I take the clipboard and the pen she seems to pull from thin air. Once Laurie and I both have our name tags stuck to our chests, Marion jumps right into a practiced monologue.

"Please get yourselves a *drink.*" She says the word like they're going on her tab and the cost of the ticket wasn't ramped up to ensure that even with the most dedicated of drinkers the event organizers are not going to be anywhere near out of pocket. Her shoulders shimmy back and forth when she says, "*Mingle.* Our cocktail hour gives you a chance to settle in and *relax* and meet some new friends among the women before you find something *more* with one of the men."

She winks at us, shoulders rising in a "what a time to be alive" movement that draws an assuaging smile from me and a look of distaste from Laurie.

"I'll let you know when we're ready for your dates to come and join you. We have some *very* handsome men lined up for you tonight and they are *eager* to meet you," she says before turning to the entryway where another woman has appeared.

"Why are the hosts *always* weird and overly happy?" Laurie mutters as we restart our path to the bar. "It's psychotic."

I can't help but laugh. "Maybe her positivity is the price you have to pay so you can do what you love: grill a man for ten minutes without him being able to leave."

"It is one of my favorite pastimes," she says with a shrug, her glossed lips pursing in amusement as she asks lightly, "Should I open with politics or religion?"

I snort just as we hit the edge of the bar, and the woman who's been there since we walked in turns at the sound of our arrival, her eyes shifting warily between me and Laurie before they settle on me. I wait for a shy smile or some sustained eye contact that usually kick-starts the social niceties that become commonplace in environments such as this, but I don't get it. What I get is her dark brown eyes flicking to the top of my head and then performing a quick once-over that ends in her plump cupid's bow lip curling up just slightly. I catch a glimpse of her name tag—Billie—in clear, though somewhat scratchy, writing before she pushes off from the bar and stalks away.

The interaction—if we can call it that—is brief, but that doesn't stop the self-conscious thoughts from arising, popping up stronger than Michael Myers after being shot six times in the chest. I glance down at my dress.

"Do I look okay?"

"What?" Laurie asks, and when the bartender turns back from cleaning up the last drink he made, I see why her attention has been drawn elsewhere. He's got a cute pair of glasses, some seriously well-styled dark waves, and black suspenders over a starched white button-up shirt. When he grins at her and she instinctively leans into the bar, I know there's no way she saw the look I think I got from Billie.

Laurie has two distinct types when it comes to men. Hot, clean-cut nerds or lumberjacks. There's no in-between. I'm just lucky the bartender falls into the former category, and she's merely distracted. She gets major tunnel vision when a man gives off wood-chopping vibes. It's been that way since college, when she was involved in a "will they/won't they" situation with a guy in her Media Ethics class (whom she maintains to this day she always despised).

And that's why, after Laurie asks for an espresso martini and I hold up two fingers to double the order, I have to repeat, "Do I look okay?"

I hold my arms out from my side, drawing Laurie's attention away from the hot-nerd bartender as he free-pours vodka into a shaker.

"That's a stupid question, baby girl."

"Not if I was just on the receiving end of some pretty severe stink eye."

Laurie allows herself one glance toward where I subtly direct my head in Billie's direction. My friend considers the odds and then shrugs in that unaffected way only someone who represses a lot of emotions can do.

"She probably just has resting bitch face."

Maybe.

I turn my gaze over to where Billie has situated herself in relation to the other women. She isn't looking back at me. She's standing on the fringes, not quite next to a redhead with a Julia Roberts smile and a brunette with an enviable blowout who are engaged in a gestural conversation.

"*That* didn't feel like resting bitch face, that felt like—"

I mimic the look, and Laurie nods, picking up the espresso martini slid in front of her and saying sagely, "A stink eye."

I frown down at my dress again as the bartender places my own martini in front of me. "Maybe I should've—"

"No." Laurie cuts me off in a tone that leaves no room for argument. She isn't being complimentary when she says, "You look amazing." Then she turns with her drink and surveys the room, the bartender forgotten now that my self-esteem is on the line. Six other women stand in the space. "Honestly, everyone looks amazing."

She's not wrong. All the women in the room have interpreted the cocktail attire dress code in their own way, but they all look fantastic. Laurie herself looks like she'd grind a guy's testicles to dust in the palm of her hand and he'd thank her for the privilege of it. Next to my flirty, floaty dress, we live up to the stereotype of odd-couple female friends. Her dark features, the long, lithe, ballerina lines of her body, her interest in the secret lives of sea moss farmers—it's all a foil to my melanin-deficient characteristics, my curves that multiple online tests have told me are considered "theatrical romantic," a term that Laurie said could double as a definition for my general demeanor, and my preference for any media that isn't boring as shit.

"If you want me to smack a bitch, I'll need at least two more of these."

Laurie's offer draws my attention away from the other women in the room. Her glass is poised at her lips, her gaze locked on mine, and the speed at which she drinks her cocktail is entirely dependent on my answer. I raise my glass to my lips and take a tentative sip. It is *strong*. Like "Jason Voorhees knocking a person's head off with a single punch" strong, and that's why I say, "Yes to the espresso martinis—"

I glance back at Billie. She still has that unimpressed expression on her face, her lip is still curled up, but maybe she does just have one of those faces.

"No to spilling blood this early in the night," I conclude.

Laurie takes a small—and therefore appropriate—sip of her drink before muttering, "You're no fun anymore."

With that we move over to the other women who've made small pockets of conversation. A Kate Hudson blonde in a cute pink knit dress spots us heading toward the mingling area and greets us with a smile, angling her body out so we can join her and her friend—aka a *normal* way to react to a stranger at a social event. Laurie and I slip into the fold, nursing our drinks as we make introductions.

"I'm Colette," she says warmly, and I'm glad she does. Even with the surreptitious glance at her name tag, I can't decipher the loose, loopy cursive she's used to fill the white space of the sticker. I do spot a heart after what I now know is an "e," but that's about it.

"Dani," the woman next to her says, playing with the ends of her light brown, mid-nineties Meg Ryan pixie cut like it's new, before catching herself and smoothing down her name tag instead. Her name is written in neat block letters with a cute, simple smiley face taking up the final third of the space.

I compliment Dani on her blue dress, she says she likes my hair. Colette asks how Laurie and I know each other, and we find out they both came alone but buddied up when they arrived at the same time. That's all it takes.

Maintaining the flow of the conversation is easy and our circle of four slowly starts to expand. First to join us is the brunette with the blowout—Jennifer—who pauses next to me on her way back from the bar. Her hand comes up in a "wait" gesture that puts me on the defensive for a second before she states, "Can I just say, I *love* your dress!"

The comment warrants an earnest thank-you from me and a smug "told you so" look from Laurie before Colette continues talking about how she can't keep a succulent alive. That lures in a new arrival, a dark-skinned woman named Nia, who chimes in with, "I'm going to change your life with two words: 'soil drainage.'"

After that, different exclamations like "That's because she's a Pisces stellium," "It's just rebranded populism," and "Me too! But my doctor told me to just go back on the pill" act as a siren call to the other women in the room. By the time the last woman arrives, the boundaries of our groups have bled into one another until we're just one big circle of voices juggling way too many topics that get louder as we move onto our second and third drinks of the evening.

Marion has to clap her hands together, calling out a few "Ladies!" to garner our attention when it gets closer to eight. Not that I'd know what time it is. It's not like clocks are high on the list of necessities when it comes to outfitting a club, and not for the first time since we've been here, I find myself looking around for my purse when I forget it's locked in a box upstairs.

"I'm sure you've all been sharing what kind of man you'd love to meet tonight!" Marion croons when we quiet down, shooting a wink at no one in particular as we stand shoulder to shoulder in the middle of the room.

In the last hour, I've had conversations ranging from appropriate indoor plant care to book recommendations. At no point did the conversation turn to the reason why we're *actually* here.

As if she can read my mind, Laurie muses out the corner of her mouth, "We were supposed to be talking about the men?"

I can't help the sound of amusement that leaves my lips before I press them tightly together on a warning look from Marion.

"*Tonight*, you ladies will stay at your designated table and the gentlemen will rotate between you. Each of your ten dates will run for ten minutes, and a bell"—she turns to a silver call bell on the table next to her and taps it—"will ring when it's time for them to move on. Once you get to your table, you will see match cards for you to keep track of your suitors. I will provide each of the men with one of their own when they join us. The names are already there in the correct order for each of you, but everyone has name stickers, so you won't have to refer to the cards during your date. Please refrain from filling in the card until *after* your date has left the table. We don't want anyone's feelings getting hurt. There will be a fifteen-minute bathroom and bar break after your fifth date at the halfway point, and we welcome you to stay for half an hour of mingling after the final date. At the end of the evening, I will collect your cards and contact you tomorrow with any compatible matches. Who knows?" She performs that same shoulder raise from before and says conspiratorially, "Tonight, you could find your *perfect* match."

I hazard a look at Laurie, who merely performs a brief eye narrow before cutting an amused glance my way. I have to look away from her so I don't make another sound that will gain Marion's ire.

It's not that serious. This night, these dates.

Laurie was the one who wanted us to come tonight as part of our pact, but the chances of either of us meeting the love of our life over the next few hours are slim to none. So that's why we haven't been theorizing about the dates. It's why I'm mentally debating whether to stick to the plan of having gyros after this or trying out the new Korean place a few blocks from our apartment. I'm not thinking about whether one of the men I meet tonight is going to turn out to be my "Oh, it's *you*" person.

Marion wraps up her talk with table assignments, directions to the bathrooms on both the basement and first levels, and encouragement to freshen our drinks while she goes upstairs to retrieve the men. When everyone gravitates toward the bar, Laurie bumps her hip into mine.

"What's on your mind?"

It's only right that I'm honest. "What we're going to eat after this."

"Gyros, obviously." Then a look crosses her face that she usually reserves for when she's choosing between a boring documentary on wind turbines or an equally boring documentary on hydroelectric turbines. "Halloumi . . . or fried eggplant if they have it."

"I'm gonna need meat," I reply distractedly as I watch Marion dart out of the room, calling over her shoulder that everyone should start making their way to their designated table. Mine's on the left side of the room, in the middle of the bracket, and Laurie's is directly across from mine on the other side. The men will zigzag between the tables, so my dates will move from me to her. At the very least, I can give her a warning look if anyone gives off the wrong vibes.

"You're gonna *need* meat, huh?"

A snort draws my attention back to Laurie. A smirk starts to spread slowly across her face, dark eyebrow arching upward, but before she can open her mouth to say something particularly heinous, I warn, "*Laurie—*"

"I was just going to say it's cute you're anemic."

I can't help but chuckle. For all her educational achievements and her penchant for dull documentaries, my girl's got a dirty mind. And I wouldn't have it any other way.

"You were gonna make a dick joke."

"Yeah." She nods solemnly. "Yeah, I was."

"You going to showcase that same humor on your dates tonight?" I ask, moving up to a free spot and ordering two espresso martinis from the new bartender who's joined his hot-nerd friend. I'm guessing he was originally up on the mezzanine with the men, and they'll be making their way down at any moment.

"Like I said, it's straight into voting preferences and belief systems. If I start relying on dick jokes to carry a conversation . . ." She tilts her head down and I get a glimpse of that same wicked smirk.

"Kill me."

CHAPTER 4

"Shut up. Just shut up . . . You had me at homicide."

—Not *Jerry Maguire*

*T*he first three dates are . . . meh.

Drew seemed to like the look of me, or at least the look of my tits. They garnered most of his attention during our exchange on safe controversial topics like pineapple on pizza (Ew. No), mountain or beach (No strong feelings on that), and cats or dogs (Dogs . . . obviously). None of our answers matched and I couldn't find it in me to be disappointed.

Stu didn't like it when I accidentally called him Drew. Given I'd only heard his name for the first time five minutes before I made the mistake, I feel like the slip hardly warranted the silent treatment he gave me for the rest of our date. I was *this* close to flipping him the bird as he stomped over to Laurie's table.

Well, fuck you, too, Drew—I mean, Stu.

His preference for plaid and the manicured beard align more with Laurie's preferences anyway, but I hope his personality puts a pin in that before it can become an issue.

And Lee, well, he spent the whole time talking about his first date, Nia. She was the woman who gave me tips on how to keep my monstera alive during cocktail hour. With her flawless brown skin and easy smile that showcases a set of perfect Gabrielle Union dimples, it's not surprising she already has someone so smitten with her. I could see her stealing glances at him from the corner of my eye, so I thought it only fair to offer to be his wingman after the last date was over. We spent the rest of our date talking through a game plan.

By the time my fourth date folds himself into the chair across from me, I'm already considering what kind of filling I'm going to get in my Gyros. Lamb? Chicken? *Both. Yeeeessss*—

"Hi."

I shake myself out of my meat-induced daydream and give bachelor number four the attention he deserves for signing up for ten blind dates, and . . . Oh.

He's *cute*.

Late-eighties Bill Pullman cute. Blue eyes, longish, light brown hair that is ruffled because I bet it won't do anything else, and when he leans over the table and offers me his hand, his palm engulfs mine. It's warm and big and just a little callused. Green flag.

"I'm John."

He says his name like an apology, his head ducking down a little, his eyes avoiding mine for a second before he looks back up and offers me the smallest of lip tilts. And it's so endearing I can't help but smile back. Things are looking up.

"I'm Jamie."

"How's your night been?" His voice is like his handshake: soft and warm and comforting, and I feel like he'd be really good at reciting poetry.

"Mediocre," I say honestly, lightly, sliding my martini in front of me and making the glass do a pirouette as the comment gains the soft, throaty chuckle I was gunning for.

He goes to say something, stops himself, looks at me for an extended moment from under his lashes, and then seems to find the nerve to say, "I hope I can make it better then."

Ooh. Smooth. I appreciate the risk and slide forward in my chair a little bit to reward him.

"How about you?"

"It's been fine; there are some interesting people here." His answer is more politically correct, but still, I can tell he's being honest.

"What's the most interesting thing you've heard tonight?" I ask, and he considers the question before looking over his shoulder and pointing out the pretty redhead with the Julia Roberts smile seated at the table next to Laurie.

"Shelley over there volunteered in Kenya helping endangered wildlife, and Dani"—he turns back to me and tilts his head to the woman with the Meg Ryan pixie cut—"has a tattoo of a chicken on her ribs that she has no idea how she got."

That makes me grin. He's been listening to these women talk. They've been comfortable enough to share intimate and embarrassing stories with him, and if that isn't a green flag, I don't know what is. I read this study on speed dating that said you can tell in the first thirty seconds whether you think you'll be a match with someone. Those numbers seem to be checking out right about now.

He shifts forward on his seat so there's only a ruler's distance between us. "Tell me something interesting about you."

I ponder the question. I've got nothing on poultry body art or frolicking with antelopes across the savanna. I am, however, a human trash can filled to the brim with film knowledge, and since John has been the most promising of my suitors so far, I pull out the big guns. "I can recite the entire film of *While You Were Sleeping*."

He squints at me, his head tilting to the side, and it makes his bangs flop across his eyes in a way that is too cute.

"No, you can't," he says softly, and I slide my glass to the side to meet the unspoken challenge.

I think I make a really solid choice in skipping a rendition of Natalie Cole's "This Will Be (An Everlasting Love)," since my talents don't extend to any aptitude for singing, and go straight for the monologue. I deliver it with the kind of confidence that comes from being halfway through my third espresso martini in ninety minutes. I don't forget the pause Sandra Bullock delivers after she comments on the sepia tone of the footage showing her idyllic childhood, or the inflection when she mentions her dad for the first time, but I make myself stop after four or so sentences. It's just enough to prove my point, and when John stares at me, genuinely impressed, I can't help but feel a little buoyant.

"That's incredible," he finally says, and I shrug a shoulder, trying not to show how those words actually mean *a lot* considering most people would probably assume I never leave my house after hearing something like that.

"I can also do *Saw*," I say, pulling my drink back in front of me. "But there's a lot more screaming and swearing."

His smile spreads, but he doesn't show his teeth. I think it would take something pretty spectacular to make this man grin. The amusement is still there, though, in the crinkle at the corner of his eyes and the glint of his pupil surrounded by an unforgiving steel-blue iris. Then he asks, "Do you like scary movies?"

"I love them."

And it keeps going from there. Back and forth. I tell him I like Taylor Swift—a topic that's somehow come up in all of my previous dates—and he tells me he likes new wave music from the eighties. I played softball in high school; he was in the drama club. He says he makes an amazing cacio e pepe, and I admit that I get influenced easily—and let down often—when it comes to viral Instagram recipes. We share little facts about our lives like they're breadcrumbs. If you like what you hear, keep following the trail. And I do like what I hear. He seems to as well because, when the bell rings and I start in my seat, he looks like he doesn't want to leave. He's too polite to idle, though, standing up with his long fingers curled around the neck of his beer, and landing that imploring stare back on me one more time. *So cute.*

"I'll see you after all this for a drink, yeah?"

I think I'd like that. I think I'd like that very much, so I nod and watch him walk over to Laurie. I watch him fold into the seat across from her, reach over and shake her hand, and I watch him glance back over his shoulder at me one more time before a shadow falls over my table, a body moving into his spot and taking his seat.

I only allow myself the shortest second of disappointment before shifting my focus back to give my new date the same practiced smile I've been giving the last four men, but then I see who sat down in front of me and . . . Oh.

Oh shit.

I have to remind myself that it's not polite to stare. To tell myself the noise in the room hasn't suddenly hushed, and the lights haven't gone hazy. There's no camera zooming in and there isn't a string quartet somewhere sustaining a long, resonant, affected note. There's nothing to suggest this date is going to be any better or worse than the others. But this guy . . . he is *something.*

And that's a very strange thing for me to be thinking because if John met the criteria of what I thought was my type, this guy doesn't check a single box.

Usually I like to be able to tell that my date spends more time in a lecture hall rather than a gym, but this guy . . . He's more muscular than lean, more athletic than academic. His white button-up shirt stretches across his shoulders and—that material isn't supposed to stretch, right? His hair is dark, short, styled. Nothing like the affable milk chocolate mess that looked cute on John. "Cute" isn't a word I'd use for this guy. I wouldn't use it for anyone who manages to look so grave within the boudoir-themed surroundings of the bar, but that's not a bad thing. He is Marvel-movie buff, Oscar-contender serious, and . . . damn . . . I guess I'm a fan.

He doesn't look at me at first. His gaze darts to every part of the room until, as if by accident, his eyes meet mine. It seems as if he's about to go back to scanning the room, but then he . . . doesn't.

He blinks. I blink. And then the grim line of his mouth curves into the smallest of smiles. He hasn't said anything yet—neither have I—but already my right hand itches to reach for my pen and fashion a big, clear, heavy-handed X in the "yes" column next to his name on the match card that lies facedown and unmarked beside me. I was going to wait until the break to assign my dates to the definitive categories of yes or no, or the more mollifying category of friendship only—but a couple of seconds of sustained eye contact and a lip quirk from the man in front of me has me thinking we should just call it a night now. Put in last calls, start flickering the lights and turning the chairs onto the tables.

Because another study I read about speed dates disagreed with the thirty-second theory. It said you know within the first four seconds of meeting someone whether you'll want to match with them. And I'm inclined to agree as I glance down at his name tag and see three capital letters: *WES*.

"Hey," he says.

His voice is deep, a little husky, and it sounds *so* good that there's a little delay before I remember to say, "Hi."

His smile widens into a grin he then tries to tamp down. It completely softens the inexplicably stern look that was on his face, and I find it so endearing I'm grinning back just as wide.

"I'm Wes."

"Jamie."

He stares at me for a second, his mouth silently forming my name until he tilts his head to the side and asks, "What makes you happy, Jamie?"

A bark of laughter shoots out of my mouth, loud enough that I see Laurie pause in her date with John across the way. Her head peeks over his shoulder, mouth pursing comically in a "*Girrrrlll,* we are talking about *that* when we get home" expression before I glance back at Wes and try to swallow down a fit of giggles that threaten to ruin any cool girl allure I may have conjured in the last thirty seconds.

"Seriously?" It's such a . . . *strange* thing to say.

What's even stranger is that I'm kind of into it.

"I—I don't know why I said that," he murmurs, color rising to the top of his cheeks though he keeps his stare on me. He's not embarrassed enough to look away, to break eye contact.

He shakes his head, eyes closing in a prolonged blink, and I take the opportunity to cast my eyes down his torso. I think there's a tattoo peeking over his shoulder—an interesting, sharp tip of something just visible at the opening of his collar. I'm not into tattoos. At least, I wasn't. But I want to know what that spike connects to, and I want to follow its path to wherever it may lead.

"It's the first question that came to mind," he says, eyes still closed.

"And you want to stick with that?" I grin, and when his eyes open again and he spots my smile, his lips tilt up into something that pulls at that ultrathin thread in my chest.

"Yeah, I feel like I need to know." His voice drops lower on the admission. And the way he says it . . . like it's the truth and, yes, it surprises him, too.

I pause before answering, highly aware that however I respond sets the tone for the rest of the date and possibly the rest of my life. God, where did *that* come from?

I should say something deep and philosophical. Something to impress him or something vaguely sexual to turn him on. But I don't, because I want to tell him the truth and I want him to be impressed and turned on by it regardless.

"Movies."

Nothing on this man's face flinches or quirks or furrows in response. He just keeps staring, and I have no desire to look away.

"They make you happy?"

"They do . . . They make the world make sense."

I drop my voice to a whisper since we're not supposed to talk about anything work related. I respect the reasoning for the rule—so we can find deeper, more lasting connections that aren't influenced by salary—but I'm willing to break it for Wes to know what takes up a lot of space in my brain. A lot of space in my life, really.

"I'm writing a thesis about film. I want to teach genre theory."

"What's your favorite genre?"

"I have two: rom-com and horror—well, slashers, actually."

His eyes narrow before his gaze drops down. He gives my pretty, rom-com-appropriate dress a once-over before raising his stare back to mine, his eyebrow quirking up as he does. I just grin. I can guess which part of that answer he's doubtful about.

"What makes *you* happy, Wes?"

While it may have been the first question to come to his mind, he doesn't have an answer ready, and after a couple of seconds of forehead-furrowing thought he says, "I like a happy ending."

At my arched brow, he clarifies. "Not that kind . . . although, yeah,

I'm sure *that's* nice. But I like when the underdog wins, when the hero beats the odds . . . I like when the guy gets the girl."

It's a lovely, loaded, answer. One that makes his gaze drop and settle on my mouth because I'm . . . Am I . . . *biting* my lip?

He takes his time to lift his stare back to mine, and when he does, I have a better understanding of the term "bedroom eyes." Soft, intense, endless pools of darkness. His eyes are bittersweet cocoa dark, and they somehow spike my blood sugar.

"What's your favorite movie?" he asks, and it's like asking me what the primary colors are, or who the three Big Bads are (Jason, Michael, Freddy). I don't even have to think.

"It's a three-way tie: *While You Were Sleeping, Saw, Shaun of the Dead.*"

I'm glad he asked me first because this is a deal-breaker question for me. Though I think Wes would have to like something *really* bad to counteract whatever is happening over this slightly sticky table right now. He'd have to be a fan of like . . . *Cats* or something.

"What's yours?"

He leans into the table, looking like he's up for the challenge when he folds his hands in the space between us. His middle finger is half an inch away from grazing against mine, and his hands look strong, capable. I recross my legs.

"Also, a three-way tie. *BlacKkKlansman*—"

"Oh shit, good choice." That's an understatement. It's a *killer* choice.

"*The Fast and the Furious.*"

I'll allow it.

"And . . ." He inhales through his teeth like he's considering not telling me. I'm on the edge of my seat, preparing for the *Cats* moment that is going to ruin this amazing first impression, and then, "*Miss Congeniality.*"

Be still, my beating heart. Be still, my equally beating vagina. My cheeks might very well burst from trying to hold back the smile that answer warrants.

"*Miss Congeniality?*"

"I love Sandy."

He says it so seriously that it's my turn to stare. The side of his mouth twitches in amusement when he asks, "Do I pass the test?"

"Depends. How do you feel about scary movies?"

They were noticeably absent from his list, and while I can overlook *The Fast and the Furious*, it'd be a major red flag if he doesn't watch *any* horror.

He shrugs. "I'm partial to one every now and then . . . I'd watch more with the right person."

I'd like to be the right person.

I'd start off gentle, maybe *Scream* or *Nightmare on Elm Street*. Eventually, if things got more serious, we'd graduate to *Creep* or *Sinister*. Break up the gore with *Two Weeks Notice* as a palette cleanser.

"Is this your first one of these?" I ask after the silence—the one caused by me fantasizing about having a three-way of films with this guy—extends. If I want that to become a reality, I'll have to, you know, find out more general information about him.

"Yeah, I, uh—" He leans in, and I match his movement. We're close, like six inches close, and I can smell his cologne, or his shampoo, or his bodywash. Or maybe it's a mix of all three. Whatever it is, it's woody and smoky and spicy and it makes me take a long—hopefully subtle—breath through my nose to try and memorize it.

"I work a lot."

My eyes are drawn down to his clasped hands as he talks. His thumb is mindlessly circling one of his knuckles and . . . Huh. That's new. I try not to squirm too obviously in my seat.

"I don't have much free time, but I got some time off recently and thought what's the worst that could happen?"

Didn't I tell myself the very same thing earlier in the night? Although there is one scenario that always comes to mind.

"We could get murdered."

I say it without thinking. Shrugging in a "Whattaya gonna do?" kind of way as I lift my gaze to meet his, expecting a thoroughly amused expression and my first taste of a low, husky laugh that would give me a greater appreciation for the deep rasp of his voice.

But I don't see it, and he doesn't laugh.

He doesn't laugh at all.

CHAPTER 5

"Nothing beats a first kill."

—Not *50 First Dates*

Wes just *blinks*. So I blink. We blink, and then his lips pull down into the smallest of frowns.

"Maybe that's just a general female fear," I say.

He leans back from the table, his brow furrowing, and I feel like this is a good time to explain that in my household—one where Laurie and I have had to find a middle ground between our two divisive interests (aka true crime documentaries)—murder is spoken about in the same way one might discuss what should go on a grocery list.

"Sorry . . . Um, I watch a lot of horror movies and listen to a lot of true crime podcasts, so when someone says, 'What's the worst that could happen?' 'Murder!' is just my knee-jerk reaction."

He doesn't respond.

I probably shouldn't have performed jazz hands on the word "murder," but here we are. There is a chance he missed it, though, because his eyes are fixed on a spot on the table, that somber expression firmly back on his face.

That should be my sign to change the topic to future travel plans, favorite foods, preferred sex positions, but does that stop me from going further down the murder spiral?

Not a chance.

"I mean, I don't know if there's a speed date killer out there."

Wes's eyes flick up to mine, the formerly soft brown depths hard and unreadable.

"But, you know, Dahmer picked up most of his victims on the club scene."

What the *fuck* am I saying?

"Rodney Alcala was on a dating show while he was active. How *many* people have died because of Tinder?"

Whatever warm, shimmery connection I thought we had is thoroughly unraveling with every word that comes out of my mouth.

Still, some dumb part of me thinks that I can save this by finishing with "I guess—what I mean is . . . dating is a dangerous pastime."

Wes stares at me, his jaw tense, as the silence drags like a body being carted down a hallway by a hulking teen murderer. When the bell dings, signaling the end of our allotted ten minutes and the start of the fifteen-minute break, he can't get out of his chair fast enough.

"It was nice getting to know you, Jamie," he mutters, rising slowly from his seat like he's actively trying not to bolt out of it.

"Yep!" I say too loudly, too high-pitched, audibly pathetic. "You, too."

He gives me one more wary look and then he's gone, striding out of the room like he's never going to come back. Laurie glances across at me and, seeing whatever expression is on my face, winces. One minute of word vomit and I've butchered any chance of introducing this smoking-hot man to a *Poltergeist/Ghost* double feature.

If someone could walk over right now and put me out of my

misery, that would be fantastic. Bring on the machete, the butcher's knife, the claw glove. 'Cause there's no coming back from that.

I use the break to regroup with Laurie, bypassing the bathroom so I can tell her about the heinous end to my date with Wes. My account garners a deeper wince and some targeted flirting on her part with the hot-nerd bartender that results in an even heavier pour of vodka into our espresso martinis. It's a consolation in the loosest sense, one that loses its effectiveness when the break is almost over and Wes returns to the bar. I try to direct an apologetic look in his direction as he makes his way to Laurie's table, but he averts his gaze from mine. Like I'm the psychotic woman who casually brings up murder with people she's just met. Which, oh yeah, *I am*.

The glimmer of hope with John and his cute eye crinkle and floppy hair seems like it's flickered out, too. While he managed to give me a shy smile during the break, I can't help but notice that his first date in the second half of the evening seems to go really well. He has his attention squarely on Jennifer with the gorgeous blowout, his head ducked and that same soft, close-mouthed smile gracing his face while they chat. Not to mention she keeps tracing her fingers across her collarbone. A classic, practiced move that certainly achieves better results than word vomiting intimate details about some of the most fucked-up serial killers in history. So when John moves on from their date and isn't shooting me looks anymore, I'm not even mad.

Still, my heart just isn't in it after the break, and that means my sixth, seventh, and eighth dates kind of blur together while I'm feeling sorry for myself. When the bell rings and the men move on to their second-to-last dates—Wes avoiding my eye and John walking across the room to go sit with the woman with the resting bitch face without giving me a second glance—I don't expect the night to improve.

And if there's one person in the room who can meet that expectation, it's date number nine. Curtis.

Because *Curtis* is a massive dick.

I'd even go so far as to say Curtis falls into a specific category of men who only appeal to a very small group of women who haven't discovered therapy, the concept of gender equality, and are color-blind in a way that prevents them from seeing glaring red flags.

He'd be perfect for that kind of girl.

In the first five minutes of the date we cover names, what we're drinking, and how his dates have been so far. Apparently, a lot of the women are bitches.

After those thrilling topics, the conversation lulls and I'm back to playing with the stem of my glass as he downs the rest of his drink.

"That's a nice dress," Curtis remarks when his vodka Red Bull (Yes . . . a *vodka Red Bull*) is nothing but yellow-tinted ice.

"Thank you?" I brace myself for what's about to come next, because I *know* there's more to come. His tongue is posed against his top teeth, his eyes narrowed appraisingly, and I just hope he's not going to be so inanely predictable and say—

"It'd look better on my floor."

Ugh.

You know what's already on the floor? The fucking bar. It's been set so low and yet this guy is struggling to jump over it and conduct a conversation that doesn't make me feel like I need a shower.

"Sheesh, really, Curtis? That's how we talk to women on this side of the millennium?"

I try to say it in a joking way. That's how we're conditioned to respond to men like Curtis. Keep it light, keep it playful. Because men like him are full of hot air and sometimes they blow up in your face and you get burned.

"I'm giving you a compliment," he replies, and I can't help but roll my eyes. I don't even try to hide it. Kate Winslet did not put in the hard work so women like me could smile and nod. Maybe I hold myself to a higher standard than ol' Curtis, but I just expect more from a date than what is currently manspread in front of me.

"The rapey undertone kind of counteracts the intent."

He scoffs, but he's jacked up on taurine and the false impression he is a ten among a room of twos.

"A guy can't even give a girl a fucking compliment these days," he huffs, shaking his head as he leans back in his chair. Even though I'm a card-carrying rule follower, and we're supposed to keep our dates "light and polite," something inside me just snaps. I'm not one to choose violence, but being a woman in academia and tutoring first-year film students—the kind who think identifying a Dutch angle in a Michael Bay film makes them incapable of receiving anything other than full marks—hasn't exactly made me shy away from confrontation, either. Maybe it's because we're almost two hours into this event and *somebody* should've put this guy in his place already. Or maybe it's because the way Wes left my table was a little bit more of a stab to my ego than I'd like. But if Curtis is going to move on to Laurie and add me to the list of bitches of the night, I want to at least give him a strong argument for that case.

"Can I give you some advice, Curtis?"

"N—"

"If you find yourself in a situation where it seems like you are surrounded by an unusually high number of bitches, there's a really good chance you are probably being an *asshole*."

He looks like he wants to say something cutting in return, but I lean in, jump-cut quick, and he flinches in his seat instead. The movement garners a few looks from neighboring tables. Even John's date—the same woman who may or may not have given me the stink eye—glances over his shoulder from where she sits near the entrance.

I shift my gaze back to Curtis, taking a page from her book and giving him a definitive stink eye.

"When a woman doesn't appreciate your 'compliment,'" I continue, "don't blame her for your inability to read the room." I make my voice softer, lighter, and enjoy his confusion at the contrast when I add, "Shut your *fucking* mouth and *stop talking*."

He stares across at me, his mouth opening and closing around arguments he hasn't formed yet as I lean back in my seat and revel in the satisfaction that comes from putting a man in his place. I swear, I'm not usually *this* confrontational. Not unless I'm calling Laurie a piece of shit, which is just one of our mutual terms of endearment. But I do have a floral Take No Shit sticker on my laptop, and the two types of films I have decided to dedicate my life to feature women who go up against odds scarier than this two in a suit could ever hope to be.

I see the moment he figures out his rebuttal, but the soft tinkling of the bell cuts off whatever unwelcome comment his underdeveloped brain could create. The other men around the room are already standing and moving on to their final dates as I direct an "eat shit" smile across the table. Before I can verbalize that he should follow their lead and leave, the lights cut off. The red velvet room is plunged into darkness.

"What the fu—" Curtis cries out among the confused rabble while I blink my eyes into adjusting to the pitch-black surrounding us. There are sounds of movement, muttered apologies, glasses accidentally clinking, and then I catch the slick, wet sound of . . . I don't even know. I've never heard anything like it before. A thick, bubbling noise takes its place, and the only thing I can liken *that* to is someone gargling mouthwash, but even that's too far removed. The lights come back on before I can think about it too much, and after a few seconds of blinding brightness, I catch Curtis's wide-eyed gaze staring, unblinking, at me.

God, some guys need a map to know where to fuck off to. I nod in Laurie's direction, trying to catch her eye to give her the universal facial expression for "this guy is a psycho" when he still doesn't move.

"It was *so* nice mee—"

Color catches my eye. A scarlet line cutting across the thick, pale column of his neck. At first I think he's used the darkness to tie a scarf around his throat—which is puzzling all by itself—but then it grows. It spreads. Dark red pouring down into the open collar of his shirt, the extra button he left undone even more obvious now.

My hand starts trembling around the stem of my martini glass before I can fully comprehend *why* his throat is slashed open in a wide curve, a crude imitation of the smirk that was cemented on his face for the entirety of our date. He opens his mouth to say something, but nothing comes out except that gargling sound. He can't talk, and a weird part of my brain has the audacity to think at least some of what I said has had an impact.

But when he hiccups and blood starts flowing from his mouth, I scream.

CHAPTER 6

"I've got a sneaky feeling you'll find that blood actually is all around."

—Not *Love Actually*

It's chaos. Like the beginning of a flash mob before everyone moves in synchronicity.

Curtis is bleeding out in front of me, and behind him is a blurred background of running bodies as different flight responses kick in.

The smell of fear hits me as I gape at the body slumping in the chair. It's a bespoke cocktail of sweat and spilled alcohol, a mix of too many incompatible colognes and something else so innately primal that it pulls me out of my shock.

I've seen scenes like this before. I've watched terror play out on a screen and I've examined each shot and analyzed every plot point. I know all the possible endings to a story that starts with bloodshed. So I stay in my seat instead of heeding a more reactive impulse and heading for the stairs, because the panicked hive mind has taken over and too many bodies start to head for the archway we all walked through at the beginning of the night.

That's a bad idea.

It's not wide enough to fit so many people at once, and watching the horde try to squeeze through the frame is like watching Bridget Jones pull on a pair of Spanx. Men and women jostle shoulder to shoulder to get away from danger, and all that polite conversation and active listening and reciprocal flirting means nothing now.

This isn't the *Titanic*.

There's no "ladies first" code of conduct when another man's neck is gaping open.

Chivalry died in that chair with Curtis.

Somewhere in the fray, over the screams, I hear the ding of the date bell—someone must have stepped on it in the rush—and the room descends into darkness again.

The screaming seems to hit a new level, a consistent piercing tone, and I drop to the ground to avoid being at throat-slitting height. Pulling myself under the table, I hit my forehead against Curtis's splayed knees as mine burn against the carpet. He would've loved for our date to end like this.

My palms shake where they're planted on either side of his shoes, and I try to ignore the warm, wet patch slowly creeping underneath my fingertips.

All I can hear is glass crunching under heavy footsteps, body parts hitting furniture, so many voices, and so many different screams mixing until it sounds like we're in the middle of a hurricane. It's a communal howl that builds and dips and then that sound from before, the one I couldn't place, cuts through it all. I know now what that sound means. I've seen the effect of it draped across Curtis's neck.

It's the sound of flesh being slashed open like the ribbon on a Tiffany & Co. box.

The alternating quick stabs and prolonged slices playing out from the darkness are performed with the same fervor of a long-suffering girlfriend hunting for an engagement ring within her Christmas presents. It just keeps happening, more gruesome sounds playing out afterward, and all I can do is dig my fingers into the tacky, moist strands of the carpet and keep my mouth shut so I don't draw attention to my hiding spot.

I met these people two hours ago and now I'm bearing witness to their last moments, and it's . . . too soon, too much, too *intimate*. I don't know them well enough to share this kind of thing with them. I don't know anyone that well except—

Oh my god.

Laurie.

I grab the strands of carpet to stop myself from crawling out and navigating the darkness to find her. I pray she paid attention to the poster I stuck on the back of our bathroom door. The one I bought as a joke: How to Survive a Slasher. Because rule seven is don't run up the stairs, and rule four is turn on the light.

As suddenly as it began, the noise stops. Then it's just the muffled sound of footsteps on the level above, like the last dancers standing are giving it their all in the middle of the dance floor before closing time, and the steady drip of . . . liquid.

A second later the lights turn on, as innocuously as the beginning of a Nancy Meyers movie. And once they do it doesn't take quite as long for my eyes to adjust, not when the lights seem dimmer . . . darkened by a red tinge.

I peer through Curtis's legs, zoning in on where Laurie was sitting. Her date's chair is knocked over, giving me an unobstructed view of her table. She's there, crouched under the table in the same position as me, her eyes shut tight. I watch as her head nods, like she's psyching herself up to open them, and then her gaze goes straight to my table. It darts around where Curtis is slouched in his chair and I shift forward— quietly, carefully—ducking my head between his legs so she can see me.

So she doesn't try to move out and find me.

She stares when our eyes finally meet, her red nails digging into the carpet just like mine, her shoulders relaxing when she sees I'm okay. Relief makes her face crumple into a silent sob that draws a lump into my throat and brings tears to my eyes because *I'm* the emotional one.

We wave weakly at each other and then I hold my palm steady.

Stay.

Rule two of how to survive a slasher: always hide for longer than you think you should. And rule three: find a weapon.

I move back from between the legs of the chair and try to find something we can use to defend ourselves. To my left there's a single block high heel. To my right is a broken Kahlúa bottle that's rolled an arm's length away. The base didn't break evenly, making it look like a jagged candy scoop, but it will do the job. All I have to do is reach out and grab it.

I look over to the archway that everyone ran through. I can see the light switch that's allowed whoever is doing this their anonymity while butchering complete strangers, and there's no one there. There's no obvious threat like a knife-holding assailant allowing their blood-soaked weapon to drip steadily on the floor.

That doesn't mean it's safe, though. The killer *could* still be in the room. They could be waiting for someone like me to crawl out of their hiding spot so they can restart the fun and games they triggered by slitting Curtis's throat. It's a risk, and that's why there's a rule warning against leaving a hiding place prematurely.

A glint of amber glass catches my eye like a wink across a bar, droplets of Kahlúa glistening on the sharp edges of the broken bottle, and it's hard to resist. Though it feels wrong, I might need to break one rule to follow another.

Inching my arm out across the space, I grab the neck of the bottle and pull it slowly and silently under the table. It's wet and smells like the top note of the espresso martinis I was drinking, so I use the bottom of Curtis's slacks to dry the glass until I can hold it firmly in my palm.

Rule three: find a weapon. Check.

Rolling from my knees to my ass, I check that there's nobody behind me (rule six: watch your back), then, when the coast is clear, I slide out from beneath the table. Once I'm standing, the bottle clutched tightly in my fist, I cast a glance around the room I thought couldn't have gotten any redder and am immediately proven wrong.

There's movement across the space, and when I tear my eyes away from the sprays and arcs of blood that are still dripping down the walls, I see Wes. He's two tables down from Laurie, closest to the other entrance of the bar, and he has the same idea as me.

Sometime during the clusterfuck he's broken the leg off one of the chairs and now holds it out like a baton. The sharp stake is steady in his fist even though his chest is heaving. I spy the dark point of that tattoo on his shoulder before our eyes meet and he straightens, the ink slipping back out of sight. He looks like he's ready to burn this whole place down, like what just happened is going to form the basis of his origin story and the jury is still out on whether he becomes a hero or a villain. It's confusingly attractive.

There's one other figure straightening from behind the table closest to where everyone escaped, and I realize it's John.

While he hasn't gone down the weapon route, his fists are curled tightly at his sides. That won't achieve anything, but I've got to give credit where credit is due. His blue eyes are wild, searching around the room, and when they land on me, he shakes his head like "did you see that?" His hair flops across his forehead, sticking to the sweat on his skin. Also surprisingly attractive.

When I take in the rest of the scene, I see figures crouched behind overturned tables and people hiding behind heavy velvet curtains before they slowly push them to the side—others who found ways to hide from the killer. On first count there are eight survivors. It's a cruel parody of the evening's previous uniformity. Before it was ten men, ten women, ten minutes per date. Now it's four men, four women, and four . . . bodies. Curtis lies terrifyingly still, as do the two bartenders. An ice pick protrudes from the neck of the one Laurie was flirting with, right in the jugular (RIP hot nerd). The other bartender, the one who was manning the end of the bar closest to me, has a long gash across his neck. A perfect match to the one starting to coagulate on Curtis's throat. Their blood is sprayed across the entire bar top. Then there's the host, Marion, who lies facedown in a booth near the doorway with a knife sticking out of her back. It's a scene that leaves everyone speechless. Shell-shocked. I think we're all still processing, waiting to see if the killer is in the room.

I mean, nobody is holding a blade stained with blood or proudly taking responsibility for slicing through Curtis's trachea, but my guess—an educated opinion, some might say—is that you don't do such a thing under the cover of darkness because you want people to know it was you. Not yet, anyway.

And so the possibility stands: the killer could *still* be in the room. The thought draws my gaze back to the table that has my best friend underneath it.

"Laurie," I call, and she pokes her head around the fallen chair, crawling out when I nod. She can't help but smooth down the front of her jumpsuit when she stands (silk creases so easily!), before casting a guarded glance around the room.

Her eyes fall upon the body of the bartender sagged against the mirrored wall behind the bar, and the sight makes a little whimper fall out of her glossed lips.

"Laurie," I say again, and she tears her eyes away from the sight. I extend one blood-tipped nail to the space next to me.

She doesn't question the silent directive. She just puts one spiky-toed foot in front of the other until she's at my side, staring at the cleanest patch of carpet in front of us. When it starts to darken from the expanding pool of Curtis's blood, she raises both her hands to cover her mouth, and the sight of her empty shaking palms in contrast to the Kahlúa bottle clenched tightly in my own makes me realize she's not following rule three.

The table on my left has a half-empty beer bottle on it, so keeping my eyes on the other emerging members of the room, I reach across Laurie and curl my fingers around the neck. Once I smash the base against the tabletop—a collective flinch rippling across the room at the sound of breaking glass—it's a travel-sized version of the weapon in my hand.

Now that all eight of us are standing out in the open, I try to identify everyone.

Me, Laurie, John, Wes, Drew—I mean Stu—the guy I would've had a date with after Curtis, and the two women I first started talking to during cocktail hour: the Kate Hudson blonde and the Meg Ryan pixie cut.

That seems like a long time ago now.

"Take this," I say, pushing the neck of the bottle into Laurie's palm as I straighten, her fingers trembling until she tightens her grip.

"Okay . . . what . . . what do I do with it?" Each word shakes as it leaves her mouth, and it just makes me focus extra hard on making my own voice sound steady when I answer, "If it looks like someone is going to attack you . . . stick it into them."

"Right . . ." She nods, as if I've told her she needs to stop believing the contouring tricks she sees on social media are going to work for her in real life. "Of course."

A scream echoes from above, and eight heads jerk up like it's the beginning strains of "Mr. Brightside." It cuts off so quickly, so abruptly, that I know that—even without the weighty thud of a body falling to the ground—whoever is doing this, whoever is *capable* of doing something like this, must be up there. And while there is a moment of relief that they're not still in the room with us, it's quickly overwhelmed by what that scream means.

They aren't finished, not by a long shot.

Curtis was just the first kill—the first of *four*—and any one of us could be next.

CHAPTER 7

"If you want to kill someone, you do it, you do it right then, out loud. Otherwise, the moment just . . . passes you by."

—Not *My Best Friend's Wedding*

"**I**s anyone hurt?"

Wes's voice is even more raspy than before, the question jarring in the stunned aftermath of what was supposed to be a normal, fun, nonmurdery night.

It's also kind of ironic given the scene around us, and the fact he's holding a weapon as he says it. I can't find it in me to point out the obvious. No one can. We all just shake our heads and then, one by one, survey the room. Take in the way most of the tables and chairs are splayed across the space, how the blood spatters on the gas lamps look almost intentional from afar, or how there is a clear distinction between the red shag of the carpet and the darker-toned stains that spread across it. Those details are going to form the backdrop of our nightmares from now on. If we can get out of here, that is.

John is the one who finally speaks, combing a hand through his hair and confirming that that cute, disheveled look is entirely by accident as he states, "We can't stay here."

"You want to go up there?" Dr— Stu, damn it, says incredulously, pointing to the shard-like section of stairs visible through the doorframe.

Aside from Curtis, the other bodies—our host and the bartenders, people who were just here because of their *job*—make heinous markers toward the exit. I saw the daters who panicked and ran out of the room going in that direction before the lights cut out again, and I think it's safe to say the killer worked their way toward the stairs just the same as those who were trying to escape.

After that initial scream, and those heavy panicked footfalls, the level above us is now eerily silent, and that prompts the question: Who made the right choice? Those who ran, or those who hid? With the killer upstairs the answer might be obvious, but there is one advantage the runners have that we don't: they're closer to accessing the outside world through those heavy double doors, while we're standing in a basement surrounded by four bodies.

"I don't think there's an exit down here," I say, memories of Laurie and me stumbling around this level after we'd had a few Kamikazes running through my head.

"You've been here before?" John asks, moving farther into the room. Farther away from Marion's body.

I nod. "It's been a few years, but I remember that. Right, Laurie?"

"Right," she replies automatically, her eyes glued to the ceiling in an attempt to avoid looking at the puddle of blood seeping into the carpet at our feet.

"There are stairs on that side, too." I point to the other archway with my free hand. Nobody tried to go that way because terror gives you tunnel vision. "We could go up that way, cross the dance floor, and try to get to the front entrance."

I don't know how my voice is so steady. I don't know how I'm thinking so straight, but I'm certain that being underground is not a good idea, and that this bar is far more claustrophobic than I first thought. There's also the voice in my head that keeps reminding me I've seen this movie before.

"*Try?*" the Kate Hudson blonde in the pink dress says. Colette. She must've been at a table close to the bar, because a heavy spray of blood covers the left side of her body. The loopy handwriting and the cute heart on her name tag are covered with it. The sticker may as well just be one big block of red, and when she gingerly peels it off and blood soaks into the untouched square of knit material beneath it, she gags. I want to pick up a napkin from the bar and offer it to her, even a paper coaster, but it would be useless . . . they're all soaked.

"Whoever did this, they're probably still up there," I say, because I doubt the killer slaughtered four—probably five, if that scream overhead was anything to go by—people and then decided to call it a night and flick through some new releases on Netflix. "I don't think they're just going to let us walk out."

I make the mistake of glancing over at Wes and he goes from looking gravely at the two dead bartenders to staring back at me with that same intense, guarded look from before. *Before.* When I *joked* about this very thing happening. God, to think I was babbling about how the very scenario we're living out would be the worst way to end our night. My manifestations about my career and love life never come to fruition, but I utter the words "speed date" and "killer" in the same sentence *once* and speak it into existence?

"Why?" sobs the woman with the Meg Ryan haircut. I squint across the room at her clean name tag and spy "Dani"—right. It's clear she doesn't expect anyone to answer. Even when she follows up with, "*Why* are they doing this?"

It's not the right question to be asking. Motive never matters, and sometimes it doesn't even exist. For every *I Know What You Did Last Summer* there's a *Slumber Party Massacre*. We could be dealing with a Ben Willis, out for revenge, as much as a mindless killing machine after some cheap thrills like Russ Thorn.

Colette wraps her least bloody arm around Dani, and again I look to the bar for something to mop at Dani's tears. The same napkins are still sitting there, seeped in blood.

Wes finally drops his arm down from the defensive position, his knuckles still white around the chair leg, and takes a step away from the table.

"Jamie's right. We need to get upstairs, get outside, and call for help."

He seems to function very well under pressure. It's an admirable quality. One I would've liked to discover under different circumstances. If only I hadn't mentioned Jeffrey Dahmer on our date.

"If we work together," he says, "look out for each other . . . it'll be eight against one."

He reaches up with his other hand and peels off his name tag. Unlike Colette, who did it out of necessity, his action feels more like a symbolic end to our time down here, and I watch as the others follow his lead and rip the sticky paper off their clothes. I look down at my own sticker and there are flecks of blood on the blank spaces between the letters of my name. I grasp the name tag and pull it off as Laurie says, "What about the others?"

Right, because there were twenty of us daters.

"They probably got out. We just have to get to the front door," John says, and his words seem to make her breathe a little easier. I'll admit, they do the same for me, too, but then I remember those footsteps I heard above our heads. They didn't sound like they were running toward the front door—they sounded like they were running away from it, and if this were a horror movie, then—

"I'll go first," Wes says, and it pulls me away from jumping to a conclusion that is not a good one. He waves the chair leg in his hand like it's a tour guide flag and we're about to walk through Manhattan to see all the hot spots of *Sex and the City*.

"We'll go up single file. Watch each other's backs . . . Anyone want to take up the rear?"

"I'll do it," John says weakly.

He shuffles on the spot and then heads to the bar. Scanning the bottles like he's picking out an appropriate aperitif for the occasion, he grabs an almost-empty bottle of Midori. After passing it awkwardly between his palms, he looks at me as if I'm the expert on bottle smashing.

I mime hitting my bottle against the table, and when he slams the frosted bottle down on the corner of the bar top, green liqueur mixes with the bright, oxidizing pools of red. His actions start off a chain reaction, and after a few more daters smash bottles on the blood-covered bar, I feel somewhat relieved. The fact that everyone looks uncomfortable holding something sharp in their hands supports my "the killer is upstairs" theory, and the panic that pushed my espresso martinis up into my chest starts to abate.

Because I know the way out of the basement, I go second after Wes. Laurie steps up behind me and I reach back to clasp one hand around her limp wrist, tightening the other on the brown neck of my bottle. After Laurie is Stu, and I get the feeling their date was much more successful than ours from the way he reaches out and touches her elbow. She manages to pull her lips into the smallest of smiles in reply, hinting at just how much Stu's combination of beard, mountain wear, and strong-looking thighs appeals to her. That makes me grimace. Laurie may be a Capricorn, but you can tell she's a Taurus moon from the way she runs headfirst toward walking red flags.

Colette and Dani line up behind Stu, then it's the guy who was supposed to be my last date. It's only from a quick glimpse of the sticker on his shirt, before he peeled it off, that I learn his name is Campbell. He hasn't spoken a word—he's just followed the paths and actions of the people closest to him. And I know four people just died in front of us, but that, paired with his unthreatening, boyish good looks makes me immediately associate him with Norman Bates. I can't help it. Maybe it's the way he goes from being fidgety one minute to distant and unblinking the next, but I'm kind of glad we're on opposite ends of the line. If he does decide to speak and his first words are about his mother, I'm pointing the finger at him.

Once John is at the back of the group, we move toward the other side of the room. There's fewer crude barricades blocking the way, less blood covering the walls, and I catch sight of the hallway when I look around Wes's shoulder. It's dark, lit only by overhead lights that make Serendipity's signature red walls a deeper red. Residual light from the upper level shines down on the staircase in a cool, white block, and the symbolism isn't lost on me. Where's the chorus of angels when you need them? This is our saving grace—if the killer doesn't decide to retrace their steps and finish us off before we can reach it, that is.

I let go of Laurie's hand and point around Wes to the bottom of the stairs. He rolled his sleeves up when we were figuring out the order of our elephant parade, and my bare forearm brushes against his as I gesture out to the hall. His skin is . . . warm. The muscles underneath look . . . taut.

Goddamn it, Jamie, there's a killer on the loose.

"The corridor goes around the entire bar down here," I say, then clear the huskiness out of my throat. Drawing my finger in a straight line across from the bottom of the stairs to what mistakenly looks like a wall in the darkness, I add, "So there's going to be a long hall running back that way."

He doesn't turn around when he asks, "You come here a lot?"

"I did. Enough to know it's literally a maze. There's *a lot* of places to hide, so just make sure you cover all your angles, you know?"

That makes him let out a darkly amused breath. "Yeah, I know."

Shit. I hope that didn't sound condescending. It's taking everything not to retreat into myself and avoid him after I showed him too much of an unfiltered version of myself. I bet he suspects I'm living out my wildest fantasies. I could live with the idea of him thinking I'm a bitch. I'm starting to accept that he thinks I'm a nutcase. But I draw the line at him believing I'm both.

"Wes, I just mean be . . . careful?"

It seems like a meaningless word and an obvious request, and I'm ready to try a more direct apology when he looks back at me and . . . he's smiling. The same smile he had when we first locked eyes and I told him what made me happy. It's almost like he's forgiven and forgotten the whole word-vomit thing. Which is a possibility considering verbal diarrhea pales in comparison to—I glance behind us—*this*.

"I'll do my best."

His voice is low, quiet, as warm as the arm that's still pressed against mine even though either one of us could have—should have—moved away by now. He leans forward, popping his head out of the entryway to survey both ends of the hall, and the cold air that slides in between us makes me shiver. I retract my arm from the doorway and rub at the goose bumps, watching Wes's hair turn a deep pinot noir under the lights before he leans back.

He glances over his shoulder to see some of the others are still psyching themselves up to leave the room before dropping his gaze down to mine. His head dips until we're closer than during any part of our date. "Are you okay?" he asks. "I mean . . ."

He doesn't have to elaborate. I had a front-row seat to the start of this madness.

"I think so."

It's hard to tell with so much adrenaline running through my body.

"If I just pretend it's a scene from a movie and not actually happening in real life, I can make my legs move."

The side of his mouth tilts up a little, and even though we're armed with DIY weapons and my hands are sticky with someone else's blood, my heart beats faster at the sight of it. He really is drop-dead gorgeous.

"Keep thinking that then. We're gonna get out of here, okay?"

It's funny. I believe him.

"Okay."

"And Jamie?"

"Yeah?" I need to tilt my head back to maintain eye contact, and he's not looking at me with that guarded expression anymore. Nor has he gone back to the gratifying appraisal from the good part of our date. This look is new, and I hope it's not wishful thinking that has me interpreting it as something better.

"You . . . the way you're handling this . . . Like, with Laurie . . . it's—"

"Sociopathic?" I say without thinking, and he grins. Maybe the true crime talk wasn't as big a turnoff as I'd initially thought.

"I was going to say it's impressive," Wes says. "It's the kind of thing that's gonna keep us alive."

Keep us alive. That's the goal of every survivor in a slasher, isn't it? And I've seen enough of them to know that the choices characters make either lead to their demise or land them a spot in the sequel. I know the formula.

I just hope I know it better than the killer.

It's too easy.

Our path up the stairs, around the boundary of the dance floor, into the entrance—it's far too easy. The first level is such a stark contrast to the devastation beneath us (completely undisturbed, as clean as a nightclub can be) that I know something isn't right. It's too quiet. Too still.

The men try to push open the heavy front doors, but they don't budge. Then they turn to grasping the huge ornate handles and pulling. Again, fruitless—they're giant, heavy, and don't have a visible lock. Then John spots something on the wall next to the coat check window and strides over to it. He digs his fingers into the top of a black rectangle and it flips open. I spot a red light, buttons that probably are numbered, then he slides in front of it and blocks my view. I don't need to see it to come to the right conclusion, though. That box is our way of unlocking those doors. Even before his shoulders droop and he turns back with a frown, I know what he's going to say.

"It needs a code."

The killer always isolates their victims and makes it impossible for them to escape.

So that means that all those daters who ran up here had nowhere to go with a guy who just killed four people on their tails.

I do the math, subtract Curtis from the equation, and figure there are eleven people who made it up here. Then I remember the scream we heard . . . More likely ten. Plus the killer. While there's always a possibility some stranger crept in during that first blackout, I don't know if they could've left the room again before the lights came back on. Returned to their seat, maybe. Hidden a knife, sure. But somebody would have mentioned an unfamiliar face. Then when you consider the proximity they had to have to Curtis before the blackout, the way they targeted the host and the bartenders . . . Whoever did this *has* to be one of the daters.

So, nine. Nine terrified people who are strewn across the club.

"Where's the girl who was on coat check?" Stu asks, and it looks like he has half a mind to click his fingers in the air to conjure up her services. It makes me frown and I can't help but look at Laurie, quirking an eyebrow when she meets my eye.

Really? This guy?

She glances at him, tilts her head to the side to try and see him from my angle, and then just shrugs. We will be having a serious talk when we get home.

Colette is the closest to the entrance of the coat check. It's cordoned off by a velvet rope the same color as the stains on her dress, and when she unhooks it, she makes it three steps into the room before stopping short, her gaze drawn to something on the ground.

"Oh."

"What?" Campbell, the Norman Bates lookalike, asks. Now that he's away from the bloodbath downstairs, he's become more talkative. Not by much, though. He's skittish, flinching at the most banal sounds. Maybe if we'd had our date, I would've had a chance to have a more neutral first impression of him, but I'm still keeping an ear out for any mention of his mom.

"She's here."

Colette's voice seems to be set to a sweet, high-pitched tone that people who work with children always have. The one where, no matter the subject, no matter the situation, they always sound upbeat and pleasant.

There's a pause, and then Campbell says, "Is she okay?"

"I don't think so."

I move into the coat check after her. There's not much room, and when we stand shoulder to shoulder, I can smell the blood on her, a coppery tang that goes straight through my nostrils and onto the top of my tongue. I can't concentrate on it too long, though, because I look down to where Colette is still staring and—*"Oh."*

"Jamie?" Laurie prompts.

"No . . ." For a second, I think I'm going to throw up, but then I remind myself I've seen this before. *Friday the 13th: The Final Chapter.* "She is *not* okay."

The woman in the coat check room was the one we heard scream. And it makes sense why, considering there is a meat cleaver stuck in her forehead. A *meat cleaver.* This place doesn't even have a kitchen.

"Phones," I say, and look away from where her face is split open like an uncooked roast. "We need to find the phones."

I find the key to the lockbox easily. It's right on top of the desk and it has a tag, with only a little bit of blood on it, that clearly identifies it as the counterpart to the box holding our phones captive. Dani and Laurie join Colette and me on the hunt for the black metal box, but even with all of us squeezed into the room, we can't find it. It's not here. The coat check attendant's phone isn't anywhere on the table or in her pockets. I duck down to check, try not to gag, and still come up empty. The iPad she was using earlier in the evening is missing, too. There isn't even a landline.

"Nothing," Laurie mutters from the back of the tiny room, extracting her hand from the pocket of a coat, pulling out the lining as she does. The satin pocket is red, spilling out against a tweed-looking material and it reminds me of . . . a lot of things I've seen tonight. She shakes her head, face ashen as she repeats, louder for those who can't fit in the room, "Nothing."

The thing is, I'm not even surprised. This is Slasher 101. The killer cuts off your ability to communicate with the outside world. Mrs. Voorhees did it in *Friday the 13th*. Killer Santa did it in *Silent Night, Deadly Night*. And now this one is following the same format. "Is there a break room farther back?" I ask. "A door to outside?"

Laurie and Dani pull the coat racks away. There's red velvet hanging along the wall, and when Dani wrenches it back like a theater curtain, all it reveals is bricks. This room is so small there is only one way in and out. There was no chance the coat check attendant could have avoided that meat cleaver. She may as well have been in a cage.

"See if the code for the door is in there," says Wes from the other side of the counter, and I turn back to the desk with a new mission, searching for a piece of paper with numbers scribbled on it, or some manual that could detail a way to bypass the lock. But there's nothing. The drawers are just filled with stationery, an obscene amount of rubber bands, and tickets used to identify our belongings. The only thing in the whole room is the rack of coats . . . and the coat check girl. Woman.

"There's got to be another way out of here," Dani pants as we all file out of the room and join the men to form a ragged circle by the front entrance. She's trying not to hyperventilate and is failing miserably.

She's not wrong, though. There will be another exit, but while I remember the hidey-holes and the dead ends of this place, my drunk girl memories do not extend to anything helpful like a back door or a fire escape or even a *window*. If we want to find an exit, we're going to have to search for one.

The rest of the group comes to that conclusion at the same time, but it's Stu who proves just how incompatible we are by planting his fists on his waist and saying, "We should split up."

CHAPTER 8

"I think I'd murder you even if we'd never met."

—Not *The Wedding Date*

"*That's* the worst fucking idea in the world."

Stu glares across the circle we've made after I say it, crossing his arms over his plaid-covered chest. With his visible undershirt and perfectly trimmed beard, he really does look like a lumberjack from the TikToks that are a core part of Laurie's algorithm. I guess that's part of the appeal for her. Things have not improved between ol' Stu and me since our date, though. He can barely keep the dislike out of his voice when he says, "We can check each level and each side of the club if we split up. We'll get out of here quicker."

It's like he's never seen a horror movie in his life.

"We can get *dead* quicker, too," I reply. "Splitting up just makes it easier to get lost or to become a target. Not to mention we don't have a way to communicate with each other if one of us does find an exit."

"I agree with Jamie."

The low rumble of Wes's voice travels across the circle and I turn to see he's propped himself against the doors. His arms are crossed, the stake gripped in one fist and resting across his bicep. His eyes are fixed on the space beyond us, tracing a path between the stairs down to the basement and up to the mezzanine, the entrance to the dance floor, the hallway leading to the back of the club, and I remember rule six, watch your back. You don't have to do that if it's flat against a wall. Why do I find *that* hot right now?

"We're safer together," he says, and it's the second time he's backed me up. Something soft and warm starts to weave beneath my ribs in response, but before I can feel too good about it, Stu lets out a dark scoff in rebuttal.

"Right," he mutters before his tone turns deceivingly light. "You do what she says downstairs. You do what she says up here. I'm starting to see a pattern, bro, and I just need to remind you it's not date night anymore."

"Excuse me?"

It seems like Wes is not a fan of passive aggression, especially in the wake of such brutality. His stare is hard after he poses the question. He pushes off the doors, arms dropping to his sides as he walks toward the center of the group where Stu has placed himself.

Stu scoffs again. "You don't have to pander to what some bit—"

"What is it you're trying to say . . . *bro?*"

While I think we all know where Stu is heading with his sentence, the offense I feel is tamped down by just how stern Wes looks again. Serious. His pace is unhurried as he moves, his head tilted to the side ever so slightly, his hand tight around the piece of wood. I don't think he means it as a threat, but Stu straightens nonetheless, the grip around the neck of his broken bottle constricting, too. While he's tall and broad shouldered, he has nothing on Wes, and he has to resort to angling his chin up as they face off, his voice tense when he says, "You're thinking with your dick."

Wes doesn't even flinch; he just moves a step closer, and I can see it takes all of Stu's self-control not to retreat. John is across the room from me, his arms crossed over his chest and a pained expression on his face. He seems more conflict averse than the other men in the room, and we share a quick "boys will be boys" grimace. I can't hold it against Wes, though. Not when he calmly—and correctly—states, "And you're thinking with fuck all."

He places two fingers against Stu's shoulder and shunts him back. The strength in Wes's shove catches Stu off guard, and then of course he's got to save face. He drops his bottle, it lands on the ground with an underwhelming clunk, and then he puffs himself up like a tulle ball gown. For a second, I think he's about to ram his head into Wes's chest until Campbell plants himself right in the middle of them.

"H-hey! Do you want to fight, or do you want to get the fuck out of here?"

If I'm honest, they both look like they want to bump up the body count, and with a barrier between him and Wes, Stu finds his second wind. "Who put this asshole in charge, anyway?"

I watch Wes move back from Campbell's palm. He holds his hands up in surrender and then squints across at Stu, who's swerving his upper body around like he's dodging phantom punches. Wes, on the other hand, looks like he could knock a guy out in one punch, and you'd only be appalled by it because it made you discover you have a new kink.

I look away so I don't have to make that shameful discovery and my gaze falls on Laurie. She's watching Stu like everyone else, her eyes narrowed, lips pressed in a thoughtful line, and I suspect she just might be developing the ick. Good.

"I don't see you stepping up to the plate," Wes says evenly. "If it was up to you, we'd still be down there standing in a bloodbath."

Dani lets out a sob, like mentioning the basement has the power to transport her back to it.

"And if it was *still* up to you," Wes says, "you'd send us all into an active crime scene, blind and alone."

That makes Stu stop. "Fuck you, man."

"Yeah? Fuck you right back," Wes replies without missing a beat, and I have to bite down a laugh.

"What if we break up into two groups?" Laurie says. Her directorial authority comes in handy, and I can't help but be a little relieved that the shock of downstairs has worn off. We need her big, boring, elitist brain. Not only that, but she's been in this building as many times as I have. Hopefully we can supplement each other's alcohol-induced knowledge gaps. "There'll be four of us in each. We can spread out and find an exit . . . Jamie?"

Every head turns to look at me. I got us up to the first level without any further casualties; therefore, I've become the unofficial authority on navigating a massacre.

After he's straightened from swiping his weapon off the ground, Stu gives me a once-over that speaks volumes. There is just *something* in the way he looks at me that makes me want to shrink. It feeds into a preexisting complex and kick-starts a montage of doubt. When I paused and reconsidered my outfit earlier tonight. When I modulated the volume of my laugh in the bar in case it bordered on being too loud. When I tried to backtrack my serial killer references so Wes wouldn't think I was a complete psychopath (and what a swing and a miss that was). I've heard that I'm "a lot" before, and it's enough to make me think maybe my informed hypotheses aren't enough to see us out of this situation.

I'm almost about to give in to my usual instinct to sit up and shut up. About to throw it back to the group and feign uncertainty, but then Wes catches my eye, nods almost imperceptibly, and I remember I shouldn't care what a man like Stu thinks.

Not when the only suggestion he's made is the leading cause of death among teens who cover up hit-and-runs or summon vengeful spirits.

"Two groups could work," I finally say, thinking back over my catalog of slasher knowledge to try to determine a plan. Those films don't usually detail the *right* way to avoid a serial murderer, so I consider each scene that comes to mind as a nonexample.

Four against one is not as strong as eight. It seems like everyone is forgetting the killer cast off four people in complete darkness. They may as well have been doing it with their eyes closed. But this place is huge, and confusing, and if we stay where we are, we're sitting ducks. Anyone could turn the lights off right now and add a few more strokes to their tally.

"If we *all* stay on the dance floor level and work our way toward the back, each group could cover one side of the club," I say, cringing as I start to play out the scenarios that could happen even if an exit is found. They all seem to end in more bloodshed. I'm speaking more to myself than to anyone else when I add, "There's still the issue of not having a way to communicate, and it's *not* a good idea to split up again and send someone to find the other group, so—"

"We should have a firm time limit on how long we look," Laurie says, and I would kiss her if I wasn't certain she'd slap me upside my head for attempting that kind of public display of affection. "Does anyone have a watch?"

Campbell and Stu do. Their dress watches weren't considered "smart" enough to be confiscated at the start of the night, so they are the timekeepers for each group by default. "How does thirty minutes sound?" Laurie says, and I bite my tongue to avoid saying that in a slasher, a determined killer can hack through a hell of a lot of people in thirty minutes. Fortunately, Wes saves me from making a comment that would really ruin the gung-ho mood that's developed now that we have a common goal.

"That sounds good. We should meet back on the dance floor when we're done, report what we find. Hopefully the people who ran up here were able to get out somewhere."

The others. More than half of the original daters ran away from the basement, and if they weren't able to get out through the front door, *where* did they go? I can only hope that there's another exit close by we'll be able to find, too, but if there isn't—if all those people are still here, hiding somewhere in the club—I hope we find them before the killer does.

Wes continues. "If we can't find an exit, we come back, move to the mezzanine, and sweep through in the same way."

It's a great idea.

It's not just me who thinks that. All around the circle, heads are nodding, hands stop wringing, shoulders are lowering from where they've been locked up against ears. The promise of safety in numbers and an exit light at the end of the tunnel is a plan easily adopted by everyone.

Well, almost everyone.

"That's what I was going to suggest." Stu's voice is saltier than movie popcorn.

"Sure it was, buddy," Wes calls across the circle, and I swallow another laugh. When I meet his eye, he's holding back a smile, too. I don't know how he does it. The switch from being an intimidating badass to cracking jokes makes that thread I thought was unraveled lace tighter in my chest.

"I'm not going in the same group as that dickwad," Stu mutters.

"You come with me then," John says, exhibiting the patience of a saint. "Campbell, you go with Wes."

Campbell flinches at the mention of his name but doesn't seem to have any preferences. He just moves toward Wes, keeping an eye on Stu like he's going to try and run across the room and fly-kick him.

"I want to stay with Colette," Dani says. And I can't help but be relieved. Laurie clasps her hand around mine and I squeeze it back. When I meet her eyes and we share a grim smile, I know we're thinking the same thing.

They'd have to pry my cold, dead fingers off you, baby girl.

"Laurie?" Stu asks, and for a second, I fear the pull of his plaid effect might be too strong and she'll want us to go with him.

I'd be fine with John, but if the killer doesn't get Stu, there is a good chance I'm going to be tempted to murder him by the end of the night.

Fortunately, the way he's acted—the fact he's been put under pressure and the result is a dusty-ass piece of coal instead of a diamond—has lessened the lumberjack effect. Laurie glances back at me and says decisively, "We'll go with Wes and Campbell." But she still puts a palm against his arm when she adds, "Make sure you're keeping track of where you're going and where you've been. It's easy to get lost in this place."

He looks disheartened she didn't choose him, and showing just how much of a dusty-ass piece of coal he is, he shrugs her hand off.

"Yeah," he scoffs. "Obviously."

When he turns and walks over to Dani and Colette, placing a hand on each of their backs and turning their group into a huddle separate from the rest of us, I direct a middle finger at his back.

"Jamie," Laurie starts, but I cut her off, still glaring at the back of Stu's head when I say:

"You dodged a bullet, there. He is *not* a nice guy."

I can tell she's a little hurt. She won't let it show on her face. She'll probably never mention it again if we get out of here, but beneath that hard, logical, "definitely a diamond too good for that piece of shit coal" exterior is a woman who came tonight with good intentions. I squeeze her hand in lieu of the tight hug I know she'd hate.

"I mean the man wants us to *split up*," I exclaim. "Next thing he's going to suggest is turning off all the lights and having a drug-fueled orgy."

She allows herself a small smile. "Yeah, I remember the rules on the back of the bathroom door. I read them every time I have to pee, thanks to you." Her eyes are drawn across the circle. "On the subject of nice guys . . ."

Laurie displays her keen ability to slip out of a situation when John forgoes the huddle and makes his way over to me. The upward tilt of his lips indicates he spotted my gesture toward Stu and, although he wouldn't do it himself, he agrees it's warranted.

"Hey."

"Hey."

It's the first time we've been one on one since our date, and I'm reminded of the nice, warm, easy feeling that came with being in his presence.

John moves the Midori bottle between his palms again. "Are you all right? After what happened with Curtis . . ."

I don't know if I've ever had so many people checking in on my well-being before. I've also never had somebody almost have their head disconnected from their body while they're in spitting distance, so the connection between the two events does not escape me. Still, it's nice he wants to make sure I'm okay.

"I'm fine." He looks like he doesn't believe me, but our physical health is a little more pressing than the trauma I'm going to develop, so I add, "I'll *be* fine."

"It was looking kind of . . . heated before everything."

So he was watching. It's kind of flattering he kept an eye on me.

"Oh, yeah . . ." I wince when I remember what I said to Curtis before the lights turned off. "I feel a little bad the last thing he heard before he died was that he's an asshole." And I do. Even though he is—was.

John's eyes crinkle in that soft eighties Bill Pullman way and he leans in—*leans in*—to whisper conspiratorially, "I'm sure you weren't telling him anything he didn't already know."

I can't help but chuckle. "Thanks." Then I fully comprehend that he's paired up with Stu to find an exit. Hotheaded "Let's split up!" "I get pissy with women I just met over the most insignificant things" Stu. And I feel the need to warn him, "Look, there *will* be another way out of here, but if this is anything like—"

"Those scary movies you like?"

He remembered. It makes my stomach do a little somersault.

"Yeah, those ones ... we just have to be smarter than—" The killer? Stu? The other daters spread out across the club? "Than whoever is doing this. You just have to keep your cool."

I don't think John has ever been anything other than cool. He's been so polite and levelheaded this whole time. He certainly hasn't let anger, or fear, or panic overcome him since Curtis was killed. He seems to think over my advice, glancing up at me from under some very nice lashes, then holds his hand up in front of me. It's as steady as Colin Firth's eye contact.

"What do you think my chances are, seeing as you're an expert on all this?"

I smile. "They're looking pretty good."

"Well, if you think so, Jamie, then I think I can put my faith in that."

That makes me blush. Over his shoulder I can see the groups are split, prepared to leave. We're the final members they're waiting for, and I realize Wes is watching us. He looks away when our eyes meet, but that doesn't detract from the fact he was looking. Watching. I return my gaze to John and try to instill some confidence in my voice.

"I'll see you soon, okay?"

"We still need to have that drink, right?"

"Right." I scoff at the obvious joke, and then with one last look at the doors, I move to Laurie's side and walk deeper into the club.

CHAPTER 9

"People who truly killed once are far more likely to kill again."

—Not *Sleepless in Seattle*

Our group takes the left side. We need to cross in front of the dance floor again to get there, and the contrast between the times when I had to squeeze myself through sweaty swaying bodies and now does not escape me. There are four of us creeping around a space that is meant to hold two hundred.

We don't talk as we walk close to the booths, forming a tight diamond shape with Wes at the front and Campbell at the back. Conversation doesn't factor high when you're trying to avoid the attention of a killer, and I hope everyone is using the silence to keep an ear out for some preview that we're going to meet this psycho face to face. The departing footsteps of the other group echo behind us and I try not to let my attention go with them, straining instead to hear sounds coming from the dimly lit alcoves ahead of us—shuffling shoes, scraping metal, a nondiegetic ominous tone that would signal impending danger.

It takes a lot of effort to keep my trembling fingers tight around the neck of my bottle when we're halfway across the room. The cool, dim white light that shone down on the stairs bathes the entire open space of the dance floor. A glimmer catches my eye, and I shoot a glance up to a disco ball on the ceiling. Intermittent gusts of air from the vents keep it moving, even if it is at a glacial pace, and faint diamonds of light spray across the mezzanine level above our heads. The slow, unhurried revolution should be calming, but it isn't. Who's to say the killer isn't going to switch the light off and we'll be stuck with no way of shielding ourselves? It was a possibility with eight people escaping the basement, but it becomes a lot more concerning now that we've halved our numbers.

We make it back to the stairs, and I try not to think about what—and who—still lies beneath our feet. But trying not to think about the bodies in the bar just makes me think about the very real possibility of finding even more bodies up here.

We round the brick wall and come to another hallway. The gas lamps, intended to foster a seductive, panty-dropping effect, look eerie tracing the wall, especially when the alcoves set into them on our left makes the crimson hallway look like toothless gums.

The first alcove contains deep-set booths, more velvet curtains, and a mini chandelier that is still and glistening. Once Wes has checked it for a threat, we continue down the corridor. As we're heading for the second alcove my heel gets caught in the strands of the plush carpet. The tangled red threads threaten to drag me into the mouth of the seating niche, and flashes of Ripley in *Aliens* and Katie in *Paranormal Activity* cross my mind as I lose my balance.

I grab the frame of the alcove, pulling myself away from the knot that's latched on to my heel, and try not to stab myself with the Kahlúa bottle as I swallow a gasp that wants to escape upon my death drop.

The "clumsy girl" trope has never been my favorite in rom-coms, and in a slasher, unsteady feet is a sign you're not going to make it to the sequel.

Wes, Laurie, and Campbell all freeze, as I land/sit/fall onto the cushioned seat, so practiced in keeping quiet at this point that their only reaction is a collective flinch. Once I've accepted I haven't fallen onto some hidden buzzsaw and nothing is going to descend from the ceiling and drill through my stomach, I push off the surface of the couch, balancing on my elbows, and notice . . .

I'm sparkling.

The bare parts of my body that hit the couch are *covered* in red glitter. The last-minute cleaners really did do a terrible job.

"*Fuck*," I spit.

Wes checks the space around us and then steps into the alcove.

"Are you all right?"

Glitter stays with you *forever*. So, no. If silver sparkles were glistening across my bare shoulders instead of red, this would be the perfect moment to turn to him with a tortured look on my face and announce that "This is the skin of a killer." But then again, we're trying to get away from an *actual* killer, so I tamp down any impulse to make a *Twilight* reference.

"Yeah." I hand my Kahlúa bottle over to him and slip my shoes off, fastening the straps around each other and hanging them in the crook of my elbow; they're heavy and the heels are pointy, and that's enough of a criterion to make them a weapon. When I'm on my feet, I immediately feel more grounded, more capable. Confident I can stay upright and outrun the killer . . . maybe even throw my shoes at him to slow him down.

"Huh . . ." I hear Wes let out an amused exhale, and when I glance up at him, he looks like he did at the beginning of our date. Surprised, pleasantly so.

"What?"

"You're . . ." He grins. "Short."

"I'm not *that* short."

I get to work trying to brush as much of the cherry-red sparkles from my arms as I can. The sweat and blood makes them stick, and then it's on my hands, and I can feel it falling onto the tops of my feet. *Fuck.*

"You're shorter than me."

I'm eye level with the center of his chest, but I don't think that would be a new experience for him. He's taller than Campbell. Laurie, too. But it's *my* height that makes his eyes seem to sparkle with amusement as I hold out my hand for my weapon.

"Is that a problem?"

"Not at all." He still looks amused, and I pin him with a warning look.

"If you say I'm cute, it won't be the killer you have to worry about."

He places the bottle back in my palm, his fingers lingering against my wrist, and for a moment I think I could forget we're trying to escape if he touched me like that again. If he touched me like that on other parts of my body, but slower, firmer, for longer. Especially when he says, "I don't think you're cute, Jamie . . ."

His eyes dart down to my bare feet and then slowly draw a path all the way back up to meet mine before he adds, "Not at all."

The way he holds my stare afterward has the potential to make my knees weak and send me back onto the booth again. Okay, so we both don't think the other is cute. Good to know.

I'd like to ask what other words he'd use to describe me, but I'm aware Campbell and Laurie are standing guard since I had my graceful collapse, and we are most definitely still being chased by a psycho. So I gesture out to the corridor and walk past him, situating myself back in formation with Laurie and hoping he can't spot the blush on my face. He walks out a moment later and heads to the front of the group, leading us to the neighboring alcove and conducting the same check he performed on the first one.

Laurie catches my eye while we wait, and though she doesn't open her mouth, her facial expressions are loud enough that I can confidently translate the dip and fall of her eyebrows—and my subsequent silent responses—as thus:

What was that?

Nothing.

Nothing? Stop eye fucking him!

I am not!

Oh, really? You're not?

No.

You liar.

But you love me.

God knows why.

By the end of the conversation, we're wearing matching tight-lipped smiles. I glance behind me and it's clear Campbell has witnessed the whole exchange and hasn't been able to understand any of it. Before, he was nervous. Now he's confused. It's not a good mix and he looks extra twitchy. More like Norman Bates before he goes full "Mother." Like he's one sudden sound away from bolting.

We reach the third alcove, and something isn't right. Wes stops a few feet away, and when he points to it with the chair leg, glancing back as if to confirm it's not just his mind playing tricks on him, I nod. I see it, too.

The curtains closest to the hallway are bulkier than the others we've seen. Lumpier. And while the flickering effect of the gas lamps against the sheen of the velvet makes all the curtains look like they're undulating, this one is definitely moving. Like blood pulsing through an artery, and the more whoever is hidden behind it realizes we aren't walking past their hiding spot, the faster it pulses.

It's most likely one of the daters, but we can't be sure it's not *him*. The killer. I know I'm making a lot of assumptions about whoever is doing this being a man, but in my defense, it *is* a more male-dominated activity. Mass murder. Not to say the killer can't be a woman. Fictional female killers like Baby Firefly or Mary Lou Maloney could go toe-to-toe with the most iconic male Big Bads. But when it comes to real life?

Women are usually just better emotional regulators.

There's a cord hanging down near the doorway, and when Wes steps forward to reach for it, looking over his shoulder to make sure we're all ready, I move into the space next to him and hold my broken bottle out. I don't even think about it, and when I'm there, there is a part of me that wants to back right out again. But I also can't let Wes be alone in the line of fire if a knife is going to appear from behind the curtain. It's not just because I lied to Laurie, and I was definitely eye fucking him a few minutes ago; it's because I know this night would be much worse without him.

He tries to get me to move back with some sharp head movements, but I ignore them and gesture for him to open the curtain already. Laurie has her back against mine to watch the corridor. Campbell is useless. When Wes sees he's fighting a losing battle, his jaw tenses in defeat and he swaps the wood to his other hand, reaching for the cord.

After one more shared look, he holds up an index finger to start the count.

One.

Two.

Three.

He pulls the cord, and the curtain draws back as sharply as an inhale.

She doesn't scream. She just lets out one of those chest-shattering gasps until she sees there's four equally terrified people staring back at her. Once she realizes we have no intention of killing her, she glances down at the broken bottle I've held up between us and just looks . . . unimpressed. Resting bitch face fully activated and name tag still in place.

Billie.

After the stink-eye episode at cocktail hour, I couldn't figure out if she was Kat Stratford standoffish or Jo Stockton shy. Dressed in all black, with her silky brown hair fastened into a low, effortless chignon, and her lips a matte shade of merlot, she looks chic and unattainable. Like she's walked in off the street by mistake and stuck around on the off chance things might get interesting. I wonder if this is what she had in mind.

I drop my bottle down to my side—maybe that's why she looks so defensive—and ask, "Are you okay?"

Because even though we're in the middle of a horror movie, it's the polite thing to ask.

Her thick, perfectly shaped eyebrows smack together in two concave swoops, and her voice has a derisive quality when she replies, "No. I'm fucking hiding from a murderer. What is wrong with you?"

Well, fuck me for being concerned. Kat Stratford it is.

Her gaze flits between the four of us, her lips pursed and her almost black eyes wary as she says, "I barely got out of there. Everyone went apeshit after what happened to"—she looks back at me—"*your* date."

"Do you know where anyone else is?" Wes asks, and after a drawn-out apathetic stare in his direction, she shakes her head.

"As soon as we got up the stairs and the doors wouldn't open, everyone just scattered. It was like turning on a light in a kitchen infested with roaches. I ran this way and hid . . . Then I heard the scream."

I see Laurie wince in my periphery. I bet the sound is as easy for her to conjure up as it is for me.

"Did you see who did it?" Laurie asks.

Her eyes snap to Laurie and narrow.

"Did I see who *did* it? I was a little busy *running for my life*." Her tone is acidic, and it's a small comfort to know she talks to everyone like that. She looks between us again. "What are you guys doing?"

"Looking for a way out."

"Good." Billie pushes the curtain to the side and steps out from the hiding spot. A few tendrils of chestnut hair fall loose around her face, and when she reaches up to bat them away, I spy blood across the top of her sweater. It's the same kind of blood spray Colette had. I didn't think it was possible, but her expression hardens even further when she notices me looking.

"I got hit when I was at the door," she says, even though I didn't ask. "How many . . . fatalities were there?"

Wes answers. "Four downstairs. One on this level."

She lets out a deep, extended sigh, her eyes falling to my dress, nostrils flaring like she's caught a whiff of a bad smell. I get the feeling Billie is not a girl's girl, but then her gaze flicks up to stare hard at the chandelier hanging from the ceiling, and I think this is the moment she cries. This is the moment we might see a small crack in the armor, a little humanity within the ice.

Instead, she just shrugs.

"The night is still young, I guess."

CHAPTER 10

"I'm scared of walking out of this room and never killing the rest of my whole life the way I kill when I'm with you."

—Not *Dirty Dancing*

$\mathcal{B}$runette blowout Jennifer is hiding two booths down from where we found Billie, and she's much happier to see us. She reveals herself when we're a few steps from her hiding spot. Turns out it's near impossible to completely soften the sound of five people moving through an echoey corridor, and she figured it was more likely a group of survivors rather than a group of killers.

It's a gamble, but it pays off for her.

I push thoughts of the pack murderers in *The Texas Chainsaw Massacre* and *Hellraiser* out of my mind as quickly as they enter.

Jennifer still looks "girl next door" pretty despite spending the last however long compressed between a heavy velvet curtain and a brick wall. Her hair is only a little mussed, her green dress easily straightened, her name easily distinguishable on her sticker because her handwriting is flawless. She must have gotten out of the bar before the tag could be hit with blood spray. When she slides out from her hiding place without any theatrics and whispers how relieved she is to see us, she's immediately likable, and our group of five turns into six.

Jennifer and Billie form a new duo behind Laurie and me, while Campbell still trails at the back. Every time I glance over my shoulder, he seems to lag a little more, like the only thing that's keeping him tethered to the group is that the alternative—being by himself—is so much worse.

We pass the last of the alcoves, and the corridor splits into an intersection, a red cross illuminated by bronze wall lamps whose flames all flicker in sync. We can keep going straight, into a claret-colored abyss that may or may not lead to an exit. We can turn left, into another long hallway that is as dimly lit as the others. Or, if we go right and trail behind a bar that lines the edge of the dance floor, we'll end up back over at the side we came from. The other group's territory.

"What do you think?" Wes asks as we idle, and I try to remember if I've been down here before. When it was less *Cabaret* chic. "Straight ahead?"

I don't see why not. It makes sense that another exit would be at the back of the building, but then the club sits on a street corner, so there could be a side entrance, too.

"Laurie?" I ask, but she's already shaking her head.

"I can't remember shit about this level."

"Me, neither." Maybe this place really is the reason I don't drink Kamikazes anymore. "We stayed up mostly on the mezzanine, didn't we?"

"Yeah."

"What if it's a dead end?" Jennifer whispers from behind me. She's dug her fingers into her clavicle, gripping on for dear life.

"*There's* a double meaning," Billie mutters, and Campbell lets out a little sniff of fear.

"I think it's more likely the whole thing connects back on itself," I say.

That's the theme of the building—a three-level maze filled with plenty of places to engage in illicit activities. I just don't think the architects who came in and redesigned the former factory were thinking it'd be as illicit as murder.

I watch Wes as he mulls over our options. He's thinking through our path before we take it, considering each route the crossroads presents to us and checking them against the way we came. He was doing that as we moved past the alcoves, at the coat check, downstairs in the bar. He's been doing it this whole time. I never thought I'd find vigilance sexy.

"It'd be good if they all connected," Wes says. "If we don't find an exit at least we come back to something familiar . . . How are we doing for time?"

Campbell glances down at his watch, looks back up. "I can't remember when we left, but it's almost ten forty-five."

Holy shit, Campbell. You had *one* job.

Before I can firmly categorize myself as confrontational, Laurie decides to be diplomatic.

"I don't think it's been that long, but let's make sure we're back to meet the others by eleven."

"Let's go straight ahead then. And let's make it quick." Since no one has the means or motive to argue with Wes, we trudge on.

Whether there's an end to the hallway is unclear until we're a few feet away and the gas lamp directly in front of us reveals that the path turns to the left. We're a few steps from the corner when I spy a shadow creeping across the carpet.

My heart doesn't clench in my chest. Not like when I saw the unmistakable movement of Billie behind the curtain. Instead, it plummets into my stomach, because I know it's not actually a shadow. I know by the way it moves across the floor without merging with the dark patches of the hallway that the faint glow of the light sconces can't reach, the way the carpet fibers bend under the weight of the shadow as it edges out farther and farther. It's a stain. And it's spreading.

"Wes," I breathe.

"Yeah," he murmurs. His back is stiff, even as his shoulders drop in a sigh. "I see it."

"It's not usually a great idea to walk toward the growing pool of blood," I say, and Wes nods stiffly in front of me.

"I agree, but if there's an exit around the corner . . ."

I hear his exhale, long and weighted, before he turns back to the group with a commanding look in his eye. It does nothing to abate the urge to eye fuck him some more, so I keep my stare trained over his shoulder. If he can't follow rule six, I'll do it for him . . . just in case.

"Stay close to the wall," Wes says. "And if anyone comes around that corner . . . *run*."

I'd love to do that right now. Turn back, or at the very least slow our steps, but there's no point delaying the inevitable, and when we get to the end of the hall, we see it. Or rather, *them*.

He's killed two more people. The matching puncture wounds on their throats makes that startling clear. If cut in the right way, a carotid artery can bleed out in two minutes. I googled it once out of curiosity, after a particularly gore-filled movie marathon. I just never thought I'd see it in person.

Drew and the woman next to him never stood a chance. I know it's Drew from the bold block letters on his name tag, and while the woman's long red hair is familiar from cocktail hour, I can't remember her name. I only know that she was the one with the Julia Roberts smile and that Drew liked pineapple on his pizza. Really superficial information about two people who are lying dead in front of us. They look like the twins from *The Shining* from the way they've dropped onto the carpet. Their blood spreads around them like one of those heart-shaped beds nobody thinks is romantic.

"What the h—"

Laurie's voice comes out in a long gust. She shakes her head in disgust, her eyes fixed on the spreading stain, and that's when I notice them. Scattered around the two bodies, sinking into the pool of blood. Red rose petals.

What the hell?

The petals aren't just confined to the bodies, either. No. They continue down the hall into the darkness, scattered delicately across the carpet. A *trail* of rose petals.

What in the *American Beauty* madness is going on?

Wes seems to have the same question on his mind. He starts to edge around the macabre mix of crimson petals and the slightly darker shade of the puddle that is swallowing them as it spreads, intending to follow the trail.

He keeps a firm hold on the chair leg, his other palm extended back, directed toward us, as he says, "Stay here."

Yeah, that's not going to happen.

"No, Wes—"

"I'm just going to check around the corner. I'll be rig—"

"Don't fucking say it," I hiss back before he can finish, willing away the sharp clench around my heart at the dangerous words that were about to come out of his mouth. He almost broke rule eight.

"Don't you *dare* say 'I'll be right back,'" I grit out, because it's a promise he can't keep. I am *surrounded* by people who need to consider watching films for their educational value and not just entertainment.

"There's no chance I'm going down there," Billie says.

"I don't want to, either." Jennifer grips her shoulders tighter, shaking her head jerkily as she looks everywhere but at the bodies on the ground. While Jennifer is avoiding the obstacle in our path,

Campbell can't tear his eyes away from them with that same distant, unblinking look on his face. I highly doubt he'll be making any moves to get a closer look, either.

"Then I'll go with you." It's out of my mouth before I've actually made my mind up, but there are too many scenes playing through my head of men like Wes walking down a corridor and never coming back that I don't regret it.

He glances back down the rose-covered corridor, his jaw tightening before he takes a step back to me, his hand gripping my shoulder, heating my skin, and he's right. He is taller than me.

"Jamie, stay he—"

"No. Splitting off is just as bad as splitting up. It's one of the rules."

I turn to Laurie, offer my Kahlúa bottle, and hold my other hand out for her travel-sized one. It's loose in her grip and easy for me to swipe, exchanging it for the larger, heavier bottle. Jennifer and Billie don't have weapons, and I'll feel better leaving them, leaving Laurie, if they have something big and sharp to protect themselves with. I already know these makeshift weapons won't hold up against the arsenal I suspect this guy has, but it's better than nothing.

"*Rules?* What the fuck is she talking about?" Billie mutters, and I ignore her.

"Jamie—" Laurie says, and I can't ignore her as easily. "Don't go."

Her voice trembles on the last word. Even in the dim light I can see the panic in her face. I know how contradictory my words are. This is exactly what I *didn't* want to do. Split up. Leave her. But we *need* to find a way out, and if Wes goes down that hall and doesn't come back, we are majorly fucked.

"He *can't* go alone," I reason, and she goes to follow me.

"Then I'll come, too."

"*No!*"

She flinches at the sound, and again I need to tell my heart to keep beating. I don't know how to do anything by halves. I'm not sure I'm capable of it, so when Laurie and I became friends I knew I was all in. I can deal with the three-hour documentaries that are lacking in any discernible conflict. I can deal with the aversion to hugs. I can even deal with the lumberjack obsession because—despite our differences, or maybe because of them—she makes me feel seen and valued and understood in her no-nonsense way. It's not like I didn't have friends before we met; it's not like I haven't made others since; but she's just a really fucking good one. The best, and if something happens to her . . . well, I don't even know. All I know is I will do everything to make sure nothing does. If there *is* someone waiting down there, I won't drag her into their path. And that's why I make myself sound calm and assured when I say, "I—*we* need you to watch our backs. The four of you just . . ."

I consider the scene setup, try to recall something that's similar and how we can avoid playing out a bloody moment that would rival the one we're all currently trying not to step in.

"Stay in the corner," I say. Johnny Castle would roll over in his grave right now. At the same time, though, I am definitely not having the time of my life.

"Keep your back to the wall and no one can sneak up on you," I add as Wes settles at my side. He's still shaking his head, like the idea of me joining him is akin to making snow angels in the sticky mess blocking the hallway, but he directs the next instruction to the rest of the group.

"If the lights turn off, hit the ground and stay near the walls. If anything else happens, run. Run and then hide. Only fight back when you don't have any other option." His eyes wander to the weakest-looking member of the group. Campbell, obviously. "But *stay together*. Somebody is going to realize we're missing eventually. Even if it takes the whole night."

Billie rolls her eyes, but she wanders over to the corner where the halls meet and slumps between two gas lamps, her back firmly against the wall.

"Fantastic," she quips. "I haven't had a slumber party in years."

I wonder why.

Wes turns back to the bodies obstructing our path with a sigh. "Come on."

We can't avoid the blood. It reaches wall to wall now, so Wes finds the shallowest part of the puddle and walks through it. There are certain personal boundaries I'd like to remain intact after tonight, and walking barefoot through a blood spill is one of them. I quickly slip my heels back on before I follow him, feeling Laurie's eyes on my back as I fasten the straps around my ankles. When I glance up, she's just staring at me, so much emotion in her eyes I fear it's going to pour right out of her.

She'd let me hug her right now if I wanted to, but it would feel too much like a goodbye. There's a finality to it that I don't want to put out into the universe. So instead of a hug, I just take advantage of our well-attuned facial expressions and silently promise *I'll be right back*, because I'd never say it out loud.

I ignore the squelching of the carpet when I edge around the bodies, distract myself from the way the blood laps at the bottom of my shoes, and feel grateful I chose a closed toe for tonight. When I reach Wes, they look like Louboutins, the bottoms stained red, and I have half a mind to just keep them on. But then I imagine myself tripping again, this time while being pursued by the killer, and I'm taking them off. I should just abandon them in the hallway, write them off as another casualty of the night, but I feel like they could defend me a little better than the beer bottle I took from Laurie. So I clutch the straps in my free hand as I move closer to Wes, trying to ignore how the soles are dripping.

We're only a few feet away from the rest of the group, but we might as well be on opposite sides of a river. The rose petals scattered before us blend in better with the carpet without the darker shade of blood beneath it, but even then, I can't ignore the fact their placement is deliberate. The way they've been dropped along the corridor, it's strategic, aesthetic. If I didn't know any better, I'd think it was meant to be—

"How romantic," Wes mutters when we start moving down the hall. His eyes are focused forward, jaw still tight, mouth thin, but he can't help looking down at the petals every now and then. When he does, he makes a point of crushing them under his heel.

"You think this is supposed to be *romantic*?" I whisper, but I don't get an immediate response when he pauses in front of me. The trail continues around the corner, out of sight. Corners are going to be the most dangerous part of our expedition because we're blind to what's around them until we're close enough to get stabbed. Wes must think the same thing, since he wraps his free hand around my wrist and pulls me behind him, drawing me in until my chest is firmly against his back.

The message is clear. *Stay behind me. Stay close.*

While that may be the intended communication, my brain still takes a second to add a very nice ass to the list of Wes's admirable qualities. Once that's securely in the memory bank, I make myself concentrate on the matter at hand.

"Wes?" I ask.

"I don't know," he murmurs, moving his palm from my arm to the middle of my back to hold me against him. Like if anyone plans to stab me, they'll have to literally go through him first. "I've never done the rose petal thing myself."

No, I don't imagine he has. Something like rose petals seems a little too showy for someone like Wes, but the thing is—his fingers grip a little tighter into the material of my dress and I feel the need to clear my throat—I don't think he'd have to resort to it, either.

"That's what they mean, right?" he says, our shoulders scraping against the wall as we move closer to the corner. I can feel the rise and fall of his back against my chest. Wes's smoky, spicy scent is so much stronger from sweat and proximity, and in the darkness my body misinterprets it all. It thinks we're moving toward a bedroom rather than to our potential demise, so when I poke my head around his arm and can see down the new hallway, see there's nothing but rose petals, it takes a lot of effort to make myself move away from him.

"The rose petals were on top of the bodies, so that means they were put there after they were . . . well . . . it has to be deliberate." He pauses, looks like he's weighing whether to say the next sentence, then the muscle of his jaw shifts as he stares into the darkness ahead of us. "Have you heard about that woman who was murdered recently?"

At first I'm tempted to ask which one. But then I remember the end of the report Laurie and I watched earlier today. As soon as I move away from him, as soon as I catch a glimpse of those rose petals tracing down the corridor, I make the connection. I barely registered it this afternoon because it was tragically similar to the countless reports of other women who have met a similar fate. The ones who become reminders that I can't walk at night with music blasting through my headphones, or that I need to hold my keys between my fingers when I walk to my car in the dark. But this one. This one's still fresh.

Wes quirks his brow, and I know he's thinking the same thing as me.

Our guy's not an amateur. He's a pro.

CHAPTER 11

"I hate your big dumb hunting knife and the way you read my mind. I hate you so much it makes me sick, it makes me commit a crime."

—Not *10 Things I Hate About You*

The rose petals are too specific to be a coincidence.

Wes shifts on the spot, and the movement makes his arm brush against mine. Goose bumps ignite across my bare skin, and not the kind you'd expect to experience after discovering two bodies and a possible connection to a serial killer.

"You think this could be linked to those murders?" I ask, gesturing to the petals on the ground.

He nods, and I don't think it's just the dim, artificial lighting of the corridor that draws the color from his face. "Yeah, they could be."

My brain starts cataloguing everything that's happened tonight with the brief snippets of information I've picked up about the other murders with the same calling card. I haven't been paying close attention to them because—and I know this sounds morbid, but—it's like watching a film you already know the ending to. One that relies too heavily on a prescriptive format. There's nothing *new* about those murders. It's the same movie, different cast.

Tonight, though?

"If this is connected, this would be an escalation, wouldn't it? Going from murdering one woman at a time to trapping a bunch of people in a building and methodically killing them off one by one seems like a change in methodology. Or a change in MO, if we want to use the correct termi—"

I cut myself off when Wes moves his gaze from the corridor back to me, his mouth set in a firm line. Heat starts to flow up my neck and I drop my stare to the petals crushed beneath my feet.

"Sorry." I shouldn't be talking so much. *We* shouldn't be talking so much. Not when our goal is to avoid the killer and find an exit. I could kick myself for almost going full *me* and—

"Why are you apologizing?"

I start when his hand brushes against the back of mine. This time the contact is on purpose, and when I glance at him that grave expression is gone. He looks confused.

"I just . . ." I pause. There's got to be a better way to say *I was about to go on a verbal tangent that would put my "dating is a dangerous pastime" word vomit to shame.* "Sometimes I get on a roll with a topic, and it seems like I'm eager or excited about things that people shouldn't be eager and excited about. For the record, I'm definitely not into what's happening. I just get caught up in my head, and when it comes out of my mouth . . ." I shrug, like the reactions I get from people who think I should speak less don't bother me. "It doesn't always land well."

Wes's eyes trace over my face. The warmth in my cheeks feels different when he shakes his head and murmurs, "It lands well with me. I don't see anything wrong with it."

He curls his hand around my wrist again, shifting his attention forward to where the corridor turns another corner, and that brings the conversation to a halt. Wes's grip tightens against my skin, mine tightens around my weapons, and we skim along the wall.

"What did you mean when you were talking about the rules before?" Wes asks quietly after we inch our heads out around the edge and are greeted by more darkness.

"It's a poster Laurie and I have in our apartment," I say once we start to move down the corridor, side by side. "How to Survive a Slasher. There are ten rules to follow if you want to survive that kind of movie. 'Don't split up' is number five."

When we're this close and I don't have to speak above a whisper, I can keep my eyes on the path ahead of us. The sight isn't a promising one. There's more rose petals littering the floor, smooth walls that are punctuated by syncopated, flickering gas lamps, and not an exit to be found.

"You really are into horror movies then."

I glance at him, spotting a smile amid the glow of the artificial flames illuminating his face.

"I really am. I never thought I'd live one out, though."

I may have watched *Only You* or *The Wedding Singer* and hoped for some semblance of those storylines to appear in my life, but not for a second did I watch *The Town That Dreaded Sundown* or *Wolf Creek* and think: *Man, just once I'd love for that to happen to me.*

"I know it sounds dumb, but following the rules, it helps with the . . ." With the reality of what is happening to us right now. That people have died, could be dying, *will* die, and that nobody on the outside—no police or *anyone*—has turned up to save us probably means that nobody is coming. I can't say that, though, not to this guy I met a couple of hours ago who is doing everything in his power to keep us alive. So instead I say, "It helps with not being scared."

If we were in a slasher, or even a rom-com, this would be the part where he tells me I don't have to be scared because he's not going to let anything happen to me. Then there'd be a series of events that would lead to him being disemboweled by an ice hook and leave me incapable of trusting men at their word.

Wes doesn't do that, though; he just shifts closer as we make it to the halfway point of the hallway.

"I count down from three." His voice is right at my ear, his breath fanning across my temple, and when I look up, I see just how close he is. His gaze is still focused straight ahead when he adds, "Whenever I'm scared or stressed or need to make a tough decision . . . I give myself three seconds, and then I do it."

It's so simple. I've only known him a short time, but it makes sense. He seems like the kind of guy who goes with his gut. The kind of guy who knows being brave isn't about being fearless, it's about doing what you need to do despite the fear.

"My parents taught me to do it when they realized I had poor impulse control as a kid and I guess it stuck."

I like it, but I can't ignore—

"*Had* poor impulse control?"

I catch the amused twitch at the side of his mouth as he lifts his head to look back the way we came. "It comes back every now and then."

His chin grazes the top of my head, and I can imagine him doing the same thing on a street corner while we wait for the lights to change, or in a café when his coffee order is called. Sans bloody shoes and improvised weapons, of course.

"Counting works every time. I can anticipate what will happen, but I don't have enough time to back out. It puts the pressure on. I work better under pressure."

"I've noticed."

His smile turns into a grin. Even though it looks like his entire body is ready to strike at the first sign of danger, his eyes are soft. I'm reminded of when we were sitting on either side of the table during our date. Bedroom eyes.

There's a sound. A rustle that makes us both flinch until I realize it's not a rustle, it's a crackle coming from the closest gas lamp. The relief that it's a loose wire, rather than a murderer, pulls a shuddering sigh from my lips.

"Let's keep going," Wes murmurs as he rolls out the tension in his shoulders. The false alarm doesn't stop his questions, though, and I'd guess maintaining our conversation is more of a fear-reduction technique than a do-over for our bad first date.

"So, what's the first rule of slashers?" he asks as we walk farther down the hallway, and that surprises me. It's the classic marker of the original slashers from the seventies and eighties. The way you can identify the inimitable Final Girl—the conventionally attractive, doggedly determined heroine who hacks down the killer—among the other nubile, soon-to-be-dead teens.

"You don't know?"

"I told you, I'm more of a Sandra Bullock fan."

He's half joking, but I get the feeling he's a *Speed* repeater.

Wes does his usual "every angle" observation before looking back down at me, one brow quirked. I try to maintain eye contact, but it's no use. I avert my gaze down to the petals. "Don't have sex."

"Sorry?"

I glance up to see the other eyebrow has joined its friend, high in the middle of his forehead.

"That's the rule. If you have sex, you die."

His eyes narrow in thought, like he's considering the two options that rule presents, then he looks over at the entrance of the corridor, breathing out a sigh.

"Damn."

At first I think he's disappointed that *that's* the rule. Like getting lucky was high on his list of things to do tonight, right under "avoid a mass murderer," but then I look down and see the rose petals have stopped at the edge of the carpet. The whole point of a trail is to lead to something, right? But we've just followed them right back around to where we were standing at that first crossroads. I can see the bar on the edge of the dance floor straight ahead, and if we turn left we should see the others waiting for us.

We would've noticed the trail if it had been there from the start. So that means whoever is doing this has been mere steps away from us this whole time. And the idea the killer could have snuck up on Laurie and the others while Wes and I were following his trail makes the espresso martinis churn in my stomach. It makes my hand sweat around the straps of my heels, but it also just makes me . . . confused.

I think Wes is right: the trail was deliberate. It was a message. If I were to go a step further, I'd say it was symbolic. You don't need to have studied romantic movies to know roses equal love. I just can't figure out why they're here in the middle of a massacre.

We complete the final turn, and I see the rest of the group exactly where we left them, standing in the corner with their backs against the wall. The bloodstain on the floor has stopped a few feet from encroaching on their "safe" area, and as we hurry down the corridor, Billie, Jennifer, and Laurie all jerk their heads in our direction. They each have varying degrees of relief and expectation etched on their faces, but all I have to do is shake my head and they know. We didn't find a way out.

Wes stiffens beside me, slows down. It draws my attention away from the three women, and that's when I realize someone is missing.

"Where the hell is Campbell?" Wes blurts out, and I can't believe I didn't notice earlier.

Well, actually I can. This is Campbell we're talking about. If anyone was going to run as soon as possible, it was him, and when

Laurie informs us that he all but sprinted away as soon as we were out of sight, I can't rustle up any kind of surprise.

Billie snorts from where she's still propped in the corner, arms folded across her chest as she remarks, "Well, he was pretty flighty during our date, so at least he's consistent."

"Where the fuck would he have gone?" I ask, but it's more a general exclamation rather than something that requires answering.

Campbell hasn't displayed any kind of instincts in the time he's been part of the group, and I just can't help but think this is the kind of decision that gets you killed *early* in the first act of a slasher.

"Should we look for him?" Jennifer asks, following Laurie and joining me and Wes in the hallway. They both immediately place their backs against the opposite wall, so they have a 180 view.

Smart women.

It's Jennifer's cautious concern, teamed with her general wholesome aura, the fact she's brunette . . . I shouldn't be thinking it, but she's got all the indicators of becoming a Final Girl. I push that thought away as quickly as it comes because there's only one way someone becomes a Final Girl. When the rest of us are dead.

"We stick to the plan," Wes murmurs as Laurie tries to swap out our weapons. I push her bottle away. Using broken bottles to defend ourselves seems laughable now. They aren't enough to go up against someone who has killed seven people in the last hour or so. It'd be like trying to fight a samurai with a toothpick. But I want her to have the bigger bottle, the sharper one, just in case.

"We go and wait on the dance floor for the others. Hopefully they found a way out," Wes says. "And we just have to hope Campbell hasn't gotten himself killed."

"Yay," Billie says, finally pushing off the wall and joining our group. "Can't wait to see how this turns out."

That's how we find ourselves moving back down the corridor,

turning away from the end of the rose petal trail and coming into view of the bar that takes up an entire edge of the dance floor. I can't help but glance up at the mezzanine above it. That's where we're going to have to move our search if the others haven't found an exit. Considering the evolution of Cravin' into Serendipity seems to be more of a facelift rather than anything structural, I know what to expect up there. It'll be larger, more hallways, more rooms, more dead ends. It'll be so much easier to get lost. So much easier to be found . . .

The glint of the railing catches my eye, and it's not the first time I've considered how dangerous it is to have this open space above the dance floor. Not when it would be so easy to fall over the edge and end up on the bar. Or maybe that's just from watching *Chopping Mall* and *Death Ship*. Those railings just give you a little more flair as you're plummeting to your death.

"What the *fuck*?"

Wes's voice is like thunder. It's a suppressed warning, the personification of a dark cloud that rolls over before a deadly lightning strike. And when I tear my eyes from the mezzanine and see what's caused his entire body to go rigid, his face to go hard, fury almost crackling off him, I get it. I feel it, too. Because there, standing beneath the disco ball, is John.

And only John.

He's already holding his hands up in surrender, the Midori bottle loose in one fist and a first aid kit hanging from the other as I try to figure out why he isn't flanked by two well-dressed women and an asshole in plaid.

"I told him we shouldn't split up."

CHAPTER 12

"Killing isn't easy; that's why they call it murder."

—Not *The Big Sick*

"**S**tu wanted to find the exit before you," John says, pausing to lift a hand in greeting to the two new additions to our group. Jennifer looks happy to see him, and I remember that before everything went down, it seemed like they had a nice date.

"He told Dani and Colette to go back into the basement together to see if any of the dead staff had phones. I stayed on this level, and he went up to the mezzanine."

While the slasher fan in me is screaming that nothing good ever happens by returning to the scene of the original kill, let alone going down into a basement, I can admit trying to look for a phone on one of the staff is a good idea—one I wish I thought of before we made our way up. But why didn't Stu tell the rest of us? Why turn an escape attempt into a competition?

He really is a dusty-ass piece of coal. And maybe he's something worse than that. I'm starting to doubt whether that scream we heard while we were downstairs—the one that made me think the killer was above our heads and couldn't be anyone in the room—is enough to reduce the number of suspects.

Then I realize—

"So, you've been alone this whole time?" I ask John.

The thought is terrifying for two reasons. The first is: What if he'd come up against the killer? What if he became the next person we found splayed out in the middle of a hallway?

The second is that unlike the four people beside me, John doesn't have anyone to verify what he's saying is true. My stomach clenches when the thought crosses my mind. Do I think he somehow killed two people, left a trail of rose petals—all while evading notice from his own group and ours—cleaned himself up, and made it back onto the dance floor to meet us?

No, I don't.

Can I discount him as a suspect because I don't think this sweet guy is capable of murder?

No . . . I can't.

"I had to navigate this level on my own, I'm afraid." John directs his crooked little smile my way, the one that's cute and humble and apologetic all at once. "The hallway made a square kind of shape after I passed some restrooms. There was another bar, and then I hit a dead end." His steel-blue gaze moves to each member of our group. We've made an arc around him, like the lifeless remains of a dance circle.

"I didn't want you guys to come back and find no one here, so I turned around, and when I came across the bar again, I thought there might be a first aid kit." The guilt of thinking he could be a suspect grips harder when he holds up the green fabric case, a white cross stark in the middle of it. "It might come in handy in case we find anyone who needs help."

"I don't think a few bandages are going to help the people we found," Billie mutters darkly, then at John's furrowed expression she says, "Bodies."

John's face drops, and I realize there must have been a certain part of him that thought the bloodshed was done for the night. That what happened in the basement was like fireworks on New Year's Eve: a sudden, explosive display of color and sound, an assault on the eyes, but over as soon as it had begun. He doesn't know about the new bodies, or the blood, or the rose petals. He doesn't know this is only the beginning.

"What do you mean *bodies*?" John looks between us all, but it's Billie who juts a thumb over her shoulder.

"Two. In a hallway over there."

Again I'm struck by how cold she is. How . . . unfeeling. If it came down to John or Billie being the killer, I know who I'd put my money on.

"*Christ,*" John mutters, his hair falling into his eyes as he shakes his head. I have the sudden urge to brush the light brown strands back from his face, but I push that thought away as he glances back up and looks around the group. "Where's Campbell?"

"He ran off," Wes says. He's turned his gaze to the mezzanine level, looking up at the rails above our heads as if Campbell and Stu are going to walk out from the shadows and wave down to us on the dance floor.

"He's probably the one doing this," Billie interjects. "It's always the quiet ones."

"What if it's Stu, though?" Jennifer says. She's gripping onto her elbows now, and the skin around her fingers has turned white. "What if—"

"Our job isn't to play detective right now," Wes interrupts. It's an instruction, a command, but he says it softly. As carefully as a man wielding a chair leg can. "We need to keep looking for a way out. We should head up to the mezzanine, but we have to have a clearer idea of what we're walking into. It's too easy to get lost in here."

Far too easy. That's what it's designed for, after all. That was the draw for me and Laurie all those years ago, and when I glance over at her and see her already looking my way, I know she has the same idea as me.

"What if we make a map?" she says. "Jamie and I can try to piece together what we remember of this place."

Wes and John already know about our history with Serendipity, but the offer prompts the women to look at us with surprise. I can't help but notice that somewhere within Billie's expression of distaste is something that looks like suspicion.

"We used to come here a lot," I say before any accusations or more dirty looks can be thrown across the half circle. I guess I'd be suspicious of anyone knowing the ins and outs of the club, too. Having control over the environment is an advantage for the killer, but it could become an advantage for us, as well. "Granted, it's been awhile, but I don't think the layout has changed too much . . . Maybe it'll help?"

"It wouldn't hurt. I think you should tell us about those rules, too," Wes suggests.

"*The* rules?" Laurie's voice is incredulous, and when I nod she raises a brow at me suggestively. The bitch knows me too well. "Well," Laurie says with a shrug, "if there was ever a time to use them, it's now. You talk and I'll draw?"

It's a good plan, and I move my bloody heels into my other hand and point to the coat check. "We can use paper and pens from in there."

I've only taken a few steps across the dance floor, which manages to be both sticky *and* dusty under my feet, when Laurie is at my shoulder, Wes and John are close at our heels, and Billie and Jennifer have no choice but to follow us.

When we make it to the coat check, I ignore the dead body at my feet, making sure not to step in her blood as I place my shoes and weapon on the desk. Opening the top drawer, I pull out some of the stationery I spotted earlier as Laurie joins me behind the desk and everyone else waits near the door or across the counter. Their bodies are angled in a way that shows the last hour or so has been enough for rule six—watch your back—to become firmly ingrained in the group dynamic.

As Laurie gets to work sketching the outline of the club, I turn back to the group, pretending that this is just a bunch of undergrads rather than a group of people trying to survive the most horrible night of their lives.

"I'm writing a thesis—which you don't need to know anything about except that I specialize in horror films. Slashers. And these types of films are pretty formulaic. The story plays out because of the characters' choices. To have conflict and to build tension, characters usually have to make more bad decisions than good ones. All that's to say, in learning from their mistakes, there are basic rules that need to be followed if you want to survive."

"Survive what?" Billie asks drily from where she leans against the counter. Laurie and I share a look and her lips purse almost imperceptibly. I'm finely tuned to the subtleties of my best friend's facial expressions, and I can easily read her opinion of Billie. She's so detached, dismissive. It might be a coping mechanism, but it makes me doubt my theory that the murderer has to be a man.

"A slasher," I say again. "Like *Halloween, Friday the 13th, Scream*. They're all films about a killer who hunts down a group of people . . . Like what's happening right now."

Billie's lip is already curled up to dislike whatever I'm going to say, but when I glance over to Wes, who's standing guard at the entry to the coat check, and John and Jennifer, who stand behind Billie, none of them seem offended by what I'm saying. So I ignore her perpetual bitch face and continue my lecture.

"Here are the rules for surviving a slasher." I decide to skip number one, since I don't think anyone is going to really have the inclination to get some action tonight. "If you end up hiding, you need to stay hidden for longer than you think you should. In the movies, people always leave their hiding place too soon and the killer is just standing there waiting for them. I'm hoping that if the others haven't found an exit, that's what they are doing."

I pick up the broken bottle. "Having a weapon is a must. So is turning on a light when you enter a room, because the killer can hide in the darkness, but that rule also has a loophole if turning on a light is going to draw attention to where you're hiding. Pretty much just be wary of dark spaces."

I turn to John. "Splitting up is obviously a bad idea—"

"Stu was the one who wanted everyone to split up initially, wasn't he?"

Jennifer's voice is neutral, but I can literally see her biting her tongue to keep from voicing her "it's Stu" theory again. It's not that I couldn't be persuaded to think he's the killer, or I don't want to try and figure out who is doing this, either. It's just that in most of the slashers I've seen, people die because they get sidetracked trying to figure out who the killer is instead of just focusing on self-preservation.

"It's dangerous to assume it's Stu or to start making accusations based on fear," Wes says. He tries to soften the gravity of his statement by directing a grim smile at her when he adds, "That's how innocent people get hurt. We just need to focus on staying alive and getting the hell out of here."

Jennifer sighs, nodding in acceptance before she gestures at me to continue.

"Splitting up leaves you vulnerable," I explain. "You don't have anyone to help you if you get hurt, not to mention anyone to watch your back. Which is its own rule. Watching your back, that is. You need to always be aware of what's happening behind you because the killer can sneak up on their victim. The next one is not to run up the stairs, because—"

"Are you fucking crazy?" Billie spits, that look of disgust etched into every facet of her face as I pause and arch a brow in her direction.

Wes and John try to defuse the situation with a matching, surprised "Hey!" but we both ignore it. Billie's had a problem with me—with everyone—since we pulled the curtain back on her. But if I didn't care about what Curtis or Stu thought about me, I'm certainly not going to back down now.

"This isn't a movie, Jamie. Are you even taking this seriously?"

She glares at me from across the counter, and I stare squarely back at her, unable to stop the scoff that falls out of my mouth. "Am *I* taking this seriously? Who's the one who said, 'The night is still young,' after they found out five people died?"

She doesn't even blink. Doesn't show a hint of remorse, just doubles down and leans into the counter. Her dark lips curl up in reproach as she hisses, "I just want to get through this night without adding myself to that number if possible."

"That's exactly what I'm trying to do, too."

"By going on about some ridiculous 'rules' that only make sense in shitty films?"

I'm about to point out that they *aren't* shitty. They're some of the most successful and influential films in the industry that set the precedent for slasher films—and for the night we're currently trying to live through. I'm also tempted to say she's currently ticking every box for the "annoying skeptic," and those characters never last very long in situations like ours.

Laurie intervenes. "Have you been paying attention *at all* this whole fucking time?" Her hand pauses over her rough sketch of the mezzanine, and she shoots Billie a look I've only seen her direct to the one Hallmark movie I ever dared her to watch.

"*Everything* Jamie has said and done has been to keep us alive and safe. You should count yourself lucky she knows what to do, because the alternative is waiting for you down at the end of that corridor."

Her voice is venom, and it brings the conversation to an abrupt end.

After a moment of dead air, Billie scoffs and says, "I don't feel very *lucky* right now." She strides over to the booth closest to the entrance of the dance floor and flops onto the velvet seat, shooting daggers in my direction. After giving me an apologetic look, Jennifer joins her.

I get it. I've got Laurie in my corner and Jennifer, by default, needs to be in Billie's. I don't want to descend into an "us versus them" mentality, but I don't think it's a coincidence the ones who stayed in the basement are the ones who still stand at the counter, stone-faced and trying to figure out our next steps. We witnessed the aftermath of the violence that occurred in the blackout. We know what we're trying to avoid.

Laurie slides the newly created "map" across the desk to me.

"That's all I can remember. Does it look right to you?"

I cast my eyes over her rendition of the three levels of the club. She's been working diligently on it this whole time, and the scale is all over the place. There are unfinished corridors, and parts of the building are blank or annotated with question marks. But she's managed to get the bones of the club to align with my faint recollection of Cravin' and the more recent experience of trying to escape the lower levels of Serendipity.

"It looks good, given we haven't been in here in years. Though—" I take the pen and draw in the bar on the mezzanine that she's missed, then I look at a section of booths she's drawn flush against the stairs on this side of the club.

"There's a wall that runs behind those booths, right?" I ask, tracing a faint line that slices the booths in half. "It makes another corridor that runs the length of the stairs."

Laurie lets out an affirmative sound and I pass back the pen so she can turn my light mark into a clearly defined line. "I think you're right. How do you remember that?"

"I found you there once. Your dress ripped and you had your back against the wall so no one could see you were wearing those weird panties with the cat face on the back. We had to leave the club with me shielding your whisker-decked ass with my body." I hear a soft huff of amusement.

"And to think," Laurie mutters, "I thought that was the worst night I spent in this club."

CHAPTER 13

"The best kill is the kind that awakens the soul."

—Not *The Notebook*

With John's help, we're able to add a little more detail to the sketch of the level we're currently on, and after a few more corrections and a lot more question marks, the map is as detailed as it's going to get. We spend a few minutes studying it, murmuring about possible exits, but my attention is drawn to fervid whispering a few feet away.

"—I *know*, but—"

"—*she* is the one who—"

Jennifer and Billie keep their voices low so I can't catch the end of their sentences, but Billie can't hide that deadly glare she shoots at me every now and again. The way they whisper in the dark, the comforting hand Jennifer places on her shoulder, reminds me that we're missing two people (that I care about).

"Dani and Colette should've come back up by now," I say once Laurie places the final question mark on the map and puts the pen back down onto the desk.

Nobody answers at first. Yes, our goal is to stay alive, but we want to make sure the others are safe, too. We've already lost too many people tonight. Then Wes starts nodding along to whatever plan he's constructed in his head, and though I have a feeling I know what that plan entails, it still makes the space under my ribs constrict when he says, "I'll go downstairs."

"Wes—"

"You're right. They should've come back by now. What if they're hurt? What if there *is* an exit down there that we don't know about? We need to check."

"Then I'll come, too—" I say, and immediately get a backhand to the tit.

"Ow! *Jesus*, Laurie."

When I turn to glare at her, she has her most serious face on. The one she usually reserves for when I try to girl math my way through dropping two hundred dollars on skincare.

"You're not leaving me again, and I'm sorry, but I don't want to go back down there and see . . ." She points to the ground. I know she's referring to what lies on the level beneath us, but the line of her finger lands directly over where the coat check attendant's foot just so happens to be, unnaturally still and splattered with red droplets. "*That*."

Jennifer and Billie rejoin our group as Laurie and I engage in a stare-off, and John makes room for them to join the discussion, clearing his throat. "Do you want me to—"

Interrupting, Wes says, "You should stay here. With whoever stays behind," and I shift my glare from Laurie to him.

"You're not about to say he should stay here and play protector, right?"

He holds my gaze for a moment before he looks away with a sigh and mutters, "I'm not going to *now*."

I roll my eyes, crossing my arms over my chest as a droll voice cuts through the unhappy silence. "I'll go."

My neck almost cracks from how quickly I whip my head around to gape at Billie. "It's probably better for a woman to get them anyway." She shrugs. "Would *you* trust a man by himself?"

I'm not going to pretend that she isn't 100 percent on the money with that point. If *I* was hiding down there and a guy walked in, shoes covered in blood, a broken chair leg in his hand, it wouldn't put me at ease. I'd probably stab him with my beer bottle first and ask questions later.

She pins me with an acidic look. "Not to mention we want to follow *the rules*, right?"

The tone is unnecessary, but the sentiment is correct.

"I don't think I can go back down there," Jennifer says quietly.

She's back to gripping her arms again, eight white circles surrounding the skin where her nails dig into her flesh. Her dark eyes are wide, rimmed with darker lashes and unshed tears, and I immediately lose some of that confrontational energy that Billie seems to stir up in me.

"That's fine," John says, reaching out and laying a reassuring hand on her shoulder. It's probably warm and comforting, and I remember again that—before the chaos—their date had looked . . . successful.

"It's fine, right?" John says, turning his attention to the rest of us. He maintains such a calm tone that I find myself nodding, even though an uneven split of the group leaves a bad taste in my mouth.

I know I'm the one who pointed out Dani and Colette were still missing. I know I'm the one who implied we needed to find them. I am still very much in favor of trying to get out of this mess with as many living people as possible. I just wish we didn't have to split up *again* to be able to do that. But since we have two willing volunteers and any further argument on my part will only earn me another swift punch in the boob, the plan is settled. After a few minutes of group discussion, it's decided that while Wes and Billie go down to the basement bar, the rest of us will move to the mezzanine. If Stu returns with an exit then we'll get them and get out, and if he doesn't, we'll be able to watch the staircases to make sure no one can follow them down. But watching the stairs isn't going to do much if the killer is already down there waiting for someone to walk into his trap, is it?

The thought has me standing behind the desk, stewing in my own discontent. Wes is over at the booth with the map, talking through possible paths with Billie. John and Jennifer study the keypad near the door like they're going to absorb the code by osmosis, and Laurie is looking around the coat check as if the phone box may have been missed in our original search.

Spoiler: it's still missing.

I open the top drawer again and pull out a handful of rubber bands to busy my hands as my mind runs through the best- and worst-case scenarios of our group splitting again. Every scene I imagine ends up aligning with a slasher that I know we don't want to emulate.

Laurie appears at my shoulder, her voice low as she asks, "What's wrong?"

"Nothing." When I look up from fashioning some knots with the rubber bands, she squints down at me and I shrug. "I didn't mean to—"

"What?"

"Go full . . . *Jamie*. With the rules and the films. I'll—"

"If you say 'tone it down,' I will punch you in the tit again," she warns, inclining her head in the direction of my current critic and adding, "Billie's a fuckwit. You're a fucking star, baby girl. I would marry you if providence hadn't tragically decided to make us both prefer dick."

I swallow a laugh as she pulls more rubber bands out of the drawer, handing them to me as I start tangling them together.

"The only reason we've gotten through tonight is because you know the formula. You know what happens next."

I do. And that's why splitting up again is gnawing at me so badly. We're getting closer to act 2 now: the confrontation. It's usually my favorite part of the movie when I'm watching it from my couch, but living it is different. There are a few things that are inevitably going to happen if we keep following the format this killer has set up:

- It's going to escalate. The kills are going to get more inventive, and no amount of rose petals are going to soften the effects of the violence.
- We're going to come face-to-face with him, and if he's smart, he's going to wear a mask.
- The tensions are going to boil over between us—they already have—and the group is going to fracture . . . again.
- We're going to lose someone . . . We might lose a lot more people.

And that's before we get anywhere close to the third act. Before we figure out who the monster is and why he's doing this, and before the roles we're meant to play are fully cemented.

This is playing out exactly as he wants.

"I know there's at least one other person who doesn't seem to mind you going full Jamie . . ." Laurie muses, pulling me out of my thoughts and drawing my eyes to the man standing on the edge of the dance floor with Billie.

"I like him," she says, and it's a little concerning that we both know who's the *him* she's referring to.

"Who?" My voice is a little too nonchalant when she turns her back to Wes and props herself against the front of the desk. She bumps her shoulder against mine and I grin until my ankle grazes the arm of the coat check attendant lying behind me. It's hard to have boy talk when there's a dead body in the vicinity.

"I don't know if I should be thinking about that right now."

"Oh, you shouldn't," she agrees, picking up another rubber band and passing it to me. I didn't realize it, but the knots have turned into braids. Weaving the elastic is relaxing. As relaxing as any activity can be when you're trapped and being hunted, so I keep doing it. "But just because you shouldn't be thinking about it doesn't mean you won't. It's called 'attraction under aversive conditions.'"

I look back toward Wes, the way the cotton of his shirt shapes itself against the broad shoulders of his back. "Attraction under aversive conditions" does seem like an accurate description of what I've been feeling the whole night.

"Essentially, fear makes you horny," Laurie continues, and nope, scratch that. "Afraid and horny" is right on the money. I just know that stripping Wes of his shirt would unveil a gift to humanity. Like when Emma Stone has Ryan Gosling take his shirt off in *Crazy, Stupid, Love*. Wes must feel my eyes on his back because he glances at me. I drop my gaze down to where I've tangled my fingers into a knot and murmur, "I'll have to look into it."

"I would've thought you'd know all about it, being a romance-obsessed horrorphile and all," Laurie says teasingly when I hold out my bound fingers for her assistance.

"How do *you* know about it?" I ask.

"I was looking up historical social psychology studies."

"Why?"

She looks at me like I'm an idiot. "For fun. I'm the smart one, remember?"

When she frees my fingers, I go right back to fashioning the elastic into a longer braid. A sigh of frustration draws my gaze to John, his eyebrows stuck together in a cute furrow as he grazes a finger across the pin pad of the door. He steps back from the wall, his fingers combing through his hair, making it stick up in every direction. The sight makes me smile as I twist the rubber bands into another knot.

Laurie follows my gaze. "He's nice, too."

He is, and it makes my heart swell in my chest. I wonder if there's a study about affection—rather than attraction—under aversive conditions.

"More my type?" I ask, even though I already know the answer. I've introduced a couple of "Johns" to Laurie in the past. All of them nice and cute and thoughtful. But I wouldn't be here tonight if any of them had worked out.

"I don't know if I invest much in types." She pauses. "Stu is my type."

"Stu is a douche bag," I retort.

"Exactly."

Laurie sighs, drawing my attention to where she's picked up her own rubber band. Her gaze is hard on the back of the room as she mindlessly threads her fingers over and under each other until the elastic cuts into her skin. "So, if we get out of here—"

"Hey. No." It's one thing for me to think it as some involuntary, intrusive thought, but it's another for her to say it out loud.

"Jamie—"

"Laurie." I grab her hand, pull the elastic from her fingers, and watch as the blood flows back under the skin. When our eyes meet I can see the fear clearly behind the brown irises that stare back at me.

"We *are* going to get out of here. If I need to smash every bottle in this fucking place or break every one of those rules from our poster or ruin my chances of having sex with any number of attractive men tonight, *we* are getting out of this place, we're going to be okay, and you are going to live a long life making boring-as-shit documentaries."

It's a terrible, unfocused, slightly offensive declaration, but it pulls her away from that dark place. And even though her tone is sarcastic, I can tell she means it when she shakes her head and says, "That was beautiful."

"I'm the dramatic one, remember?"

Maybe that's why I'm finding this a little easier to navigate. Laurie likes certainty. She lives her life in reason and pragmatism, and none of what has happened so far tonight falls into those categories.

Laurie suddenly shifts away from the desk, and that's my indication that Wes is moving back to the counter. She stays within earshot at the doorframe, though, because voyeurism is inherently linked to liking documentaries.

The chair leg slides into view on top of the counter while I'm twisting two braids together—so does the map—but Wes waits until I look up, until I meet his eye, before he says, "We'll be as quick as we can. Maybe Dani and Colette have found a phone by now. There might be a flashlight, or an evacuation map. Something that can help us."

I hadn't thought of any of that, and it's the kind of problem-solving you don't see in most of the slashers I watch. What is "logical" doesn't play a main role in the escapism I gravitate toward.

Maybe that's why I relent a little. "Good point."

He looks like he wants to say more, but then he grabs the broken chair leg and gets ready to go. I look down at the length of plaited elastic in my hand so I don't have to watch him leave, and then it hits me. What I've been making this whole time.

"Hold on."

He pauses readily, and I try not to read too much into it when I grab hold of the piece of wood in his hand and pull him back to the counter.

I never thought my friendship bracelet skills would come in handy outside of elementary school or to prepare for a concert, but all that nervous knotting and twisting has resulted in a braid of rubber bands that could make a too-big bracelet, or—

"Here." I tie one end around the handle of Wes's handmade weapon, working in a cradle knot to make sure it doesn't slip out, and then hold my hand out for his. Trying not to be distracted by the warmth of his skin against the pads of my fingers, I make a loop on the other end, then fasten it around his wrist.

"Wh—"

"*Cabin in the Woods, The Strangers*—" I stop with the examples when I remember he prefers Bullock-fronted films. "They all drop the weapon. This way you won't drop your . . . stick. Stake? Shaft?"

"Please don't call it a shaft."

"You can adjust it." I start tightening the bracelet, only looking up to take stock of the leftover materials on the desk. There's not enough to make another. I probably should have kept it for myself. Self-preservation and all that. But I'm not one to take a gift back. Not to mention he's going down into the depths of the club while I'm going up to an open, easily accessible (and potentially escapable) level. Even though Wes volunteered for the basement run, I feel like he drew the short straw.

When the bracelet is finally tight enough to reassure me it won't slip, I look up to see Wes's mouth splitting into a grin. "How . . . *How* do you know how to do that?"

I shrug. "I went through a macramé phase, and a friendship bracelet phase, and a—"

"Jamie . . ."

His voice is soft, low, warm. So warm my mouth goes dry.

"Yeah?"

He pauses a moment, scanning my face.

"Don't listen to Billie. Laurie's right. Everything you've done tonight . . . I don't know how you do it." He points down to his weapon wristlet. "Do this."

That makes me grin. Because having Wes gesture to a shitty friendship bracelet like it's an Academy Award is incredibly gratifying.

"I could ask you the same thing," I say with a smile. "How do you do it? How do you know how to look out for everyone and keep your cool?"

He stares at me. Hard. More than I would've thought the question would warrant, then he seems to find the words.

"It's just part of who I am."

And that's why I'm drawn to him so much.

"Same for me. But we need to test this thing. Drop your weapon." He lets go of the stake, and it bounces right back up into his palm. I have to stop myself from doing a little clap since there was a very high chance that wouldn't have worked.

The grin is back on his face. "You're pretty incredible."

Okay, that was far more gratifying than his reaction to the bracelet. Why do I feel like I'm the one winning the Oscar now?

"Thank you." Heat spreads out underneath my collarbone, and I raise a palm to cover it, but it just increases when his eyes drop to watch my movement.

"You're pretty incredible, too." I should leave it at that, but the next part is out before I can stop myself. "It'd be incredible if you didn't die."

"I'm determined not to." He grants me that grin again, but then it's gone just as quick. His expression turns serious, the same look as the one before when it seemed like he wanted to get something off his chest. This time he decides to say it.

"Look, I'm . . . I'm sorry for how our date ended—"

"It's okay," I say—too quickly. Partly because I don't want to relive the mortification of the final minutes of our date when things—

ironically enough given our circumstances—seem to have gotten back to more promising ground. But also because if this is his way of having no regrets in case something does happen downstairs, I don't want to hear it.

I continue. "I kind of screwed it up at the en—"

"No." The force of the word makes me start, but it also makes my heart beat fast and furiously beneath my ribs, especially when he follows up the outburst with a soft "You didn't screw anything up, Jamie. I just . . . I'm—"

"Wes?"

Billie is waiting a few steps behind him, one fist propped on her hip, the other grasping the handle of the first aid kit. John must have given it to her, and I try not to think of what she and Wes are about to walk into. She grants me one more narrow-eyed look before tilting her head in the direction of the stairs.

"Yeah . . . Yeah, I'm coming." Wes nods. We share one more second of eye contact before he clears his throat and pushes off the counter.

I can't tear my eyes away from him. I don't know if this is the last image I'm going to have of him, and that's why I say, "Wait."

He does. Instantly. *Again.* And now I need to scramble for a reason why I stopped him. Fortunately, I find it right in front of me.

"You guys should take this." I pick up the map on the counter and fold it into thirds. "Since Laurie and I are staying with the others."

When I hold it out it looks like he's going to fight me on it. The map is one of the very few advantages we have at the moment, but then he takes it, and I don't miss the way his fingers linger when they brush against mine as he pulls the paper out of my hands.

My fingertips are still tingling from the contact when he lifts his gaze back to mine and points his baton at me. "I'm not going to say that thing you told me not to say."

I try not to smile and fail. "I appreciate that."

He slides the map into his back pocket as he joins Billie and—making sure not to disturb the corpse at my feet—I exit out of the coat check to watch them walk toward the stairs. Wes moves slowly, purposefully, each step taken with care until they pause at the top of the stairs. I stop breathing when I realize he waits for three beats—I know what that means—but then he descends the staircase with those same slow, purposeful steps, Billie one step behind him. It's only when I can't see them anymore, when their departure isn't immediately followed by a horrifying sound of metal puncturing flesh or a pained yell, that I let out the breath I'm holding.

"Jamie?"

I turn back to John, fashioning a smile on my face. "Yeah?"

Over his shoulder, I glimpse Laurie pointing above her head, tracing invisible paths on the ceiling, as Jennifer nods.

"Look, before we go upstairs, I just wanted to say . . ." John rolls his bottle between his palms—a nervous tick I'm starting to recognize—before he meets my eye. "I know I should've insisted that our group not split up. Maybe if I fought more, Dani and Colette would've agreed." He swallows, regret etched into the furrow of his brow, and I'm shocked that he thinks this is *his* fault. "I'm not like Wes or Stu. I'm not really the kind of guy who—"

"I like the kind of guy I've seen so far," I say, and the way his blue eyes lock on mine, the way his spine straightens after my words, I'm glad I did. I don't need my complex to be catching. I don't want John thinking it's a character flaw that he's not like Stu, of all people.

"What I mean is," he starts again, "I don't think I'm a particularly fearless person. I don't take a lot of risks. I've never needed to, you know? I plan things out. I stay in my lane."

I had the feeling he was more reserved in comparison to some of the more extroverted suitors of the night, but it was his quiet composure that made me like him in the first place.

"But . . . I *promise*," he says. "I'm gonna try to be a little more fearless. I'm gonna do whatever I can so we make it out of this."

I nod, but still, I can't help but look over my shoulder at the empty staircase.

The silky, ebony sheen of Laurie's jumpsuit shimmers in my periphery as she and Jennifer move closer to the counter, a nonverbal indication that they're as ready as they'll ever be for us to move up to the next level of the club. The one that's even more mazelike than the last two we've been on.

"We're going to be okay, Jamie."

The certainty of John's words draws my eyes back to him, and the warmth of his stare dissolves some of the uneasiness. I said the same thing to Laurie, but John makes me believe it. I want to believe there's another side to this, one where we get to have that drink and talk about this night in the past tense.

I just don't know if this is that kind of movie.

CHAPTER 14

"I wish I knew how to slit you."

—Not *Brokeback Mountain*

*T*he mezzanine level of Serendipity affords us a bird's-eye view of the dance floor. When I came here when the club was still Cravin', the railings circling the open space allowed you a great vantage point to spot your prey. Back then, the predators were fuckboys and older men ready to feed on inexperience and female politeness. Now we're dealing with a whole other breed of predator.

When we get up to the top level, we move to the booths that trail the wall along the front of the club. It has the best view. There's a bar to our left where the men were served during cocktail hour, more booths sit against a partition wall on our right, and on the other side of the open space—allowing us a full view of the lower level and the staircases leading down into the basement—is a wall punctuated by five corridors leading into the back of the building.

From what I can remember, the corridors are more complicated up here. I know the hallway directly in front of the stairs—dark scary hallway number one—leads to some VIP rooms. The others I can't be sure of. From our spot, I can see dark scary hallway number two and dark scary hallway number five are roped off, and that just increases the mystery of what might lie within their gas lamp–lit depths. An exit, ideally.

"I know we're not supposed to be focusing on this," Jennifer says, perched on the top of a table in one of the booths. "But who do you think it is?"

John stands in the space between the barrier and the booth, and Laurie and I are shoulder to shoulder between Jennifer's booth and the one next to it. It grants the ability to run if the occasion calls for it, but it also has the clearest view of the dance floor. I can dart my eyes between the two sets of stairs that feed into the belly of the building, hoping Wes and Billie come up at any moment with Dani and Colette in tow.

"The person doing this?" John asks, even though we all know who Jennifer's referring to.

"It has to be one of the people who was on the dates." Jennifer's eyes are wide, the tears long dried up, and her enviably long and thick eyelashes bat nervously. "But why here? Why tonight? And what about those rose petals? Down near those bodies in the hallway? Where did they come from?"

She keeps going, but I don't think she actually expects any of us to respond. She's full of questions none of us have the answers to. Well, not concrete answers, anyway. Nobody else was there when Wes and I were drawing connections between the rose petals left near the bodies and the murders of the women that happened before tonight. And I don't know if I should tell them. I don't know if it will make things worse, telling them a person who sat across from us tonight has probably been killing people—women—for months. That he's had a lot of practice, and maybe this is just a normal Tuesday night for him.

Maybe it's the horror fan in me, but something in my gut is telling me tonight is not just an escalation of those murders. It's not the next logical step in the path to getting full marks for psychopathy.

There has to be some reason why he's flipped the script.

I just don't know what it is.

"And also—"

A sound, like shoes scraping against carpet, filters out from the corridor on our left and cuts into Jennifer's monologue. Laurie stiffens beside me, whispers, "Did you—"

I hold a finger to my lips—well, *near* them, since I've still got blood on my hands—as we all turn toward the dimly lit hall. The sound of Jennifer sliding off the table is audible behind me as I squint through the darkness, trying to see if a figure appears in the corridor. There's nothing. Of course there's nothing. But then the sound, which is just as likely to be cautious shuffling as it is meticulous creeping, happens again. This time it's a little softer, and I don't know if they're moving farther away or they're just being more careful as they sneak up on us.

Either way, it's never a good idea to go toward the unknown sound. There's never a good surprise on the other end. I hear a deep inhale behind me, like someone steeling themselves, but when I turn around, John is already moving past me, his hand gripped so tightly around the neck of his bottle his knuckles are ghostly white.

"Stay here," he whispers, approaching the sound, moving *away* from the rest of us and any possibility of safety in numbers. It's the quickest I've seen him move all night. Every other action, every other smile and nod and that fantastic *lean* has been slow and unhurried. But now he's at the edge of the corridor before I can even shape my mouth around his name. Before I can convince him to stay with us and not go headfirst into danger, alone, *again*.

Then, when I thought it couldn't get any worse, he says over his shoulder, "I'll be right back."

"Shit," I whisper. "Shit. Shit. *Shit*."

It's been ten minutes since John strode into the darkness before any of us could stop him. Even without a watch, I know it's been that long because I've counted every second since he left.

When I was going through the rules, I should've led with number eight: don't say "I'll be right back." If I had, then maybe John wouldn't have made the empty promise and walked down that corridor. If he hadn't been surrounded by men who have more bravado than sense (Stu), then he probably wouldn't have felt the need to display some fearlessness by investigating a sound that could be a psychotic killer.

If. If. If.

The word stabs into my brain like the shower scene in *Psycho*. "What do we do?" Jennifer asks.

She started pacing along the booth as soon as John disappeared, and if I wasn't preoccupied with that same question, I'd be really concerned about whether the marks she's digging into her arms are going to be permanent. There haven't been any more shuffling noises coming from the hall. There haven't been any screams, either, so that's promising. But I don't like to wait around for men to text me back, let alone wait for one to return from a dark, dangerous search party.

This is why you don't say those stupid words.

The second John walked down the hallway I knew what would happen next. Just like when Wes and Billie went downstairs. The splitting of the group is part of how the plot progresses. It's like in a rom-com where the romantic leads are forced into close proximity or get caught in the rain or share one bed. You need something to move the story forward.

And how do we do that so it works in our favor?

"I'll go look down the corridor." It's the only answer I have for

Jennifer, and I'm not fully committed to the decision. Laurie opens her mouth to protest, but I power through. "I'll be gone for a maximum of five minutes. I promise."

"Not on your fucking life," she growls, and if there wasn't so much acid in her voice, I'd be touched by her concern. But the first act is done. The main players have been introduced, the conflict is clear, and now—I hate to say it—if we want to get closer to an ending, we're going to have to move onto act 2. *Fucking* act 2. It's not called the confrontation for nothing. My hand's been forced now that we've reached this point.

Jennifer tries a different approach from Laurie to get me to stay. "Jamie, we told Wes and Billie we would wait here—"

"And you two should," I say, "while I check the corridor. There are only three of us, so one of us inevitably has to be on their own. Better for that person to be me."

"No fucking way." Laurie shakes her head, her straight brown hair flaring until I grab her shoulders and halt her full-body refusal.

"Baby girl—"

The endearment makes her recoil, but she doesn't try to get out of my grip.

"I'm *not* going to disappear. I *will* be five minutes. Less than." When she starts to puff up in agitation, I say, "You know I know all the ways this could play out. I'm not doing this to whip out my dick"—*Stu*—"or to prove anything"—damn it, John. "I'm going to look and come back."

She's been with me through the in-depth analysis of countless slashers. Yeah, she covered her eyes a lot or left the room, but she knows I *know* my shit, and that's why I say, "I just need to make sure I don't make the same mistakes every other blonde who's ever walked down a dark path toward an unseen danger has made."

I manage to get enough confidence into the statement that Laurie doesn't reach for me when I take a step back and turn toward the dark corridor.

"And if you *don't* come back?" Jennifer murmurs.

"I will." It's a promise, a loophole in rule eight because I don't actually *say* the taboo statement.

"If—" Laurie says, and the hitch that follows the word tempts me to look back at her. It doesn't matter what comes after the "if," because anything other than me coming back in five minutes will be unacceptable to my best friend. So she doesn't finish the statement. Her face just gets tight, and she pins me with a warning look. "I'm going to be *so* fucking mad at you."

I nod as I turn back to the hallway, fully determined to avoid her wrath.

"Five minutes," I say again. A promise not just to them but to myself. I move toward the hallway that swallowed John, slowing my steps when the path turns into an L once I pass the bar. Laurie and I sketched this side of the building onto the map and then covered it with question marks because we couldn't remember what lay in the hallways behind the bar. The dramatic irony doesn't escape me. It does nothing to stop the skin of my arms breaking out into goose bumps.

John walked straight ahead, and I make to go that way, until a sound echoes from the other direction. It stops me in my tracks. This sound is . . . different. It's nothing like what we heard before because, if we had, John wouldn't have followed it. Not when the thud of a punch mixed with a juicy squelch resounds from a corridor farther down the hallway.

Shit.

I look back over my shoulder, but it doesn't seem like Laurie and Jennifer can hear it. They're just standing there in their newly formed duo, arms crossed, trying to avoid watching my departure. We've watched too many people walk away and not come back.

Even though every fiber of my being is telling me not to, telling me to turn back, I turn right and walk deeper into the darkness. It has nothing to do with morbid curiosity.

Maybe seeing tonight through the lens of a slasher has progressed further than a coping mechanism, because there's a part of me that wants—*needs*—to see the threat so I can compare it against all the Big Bads I've seen and figure out what we're up against. Who we're up against. Part of following the format is deciding to become a part of the story, playing an active role, and I don't think we can avoid the monster for the whole night.

My bare feet are silent against the carpet as I pass an empty corridor, bottle clenched in one hand, shoes in the other. With every step I get closer and closer to the hallway the noise comes from, and when I finally reach the entry, I see it. The dim gas lamps cloak me in shadow, but they also cast a dark veil over the moving shapes down the hall from where I stand.

And they are moving. Surging. At first glance, I'd think the two people propped against the wall have given into their "attraction under aversive conditions" and are breaking rule one. The likelihood of two of the men finding a match tonight rather than during the queer event next week has the same odds as anything else that's happened in the last few hours. And I can tell it's two men at the end of the corridor. I can see enough of the face of the man against the wall to know that it isn't John. And if I wasn't witnessing what I'm witnessing, maybe I could feel some relief about that. I *do* recognize him as one of my dates from the second half of the evening, but that's about it.

The guy holding him up against the wall is shrouded in darkness, his head just a black blob. But given his height, the way his shoulders are broad even under the oversized dinner jacket—he's unmistakably masculine. It'd be nice to think it is just two of the guys who have unexpectedly connected and given into their carnal urges, but there's also the fact the guy against the wall's head is thrown back in an unnatural position and the sound—that heavy, wet sound—is coming from the repetitive thrust of a blade into his belly.

This is different from Curtis or the coat check attendant or the bodies in the corridor. I could look at the gore of their injuries and pretend they were Tom Savini masterpieces, convince myself what I was seeing was just the magic of makeup effects. But this . . . this is like watching how the sausage gets made, and the sight makes me gasp.

The man pauses shoving his knife into his companion's stomach, the black shadow of his head tilting to the side as if he's heard me. He's heard me, but he's contemplating sticking with the task at hand rather than turning to greet me at the end of the hall. After a moment, he pulls his knife out of the guy's gut in one slow, graceful motion. The blade glitters like a ruby under the dim recessed lighting overhead as the body slides to the floor with a dull thump. He flicks the knife to the side instead of wiping it, and even from where I'm standing I catch how the blood splatters against an ornate mirror, countless red jewels pouring down the silver surface. Bile rises in my throat, and I swallow it back down. Red is dripping from the ceiling and spreading across the carpet and sprayed across the walls.

Run, Jamie.

I know that's what I should do, but I can't get the message down to my feet. Goddamn it. I judged all those characters who just stood there while the killer moved closer to them. The ones who screamed and held up their hands and ended up with a knife—not unlike the one he's holding—buried in their chest. I confidently assured myself I'd never do that, but now—

He turns fully toward me.

RUN, Jamie.

A rose-red halo backlights him as he starts slowly down the hallway.

He isn't in a hurry, and as he passes one of the antique lights, the romantic glow illuminates his head, revealing a mask.

Of course he's wearing a mask. They all do. In the shadows it looks like a deep burgundy ski mask, the color of dried blood, but when he passes another lamp I can see it isn't burgundy at all. It's pink.

A hot, fun, feminine pink.

The bottle slips from my grasp as my hands start to shake, and my shoes follow. They don't make a sound when they fall to the ground, and even though part of me is still screaming to run, another part is cursing the fact I didn't keep the bracelet I gave to Wes. Another small, delusional part is telling me to just bend down, pick the bottle back up, and meet him halfway, arm outstretched, but I can't stop looking at that mask.

A zipper makes a grim silver line where his mouth should be and his eyes . . . they are deep, black, endless pools. Not just his eyes, but the space around them; there's some material stretched over the holes that obstructs my view of his eyes but clearly doesn't impact his vision. When he strides past another light, and I'm able to distinguish the shape of the eye holes, why they look different, that's when my brain flicks over from freeze to flight mode.

RUN, JAMIE!

The hem of my dress flares out around my thighs in a wide arc as I spin on the spot and leg it back the way I came. I know then, sprinting across the plush crimson carpet, that the image of his mask is one I'm not going to forget anytime soon. If I survive this, if I make it to the end, I'm going to see that mask every time I close my eyes.

Because the holes around his eyes aren't circles.

They're hearts.

CHAPTER 15

"You make me want to be a better murderer."

—Not *As Good as It Gets*

"*R*un!"

The word rips from my throat, a strangled command as I turn the corner and catch sight of Laurie and Jennifer waiting for me. Laurie takes off as soon as she sees me sprinting out of the corridor. She dashes past the booths, glancing over her shoulder every now and then, her hand thrown back like she's running one of those relay races we were forced to do on track-and-field day at school. When I reach her and she grabs hold of my wrist, pulling me in line with her instead of bolting forward on her own, it's clear I'm the baton in this race. Jennifer doesn't need to be told twice, either, and in an instant the three of us are almost shoulder to shoulder, sprinting along the carpet in our best date outfits. With the red velvet surroundings and our hair flying behind us, it'd make a perfect album cover for a girl group if we weren't absolutely terrified.

The hall makes a sharp left, and we have no choice but to follow it around the corner, jostling each other like bumper cars.

"Ah—" I grit my teeth as a hot, sharp pain cuts across my arm. White sparks burst in front of my eyes. My steps falter.

Fuck.

"Shit—" Laurie pants, the Kahlúa bottle falling out of her hands when she sees blood on the jagged edge and then the corresponding red gash splitting my bicep. She goes to circle back to pick it up, but I use my good arm to grab her jumpsuit, wrenching her back into line. I'm *really* kicking myself for giving Wes the bracelet now.

"*Don't* stop," I grit out as we keep running down the hallway. The stairs come into view just beyond Jennifer's shoulder, but by the time it hits me that going back downstairs is an option, we've already passed them. Stopping, turning back, making for the stairs—all things that lead to death in a slasher.

So we keep running. Right down dark, scary hallway number one.

As we head deeper into the club, flashes of past adventures down these corridors come to mind. This is where we spent most of our time in Cravin'—hours of drinking and dancing and giggling and screaming in glee every time we came across a friend we'd thought we'd lost. Unlike the people we've lost tonight, they always returned, armed with a cocktail and a new story to regale us with in one of the seating areas.

The rooms in the VIP section are larger than the alcoves downstairs. Some have private bars, others are fitted with dancing podiums or stripper poles. We pass one and I spy a promising feature, so I stop in front of it, grabbing Jennifer's and Laurie's shoulders and wrenching them back.

"In here."

Laurie hits me with a "What the fuck are you doing?" expression before I hop over a velvet rope in front of the entrance and look for a place to hide.

The middle of the room is occupied by dark wood chaises covered in burgundy velvet. They circle a low table set up with an ice bucket and champagne flutes ready for the next VIP group to drop some serious cash on bottles of Dom. But it's the recessed arches built into the back wall that caught my eye. Each arch is crowned with two smaller versions of the gas lamps from downstairs and covered by a heavy velvet curtain. I remember them. I remember throwing up in the one on the far left, and I remember making out with a guy who tasted like blue raspberry vape in another. Unlike the alcoves downstairs, they aren't deep or wide enough to hold a couch or a booth, but they can definitely hold two women shoulder to shoulder. I stride over and pull back one side of the curtain in front of the middle arch and—*Yes!*—it's empty.

"Get in."

I push Jennifer ahead of me and she slips easily into the corner, planting her back against the wall. My heart is beating so loud, and the pain from the wound in my arm is throbbing like a Bernard Herrmann composition, but I gesture to the other side of the archway as warmth trickles down into the crook of my elbow.

"Go," I say, pushing Laurie in next to Jennifer, but she already knows what my intention is: get her out of sight while I act as lookout. She shoots me with that stubborn, intense stare she gets when she refuses to watch my Matthew McConaughey–themed double feature with *The Return of the Texas Chainsaw Massacre* and *The Wedding Planner* again. The one that ends up with me having to suffer through a three-hour documentary about coral bleaching.

"*No*. I'm staying with you," she hisses, and we allow ourselves one moment to stare hard at each other. The "who didn't replace the toilet paper again" glare. Her gaze drops to my arm, her lips pursing in remorse at the sight of it. It's not a deep cut—at least I hope it isn't—but that doesn't stop heat from flaring up under my skin or blood pouring down my arm.

"Jamie—"

I cut her off. "It's fine." It's not her fault. We don't have time to worry about my accidental cut when someone is on a mission to give me a much deeper, purposeful, life-ending one. "Jennifer, do you want to hide here or stay with us?"

"What do you think?" she yelps quietly, stepping back out of the archway and wrenching the curtain closed.

I don't know how much time has passed or how close the killer may be to finding us. He wasn't in a hurry when I left him, and at the very least, I've learned he's a slow-stalking killer. That doesn't put my mind at ease, though, because he sure as hell was quick in the basement bar. His lack of urgency means he's either overly confident in his ability to kill us, or he knows there's nowhere for us to escape. And if we can't escape, we need to be out of sight so what happened at the end of that hallway doesn't happen to us.

Turning back to the empty room with a new, shared task at hand, my eyes hone in on the bar that takes up most of the left side of the room. Red neon lights outline the edges of the bar itself, and though it's off-brand with the replica period pieces in the rest of the room, it may as well be a neon arrow pointing to sanctuary.

Laurie spots it the same time I do, and we both take hold of Jennifer and pull her along with us, circling the corner of the bar and dropping down onto the rubber mat with a soft thud that I hope hasn't echoed into the corridor. The shadow of the bar covers us, reaching a good foot away from where I'm sitting with my back flush against a mini fridge, and I think it's enough to conceal us.

I'm closest to the edge of the bar, positioned so I can see the entryway. Laurie crouches beside me, and when I glance over my shoulder I see her head tilted back against an ice bin. She has a hand pressed across her mouth, her shoulders rising and falling rapidly as we wait. Jennifer is in the farthest corner, her arms wrapped around her legs, head dropped into her knees. Her hair is draped on either side of her face, like it's enough to shield her from the threat that looms outside. Once I know they're not going to be moving anytime soon, I turn and watch the corridor. My eyes lock on the bottom of the velvet rope as it swings. It's subtle, but I hope it stops before anyone comes down the corridor.

Before *he* comes down the corridor.

I can't tell if we're silent enough. My heartbeat seems loud enough to provide a steady bass line to the songs we used to dance to down on the ground level, and even the scratch of my dress against my skin could double as television static. I don't have time to worry about that, though, when a burgundy shadow seeps across the crimson carpet of the hallway. I clamp my palm across my mouth to stop a cry from escaping.

Oh god.

His shoes come into view first, the lighting too dim to pick up any distinguishing features except for the fact they're stained with blood as they settle into the carpet.

For a second I think we'll get lucky. He'll amble right past, continue down the hall so we can circle back and find the others. But of course I'm kidding myself. Now that we've seen the monster, the action is only going to intensify, and that starts with him pausing in the center of the entrance. I glance up from under the bar, my eyes straining to see higher. The pull at the back of my eyes does nothing to abate the throbbing pulse and panicked thrum that's taken over my brain.

The top half of his head is cut off from sight by the corner of the bar, which is fine since I don't want to see those black heart-shaped eyeholes again. I can't move to see him better anyway. Not when it could make a noise or shift the material of my dress into his view. From my vantage point I'm able to see that beneath the gray, ill-fitting dinner jacket, he's wearing a pair of black coveralls. It's a deviation from the iconic dark green color favored by Michael Myers in the original *Halloween*, but it's a smart choice, I guess, given that he's decided to engage in some messy business tonight. His shoulders twist toward the room, and that's when the knife comes into view. It isn't dripping anymore, but the stain, the sheen of blood, still darkens the blade.

It may be the fear, but I swear I can hear him breathing. A muffled inhale and exhale of someone recovering from the exertion of gutting a fully grown man against a wall. But even though it's heavy, it's even. He isn't rushed, he isn't ruffled—he just moves into the doorframe and waits. Idles with an eerie stillness until the same hand holding the knife reaches out toward the rope and a light, devastating clink of metal unhooking from metal brings tears to my eyes. The rope falls to the ground with a muffled thud, but he doesn't step into the room.

A glimmer out the corner of my eye draws my gaze away from his frozen stance to where the red carpet and the dull, black surface of the bar area meet. The way the light from the neon strips overhead hits the single drop on the floor makes it look like a discarded sequin. It shimmers under the light like the glitter that's speckled across my skin, but it's unmistakably blood.

My blood.

And the sight makes my breath catch in my throat and those tears push closer to the rims of my eyes. There's another drop a foot or so away from the first, and then another, all of them glowing like black jewels beneath the overhead lights, forming a subtle arch around the corner of the bar.

Leading straight to me and Laurie and Jennifer.

A soft rustle draws my eyes away from the trail of blood, glancing up to see him still standing in the same position in the doorway. I can't tell what made the sound, but that doesn't matter when Laurie's hand drops down on top of the one I have propped up on the rubber mat. It takes all my self-control not to scream into my palm from the contact. Her hand is slick with sweat, shaking on top of my own, and then her nails dig into my skin. Hard. Hard enough I have to bite down on the flesh pressed against my mouth to counteract the sting of the almond-shaped points. I slowly turn away from the killer—his pink wool-covered head starting to move across the room in a slow, steady sweep—to silently request that Laurie pull her talons *the fuck* out of my hand.

It's when I notice her shoulders silently heaving that I know something's wrong.

Well, *everything* is wrong right now, but something is worse. Something is scaring her more than the killer standing on the other side of the bar.

Her other palm is still clamped tight across her mouth and her wide eyes are locked, unblinking, on the space above her head. Even in the darkness I can see the stark whites of her eyes. She looks this close to hyperventilating, and when I follow her gaze I understand why. Digging my nails so hard into the rubber beneath us that the gel tips slice straight through the surface, I try not to hyperventilate myself.

If I thought the blood trail leading the killer toward us was bad, this is worse. Much, much worse.

Laurie must have brushed against the edge of the bar when we ducked behind it, because a bar towel hangs over the edge, stuck between her head and the ice bin she's propped against. That's not the issue, though.

The issue is the martini glass lying on top of the towel, hanging precariously over the edge of the bar, teetering over her like a guillotine every time she takes a panicked breath, slipping closer to the edge and primed to fall.

It's the same obnoxious, wide-rimmed style I was sipping out of downstairs. The stem is heavy, the rim is paper-thin, and the diameter is just a little wider than the span of my palm. If it falls—*when* it falls—it could land soundlessly in Laurie's lap. But the more likely scenario is that it smashes against the ground, and even if he misses the red trail I've left behind, he'll know exactly where we're hiding.

My eyes dart to Jennifer, but if anyone's going to give us away it isn't going to be her. Her head is firmly between her legs, her body so tense she looks like she's frozen, and she's completely unaware of what is happening next to her. A luxury I do not share.

I turn my attention back to Laurie. Her eyes drop down from the glass to meet mine, and I don't want to see that expression on her face ever again: *We're going to die.*

So even though I'm afraid removing my hand will release every possible sound of terror from my mouth, I bite down on my lip, slide my hand away, and pin her with a look of my own.

No, we're not.

I reach my injured arm out across my chest, my forearm brushing against the material of my dress and making a hushed scraping sound. I pause. There's another rustle of clothing, but this one is farther away. When it's followed by the slow, repetitive sound of heavy soles hitting soft carpet, I have to make myself concentrate on the glass above Laurie's head. Ignore that the killer is walking around on the other side of the bar.

Blowing out a silent, shaky breath, I angle my arm away and restart my efforts to move toward the glass as my heart slams steadily against my rib cage. Laurie is almost puncturing the skin in my other hand while I stretch my arm across her, but I've become almost acclimatized to it. Numb to it.

I reach until I think I might hyperextend my shoulder. I reach until my skin stretches and the freshly coagulated wound in my arm rips, allowing fresh blood to seep down my skin. I reach until I'm half an inch away from the edge of the glass and I can feel the heat of Laurie's breaths escaping from between her fingers against my skin. The whole time the glass hovers over the edge of the bar, until it dips a final time and slips farther down against the towel. Like me, it's unable to resist the force of attraction. But instead of dark eyes and hidden tattoos or tamped down smiles and messy hair, it's powerless against gravity, and when it finally gives in, I catch my breath as it falls.

CHAPTER 16

"*The greatest thing you'll ever learn is just to kill and be killed in return.*"

—Not *Moulin Rouge!*

I jerk forward, hand outstretched beneath the glass, and it hits the surface of my skin.

Soundlessly.

My fingers lock, my arm drops just in front of Laurie's face, and then I freeze. The rim digs into the crease of my thumb and the nail of my pinkie, and I squeeze, gripping my other fingers into the perimeter of the glass until my hand shakes. Drawing my arm back into my chest, I place the glass lightly in my lap, and it takes all my self-control to keep from sighing in relief when Laurie extracts her nails from my hand.

That was too close.

When I meet Laurie's eye and see the look of shocked, apologetic gratitude, I know she thinks so, too.

Flexing the feeling back into my hand, I glance over my shoulder just in time to see the killer hook the rope back into place across the doorframe. Whatever he was doing in the room, he's done for now, and he takes a step back—a step away from us—before turning on his heel and continuing down the corridor. A hot, wet trail drips down my cheek, and my first instinct is that I've cut myself again. When another follows on the other side of my face, I realize the tears I've been holding back since he unclipped the barricade have finally fallen.

That was *way* too close.

We don't move. Not when his steps eventually turn inaudible. Not when the pins and needles start up in my legs. Not when Jennifer lifts her head, spots the martini glass in my lap, and confusion crosses her pale face. And not when my breathing comes back to normal, my shoulders settling against the bar. I can feel Laurie's eyes on the side of my face, awaiting further instruction, but I keep waiting.

Rule two: always hide for longer than you think you should. I broke one rule by splitting away from the group and this is where it got us. I fucked around, and holy shit, did I find out. So I wait to make sure he doesn't circle back, that he's not idling just outside the entry, or any of the other endless killer tricks I've watched that would leave us dead for moving out of our hiding place too early.

When there hasn't been even a hint of movement or sound after what might be ten minutes, I place the martini glass on the ground and slowly rise from behind the bar. I instantly wish I hadn't, though, because when I do, I spy an addition to the champagne flutes and ice bucket that are carefully displayed in the middle of the chaises. A bloom of color. I *know* it wasn't there before, and the sight makes me feel sick. More so than when Curtis was bleeding out in front of me, or when we came upon those bodies discarded in the middle of the hallway.

Because there in the previously empty silver ice bucket is a single crimson rose.

It's only after we've checked that the hallway is clear that I move toward the rose. There's a card, too, propped in front of the bucket, and I hesitate before picking it up. It's rigid, weighty, a perfect pure white, and I can't stop my hands from shaking as I slip a finger into the fold and prepare to open it.

This isn't like the rose petals downstairs. This feels more like a gift. A gesture.

He wanted us to find this. He knew someone was hiding in this room, he knew we were in here, and he didn't *look* for us. He's killed so many people tonight, but when he had us cornered he just . . . left. There *has* to be a reason, and I feel like we'll find it inside this card.

"That wasn't here before." Laurie's voice is steady as she situates herself near the doorframe to keep watch. Her eyes are locked on the card in my hand.

No, it was not. And the appearance of a rose is completely uninspired. This whole night is uninspired. Even the mask is uninspired. I'm sure there's a slasher flick where the killer wears a mask like his. I can't remember it right now, but I'm certain it's out there. That's why I know for sure that I was right in my predictions for the night.

He's following the formula.

"Should we open it?" Jennifer whispers, stepping up next to me and leaning over the table. She reaches for the flower, sliding it out of the bucket, and looking at it like she's never seen a rose before. Pinching a petal between her fingers, she pulls it away from the bud. It's real. He's spared no expense.

It's not like the killer is going to jump out of a greeting card, but I have to psych myself up to open it as if he was. With a stunted exhale I flick my thumb up, and I'm immediately struck by the familiarity of the single line that's etched in black ink. I hear a choking noise at my shoulder, and when I glance away from the card, Jennifer is staring at it with terrified incredulity.

"Is that—" She gasps. "Is that a . . . *Taylor Swift* lyric?"

Can't you see? You belong to me.

Disregarding the misquote, I'm struck by the handwriting. I feel like I've seen those sharp letters before, caged within the red barrier of a flimsy name tag. We all agreed whoever's been doing this must be one of the daters, but this confirms it for me.

The killer is one of us.

Jennifer stares at me with wide eyes, the petal dropping from her fingers when she says, "Why would he leave song lyrics and a rose?"

It's the same question playing on my mind, and when I look down at the card again, rereading the lyric that is meant to be a declaration of romantic compatibility, different film scenes start playing through my head. Ones with less blood and more makeover montages. Ones with soft, gentle lighting rather than a reliance on underexposure.

Marion did say we could find our "perfect match" tonight. So what if someone did?

What if somebody was so enamored with one of their dates that they're doing everything in their power to get rid of the rest of us?

Shit. This whole time I've thought that the murders were a deviation from the main event, but what if they're just *part* of it?

"Those rose petals downstairs, and now this . . ." Laurie's contemplative voice pulls me out of my own musings, and while I planned on keeping my theory to myself, I'm flanked by two smart women. Jennifer's sharp gasp is indication enough that she's come to the same conclusion.

Her eyes dart between the card in my hand and the rose gripped in hers. "He's leaving them on *purpose.*"

Speaking the theory into existence kicks me into gear, and I slide the card into my bra for safekeeping. If we meet back with the others—*when* we meet back with the others—we can see if anyone recognizes the handwriting. But first, we need to find some more weapons to replace the ones we lost. I stride back over to the bar and start searching among the tools for swizzling and muddling to find something more akin to slitting or stabbing.

"My god," Laurie says, slumping against the doorframe where she still keeps watch. "Is he . . . Is this whole thing *for* someone?"

She turns to me, and whatever look she sees on my face when I glance up from trawling the bar makes her shoulders drop farther.

"Jamie?"

"I think so. When Wes and I were following that trail downstairs, we thought the rose petals might be a calling card, but this is different. I think . . ."

I think a lot of things.

I think the broken bottles haven't worked for us so far, not when we're up against the never-ending supply of knives this guy seems to have. There's a reason all the Big Bads prefer metal blades, and it's not just for the theatrics. Freddy's were crafted onto his hand, Michael and Jason always sourced something that had a great ergonomic grip. Even Leatherface utilized weapons that could be found at your local hardware store. They all chose their weapons based on ease of use, and I don't think our guy is any different.

"Jamie, *what* do you think?" Laurie asks from the doorway, her gaze locked on the hall beyond it. I couldn't be prouder of her for developing a keener sense of her surroundings in the last couple of hours. At home she trips over our robo-vacuum even though we've had it for two years. "I think," I say as I continue rummaging around the bar, "the killer met someone at one of the dates tonight and this is his way of showing he's interested." I spot a corkscrew and place it on the bar top. When I find two more stacked near some slightly dusty wineglasses, I put them next to it.

"I think the killing is just a means to an end," I say as I try to find a paring knife or *any* kind of blade that could do even a fraction of the damage the killer has managed so far tonight, but it's no use. It would be bad business practice to leave out anything that could be used as a weapon. Still, I slide the spiral of one of the corkscrews between my index and middle finger, gripping the handle in my hands as I circle back around the bar. The tip is dull, but it's better than nothing.

"We need to get out of here. If he comes back, we'll be cornered," Laurie says once I've handed her one of the other corkscrews and passed the spare to Jennifer. "Did you see which way he went?"

The question is directed at me because I'm the only one who has seen him so far. The only one, that is, who has seen him and lived, and that makes my stomach curl in on itself. I don't know what that means for me. What it means for the three of us. Or maybe I do, and I just don't want to admit it to myself. I don't want to admit he probably could've chased us down if he wanted to. He could have walked around this room and found us. He's killed eight people so far and I can guarantee at least one of them would have had better cardiovascular capabilities or been able to find a better hiding spot than the three women in this room. There's only one kind of person who's able to have so many near misses. One kind of woman . . .

One kind of girl.

I ignore the twist of suspicion in my chest and point down the corridor. "That way."

"Should we go back to where we were then?" Jennifer asks as we start to move out. She looks like she's about to leave the rose behind, but I gesture for her to bring it with us. It's a gift. One that is clearly unwanted, but it's a clue, too, and despite what Wes said downstairs, we might need to start playing detective soon. The problem-solving in a slasher usually does begin in the second act anyway. "What if he's waiting there?"

"He could be anywhere," Laurie says, and it's good she can take the lead while my brain is still running through the improbability that we survived the killer coming into the VIP section.

"But," she continues, "we need to see if Wes and Billie have come back. If they were able to find anything. If John's okay. If they're..."

I can tell what she was going to say before thinking better of it and deciding not to jinx it.

If they're still alive.

And that makes a sharp twinge, not unlike when my arm was sliced open, tighten inside my chest. We've been in such a state of panic I haven't allowed myself to consider something has happened to them. A small, intrusive thought breaks through my survival mode: *We didn't even get to have a* real *date.*

It must come from some part of my brain that believes it's possible for boom boxes blasting Peter Gabriel and meetings on top of the Empire State Building to coexist in a world where twenty strangers can be trapped in a club while being methodically slaughtered by a masked killer. I adjust my grip around the corkscrew. That kind of thinking isn't going to help us in this situation, so I turn in the direction we came from and start down the hallway.

"Let's go."

We walk in a straight line. Me, Laurie, then Jennifer, armed only with corkscrews that I doubt could even pull a thread on that huge dinner jacket the killer was wearing.

The minutes extend while we retrace our steps to the front of the building, and I realize we ran a lot farther than I'd anticipated. Either that or the journey just feels longer without terror propelling us. When we reach the end of the hallway and we haven't been attacked by some hulking, murderous asshole, we pause a few feet from the top of the stairs, deciding to wait a couple of minutes to catch our breath or in case any of the others come back. Our backs are flat against the wall. Jennifer is propped up on the wall across from us, giving us the option of four different escape routes in case the killer presents himself again.

"Jamie?" Laurie says.

"Yeah?"

"Who do you think the card was meant for?"

The question prompts Jennifer to look over at us from where she's had her eyes trained on the corridor we came from. Her brows are furrowed, hands balled into fists—one clutched around the corkscrew I gave her, the other around the rose—instead of gripping her arms.

"I don't know."

But I think if I had to guess, I'd have a one-in-three chance of being right.

I can't ignore that every other person who has come as close to the killer as we did is now dead. I can't ignore the fact that a man doesn't whip out Taylor Swift lyrics on a whim, especially not in the middle of a killing spree. And I can't ignore that the intended recipient of that card, of the rose in Jennifer's hand, is most likely standing in this corridor right now. And if that's true, one of us is in the deepest shit imaginable.

"What's the end?" Jennifer asks. "Before, you said that the . . . *killing* was a means to an end. What's the end?"

"For him? Getting the person he thinks he belongs with." I tap my chest where the card sits, wincing at the idea that this murderer has bastardized a Taylor Swift lyric and ruined an objectively catchy song for everyone standing in this hallway.

"And for us?"

That's a more complex question. If I'm right, and he's trying his hardest to woo one of the women here tonight, there is no way a sane person could appreciate any of these grotesque offerings. And when he realizes that . . . Images of sad, dejected men with wet, wilted hair from any number of romantic comedies pop into my head. In the movies, the guy who doesn't get the girl bows out gracefully, but I can't see that happening here. All I see is more blood.

I'm not sure how to word that in a way that won't send them both screaming down some dark hallway never to be seen again. I don't want to worry them, and I'm saved from having to make the decision when there's a sound to our left, and then—

"Jamie?"

The voice is unmistakably male, and my back stiffens against the wall. I've only recently become familiar with the deep tone, so it takes a second for relief to cut through the initial, instinctive fear, and when I turn toward the source, I let that relief audibly leave my mouth.

He's back.

Wes is back.

Billie stands behind him, but he's the one who captures my attention, standing at the top of the stairs, face grave, his eyes locked on my arm. I'll admit, it looks worse than it probably is: the bloodstain starts a hand's width away from the top of my shoulder, spreads wide over my bicep, and then dribbles into trails of red reaching my wrist. Add that to holding a dull corkscrew, and this isn't exactly how I wanted to look when we reunited. But then my gaze drops to see the blood on *his* shirt. New, fresh stains mar the white material, and then of course there's his missing weapon. Rod? Shaft?

The chair leg is gone. Well, not so much "gone" as upgraded.

Now it's a blood-tipped knife.

CHAPTER 17

"If you find somebody you can hunt, you can't let that get away."

—Not *The Wedding Singer*

"**W**hat the *hell* happened?"

I move toward him but stop short, glance down at the knife hanging from his weapon wristlet, then take two steps back. It was too dark in the corridor to be sure, but the knife in Wes's hand doesn't *look* like the one that was used on the guy at the end of the corridor. The one that was able to paint an already red wall a sticky coat of dark crimson. It's still a knife, though, and there's still blood on it. There's blood on *him*.

"Why do you have that?" I ask, trying and failing to keep my voice even as he shifts to take the final step up to the mezzanine.

He pauses before his foot hits the floor, a brief look of hurt crossing his face, but then he glances down at my arm again and moves back onto the previous step. Billie presses herself up against the wall to accommodate him, her eyes darting between the corkscrews in our hands. Wes's gaze shifts behind me to the other women who look like they've been dragged through hell and back, and then he holds him arms up in surrender. The handle of the knife becomes loose in his hand—though the bracelet I made him would make it impossible for any of us to get the weapon out of his grip anyway— and I see he's holding the small first aid kit and a flashlight in his other hand.

Something moves behind them. Someone.

"Dani?"

She looks like hell, too—her Meg Ryan pixie cut is looking less nineties rom-com cute and more like an eighties slasher heroine who's seen some shit. She does not look like someone who'd accidentally get a chicken tattoo on a fun night out, and when she squeezes past Wes and Billie, I see her face is gaunt and pale. I crane my neck to look over Wes's shoulder, hoping to see that familiar pink dress. Because if they've found Dani, then—

"Where's—"

The question dies on my tongue when Wes shakes his head almost imperceptibly, his eyes closing in a "don't ask" blink, but the word alone is enough to bring Dani to tears.

There's blood on her hands so she doesn't try to wipe at them as they fall down her cheeks.

"You were right," she sniffs. "We shouldn't have split up. We thought we could check both corridors at the same time, but Colette didn't come back. She didn't come back."

Fuck.

She climbs the final step and joins us on the landing; Billie, too. But even though he's been with them this whole time, and I'm sure Billie and Dani would tell us if he went AWOL at some point, Wes stays where he is. I have a feeling he won't take another step closer until we invite him to, like a polite yet cautious vampire. And I appreciate it. He's not a threat, but he knows we feel threatened. So that's why

I hold my hands up to mirror his and make my voice soft when I ask again, "What happened?"

"Dani was hiding under the bar," he says, using the hand holding the knife to gesture to the stains on his shirt. The way they cut across the white material in straight gashes, it's like he was brushing against wet paint. "It was . . . messy."

Not wet paint. Spilled blood.

"When Colette didn't come back, I didn't want to go back upstairs alone," Dani says from behind me. "I thought I could just hide and wait it out."

Considering I didn't get to tell her about the rules, those are some good instincts.

"When we found her, she almost got me." Wes points down to a spot of blood near his collarbone. His shirt is sliced open an inch or two, but the stain has stopped spreading close to the cut, so it's only a superficial wound. "A broken bottle. Inspired by you, no doubt."

How he still manages the smallest of smiles at me when he's explaining how he got stabbed, I'll never know.

"I'm sorry . . . again," Dani says, and when I look back at her she's wincing, apologetic, but the soft chuckle ahead of me draws my eyes back to Wes.

"It's fine. You did the right thing." He's shaking his head like they've already had this conversation before his eyes laser in on my arm again and his amusement vanishes. "What happened to you?"

"I got cut by Laurie's bottle." I try to wave it away like it's not a big deal, but the movement just makes me wince, and a thin, fresh line of blood trails down my arm. I'm not trying to underplay it. It's just that me getting accidentally sliced open by my best friend doesn't feel like the key plot point of what played out on this level while Wes and Billie were down in the bar. We came within slashing distance of the killer, and though it feels like I'm burying the lede right now and I want to tell him what happened, no one else has invited Wes up onto the landing.

He's still in exile on the last step.

His stare lifts from my arm to look over our heads, but whatever he does or doesn't see just makes his expression get darker. "Where's John?"

"We heard a noise, he went to go check, and then he . . ." I shake my head. I don't want to say the same words as Dani and take him out of the equation just yet. He walked into the side of the club that Laurie and I couldn't remember. Maybe he got lost. Maybe he found a phone or a way out, or maybe—

"Did you find anything downstairs?" Laurie appears at my shoulder.

Wes drops his hands but still stays where he is.

"No maps. No fire extinguishers. No phones on any of the bod— people down there. We found a flashlight?" He says it like he knows it isn't enough to make up for all the things they *didn't* find, then he directs the next statement to the landing. "I—I took the knife from . . . from the host." *Jesus.* He means he took it *out* of her. Wes looks back up at us, worry written all over his face. "I think . . . I think this was planned. I think they planned out everything."

Hearing it feels like a punch to the gut, but I think so, too.

I thought so when I saw the rose, and it may have even crossed my mind earlier.

"I realized I haven't seen an emergency exit light all night, so we checked the perimeter of the basement and found the remains of a mount on the ceiling." He blows out a frustrated breath. "It looked like it had been removed. Not to mention—" He nods above my head, and when I look up I see something that pulls my heart all the way up to the top of my throat.

The dome of a security camera. They're designed to be subtle, a reminder that someone's always watching, but if you're not doing anything wrong you have nothing to worry about. The shield over the camera doesn't look like it should; it doesn't have that smooth, glossy finish with a light glowing from within. It doesn't look like that because it's covered in black spray paint, some of the dark flecks flicking across the deep scarlet ceiling. The killer really wanted this to be a once-in-a-lifetime experience.

"Each one we've come across looks like that," Wes remarks, and everything he says just makes our situation sound more and more dire. Because when you put all the pieces together—not just killing off the employees (the people who would know how to get out of here) first, or taking the phones, or locking the door and swiping the code, but also the roses and the mask and the never-ending supply of equipment he's brought to play with—that kind of thing requires preparation. It requires forethought.

And that changes things.

It means we've fully ruled out that this is a crime of opportunity. It means the format is more *Hostel* than *Halloween*. He's not the kind of killer who counts on his victims making dumb decisions like Ghostface, or who relies on brute strength like Michael Myers.

He's planned this, set it up, and we are all just side characters in the romantic evening he's orchestrated for some poor woman who's captured his obsession.

"Can I . . ." Wes's voice breaks me out of my thoughts.

Both his hands are back in the air when he turns the first aid kit toward me, the other hand holding the knife pointing to the wound in my arm. It's deeper than his, but I've gotten used to the pain. I'm about to say we should concentrate on finding a way out. That time is against us, and it's dried over anyway, and it must be my lucky day since I wore a dress that hides the stains so well.

But Laurie answers for me.

"Yeah. Clean her up."

I shoot her a dry look that just makes her say, "You're a mess."

I look back at Wes. He hasn't moved from the last step, waiting for my go-ahead.

Even if he had gone down to the basement alone, he's not the kind of guy who makes your figurative hackles stand up. His presence doesn't pull at the intuitive divining rod of danger in your gut because *something* is a little off. Not to mention, I just don't think I'd eye fuck a guy who would turn out to be a killer. So I nod and watch him step up onto the mezzanine.

It's a slow, stunned, exhausted expedition to the booths that line the side of the mezzanine across from the bar, and when Wes points to the middle one, I move toward it without argument. Laurie, Jennifer, and Dani file into the one next to us within earshot. Laurie offers to hold my hand while Wes works on my arm, but we both know it isn't her strong suit, and if anyone needs emotional support it's Dani. She's still crying. It's one thing to be caught up in someone's killing spree. It's another to lose your new bestie in the middle of it. So Laurie sits with Jennifer while she tries to comfort Dani, offering practiced sounds of consolation and awkward back pats. Billie situates herself against the railing. She says it's to be a lookout, but I think it's more because she hates everyone's guts.

"What exactly happened up here?" Wes asks.

I slide onto the seat and lay my arm on the table. It sticks to the surface, and I don't know if that's because of the blood or some residual spilled alcohol. He unzips the kit and takes stock of the contents, removing the bracelet from his wrist, his fingers skillfully loosening the strap like I taught him before he places the blade on top of the table and lowers himself into the booth beside me. His thigh is flush against my own, his shoulder at just the right height to rest my head on, and it's a struggle to refrain from moving even closer.

"We heard a noise, and John went to look," I say, shaking the image of his back disappearing into the corridor out of my head and concentrating on what Wes pulls out of the first aid kit instead: antiseptic wipes, gauze, adhesive dressing, a pair of gloves. Once he has them laid out in front of us, he pulls the gloves on, and for some reason, his consideration of hygiene despite the circumstances makes me smile.

Wes takes my arm, one hand on my elbow, the other at the back of my bicep, and lifts it off the table, turning it in his grip to get a better look at the cut. Even through the gloves, his hands are warm against my skin.

"And?" he asks, resting my arm back down on the table and ripping open the first antiseptic wipe. He starts at my wrist, slowly erasing the red, working his way up toward the actual cut.

"He didn't come back," Laurie says from the other booth, and it prompts a responding sob from Dani.

"I went to look for him," I continue, "but I heard something down the other corridor. I went to make sure . . . I don't know what I was making sure of, but I found one of the guys from tonight. The killer was—" I tilt my head, and Wes nods in understanding. "So we ran. I got cut by Laurie's Kahlúa bottle in the panic, and then we hid."

As I'm talking, he strokes the antiseptic wipe softly against my arm. It's methodical, meticulous, and he doesn't need to rest the thumb of his free hand on the inside of my elbow to keep my arm in place, but he does. The way he mindlessly strokes it against my skin takes my mind off the fact he's doing it while he's cleaning my wound. It makes me swallow thickly and consider grazing my fingers against his forearm in return. Again, I'm reminded these aren't the kinds of things that should be running through my mind after narrowly avoiding a killer.

"It might sting," Wes warns when he gets close to the cut.

"This isn't the first time Laurie's almost sent me to the ER," I say, and ignore the *pfft* she emits from the other booth. Though in her defense, it is only the second time. The first was an unfortunate cooking adventure that gave me food poisoning and dehydration. "I think I can handle it."

His eyes are locked on my arm, but he still grants me a grin. "Yeah, you're tough."

Being tough doesn't stop me from gritting my teeth when he wipes the edge of the open skin. I blow out a breath as Billie asks, "And what is that?"

She's pointing to the table the other women are sitting around, and when Jennifer lifts her hand, I spot the rose that's captured Billie's attention.

"The killer left this in the room we were hiding in," Jennifer says. "He left a card, too. Jamie?"

As Wes keeps working on my cut, I use my free hand to pull the card out of my bra. All eyes focus on the folded note. Well, almost all eyes. In my periphery, I spot Wes's gaze drop to the neckline of my dress for a split second before he shifts it back to the antiseptic wipe. I can't be mad. I'd look down his shirt, too, if given half a chance.

Billie strides over to the table and plucks it from my hand, pulling the top flap up and reciting the line in a monotonic cold read: "Can't you see? You belong to me."

There's a sniff. Dani lifts her head from her hands, and while her face is pink and tearstained, her voice is uncharacteristically sober when she says, "Isn't that Taylor Swift?"

"That's what *we* thought," Jennifer says. "What do you think it means?"

"I'd say it's meant to be romantic," Billie quips, tossing the card onto the table in front of the others and moving back to the railing. She bends her back over the edge in a leisurely stretch before she straightens, her arched eyebrow visible despite the curl of hair that falls in front of her eye. "Who doesn't love roses? I know I do." I'm about to counter that roses lose their appeal when they're left by someone who's killing off everyone in the building when she adds, "And how does this all fit in with your movie, Jamie?"

I glare at her as Laurie beats me to the punch and flips her the bird.

"Hey! You know what we should do?" Jennifer says pleasantly before Billie can turn her ire onto my best friend. "Let's see if anyone recognizes the handwriting on this card. That'll be ... fun ... kind of."

It's a weak excuse, but it deescalates the conflict and gives the others a common goal while Wes keeps cleaning my wound.

"There's something else," I murmur to Wes, and he pauses. His gaze flicks up to mine. Dark, serious, restrained. It almost makes me not say it. Almost, but I need to tell someone, and I can't tell the others without upsetting Dani or getting scoffed at by Billie.

"He was wearing a mask," I say quietly as the women huddle around the card in the booth next to us. "Like a ski mask, but the eyes were hearts."

Saying the words easily tempts the image of the pink woolen head to the forefront of my mind. I feel like I need to give him a name. A placeholder until his actual identity is revealed.

"The Bloody Suitor" actually sounds really cool, so I'm not going do him the favor of granting him such a badass name. After tonight the media will call him something like "The Serendipity Slayer," but right now, still in the midst of the action, it's a bit of a mouthful. I need something fast, something that immediately conjures the figure that's been hunting us all night. In slashers, before any real identity is revealed, simple, visual monikers are the norm. That's how we got Ghostface, Pinhead, Leatherface. Hell, Michael Myers was referred to as "The Shape" in the credits for *Halloween*. So while it is low-hanging fruit, unoriginal to the nth degree, I can't ignore the first name that comes to mind.

Heart Eyes.

"Remember when you first said the rose petals were romantic?"

Wes nods and then drops the bloody wipe onto the table, peeling open the adhesive dressing and suspending it over the cut. I wait until he sticks it to my skin and carefully presses down the edges before asking, "What if that was his intention the whole time?"

Letting go of my arm, Wes reaches for a bandage and unfurls it carefully, placing one end on top of the dressing. "What do you mean?"

I'd thought a motive wasn't important in the grand scheme of things because the reason was most likely one of two possibilities. Mindless psychotic outburst? Checks out. Bloody revenge plot? I can rationalize that. But what if there is a third?

"The roses, the card, the fact tonight was clearly planned out— There's a lot of effort behind everything he's doing, and it makes me think that maybe killing isn't the objective."

That makes Wes's hand tighten around my bicep. His gaze darts up to meet mine, those dark pools suddenly hard as he says, "It's not a slasher to him. It's a romance."

CHAPTER 18

"I'll kill you."
"For what?"
"Your heart."

—Not *Love and Basketball*

*I*t's nice to hear Wes speaking my language, and when he glances up from winding the bandage around my arm, I nod. "Right? This night might be one big romantic gesture to him."

"The most fucked-up rom-com ever?" he replies with a dark smirk that I match as he fastens the end of the bandage with a clip.

"Something like that . . ." I say. "But then what's the endgame for *her*? The woman he's doing this for? Does he want her to make it out alive, or is he saving her for last?"

"I'd say he's doing this *for* her, but if she doesn't reciprocate, if she doesn't appreciate what he's doing . . ." He pauses, then murmurs, "Remember how I mentioned the woman that was found a few days ago? It was on the news."

Blond, pretty, lights up the room. "Casey something—"

"Langenkamp," he supplies. "Casey Langenkamp."

I look down at the work he's done on my arm. The blood is gone, the wound is covered, and—not that I'm an expert on this kind of thing—the bandage looks secure. Like if I have to run for my life again, it'll hold up.

"On the news they said the police suspect that it's connected to four other murders," I say.

"It is."

The way he says it—assuredly, conclusively—draws my eyes away from my arm and I watch as he sets out replacing the unused items back into the first aid kit. This isn't the first time he's done this.

"How do—"

"Let's assume we're right and tonight is connected to it, too?" he says, hand paused over the first aid kit, his intensely dark gaze meeting mine again. I wonder whether he's been thinking this for a while. Whether this is what was going through his mind when we were following those rose petals away from the bodies in the corridor.

"What if he pursued those women and then killed them when they couldn't live up to his expectations? What if he's looking for 'the One'?"

I mull that over. His theory aligns well with mine. What if we've unwittingly entered into a slasher version of *The Bachelor*?

The rose theme is on brand, after all.

"In this case, the One is going to be a Final Girl," I say. "And they're not always considered the ideal woman."

Although maybe the killer—Heart Eyes—wants the jaded "walking out of the ruins," "the shit I've seen" kind of girl at the end of this.

It's clear Wes has no idea what I'm talking about. Not when one of his dark eyebrows quirk up in confusion.

"A *what* girl?"

This is why he'd benefit from dating me. I could fill in these knowledge gaps.

"The last person standing at the end of a slasher. It's usually a teenage girl, so they call her the Final Girl. The one who against all odds survives all the traps and all the killer's attempts and ends up defeating him . . . Killing him."

Wes considers that as he peels off the gloves. Despite the wipes, the latex is covered with my blood.

"So you think he *wants* her to kill him?"

If only it were that simple.

"No, because this isn't *just* a slasher. You said it yourself; this is supposed to be romantic."

"You're losing me, Jamie," he says, starting to slide out of the booth before I grip his wrist and pull him back onto the seat. He could move away easily if he wanted, but he settles beside me without much effort on my part. Digging into the first aid kit, I hold up one of the unopened wipes and point to where his shirt is stuck to his collarbone.

"Your turn."

"It's fine."

"It would suck to make it through all of this just to die of an infection you picked up from this dirty club. That's what we call situational irony," I counter. The corner of his mouth twitches.

"It *would* suck, wouldn't it?" he says, but doesn't move. His eyes dart down to where my fingers are still circling his wrist, and when he looks back up they're amused for some reason.

"Can I unbutton my shirt, or are you going to do it for me?" he murmurs, the slow spread of his smile and the rasp of his voice seeping deep into my pores. Apparently that's all it takes to make my nipples harden beyond belief. I quickly glance down to make sure they aren't visible through the material of my dress.

While he's made a fantastic suggestion, I remove my fingers from his arm and pull out one of the larger Band-Aids from the kit. The top button on his shirt is already undone, and he only needs to loosen two more and pull the collar to the side for me to spy where Dani was able to get him. I tear my eyes away from the tip of the tattoo that peeks over his shoulder and see he's right—it's a minor cut in comparison to mine—but it still needs to get cleaned and covered up and . . . yeah, maybe I do just want to reciprocate the effort he's spent on me.

When the packet doesn't rip open between my fingers, I use my teeth. That draws his attention to my mouth, his gaze unwavering until I free the wipe from its packaging and swipe it across the very top of his pec. He clears his throat. "You were talking about . . . romance."

"So he wants the girl who's going to make it to the end of this, right? The Final Girl," I say, trying not to let my fingers linger on his skin as I clean the wound. There's only so much I can get away with under the guise of medical attention. But my efforts garner a sneak peek into the gap of his shirt—I did say if I had half a chance, I would—and what I see . . . it's good. It's very, very good. We've moved from afraid and horny to decisively horny. Well done, Wes.

It's my turn to clear my throat. "But what if he wants the Leading Lady as well? What if he's like most men and expects a woman to be everything for him?"

"Ouch." He faux-winces, straightening his collar after I've placed the adhesive onto his skin. He's clean and covered up in no time, and it's hard not to think I should've slowed down and enjoyed the procedure a little bit more. "I take it the Leading Lady is found in a rom-com?"

"You don't have one without her," I say, discarding the wipe next to the other used ones. "She's your Meg Ryan or your Julia Roberts. Your favorite, Sandy B. Beautiful, assertive, independent in a non-threatening way, emotional, vulnerable, and any flaws she has can be overlooked because of all her other redeeming qualities. At some point tonight he decided he found her. Or . . ." A chill runs down my spine. "He knew her beforehand and followed her here."

I mean, Laurie and I came together. Who's to say some of the other daters didn't tag along with their friends, too? What if some poor woman brought some guy who thinks he's been unfairly shafted into the friend zone, and he wanted to use tonight to prove his love for her?

The other women are listening in now, leaning over the booth or on the table to take in the twisted theory we've been working on. Given none of them have made any exclamations in relation to the handwriting on the card, I'm guessing they weren't able to identify anything, so I look across at them while I zip up the first aid kit and ask, "Did anyone come here with one of the guys tonight?"

They all shake their heads, except for Laurie, who just gestures to me with a *"you're* my guy" look.

"So he's decided someone here is his dream girl," Wes says, working at retying his bracelet around his wrist as he slides out of the booth and leans against the table. With the knife tied firmly to his wrist, Wes grips the handle, placing it carefully across his forearm after he folds his arms over his chest. I watch him turn his head to survey the bar on the other side of the mezzanine as he mulls over the theory, shaking his head as he comes to some conclusion. "And he probably thought the same thing about those other women who he . . . well, whatever he thought, it didn't last."

Because we can't be everything. No one can. And that's the difference between real life and movies. Anyone can pretend to be perfect for the ninety-minute run time. The story plays out a lot differently after the credits roll. Wes seems to realize this, too.

"And if that's the case, then whoever he's doing this for, they're in more danger than the rest of us, because as soon as he realizes she's not perfect . . ."

The illusion will be shattered, and we'll be firmly in slasher territory.

"We need to figure out who it is." Billie says. "Which one of us he's killing for. She's making the rest of us targets and I don't want to be anywhere near her."

At least we can all agree Billie probably isn't the cause of all this.

"What does that make us, then?" Dani asks. "Why is he hunting *us* if he wants her?"

"Because he sees us as obstacles," Laurie says. I can tell she's trying to keep her voice calm and even, but the way she catches my eye, the stoic fear behind her gaze—she's sat through enough slashers and rom-coms to know that secondary characters aren't guaranteed a happy ending.

"Fuck that," Billie spits. "If he wants her, he can have her."

Yeah, let's throw some poor innocent woman to the wolves. Or wolf, singular. I stop myself from taking the bait and turn to see if Wes has anything to say to minimize a potential witch hunt—since Billie sure as shit isn't going to listen to me—but his gaze has dropped down to the dance floor, his eyes locked right beneath the disco ball, and when I stand up and slide out I can see a sliver of color that's captured his attention.

Wes moves slowly toward the railing, his hands gripping the top bar, the knife around his wrist letting out a soft clank as it taps against the metal. The sound repeats again, but Wes does nothing to stop the weapon swinging back into the steel barricade. I push away from the booth to stand next to him to see what's rooted him to the spot, and I get a clearer, unobstructed view of the space beneath us. It should be empty. We walked across the floor maybe an hour ago and it was a clear path, but now—

"Holy shit," Wes utters, and that's enough to capture the attention of the other group members. One by one they move up to the railing and look down at what's taken over the center of the dance floor.

Heart Eyes has been very busy. If the aim was to take someone's breath away then he's succeeded. The effort he's put into this newest gesture is unparalleled. I'd say it was on par with anything Richard Curtis could write. On par, that is, if he hadn't been murdering people alongside these romantic gestures. Murdering them as *part* of it.

At first I can't distinguish what the letters spell out. The shape encasing them is easy enough to see; it's a universal symbol, after all. The fact the heart appears to be fashioned out of intestines doesn't change that, and the mix of the red and pink of the innards conjures up images of Valentine's Day.

A rose petal–like path of blood droplets trails from the heart to a booth off to the side of the floor, one that's underneath the mezzanine and hard to see. When I lean over the railing, look straight down, I see a similar red and pink mix discarded across the booth's circular seat.

Colette.

Dani lets out a sharp gasp when she sees it. When she sees her. It pulls my attention from the tangle of insides that decorate the floor. Dani sobs into Jennifer's shoulder, the latter trying to hold back her own tears, as Laurie moves to my other side. Her eyes lock on the letters inside the heart, head tilted to try and decipher them, and I turn back to it, too, trying to read the cursive that the tubes of tissue have been twisted into. They could be a clue as to who is doing this. *Who* he's doing it for. This display isn't just a message, it's a declaration.

I figure out there's either five or six letters. He's managed to dot the "i" and connect the end of the "e" to the inside of the heart. Once I determine the vowels, it's just the first letter—it kind of looks like an "L" but it's hard to tell—and the middle—

No.

"Oh shit . . . Oh my god. *Oh my god*," Laurie gasps when she recognizes the name, then she does what I want to do and throws up in an empty ice bucket on one of the tables.

"Well," Billie drones. "At least we know *who* he's doing it for."

The sound of Laurie's retching is still bouncing off the bucket by the time I wrench my eyes away from the name spelled out with Colette's intestines. I turn away from the railing, but the image is burned across my retinas.

Billie's voice is acidic in my ear when she adds, "You must've made quite an impression."

CHAPTER 19

"You have butchered me, body and soul."

—Not *Pride and Prejudice*

$\mathcal{I}$'d consider myself well versed in what makes a romantic gesture.

Noah Calhoun restoring an entire house for Allie Hamilton in *The Notebook* in the hopes it would bring her back to him after years and parental prejudice separated them?

Swoon.

Mia Thermopolis, princess of Genovia, apologizing to Michael Moscovitz with an M&M's-studded pizza that leads to their first foot-popping kiss among a garden of fairy lights in *The Princess Diaries*?

Iconic.

But fashioning a giant heart out of intestines with the entrails forming your prospective lover's name?

Yeah, that's downright psychotic.

"How did *none* of you see that when you came up from the basement?" Jennifer asks, shock audible in the shaking of her voice.

"There's a wall that runs along the dance floor," Billie replies. "You can't see anything when you're on the stairs."

"Jamie—" Wes says.

"Oh my *god* . . . he could've been there when we came up," Dani cries.

"Did anyone see anything from up here?" Wes asks, but then his voice drops to a low murmur—one meant just for me—as he says, "Jamie—"

"It's not like someone just sat by and watched him do that," Billie says irritably. "It's out of the sight line when you're not standing at the railing."

"Well, it's in our fucking sight line now!" Laurie's agitated voice sounds echoey so she must still be propped over the ice bucket.

"Jamie!"

"Just give her a minute, Dani." Jennifer's voice is quiet, tight, trying to remain calm, while I'm standing here with my eyes closed, squeezing them tight like I might be able to wring out the image of the heart from under my eyelids. It doesn't work. There's another retching sound and I'm reminded of the times in the past where Laurie and I have swapped some of our red flag stories. The ick some guys give off really can make you sick to your stomach.

"She can have all the time she wants, 'cause I'm out of here."

"Billie—"

"No, I'm not sticking around and getting slaughtered because of *her*. I'll take my chances."

My eyes are still closed as I hear her footsteps. Hard, determined footfalls aimed at putting as much distance between us—between her and me—as she can, because it's me.

He's doing it all because of *me.*

This is not exactly what I had in mind when I said I wanted a man to go the extra mile for me. I meant unprompted good morning messages, noticing when I've done something different with my hair, buying tampons every now and then. Not slowly but surely knocking off complete strangers in creative and gruesome ways.

"Billie!" Jennifer calls out, but even with my eyes closed I know she doesn't follow her. Everyone who has left our group alone hasn't come back. Everyone except me, and that's when I should've known the role Heart Eyes had cast me in. My name spelled out on the floor is as good as top billing on the film poster. I know now what he's been trying to say this whole time.

You're the One.

"Jamie?"

Wes's voice is soft, close, and when I exhale a shaky breath, start nodding, willing myself to open my eyes, a hand slides under my jaw. Even though the contact is light it makes me flinch. I open my eyes and he's right in front of me, his thumb on my cheekbone, his fingers on my jaw as he pulls my head up to meet his gaze. It's concerned, serious, and I don't want him looking at me like that. I don't want him looking at me like I'm primed to be another statistic. I want the soft, warm, inviting glaze over his eyes I saw before. Not this. And I certainly don't want him to say, "It's going to be oka—"

"It's not," I croak. "I had a feeling that—*fuck*—I had a feeling it was one of us. After he left the rose, I thought— This is bad, Wes, it's really, really bad."

Because everything I predicted is coming true.

Coming face-to-face with the killer? Check.

Escalation? Check.

The group fracturing again? Check.

Not to mention who we've lost. Two more people—Colette and the guy in the hallway—are gone.

"We're going to find a way out."

Wes's voice is assured, soothing, but already I'm starting to see the repercussions of this plot twist. The consequences of being the object of Heart Eyes's desire. All of them—Laurie, Wes, Dani, Jennifer. They're all in so much more danger now.

"You should—"

"No." Laurie doesn't even let me finish, and I watch as she extracts her head from the bucket to shoot a watery glare at me.

"Whatever you're about to suggest. *Fuck. No.*"

"Billie's right."

"She hasn't been right all night!"

Laurie spits into the bucket one more time and pushes off the table. Her palms instinctively drop to smooth out the front of her jumpsuit, and I can see the gleam of sweat they leave behind. "That's not going to change now."

While I appreciate the sentiment, the fact remains. He's chosen me. Out of every other person here tonight, I'm the one he wants, and that makes the rest of them obstacles between us.

For the first time *ever*, I disagree with Kate Winslet. I do not want to be the Leading Lady of my own life if *this* is what my life has led to.

Not only that, but I don't think I'm even capable of being a Leading Lady or a Final Girl anyway. Not just because Heart Eyes has got it wrong and I'm too old to be a Final Girl and too young to be a Leading Lady. And while I've studied them, wanted to be like them, used the fictional life lessons and motivational messages to pump me up before anything that induces social anxiety, I've *never* put myself in either category.

"It's dangerous to be around me," I say, trying to keep my voice even as I reach up and wrap my fingers around Wes's wrist. Last time it was to pull him closer, and now I'm pulling his palm from my cheek. Before I drop his hand he manages to twist in my grip until he grabs mine and squeezes. Then he doesn't let go. Even though I mean the words, I can't bring myself to let go, either.

"It's deadly *not* to be around you," Laurie says, moving forward and grasping my free hand. She squeezes it almost painfully.

"Everyone who has died . . . well, it wasn't when they were close to you, was it? I hate to say it, baby girl, but you're our collateral."

It's brutal and factual and *so* Laurie but—"It's not going to stay like that," I say. "If anything, it's a fluke. In a slasher, when the—"

"Nothing has changed, Jamie," Wes says, but judging by the tight expression on his face . . . Everything has changed. "We're just . . . better informed."

That's one way of looking at it.

"Jamie?" Jennifer says, and when I look across, she and Dani have inched closer.

They're looking at me differently now. Wary. Afraid. As if I'm as good as the killer. They walked into this building expecting a mediocre date at best, some awkward silences at worst, and now Dani's blue dress is covered in bloodstains and Jennifer's blowout has gone flat from too much time pressing herself up against walls. God, none of us were prepared for this.

"I understand if you agree with Billie—"

"I don't," she says, cutting me off. She's far more composed than I've seen her since we found her hidden in the alcove. Less anxious. And I can't help but think that kind of character growth is to be expected this far in. "I think we're safer together. Like you said."

"Me, too," Dani says, but she's still wringing her hands so hard I can see the skin turning red.

"But now that we know he's doing this *for* you—"

"Which is *not* your fault," Laurie interjects.

"Definitely not your fault," Jennifer agrees, gritting her teeth almost comically. "Men are crazy . . ."

We sit in the silence of the statement a little longer than is comfortable, until Jennifer realizes Wes is still very much a part of our group and the conversation. She winces.

"No offense."

"None taken," he replies, and the low, accepting tone of his voice draws the smallest of smiles to my lips. When he spots it, it doesn't take long for him to match it.

With Wes's eyes on me, my back to the dance floor, and the group clustered in an intimate huddle, it's easier to swallow the panic. It's easier to push aside the implications of my name inside that heart and focus on how to use this new knowledge to our advantage.

"Was there anyone who was just . . ." Jennifer struggles for the right word until her eyes drop to mine knowingly. "*You know*. On any of your dates?"

What she means is if I got the pull with one of the guys tonight. Not the giddy, unbridled kind that makes everything rose colored, where all you have is possibilities and romanticized ideals. The kind that conjures up images of prolonged eye contact and slow smiles and light, tentative touches. I thought I was lucky enough to have two of those tonight.

Jennifer means the kind of feeling you get from a date that makes you keep an eye on your drink. The kind that makes you censor the personal information you include in small talk, so you don't end up "accidentally" running into the creep in a less-controlled environment.

"I didn't pick up any serial killer vibes," I say. "But it's not like I can remember everyone I had a date with tonight, either." There's only so much space in my brain after all, and the majority of it is taken up by film quotes and genre tropes. Wes drops my hand, his palm digging into his back pocket to draw out two postcard-sized sheets of stiff paper.

When he turns them over, I recognize them even though there are red smudges marring the yes/no columns.

The match cards.

"I grabbed these when I was downstairs," he says, handing them over. "I thought it might come in handy with figuring out who is still unaccounted for, but maybe it'll help jog your memory."

The card on top has the male names, and Stu's is the first one listed. Whoever originally owned this card has put a large tick in the "yes" column next to his name. I'm guessing they didn't accidentally call him Drew, then. I tap my finger against his name, looking up to the find the others waiting expectantly for me to go through the suspect list.

"Stu and I did not get along. I thought he was a dick." Laurie waves away the apologetic look I shoot at her when I say his name. The murders have taken away any fleeting attraction she may have had to the wannabe lumberjack.

"He could've been pretending to not like you," Jennifer says, and I can't help but cringe. At what point do we evolve from thinking yanking someone's pigtails is still an appropriate form of showing interest?

"It's not like he was negging me or pulling some schoolyard bull-shit. We basically hated each other by the time our group split."

Jennifer isn't convinced, though. "*You* hated *him*. What if he felt differently?"

That doesn't sit right. I'm well versed in enemies to lovers, but this doesn't feel like *The Hating Game* or even *Pride and Prejudice*. There was never a simmering undertone of attraction with Stu, and not just because he wears too much plaid, but because he's too much of a dumbass. Not to mention, that setup gets *less* violent as the rela-tionship progresses.

I glance down at the list, scanning the names and mentally remov-ing Drew and Curtis from the lineup since bleeding out takes you off the suspect list. There are three names that don't bring to mind any faces when I read them—Ari, Jason, and Michael.

"I don't remember these three at all," I say, neglecting to mention that I can't remember the first three dates after the break because I was still focused on the one I had before it. With Wes.

"Ari was a little weird," Laurie offers. "He spent our whole date talking about his aunt's hysterectomy."

"Oh my god, he told me that story, too," Jennifer says. "It seemed like he was nervous. Maybe because he was about to . . . *you know*."

It seems like a stretch, but I don't know if any of us have the skills to tell the difference between normal "first date" nerves and "about to commit a massacre" nerves.

"Michael was kind of quiet," Dani says after a moment. "So was Jason, honestly. He was the blond one, right?"

Laurie shakes her head. "I thought *Jason* was the brown-haired one and *Michael* was the blond."

Jennifer cringes. "I am just picturing the same person."

"Michael was blond, Jason had brown hair, and Ari must have been telling everyone about his aunt," Wes says, and I remember he met all the men during cocktail hour. I don't know if their conversations were as robust as the women's down in the basement, but even if they were, the way men act around other men is different from how they act with women. While there's every chance that Ari, Michael, or Jason is Heart Eyes, it's just as likely that one of them is the dead guy in the hallway on the other side of the mezzanine.

"Who's next on the list?" Laurie asks once we reach a communal impasse on the guys I can't remember.

I point to another name.

"Lee and I were figuring out how he could get Nia's attention—"

"Oh really?" Dani says, and when all eyes turn to her she looks a little disappointed. She tries to shrug it off. "I liked Lee."

"He was sweet," Laurie agrees, and when Jennifer nods, I know they're all thinking that disqualifies him from being the killer. Being sweet and being interested in another woman shouldn't make him a suspect, but we also haven't seen him at all since the night took a sharp turn. He's had just as much opportunity as anyone else to be the killer.

"There was John," Laurie says.

John.

Since he left—since he hasn't come *back*—I have to admit the idea that it could be him has bullied its way into my brain. I can't tell if the foreboding twist in my stomach is because he hypothetically had the opportunity to kill the guy in the hallway and leave the rose and card in the VIP room, or because he's completely innocent and probably slashed to pieces somewhere.

"How did that date go?" Dani asks, and I feel the weight of Jennifer's and Wes's stares on the side of my face. My cheeks heat up and I hope no one can see it when I drop my attention back down to the card and shrug. We had a good date, I told him I liked Taylor Swift's music, and he's been missing for *so long* . . .

"It was fine." Then on second thought I look up. Laurie got to experience all my dates after me. If I made such an incredible impact on one of these guys, you'd think she'd be the first to know about it. "How was he with you?"

"Nice." She shrugs. "He seemed interested in our conversation. Present. Bare minimum stuff."

"Our date was *really* good," Jennifer says, then she blushes. I don't think she meant to put that much emphasis on the word. "I mean, it was good, too. Nice."

"He was nice to talk to," Dani adds. "I felt more comfortable with him than some of the other guys."

Nice. Nice. Nice. It's a unanimous assessment, but it doesn't take that twist out of my stomach, because if he was standing here now, we wouldn't be having this conversation.

My mind flashes back to when we were all in the basement after Curtis was killed. John was a few feet away from me when we heard that scream, the one I'm sure belonged to the coat check attendant.

Unless he can be in two places at once, there's no way he did it.

Not to mention, there are five other men who have been gone just as long as he has. I told all of my dates about my music preferences. And John and Jennifer's date was clearly *really* good.

The guilt for thinking that he's a suspect, especially when everyone else is singing his praises, is quickly overshadowed by the guilt that I should have done more to make him stay. I should've gone after him instead of following the sounds of that unfortunate disembowelment. But then again, Heart Eyes could have found the others if I hadn't caught him in the act. He could have snuck up on them and cut everyone down if I'd followed John. More people would be dead. *Laurie* could be dead, and I'd never forgive myself if that happened because I was chasing after some guy.

Laurie moves in to look at the card. "Who's left?"

"Me," Wes says, and when the other women all glance at the space between the two of us, what little of it there is, I think it's pretty obvious that for the most part our date could be considered successful. That could be a strike against him, but Wes was with Billie and Dani in the basement when Heart Eyes crafted his little display. He's the only man we know of who hasn't gone off on his own.

Laurie clears her throat, fully recovered from her spewing spell, and the slight quirk she performs with her eyebrow is a taunt I hear loud and clear.

Eye fucker.

Instead of dignifying or affirming her accusation with a response, I simply purse my lips and go back to the list of names. There's only one more familiar one left.

"Campbell was supposed to be my last date, but then . . ."

"Curtis," Jennifer and Dani say in chorus before we all fall silent.

"He *was* acting shifty, and he *did* leave the group as soon as our backs were turned." Laurie has returned to her logical mode. It doesn't fully check out for me, though. Even though the Norman Bates vibes were strong with him, it feels a bit too anticlimactic for a slasher. These days the shifty guy is rarely the killer.

"I hadn't spoken a word to him," I reason. "I don't think I even looked at him until after—"

"That doesn't mean he wasn't looking at you," Wes murmurs. The knife is lying against his forearm again and I watch the tendons of his hand shift as he grips it tighter. "If this is a rom-com, like you said, and he saw you from across a crowded room . . ."

Then we're looking at love at first sight.

Moulin Rouge! Titanic. Romeo + Juliet. Whether it was from a trapeze, or the deck of a doomed ship, or through a fish tank, the male lead decided they were meant to be before the female lead had even spoken a single word. None of those films had a happy ending, though.

I know beggars can't be choosers, but I don't want *that*. I don't want *this*. I can understand seeing someone and having an instant attraction, but not falling in *love* with someone before you know anything substantial like their last name or their birthday or if they actually do appreciate mass killing as a way of being wooed.

Wes blows out a sigh. "Look, I still think we need to assume it could be anyone, but—"

There's a squeal of shoes against vinyl that makes everyone jerk their attention down to the lower level. For a second, I'm struck by the horror of my name traced out on the ground, as if I'm seeing it for the first time again, but then a figure appears from the shadows. He stops short, chest heaving, hair disheveled, eyes locked on the artful tangle of insides, which must look like a mess of red without the vantage point we have, before he tears his gaze away and turns it skyward.

When he sees us lined up against the railing, his sigh of relief is audible. He rolls the broken Midori bottle from one hand to the other, then lifts his free one in greeting.

"Hey."

CHAPTER 20

*"In my opinion, the best thing you can do is find someone
who kills you for exactly what you are. Good mood, bad
mood, ugly, pretty, homicidal, what have you."*

—Not *Juno*

$\mathcal{W}$es is furious.

"Where the fuck were you?"

It's subtle, slow, but I notice the way he shifts so he's standing between us—the women—and John. I notice the way he isn't holding his knife flush against his thigh, either; his arm is slightly raised, preparatory, and it makes my palms sweat around the match cards still in my hands.

"I found another set of stairs," John pants, having run up to the mezzanine level and joined us near the booths as soon as he dropped his hand. Sweat beads against his forehead and glistens across the top of his chest. I always thought he was the "academia lean" that I'm usually drawn to in men, but the way the muscles in his forearms stick out while he's clenching his fists, the tendons stark beneath his skin hinting at reserved strength . . . Now I'm not so sure.

"That side of the club wasn't on the map, so when I saw the stairs I thought maybe it was an employee section, and it might lead to an exit." He turns to Laurie and me, but he can't bring himself to meet our eyes. "That's why you wouldn't have known about it. But they just led downstairs, so I circled back, and I must've gone down a different hallway . . . I got all turned around. I thought I was lost and I . . . panicked." Color rises in his cheeks, his hair flopping down into his eyes, and he looks so shamefaced admitting it that my first instinct is to feel sorry for him. He rakes a hand through his hair, unable to lift his gaze to mine even when he says, "I'm so sorry, Jamie. I heard you scream but I couldn't find you. I tried—I tried to get to you."

His voice cracks on the last word, and that's when his blue eyes finally meet mine. They are just as gorgeous as they were on our date, bright and appealing. But I've seesawed between thinking he could be a killer and thinking he's dead in a corner somewhere, so I can't find it in myself to reach out and console him. Casual touching feels a lot more dangerous when you've caught the interest of a serial killer. Jennifer doesn't have the same issue. Especially when he starts apologizing to the other women and saying that he should've been there. She grips his shoulder with one hand, smooths her palm across his bicep, and he looks up at her with a grateful grimace. The way John places his hand over Jennifer's does work in his favor when it comes to discounting him as a suspect, though.

"Look, it's fine. We're all fine," I say, looking around at the frazzled group and figuring it's as true as it can be in these circumstances. Wes isn't actively trying to block John from joining the group anymore, and Dani and Jennifer look perfectly comfortable standing on either side of him.

"We know what he wants now," I say. Even though the discovery that *I* am what he wants is absolutely insane. "We can work with that to get out of here."

John looks between us for the answer, but I just point over my shoulder and shift away from the railing, slipping the match cards into my bra for safekeeping.

He looks down at the dance floor—at the mess that as I suspected doesn't have the same effect on ground level. It takes him a few seconds, but when he comprehends what the (literally) twisted message says, he turns around slowly, looking at me with new eyes. "You."

"Me." I pull my mouth into a grim interpretation of a smile and shrug. "Every girl's dream, right?"

He allows one more glance back at the heart before he turns his back on it for good.

"This is probably the worst time to say this," Laurie says from my side, her leg bouncing rapidly next to mine, and I know what's she about to say. It hits me suddenly, like the flick of a switch. They never cover this in horror movies. No matter how long people are trapped or running or searching. It really is a glaring plot hole.

"I *really* need to pee."

Bathrooms don't have a great track record in horror.

While my thesis adviser, Jordan, would argue that zombie films are in a different class from slashers, there is some crossover when it comes to the danger inherently connected to restrooms. There's a reason rule number three in *Zombieland* is Beware of Bathrooms. I think he'd agree with me that the risk is far greater when the killer isn't a member of the undead, though. The scenes are easy enough to conjure up: *Scream 2*, the 2018 *Halloween* reboot, *Bloody Homecoming*, *Maniac!* . . . I could keep going. We're just lucky there isn't a shower involved.

As soon as Laurie mentions she needs to go to the bathroom, Dani almost cries again as she admits that she is moments away from peeing herself. Avoiding that becomes our interim goal while an exit is still out of reach. There must be bathrooms on the mezzanine level, but I can't remember whether we go down one of the middle corridors or go back around near the VIP rooms to find them. Laurie can't remember, either, but she can vividly recall where they are on the first level, and John confirms that he located them on that first sweep he performed earlier in the night. After a short discussion, it's agreed that we'd all rather walk a known path than try to navigate the unknown parts of the building and come face-to-face with my admirer. Wes takes the card from the VIP room and slides it into his back pocket, but we leave the rose where it lies on a table. I don't really feel like claiming it as my own now that Heart Eyes has decided I'm his girl, and I don't give it a second look when we leave the mezzanine.

When we get to the bathrooms on the first level—without coming across any more bodies, messages fashioned by someone's vital organs, or slow-walking, statuesque killers with a preference for pink masks—it makes sense to have half the group keep watch outside the narrow hallway while the other half does their business. John, Dani, and Jennifer go in first after checking that the bathrooms are vacant (on Wes's instruction) and ensuring nobody is hiding on top of the toilets inside the stalls (on my instruction).

Wes and Laurie stand on either side of me while we press our backs against the wall and keep watch in the main hallway, armed with one knife and a couple of corkscrews between the three of us. I shift my corkscrew into my left hand to scratch at the residual glitter on my arm, ignoring how the pull of my skin makes my cut throb in warning. Even Wes's efforts with the antiseptic wipes haven't been able to get rid of the red sparkles, and the layer of sweat on my skin acts like glue.

"Stop it," Laurie whispers. "You're not getting it off."

"It itches."

"You're being a little bitch," she says solemnly.

I mimic her tone when I reply, "Don't call me a bitch, you're a bitch . . . bitch."

An amused exhale sounds above my head and Laurie lifts her gaze. Wes shifts next to me, and when I look back at him, I can tell he's been watching the whole interaction keenly.

"Is this normal?" he asks, extending a finger from where he's grasping the first aid kit and the flashlight, gesturing between us. For a moment I appreciate the skill and dexterity needed for him to hold everything in one hand. I wonder what else that dexterity extends to.

When I glance back at Laurie she nods her assent, allowing him a little insight into our lives, and I reply, "It's pretty standard, yeah."

"We've lived together for . . . five years?" Laurie asks, and I nod in confirmation.

"Almost. Since we were twenty-two."

"Five years," she repeats before adding, "I can tell you every disturbing, disgusting, dirty detail about this woman."

It sounds like a promise, and even in the dim light of the hallway, I catch the way Wes's eyes flash with mirth. "I'd like th—"

"But she won't," I say, whipping my head between them to find matching shit-eating grins on their faces.

I'm hit at once by the heart-pounding fear of Laurie divulging something that would make Wes balk like he did on our date and the equally heart-pounding encouragement that, if she's threatening to release potentially embarrassing information about me, she really must like him after all.

"I don't have any flaws in any way, shape, or form," I finish soberly—the first time those words have ever left my mouth—and aim an elbow back into the ribs of my best friend when she responds with an exaggerated *pfft*.

Wes seems to enjoy the interaction, and it makes me wonder: Does he have his own Laurie? Does he have someone who would stay by his side and make him laugh or give him a brief moment of relief in this hellhole of a situation if they had come with him tonight?

It's the kind of question that weighs on my mind and brings another, more prevalent thought to the forefront: I didn't get to find out that kind of stuff about him during our date. I don't know that much about Wes at al—

"Of course you don't have flaws." His gaze drops down to meet mine, and that grin turns soft when he says, "'Cause you're a Leading Lady, right?"

That sinister thought is gone. Replaced by warmth in my chest and my cheeks and the feeling that my spine might melt right down this wall if he keeps smiling at me and looking at me with those deep, dark, *hungry*—

Quick footfalls pull our attention to the right, and when a shadow slices past, Wes's finger on the flashlight is trigger quick. The end of the hallway is bathed in light, catching the figure for a split second, but it's too late to decipher who it is before they disappear down the corridor. I almost doubt I saw anything at all when the flashlight illuminates the smooth red surface of the wall, the tarnished metal of the lamps, and nothing else.

"Did you see that?" Wes turns back to us for confirmation.

Already my brain is trying to rationalize what we saw to counteract the fear that starts to simmer below my throat. I tell myself it could be one of the remaining daters, somebody to rescue us, or just a trick of the light caused by the convergence of the flashlight and the gas lamps.

Anything but the killer.

"I saw *something*," I whisper back, turning to check over Laurie's shoulder just in case it was a distraction meant to draw our attention away from the real threat coming up behind us. A real-life misdirection. An old-fashioned jump scare. But the other end of the hallway is quiet and empty.

"I think . . ." Laurie says. "I think it was *Billie*."

It'd be hard to tell if it was.

Billie is the only one of us dressed head to toe in black aside from Laurie, whose shiny silk jumpsuit turns her into a night-light—albeit a gorgeous one. Billie pulled off the all-black look. She looked chic as all hell, but she could have doubled as a cat burglar, and she is the only one of the daters who could camouflage herself into the dark corners of the hallways if she wanted to.

"Do you think she came back?" I ask, though that seems highly unlikely.

"She seemed pretty happy to be getting away from us," Laurie points out, and then verbalizes what I was already thinking. "Well, from you."

"I'll go check," Wes says, pushing away from the wall before I grab his shirt sleeve and almost wrench him back.

"The fuck you will," I snap, and I don't know why that makes him laugh. He tilts his head down to look at me and his eyes have that warmth again. The kind that makes me think they could use the dark cocoa color as a reference for every confection in *Chocolat*. Even though he's the same distance away as Laurie, it feels like it's just the two of us. Me and Wes.

"We could lose her if I don't catch up," he says. "Billie may be—"

"A raging asshole?" Laurie offers.

"—*difficult*. But . . ."

"*Wes*," I stress. "The *rules*."

How are we supposed to survive when people keep breaking them? It's what's kept me from falling apart so far. It's what's kept us alive. I tested the theory myself when I split off from Jennifer and Laurie up on the mezzanine and the result was conclusive: bad things happen when the rules are broken.

"I know." He shifts closer, and I look away to avoid meeting his eyes. I don't want him to know how the thought of him leaving scares the hell out of me. I barely know him. But when I can't resist the pull of his stare on the top of my head, I force myself to meet his eyes. He smiles softly, ruefully, and says, "We might need to break some of those rules to make sure people don't get hurt."

And that's the kicker.

Our goal is to get as many people out of here as we can. Wes is right. Being a raging asshole is not a good enough reason to let Billie die at the hands of a monster.

"This hero-complex shit is getting old," I say only half jokingly, but he's already passing the first aid kit to me and adjusting the flashlight in his palm. He meets my exasperated look with a smile that is far too relaxed given our situation.

"Is it a turnoff?" he murmurs, and I'm very aware of the irony that arises by him saying those words in that tone and the resultant shiver I suppress from running down the full length of my spine.

"Yeah, it is," I reply. "It's a glaring red flag, to be honest."

He aims a grin at me, tilting his head in acceptance. "Noted. Any tips for navigating these hallways?"

"The path makes a square back around to the entrance," Laurie answers, gesturing out with her pointer and middle finger like a flight attendant. "But there may be some random corridors, if I'm remembering correctly, and the bar area where John must have found the first aid kit."

"Those corridors were really short though, right?" I ask, remembering that that was one of the reasons we gravitated more toward the second level of the club. We didn't like the dead ends so much down here.

Laurie nods. "Just keep in the main hallway and you'll come back to us."

I stop myself from adding: *Please, just . . . come back.*

"Right." He nods once before pushing off the wall again and turning to face us, knife poised in one hand, flashlight gripped in the other, back straight and looking intimidating as all hell.

At first I think he's going to say it, the taboo promise nobody has been able to uphold all night. But then he clamps his mouth shut and just holds up three fingers. It tempts an amused scoff from my lips. I hold up three of my own and curl them one by one.

Three.

Two.

One.

With another nod, he turns and strides down the hallway.

CHAPTER 21

"Why would you want to murder me for, anyhow?"
"So I can kill you anytime I want."

—Not *Sweet Home Alabama*

*T*he card from the killer and the map are stark white as they stick out of Wes's back pocket, and I tell myself that I'm focusing on them rather than his ass as he walks away. If I were the killer, I wouldn't want to be up against Wes in a dark hallway . . . Since I'm me, though, I'd actually *love* to be up against Wes in a dark hallway.

"God, just jump each other's bones already," Laurie mutters when he's out of earshot, and I turn back to see she's caught my—okay, not completely—innocent observation of his departure.

With a faux simpering smile, I say, "Haven't you heard? I'm already taken."

Laurie shakes her head, eyes still surveying the dark hall. It's the first time we've been able to debrief this whole crazy night with just the two of us, and we fall into the easy pattern of conversation we usually reserve for our failed dates.

"Fucking *wild*, man," she mutters, and I shift the first aid kit into my other hand to grab her wrist.

"What. The actual. *Fuck*, Laurie?" I tug her arm on each word even though I already know we're both firmly on the same page. "Why *me*?"

She's still shaking her head, rapid, jerky movements against the wall that make her hair go staticky. The bounce of her heels against the carpet reminds me she still needs to pee, and the anxious movement probably has more to do with not wanting to piss herself on top of everything else that's happened tonight.

Even then, she pulls her gaze from the end of the hall, her voice almost consolatory when she says, "I mean, I think you're pretty perfect, but *God*, Jamie ..."

She pins me with a serious look we usually reserve for the times either of us need to intervene with the other's bad life decisions. Like when I was going to laminate my eyebrows, or when she was going to join an MLM.

"You are *not* worth this," she says, and I have to stop myself from smacking the wall in agreement. Thank *god* somebody said it. You can always count on your best friend to tell you what's what. And what's what is that this is *far* too much effort to try and acquire the affections of one person. *This* person.

"*Thank you*," I spit. "Thank you. My thoughts exac—"

The bathroom door swings open, cutting me off as I peek around the corner and catch sight of the others walking back down the corridor. John stops when he sees it's just me and Laurie idling against the wall.

"Where's Wes?"

Even though I catch the slightest note of annoyance in the question, his voice is still calm as he closes the distance and leans against the wall on the other side of the hallway.

When he tilts his head back and looks across at me, eyebrows raised expectantly, I can't help but appreciate the way his hair falls into his eyes. The strands at the back splay in every direction from the panicked pulls of his hands, but it works for him. So much so I could be tempted to ignore his former MIA status. Before my appreciation can extend too long, Laurie leans out from behind me, her voice strained.

"We thought we saw Billie, so he went to check." She turns to me. "If we don't go now, I *will* pee myself."

I catch a glimpse of John's eyes narrowing, no doubt over the slight hypocrisy of Wes's disappearance, before Laurie drags me down the hallway. As we pass Jennifer, I manage to hand the first aid kit to her, following Laurie into the bathroom after she barrels through the door.

When the door closes I throw my corkscrew onto the side of the sink before turning to unzip the back of Laurie's jumpsuit. She bolts into the nearest stall, her sigh of relief echoing out the half-open door a moment later.

It's only marginally brighter in the bathroom. The gas lamps have been completely foregone for the same neon strips we saw in the VIP rooms and they make the bandage on my arm glow like it's under a UV light. They also make the dark stains of blood on my nails look sickly and brown and unbearable. Washing my hands has never been such a luxury. I flick on the faucet and scrub my palms, digging at the space underneath my nails until they're red from the overhead lighting rather than the mix of too many people's blood. It's not until the water runs clear that I turn off the sink and go pee.

When I come out again, Laurie is washing her hands. I catch a glimpse of the telltale signs of what we've been through etched across my face in the mirrors above the sinks. It's not just the downlighting that makes my cheeks look pale and drawn. My winged eyeliner is smudged into the crease of my eyelids and there's a dark mark on my cheek. Another on my chest. Another an inch or so away from my mouth. At first I think it's some of my lipstick, but it's a few shades too dark.

I rub at the stains before I allow myself to debate whether the blood is mine or Curtis's, and when Laurie hands me a paper towel, I'm able to blot away most of the marks. I'm even able to remove some of the glitter on my arms—with only one hiss at a misjudged tug to my wound. But as soon as I think I've got them all another one hits the light and I eventually give up on the task. If the only thing I leave with tonight is a fine-line scar and permanent glitter, then I've gotten out relatively unscathed.

I turn from the sink and take in the new design of the restroom. The formerly brushed metal walls of Cravin' had borne witness to a lot of heightened emotions, tactical spews, and heated debates about whether it was *that bad* to send a WYD message to an ex at two a.m. These new red walls seem lighter than the ones outside, but maybe that's because there's a false sense of safety being confined in here and away from what is sprayed and strewn and splattered across the hallways in the rest of the club. I'd take those ugly cries, dry heaves, and drunk texts over whatever the hell is happening tonight.

"You ready?" Laurie asks, and I'm about to nod when my gaze shifts across the wall and I spot it. My heart jolts up into my throat and something worse than fear, worse than panic, worse than dread floods through me. *Oh my god.* I haven't felt much of it for the last few hours, but it feels, distantly, like hope.

"Laurie?" I whisper.

She mistakes my breathless anticipation for fear and flinches away from the sink, lunging into a defensive position she more likely learned from a body attack class rather than any form of practical self-defense.

"What?" she whispers back.

"Do you see that?"

I jerk my chin up to the space above the tampon machine and she follows my gaze. A few feet above the dispenser, painted in the same red as the rest of the walls, almost camouflaged if not for the slats that cut horizontal lines of black—no, not black, but a muted darkness that hints to space behind the wall—into the messy, mattered brushstrokes . . .

A vent.

Very clear, claustrophobic scenes come to mind: *Aliens. Dawn of the Dead*. And one of the most iconic Christmas movies of all time: *Die Hard*.

Her eyes drop back down to mine, and I can tell she's already come to the same conclusion. The solution to this horrifying maze we've been stuck in. She may have dedicated her life to the most boring kind of filmmaking, but at least she's capable of creative problem-solving.

Her voice is still a whisper, but I don't miss the tinge of excitement that laces her words.

"We could—"

"I can't," I say. Just from looking at it, I can tell it's too small for me; it's too small for pretty much anyone. Except for Laurie. She's willowy. Waifish. And she's not going to be jealous of my bubble butt after this. That's why I'm already looking around the bathroom to find a way to get her up there.

"No."

Maybe if she climbs onto the toilet or—no, we'll have to use the sink, it's taller. Then she can use that upper-body strength she's always lording over me to pull herself into the shaft and—

"Jamie, *no*."

I almost think she's trying to argue I would fit into the vent, but when I look back at her, I realize it's a more petulant no. Like an "I'm not going if you're not going" no, which is so damn stupid for someone so smart.

"Don't even start with that shit, Laurie."

I push her over to the sink, then bend down to undo the high heels I can't believe she's been wearing this whole time.

"No, no, no." She's just being hysterical now. "First rule of slasher movies: Don't. Split. Up."

That makes me pause with my fingers gripping the buckle of her shoe, and I squint up at her from the ground, the tiles cold against my bare feet.

"Rule number one is don't have sex," I say slowly, deliberately, because she would know that if she paid as much attention to the poster on the back of our bathroom door as it deserves. Moving back to working the strap of her other shoe away from her ankle, I can't help but feel hurt. "God, Laurie, it's like you never listen when I talk—"

"It's still a rule!" she grits out, but it's too late, she's going into that vent if I have to shove her into it like an uncooperative tampon.

I pop back up from the floor and smack my palm against the countertop, using all my first-year-theater elective skills to sound sunny and confident and not shit-scared that I'm about to make my best friend slide into a metal tunnel and *Die Hard* her way out of this massacre à la John McClane.

"Well then, rule number eleven: take the goddamned escape route when it presents itself to you."

Her bottom lip starts trembling, tears rimming those pretty eyes I've practiced some of the more difficult eye makeup tutorials on and laughed hysterically at the results. I know they won't fall, though. It would take something truly insane for my girl to cry.

"You made that rule up."

Her voice is a wisp of her usual cool, confident, measured tone. It makes my throat feel tight when I say, "I did. But I'm the expert on this, remember?"

The grin on my face is so obviously for show I can't make myself look at her when I push her toward the sink again. Well, it's more like a shove.

"Air vents connect to outside, so you just have to keep crawling until you come to the end."

"I will. I will." She's on board now, nodding and kicking off her heels. Showing exactly how someone who does YouTube Pilates three times a week can balance and bend, she swings her leg up, plants a foot onto the counter, and pushes up to a stand over the sink.

"Then just get help, okay?"

"Jamie—" She looks down at me, her hands reaching up to the vent cover, her bottom lip shaking. I know what she wants to say.

Stay safe.

I'll do whatever I can to save you.

Don't get murdered . . .

Please, *don't get murdered.*

But none of the words come out. She's never been great with verbalizing her feelings. She's the smart one. I'm the dramatic one. She's logical. I'm emotional. It's been that way ever since we met in Intro to Cinema Studies. Since we stood across from each other in that first tutorial and realized that despite our incompatible aspirations and interests, a mutual distaste for icebreakers was enough to build a friendship on. One that—so many years and major and minor life events later—has become real and deep and so, *so* important that if our roles were reversed and I could fit and she couldn't, I have no doubt she'd already have her shoulder in my ass pushing me through that vent. And that's why it's so easy for me to smile up at her. It's genuine this time because I can read every involuntary movement of her facial features. I know what she *wants* to say. So, I make myself swallow down the lump in my throat, blink away the tears in my eyes, and say, "I love you, too, baby girl."

CHAPTER 22

"You should be killed and often, and by someone who knows how."

—Not *Gone with the Wind*

The corkscrews finally come into use. While they're too dull to cause any damage to a human, the ends of the spirals are pointy enough to dig underneath the cover of the vent. They loosen the paint around the edge and allow enough room for Laurie to dig her fingers into the gap so she can pry the bottom of the cover away from the wall. The hinges at the top whine in protest, but once I hop up onto the counter and maneuver around Laurie to hold the vent open, it takes us no time to figure out a way to get her into the metal shaft.

Half of her body is hanging out of it when matching screams echo from outside. The muffled *Run!* that follows them freezes me in place on top of the counter, my hands gripping the bottom of her thighs as my heart leaps up into my throat.

"*Fuck*," I breathe.

"Jamie?"

Her head is so far into the vent she probably didn't hear the sounds, but from the way her body tenses, she definitely heard me. I know her so well that even though her ass is in my face I can visualize the panic on hers. It's only when I hear a dull thud, a pained grunt, that squelching sound that is starting to sound too familiar, that I push with renewed vigor. What if Heart Eyes comes in here and sees her escaping? What if I can't stop him from getting to her?

"Laurie, don't stop."

She starts to shimmy the top half of her body farther into the vent, picking up on my urgency. As expected, her upper-body strength works in her favor, as does the slippery silk of her jumpsuit, and she slides easily across the metal with very little assistance from me. Her feet are in my face when I stick my head into the vent after her. It's dusty, dank, and I can see it isn't completely smooth like I thought. There are jagged edges jutting out from where the sections of the vent are welded together, and while I can hear her hiss in pain, she doesn't stop. She can't.

"You're going to get out of here and get help, okay?"

I don't know whose benefit I'm saying that for, but I pull my shaking fingers from the painted plastic that leaves blood-like stains on my hands and reach down to the counter for something to use as self-defense against whatever—*whoever* is outside. Bypassing the abandoned corkscrews and grabbing Laurie's shoes, I pull them toward me, almost toppling off the counter for my efforts. I wait until she's moving more easily through the vent before I push the cover back in place, wincing at the high-pitched squeal of the hinges. Laurie's feet disappear into the darkness as I peer through the thin slats of the cover, needing to make sure that whatever happens next, at least she has a chance.

"Jamie, please . . . *Please!* Jamie! *Jamie!*"

Her cries of my name turn into nonsensical pleas, echoing back out and sounding deafening to my ears, but then the desperate calls move farther away.

She's getting away.

The realization draws a choked sob of relief from my throat that gets drowned out by the long groan of the bathroom door swinging open.

My entire body goes rigid against the wall as the room falls into a heavy, deadly silence.

Look behind you, Jamie.

For the first time tonight, there's no screaming, no pounding pulse in my head, no sound of metal slicing through flesh. It feels almost like if I *don't* turn around—if I keep my eyes locked on the blood-red wall in front of me, then whoever is standing in the entrance of the bathroom doesn't exist. If I don't look, they can't hurt me.

That's not true, though.

Jamie, turn around.

I know what happens when you turn your back or close your eyes or curl up in a ball and wish you were somewhere else.

You don't make it to the credits.

So that's why I turn and face him.

Heart Eyes stands in the doorway, using a gloved hand to keep the door from swinging closed, but that still leaves the other free to hold the second meat cleaver I've seen tonight. This one, at least for now, is still an unmarked steel rectangle. And I can't help but wonder what was used to make that sound before. Did he leave another weapon outside?

Did he leave it *in* someone outside?

That pink mask, bathed in the glow of the neon light, is just as terrifying up close. I still can't see his eyes, but I don't miss the way his head tilts up to see one of my hands still pressed against the vent. It must look like I'm trying to take the cover off for myself. At least

I hope that's what it looks like, and he has no idea Laurie is army-crawling her way farther and farther from this lovesick asshole. Farther and farther away from being another one of his victims.

I need to draw his attention away from her escape route. Away from the scratches around the edges of the vent that look like claw marks cutting through the red paint and revealing the brushed metal underneath. So I jump down from the sink counter, a dull ache throbbing in my feet as I straighten, keeping my eyes on him the whole time.

He doesn't move. He just stands there, Michael Myers still, and watches me.

I can't say I have the same composure, my chest heaving, eyes darting across to the two corkscrews left on the countertop that couldn't do shit anyway. I'm armed with nothing but an encyclopedic knowledge of this exact situation ending in bloodshed and a pair of *fucking* shoes, and—

The shoes.

I look down at them just as he takes a step forward, off the carpet and onto the tiles, his hand smoothing down the surface of the door when I glance back up at him again.

It's a long shot. Something that would only be used for a moment of comic relief within an actual slasher. An absolute fluke completely reliant on my pitching skills, which haven't been required since my high school softball days. Batting was always my strong suit anyway. Regardless, as he takes another step forward and the door swings closed behind him, I wrench my arm back and hurl Laurie's shoes at his head.

The shoes fly across the space between us, the heels aimed straight for those heart-shaped holes. They almost meet their mark, smacking against his chin and eliciting a sound of pain that's muffled by the closed zipper across his mouth and—Holy shit, it *actually* worked.

He stumbles back, falters against the door, but as the heels fall to the ground with a heavy thud he's already straightening. I think it was more surprise that sent him backward than any skill on my part. When he steps over the shoes at his feet, his gloved hand raising the meat cleaver into clear view, he doesn't need to say anything for me to know he's pissed.

This is our first lover's spat.

He barrels toward me, slamming into the tampon machine when I veer to the right at the last possible moment and throw myself into the closest stall. A spray of superabsorbent torpedoes shoots out and hit his chest when he pushes off the machine, his pink-covered head jerking toward me as he resituates the cleaver more comfortably in his hand.

This is the closest we've ever been. The clearest view I've had of him. And my eyes must have been playing tricks on me when I saw him gutting the guy up on the mezzanine. He looks shorter, smaller, not as big and broad as I expect a bogeymen to be, but maybe that's just the magnification of fear. Because the mask, the too-big jacket, the baggy black coveralls, the *knife*—they're still very much the same as what I saw in the hallway upstairs.

I slam the door in his face when he lunges for me, flicking the lock into place and climbing onto the toilet seat. There's one moment of gratitude to the universe that the stall doors extend too close to the ground for either of us to crawl under, and they reach too high for him to climb over, before all the sounds of the bathroom rouse together to form a terrifying symphony. One that could become the soundtrack to my demise. The cleaver he's holding clangs against the door as he throws his body against it. It shakes from the power of his ramming, the hinges scream, and my heart beats so loud it's like a war drum over the top of it all.

If he manages to bust this door down, my options are limited.

No scenes are coming to mind, and if they did, they aren't going to have any satisfactory outcomes for me. I could throw myself over the wall into the next stall, but the door is open, and by the time I find my feet, either he'll be in there with me or I'll just have the same problem in a different location. I gauge the gap between the ceiling and the stall anyway, but when I do, I realize I have the same issue as the vent situation. Laurie could fit through the space, but I'd get stuck.

The door continues to heave under the strain of Heart Eyes's continuous battering, and there's nothing I can do to stop it. There's nothing in the stall I can use to defend myself, not even a toilet brush. I'm completely alone, completely unarmed, completely fuc—

The banging stops.

The only sounds left are the throbbing of my pulse between my ears and a final impetuous smack of Heart Eyes's hand against the door. I force myself to get my breathing back under control, and the reprieve allows me to consider the situation Heart Eyes has put us both in with a little more clarity:

If I'm the Final Girl, this can't be the final showdown.

It doesn't have the makings of a finale. It's too early, it's not "grand" enough, there's—hopefully—still a lot of people alive.

He's either just playing with me, testing my aptitude to be his Leading Lady, or my name on the dance floor was a red herring. And that thought sucks the air out of my lungs.

What if I'm *not* the Final Girl? What if I'm just Casey Becker at the beginning of *Scream* and this is the plot twist none of us saw coming?

I flick my eyes down from the stall door to my dress. Hitchcock once said that blondes make the best victims because they make the blood show up better on screen. "Like virgin snow that shows up the bloody footprints" is the exact quote. If we're operating by that logic, then I am *covered* in red. My dress, both my own blood and other people's, the *fucking* glitter—it marks my skin, mapping the last few hours of terror across my body. But even with all that, I don't *look* like a Final Girl.

I mean, I didn't *want* the part, but I don't want the alternative if it means being demoted to Dead Blonde Number Three!

A sickening scratching noise starts up, metal on glass, and all I can do is clamp my hands over my ears. It does nothing to muffle the sound. It goes on for what feels like hours, the screech and scrape of the blade tearing through me as I crouch on top of the toilet.

My feet are stuck to the seat, my hands trembling at the sides of my head, when it eventually stops. There's a pause, a shuffle of clothing, before footsteps move out across the tiles. A long groan emits from the door hinges, the same one that preceded his entry into the restroom, before it's followed by a dull, conclusive thud. The whole space becomes silent.

I don't move.

I may be scared, but I'm not fucking stupid.

I don't get down off the toilet. Instead, I stand up, using the walls on either side of me to maintain my balance and peek over the side of the stall. I look over into the other stall, across to the sink, anywhere he could've hidden to draw me out, and the air rushes out of me when I can see he's gone. He really did leave.

If he can't get in, he's got to give up and move on, right? You haven't got a slasher if there isn't any slashing. You haven't got a rom-com if the love interest isn't responding to the romancing.

Minutes pass before I get the nerve to grip the top of the door, lean forward, and see the tiles. The asshole took Laurie's shoes with him, but he left the corkscrews on the sink counter. Even he knows they're useless. Glints of light from the mirror draw my gaze higher and I realize the corkscrews are not all he left behind.

Not again.

The bathroom door slams open and I almost fall off the toilet in shock, but when a tall, maskless figure moves into the restroom, I jump down and unlock the stall door before I can stop myself.

"Wes!"

He's pulled me into his arms before the door is fully open. They're tight, almost restrictive around my body, and I can feel where he's tucked the flashlight into his pants when it jabs into my ribs, but I don't pull away. I need him to take my weight and hold me upright, because I feel like I might fall apart and spill onto the floor if I'm given one more second to process what just happened.

Heart Eyes left me alone.

He left me *alive*.

He terrorized me, yeah, but it was a game to him. It was foreplay. Now that he's made the decision *not* to kill me twice, I can't deny I'm the object of his affection. I can't deny that even if I don't look the part, even if I don't know if I can live up to the title, he wants me to be his Final Girl.

"I couldn't find Billie, but I thought I found a way out," Wes grits out before I can ask where he's been, how he avoided Heart Eyes. He steps away to check if I have any visible damage, holding his knife away from us, almost behind his back, as I perform my own once-over. "I turned down a corridor and found a door, but it was fucking jammed, and when I came back everyone was gone and there was blood on the floor, and I thought . . ."

His eyes are wild, his breathing jagged, but otherwise he's unharmed, and when he comes to the same conclusion about me, we let out matching breaths of relief and move back into each other's space. We've escalated from accidental grazes and lingering touches to a full embrace. This is the closest we've been all night. The pull must be a symptom of the attraction under aversive conditions, and even though the fear hasn't had a chance to fully work itself out of my system, I let my body relax against his. I wrap my arms around his waist, duck my head into his uninjured shoulder when his arm curls around my back and his hand slides up to grip my ribs. He still holds the knife in his other hand, angling it away from our bodies as he drops his chin to the top of my head. We stay like that for a heartbeat, and it feels . . . right.

"Are you okay?" he murmurs into my hair, and I lift my head to meet his gaze.

"Yeah . . ." Maybe if I say it enough it'll stick. "Yeah."

His palm moves from my ribs to my jaw as his eyes dart across my face. His head dips just a fraction, almost like he wants to kiss me, and it's more instinct than anything else that makes me tilt my chin up. A second later my senses kick in and I move to pull back, but he's already let go of me, gripping the handle of his knife and rubbing his free palm over his mouth. His shoulders are up around his ears, his voice low and gritty when he asks, "Where are the others?"

I can't help the sigh of relief that tears from my throat. If he's asking, then he didn't come across any bodies in the hallway. I heard the sound of someone being attacked, I heard that familiar sickly sound of flesh being torn by metal, but maybe they got away. Maybe Heart Eyes was too preoccupied with finding me so we could engage in a little flirtation in the bathroom and he didn't get to finish the job. God, I hope whoever it was has that first aid kit handy.

"I think they ran," I say, but that doesn't take the darkness out of his expression.

"Did you see where they went?"

I saw where one went, but I'm shaking my head before the attraction under aversive conditions can make me spill, moving to the counter to collect the corkscrews.

"We have to get out of here," I say over my shoulder. "He could come back."

Wes watches my movement toward the mirror and sees the message Heart Eyes left etched into the middle of it: a rough, crooked heart with a "J" in the middle, and underneath it, something I don't think I've seen since middle school: 4EVA.

It's different from the time and effort invested in the display on the dance floor. This is juvenile, a more possessive assertion than the idealistic declaration from before. I'd think it was done by a different person if not for the fact it's once again directed toward me.

"Fuck this guy," Wes mutters, turning his back on our somber reflections as I take one more look at the rounded points of the corkscrews and decide to abandon them. I don't want to get close enough to Heart Eyes to see if they could do anything.

Wes holds his knife in front of him, gesturing for me to stand behind him as he pulls the door open.

We don't get too far once we step out into the hallway, though. The bloody handprint marring the male icon on the door across from us, a smack-and-drag stain akin to the car scene in *Titanic*, stops us in our tracks.

CHAPTER 23

"I would have slaughtered with you forever. I would have turned myself inside out for you."

—Not *Hope Floats*

"**S**hit."

Wes curses when he pushes the blood-marked door fully open.

The white tiles of the bathroom look like a Jackson Pollock painting, smeared and streaked with red. The source of the color is instantly apparent. I only need to lift my gaze from the example of abstract expressionism to see John propped up against a urinal.

When he looks up, flicks his hair out of his eyes, and sees us in the doorway, I spot the dark stain spreading out underneath his left shoulder and through the gaps of his fingers. It's almost exactly where Wes was cut, but I can already tell this isn't going to be fixed by a Band-Aid.

"I—" John winces as he tries to straighten, pain etched across his face, blood gushing out of his shoulder. "I tried to stop him from getting to the bathrooms, but he—he got me. Dani and Jennifer ran. I think . . . I think they got away."

They did, but he didn't.

"I don't think he even realized I wasn't . . . He just wanted to get to you, Jamie."

He stayed to try and protect me and Laurie, and this is what he has to show for it. He said he doesn't take risks, but he's the first of us to go on the offense against the killer, to try and save us from an attack, and I couldn't be more grateful.

"John." His name falls out of my mouth in a sigh as I move forward and almost slip on the trails of his blood. Dropping to my knees in front of him, I try to ignore the way they hit the ground too hard when I do. Even though I have the best intentions, I can't figure out a way to make the bleeding stop. I gave the first aid kit to one of the women, and if they're smart, they're far away from here and hiding.

Looking back to Wes for assistance, I almost lose my balance, but his free hand grips my elbow before I can, and I can't help but grasp his arm and smile in gratitude. I never thought reflexes would rank highly when it comes to hotness traits, but his are certainly coming into the top five.

"Where's Laurie?" John pants, drawing my eyes from Wes and the kind of thoughts that aren't going to patch up his wound or get us all out of here. Catching sight of the paper towel dispenser, I point toward it, but Wes is already striding two steps in its direction without any chance of slipping. His hand goes into the slot, but it comes out empty. Fuck.

"Where's Laurie?" John asks again, the concern in his voice still clear despite how weak he sounds. I open my mouth but the answer dies on my tongue. It's not that I don't trust him or Wes. They've been narrowly avoiding death with me all night. It's just that I love Laurie more. I will lie and omit and play dumb for that bitch. I would've let Heart Eyes gut me like a fish if I thought it would help her escape.

The only way I can buy Laurie time to get out of this clusterfuck is if no one knows where she is.

So I lie. "She ran, too." Finally biting the bullet, I press my palm into John's shoulder. His blood coats my hand like syrup. Somehow he still has the Midori bottle in his hand. It's covered in blood, too, but I suspect it's his rather than Heart Eyes's. The broken bottle would've been useless up against whatever is making red run out of his shoulder in a steady stream.

Wes walks past where I'm trying to stanch John's wound and into a toilet stall. The wall shakes, there's a resounding plastic snap, and then he comes back out with a full roll of toilet paper and the broken cover of the dispenser. It's more hysteria than humor that makes me laugh, but I still catch the roll in my free hand and press it into the wound. The white two-ply paper soaks up the blood and almost falls apart in seconds. I toss it onto the floor and the damp paper hits the tiles with a wet smack.

John groans when I push the heel of my palm deeper into his wound to try to constrict the flow, and Wes drops to the floor on his other side. He falls back into first aid mode by tilting John's head back to look at his pupils, pressing two fingers to his neck to check his pulse.

"Keep that pressure on. That's good," he instructs, and I look up to meet his gaze. He looks like he's proud of me for shoving my fingers into some guy's open wound. Like he wants to kiss me. I'd even say it's the kind of look that makes me think that if he knew I forced my friend into an air vent it would factor high on his list of hotness traits. It's a fleeting thought when John tries to shake out of Wes's grip. He looks like he's annoyed with being fussed over, which is pretty badass considering he's just been stabbed, but then I notice he also looks like he's going to throw up. Blood keeps seeping out from around my fingers. He doesn't wince when I increase the pressure. He barely reacts, and that's when I start to get worried.

"We need to get you out of here," I say. "We need to find something that will stop the bleeding."

John nods slowly, drunk from blood loss, his eyes narrowing as he glances up at Wes and mutters, "Funny how you're gone, and I get stabbed."

It's the first time I've heard him sound hostile all night and it's jarring, uncharacteristic. It's an indication of how much pain he's in, how scared he is, but still, I can't help but be a little shocked.

"John—"

"It's fine, Jamie," Wes says.

He isn't offended; he barely even blinks at the unsaid accusation as he bends down, instructs me to keep the pressure on John's shoulder while I push up from my knees to stand, then pulls John off the ground without breaking a sweat. It's not the time to be thinking Wes is very strong. If he can pick up a fully grown, limp man he'd have no issue with me . . .

My priorities are very warped.

"I thought I found a way out," Wes says as he takes most of John's weight and we move as one toward the door. I reach down and grip John's hand with my free one, keeping my left palm firm against his wound and feeling a little comfort from the way he's able to slip his fingers through mine and give a weak, assuring squeeze.

We push through the bathroom door and back into the corridor, Wes holding his knife out in front of us as we head toward the main hallway as a unit. John's grasping the broken bottle again and his arm is looped around Wes's shoulder for support. The edge of the glass is dangerously close to Wes's neck, and an unwelcome thought of how John could easily nick an artery if he wanted to comes to mind. We're lucky we're all on the same side.

"I found a door," Wes continues. "A normal one without a code, but the lock was jamm—"

206 · **SHAILEE THOMPSON**

"—and the killer just happened to reappear at the same time," John murmurs as we move back into the main hallway.

Wes stops to prop John against the wall so he can extract the flashlight from where it's tucked into the side of his pants. I catch a glimpse of his abs when his shirt gets caught in the process and rides high over his ribs as he jerks the flashlight out. He squints at John.

"You honestly think I'm the killer after all this shit?"

"You always seem to be gone when he's around," John mutters, his head lolling against the wall.

When we were in the bathroom it seemed as though Wes was willing to overlook the slight, but now he's ready to get offended. He scoffs, slipping the flashlight under his arm as he pulls his shirt up again to tuck it into his pants properly, and I can't help but stare at the second preview I'm afforded of his muscled stomach. It is . . . defined, and looks like it'd be fun to run your fingers over. Maybe even your tongue.

Mine goes dry at the thought, and when I try to get my mind back onto something other than body parts like tongues and stomachs and fingers, I'm reminded that *my* fingers are sticky and stained red with John's blood because I'm still trying to plug a wound I can't see, and I wouldn't know the severity of it even if I could.

Wes uses the flashlight to point accusatorily at John. "*You* said there wasn't a door down there."

I'm about to suggest that this conversation could be delayed until a later date, but then the slightest movement at the edges of my vision draws my eyes to the end of the hallway where Wes went to find Billie.

"I said it was a dead end," John says, but I suddenly no longer care about Wes's abs or missing first aid kits or dead-end doors.

"Guys . . ." I breathe.

There's something standing in the darkness. Idling in the shadows and watching us as Wes and John continue to snap at each other.

"And you didn't think to tell us *why* it was a dead end?"

Maybe it is just a shadow, or one of the other daters, but if that's the case, *why* are they just *standing* there?

"What are you trying to say, Wes?"

"Guys."

Wes and John glare at each other, completely unaware we have an audience, and once again my brain is frozen, trying to rationalize what I can see at the end of the hall, when the most obvious explanation is the most terrifying.

"What I'm saying, *John*, is that you—"

"Boys!" I hiss, and somehow that makes them stop and turn their heads in my direction. Whatever Wes sees on my face is enough for him to flick out his elbow and point the flashlight down the hall.

A click sounds out in the silence, a sphere of cold, white light bursting out of the flashlight, down the hallway and illuminating it to the very end. While the familiar tones of red and black and brushed bronze take up most of the visible space of the corridor, my eyes are drawn to a color that never used to instill any kind of emotion in me but now has the power to make my skin prickle in fear.

Pink.

CHAPTER 24

"It's complicated. All this murder shit's complicated. And that's good. Because if it's too simple you've got no reason to try, and if you've got no reason to try you don't."

—Not *What If*

eart Eyes still doesn't move, and it's the *not* moving that's terrifying. The meat cleaver from before is gone and a regular *Halloween*-style kitchen knife has taken its place, similar to the one gripped in Wes's hand. Even from so far away, I can tell Heart Eyes's grip on the handle of the blade in his left hand is loose, casual, and his right arm is behind his back, like he's some character from a Regency-era film who's going to confess his feelings in the rain or in a crammed tearoom.

It's only the slight shift in where the light reflects off the blade that alludes to the fact Heart Eyes is breathing, he's real. Otherwise, he is dead still. The slow walk, the ramming into the bathroom wall, the meticulous pummeling of his knife into hallway guy's stomach—it was all so active. It was something we could react to.

But this . . .

"You're gonna go back to the entrance," Wes murmurs. His voice is barely above the sound of a breath and I need to lean in to hear him, shift away from John and the way the drying blood on his shirt makes my hand stick to the material. I peel my palm away from it.

"Once you're there, go back upstairs. You hid before, you can do it again."

It's rule seven all over again: don't run up the stairs. Not to mention all three of us trying to climb them—Wes and me holding John's weight as we do, with Heart Eyes on our tail . . . It's a death trap. Then I realize what he said.

You. Not us, *you.*

He's taken himself out of the equation.

"*We* are going to go together," I spit back. His hero-complex shit is *really* getting old. I don't know if his abs can even make up for it at this point.

I look at John. His focus is firmly on Heart Eyes, too, but his eyelids keep drooping into prolonged blinks, his breathing heavy. At some point he dropped the Midori bottle on the ground to take over trying to stop the bleeding from his wound.

"I can't carry John by myself," I say as Heart Eyes keeps idling at the end of the hall. "And you're not going up against that asshole; he's got a knife."

"So do I," Wes replies, taking a step away from us, turning toward Heart Eyes.

Wes brings his knife into view and there's a moment where, still caught in the middle of the spotlight glare of the flashlight, Heart Eyes shifts on his feet. His round, pink head tilts ever so slightly to the side. Like he sees Wes, he sees the knife, and he accepts the challenge.

"You guys just have to hide until help comes," Wes whispers. "And help is going to come, okay?"

I can't even bring myself to shake my head, not when we don't know what will act as the starting signal for Heart Eyes to close the distance between us.

"Not okay," I grit out. "Not okay in the slightest."

Wes takes another step away and it takes me to a place of such unbridled panic I almost miss it when Heart Eyes moves his arm from behind his back.

A blade—the long, broad *Friday the 13th* kind—slides out from behind his thigh and glints like the disco ball currently hanging over the personalized intestine heart he made for me. His shoulder dips from the weight of his weapon, and Wes freezes.

Of course he brought a machete.

Wes's knife is as good as those corkscrews I left in the bathroom, and he knows it. That's why he doesn't take another step forward, why he drops the knife to his thigh again as his back straightens, and why both he and John let out heavy sighs.

Wes takes a step back and I let out a strangled exhale. The sound makes him look over his shoulder and meet my gaze. The expression on his face, the emotion in his eyes—it makes me irrationally, intensely angry because how dare he look at me like *that* when he's just all but told me to leave him to die?

"Jamie, you *need* to run," Wes says, and I don't like the way he's using that soft, low voice. I had hopes we'd be alone, away from here, wearing fewer clothes and not covered in blood when I eventually heard it. His expression is still intense, meaningful, steady, and made to make my heart ache, and *again* we're in the entirely wrong context. It's more suited for confessing that I complete him, or that he likes me very much, just the way I am, or that if I'm a bird, he's a bird. It's not the right expression for a situation involving a machete. And I refuse to let it be the last thing I see of him. If I'm the Final Girl, then I get the final word. *I* get the final say. And I'm not ready to be alone yet.

"I'm *not* leaving wi—"

"We'll slow you down."

"*I'll* slow you down," John says, and again I'm brutally reminded of the fact he's here bleeding out against a wall while I'm making intense "I don't know if I want to stab you myself or turn our eye fucking into real fucking" eyes at Wes.

Damn it.

"John. *No.* We're—"

"Jamie, *look* at me." He moves his hand from his shoulder and there's still so much blood. Sticky, bright, corn syrup–looking blood. There was so much on the bathroom floor, on my hands, soaking through the sleeve of his shirt. He's lost too much, and it's a miracle he's even still upright at this point.

"It's okay." He lifts his gaze to mine, those steel-blue eyes, that Bill Pullman entreating stare, focused solely on me. "Everything will work out."

"John—"

His face crumples in pain just for a second, and it's the only indication I have of what he's planning to do before he pushes off the wall. I reach for him, Wes does, too, but John's already propelling himself along the carpeted hall, using all his strength to stagger-run past the flickering gas lamps, past the curlicue frames of the antique mirrors, right into the path of Heart Eyes. Right for the knife he holds out like he's offering a rose on *The Bachelor*. My scream cuts down the walls like razor-sharp nails on a chalkboard.

"John!"

Wes grabs me around the waist, showing just how strong he is when he pulls me into his chest and my bare feet leave the carpet. He turns and starts running before I can see John make impact with Heart Eyes, but I can still picture it. Vividly. The way John would throw his body into Heart Eyes, lurch over his shoulder like they were sharing an embrace in the airport arrivals gate. I can imagine the sound of the knife going into his belly. The force of it. I can see it so clearly, even though all I actually see is the red and gold blur of the walls as Wes runs down the corridor carrying me like oversized luggage against his chest until I can pull myself away from replaying the image of John staggering right up to the killer and just . . . sacrificing himself.

I wonder whether Heart Eyes knew Wes and John were the ones I liked the most tonight. Whether he watched our dates and saw the way John made me blush or Wes made me laugh and planned it so all three of my suitors could end up here and he could cut down the other two in front of me. Give me no choice but to choose him by default.

When Wes sets me down and I find my feet, I grab the hand he thrusts toward me and we keep running. My pulse pounding in my ears, my breath ragged, we sprint back to the entrance of the club and head for the stairs to the mezzanine (rules be damned). As Wes and I are taking the steps two at a time, a quiet voice breaks through the haze of fright again to remind me that John and I didn't even get to have that drink.

CHAPTER 25

"That thing, that moment, when you kill someone, and everything around becomes hazy and the only thing in focus is you and this person and you realize that that person is the only person that you're supposed to kill for the rest of your life."

—Not *Never Been Kissed*

"**F**uck," Wes mutters as we catch our breath in another VIP room.

When we made it up the stairs, we bypassed the hallway I had run down with Laurie and Jennifer. It's important not to retrace your steps too much; what was a safe place in the past can turn on you this far into the film. Instead, we headed for dark scary hallway four, Wes's hand locked around mine until we spotted a room that had a partition in front of the doorway. The top of the solid divider stands at my chin height, obscuring the view of the room from anyone stalking the hallway, and as soon as we're on the other side of it, we plant our backs to the surface and slide down to the floor.

"Wes—"

Still trying to catch his breath, he gasps, "I can't believe— Another person— And we were arguing— And he just . . . *Fuck*."

He rubs his least bloody palm against his forehead, like he's trying to erase the sight of John running toward Heart Eyes from his memory. Maybe he's trying to erase this whole night while he's at it. Wes has taken the lead on so many things, and I can see it's starting to take its toll. It's a weight he shouldn't have to shoulder—it's not like he's more equipped to handle this than the rest of us. If anyone should feel responsible, it's me.

"You couldn't have done anything," I murmur.

I don't know if we could have left that corridor with John and still have made it here, but I do know if Wes had done anything other than drag me away we'd both be dead. Or at least he would be. Heart Eyes may have kept me around for a spin on the dance floor before he realized I can't be what he wants me to be and murdered me on it instead.

"I could've done *something*."

"You did. You got us out of there."

He doesn't say anything, but when he lets out a deep, accepting sigh, one that ends in a little shake of his head, my words are enough to pull him back from the corridor downstairs.

His hand slides over the carpet and finds mine again, enveloping my fingers in heat and soft pressure that makes it easy to ignore that both our hands are covered in blood. He doesn't make a show of it. There's no extended eye contact or slow intertwining of his fingers with mine. He just grabs my hand and tilts his head back against the wall, like it's the thousandth time he's done it, like this kind of touch is a normal part of our interactions, and the idea it could be, one day, makes warmth bloom in my chest.

"Are you okay?" he asks, and for some reason that makes me laugh. Such a simple question that doesn't have a place here. Not now that John is gone. Not now that Heart Eyes has performed the "emotional kill" of the evening. The one the audience feels the most deeply. Annie in *Halloween II*, or— As soon as the thought enters my head, I push it out again. I don't *want* to compartmentalize what just happened as another part of the formula. I don't want John's story to end this way. But the fact it has makes my voice crack when I reply.

"No, I'm not okay. You?"

"Not in the slightest," he says, and when he tips his head down to look at me and smiles, it's nice to see our gallows humor matches. It hints that we may be more compatible than a guy who likes *The Fast and the Furious* and a woman who's read every single one of the forty-eight essays in *My Favorite Horror Movie* four times should be. It also reminds me of his hero complex and that before John stole his thunder, Wes had every intention of going head to head with Heart Eyes.

"Were you actually going to . . ."

I don't even know if I can say it.

"What?" His thumb starts drawing circles on my knuckle, the same kind that caught my attention during our date, and it has the power to pull the question out of my mouth before I can second-guess it.

"Try and stop him? Fight him? The killer."

". . . Yeah," he finally says after an extended pause. I watch the muscle in his jaw tighten when he adds, "I still might . . . If it means that you—"

"Please, don't." I grip my fingers tighter into the back of his hand and his thumb stops moving. I don't want to hear the rest of that sentence, and I don't want to know what part I play in Wes's version of how this night ends. It's getting harder and harder to convince myself what is happening isn't my fault when so many people keep dying and I'm still alive.

"Jamie—"

"It's not going to end that way, Wes. Not with a single kitchen knife and a can-do spirit."

He doesn't try to argue, but his thumb starts back up on my skin. I interpret that as him accepting he can't bring a knife to a machete fight and expect to win.

"Then I'll figure something else out," he says after a few more heavy seconds of just breathing and holding hands. "We'll figure something out, and I'll do whatever it takes to make sure as many of us get out of here as possible."

Right.

Because there's still god knows how many people spread out across the club who are either dead or hiding.

It's never just been self-preservation for Wes. From the start it's been about escaping this hellhole with as many people as possible. It's noble, another thing that messes with maintaining the balance between afraid and horny, but it also puts a target on his back.

Wes is the confident, capable, attractive male lead. He might make it to the third act, he might be in the foreground of the poster, but if he tries to take down the killer he won't make it to the credits. I know he won't survive it, and the thought of him going up against Heart Eyes and not making it terrifies me.

I glance over at him. His eyes are trained on the ceiling, his eyebrows are furrowed in thought, and again I'm struck by the same realization I had when he first slid into view down in the basement bar. How he is not the type I usually go for. How he is imposing and inviting and all these other descriptors that shouldn't go together, but they do, and somehow, I really, *really* like how the way they're put together results in Wes.

I liked John, too, but there was only one scenario that would've played out: a nice, safe, mutual affection. One I've had before with other Johns. We'd excel in small talk and compliment exchanges, but eventually come to the conclusion our connection was pretty mild and more attuned to friendship.

With Wes, it's not mild. It's not safe. It's risk and reward, desire and depth, foreign and familiar. When I think of Wes I can't settle on one scenario. The possibilities are endless.

But I can't tell Wes that. I can't let on that's how I feel, because even if I haven't seen a clock in this godforsaken death maze, I know it's only been a few hours since we met. And it would be crazy to be having those kinds of feelings about someone you've known for only one night.

Spelling-someone's-name-out-with-intestines kind of crazy.

Wes turns his head and his eyes meet mine, the corner of his mouth tilting up, and it's then I realize I'm staring. The running brought out a sheen on his skin that makes his jaw look sharp enough to go up against that machete, and his lips are parted in a way that I could just lean in, slip my bottom lip right into the space between them, then close my top—

"What are you thinking?" he asks.

I'm thinking that even after everything, the afraid/horny balance is still leaning heavily toward horny. I don't say that, though. Instead I say, "I think we still have a chance of finding a way out of here."

He nods. We both know this is just a pit stop to get our bearings before we go outside again, but that doesn't stop his eyes from narrowing, or his head from ducking closer to mine as he asks, "Is that a Leading Lady or Final Girl way of thinking?" Maybe I shouldn't have told him my theory, not when our lives depend on it being correct, but I can't deny that the thrill of hearing him speak my language hasn't worn off. I still don't know if I have what it takes to be the Final Girl, and while I'm dressed the part, Leading Lady seems a little out of reach now, too. Still, if I had to choose one, "Blind optimism? Definitely Leading Lady."

"Right." He grins.

He's close, and it doesn't seem as if he's in a hurry to move his head away. If my confidence was at its peak state right now, I'd think he'd want to kiss me. But there's a part of me that refuses to forget how our date ended earlier tonight. How he couldn't get away from my table fast enough. He hasn't explained why he left so abruptly, and no matter what form it takes or whether it's retracted, rejection stings.

But it would sting a lot less if he kissed me and made it better.

As if he can read my mind, his eyes drop to my lips and the amusement leaves his face.

"I don't know how to word this without it sounding crazy, but ..."

His voice is a low murmur, the same one he used when he was trying to get me to leave him in the hallway. We have all the right elements for a situation that warrants that kind of voice: we're alone, the room is dark, his mouth is a few inches from mine, his fingers are threaded through my own. This should have been the first time I heard it.

"I'm glad that it's you and me. Here. Together. I hate that this is happening, obviously, but since it is ... I'm glad you're here. That you're with me." He says the last sentence so softly my heart starts to thump rapidly beneath my ribs.

"That does sound crazy," I say. He's still looking down at my mouth, and when his teeth graze his bottom lip, I swallow thickly. "But no crazier than ..."

Pulling my gaze from his mouth, I look up, into his eyes, and all I see is pupil. Blown out to the edges of his iris. Endless pools come to mind again, and it does nothing to calm my heartbeat. It's pounding like we're running away from Heart Eyes again.

"I'm glad you're with me, too."

Something changes in his expression as soon as I say it and I get to see that look. The one from the hallway downstairs. The "as you wish," "give you my coat when you are cold," "want the rest of your life to start now" look that makes heat flare up under my skin and my pulse race. Up close it's even better. If he wants to kiss me, I can't remember if there's a reason I should stop him.

One thick eyebrow performs the smallest of twitches.

"Guess we have matching kinds of crazy then, huh?"

It doesn't matter if I'm nodding because I agree with him or to let him know he can close the distance, because the space is already disappearing between us. Our noses bump, heads tilt, the weight of his breath is on my mouth, heat hits my lips, and then the scuff of a shoe sounds from the hallway outside.

# CHAPTER 26

*"Do you think—after we've dried off, after we've spent
lots more time together—you might agree 'not' to
murder me? And do you think not murdering me might
maybe be something you could consider doing for the rest
of your life?"*

—Not *Four Weddings and a Funeral*

*E*yes snap open, pupils constrict, chins jerk apart as both of our
backs press against the partition. He doesn't need to, but Wes
brings a finger to his lips after he untangles his hand from mine. The
same lips I had planned on preoccupying myself with for at least a
few minutes.

Of course.

Masked killer.

Dead bodies.

Worst speed date ever.

That should have been at the forefront of my mind instead of
debating whether it would be more comfortable to straddle Wes on
the floor or if he'd prefer we move over to one of the chaises. Those

kinds of musings should've been the furthest thing from my mind. They aren't, but they should've been.

Wes pushes himself up the partition, making sure to stay crouched below the top of it as he brings the knife up to his chest and looks around the room for a better vantage point. I push my back against the same surface and manage to slide up to a similar bent-over position, brutally pulled back to the present. Back to the fact we're still being hunted and the only weapon I have, aside from my brain—which wasn't concerned about anything other than where I was going to place my bloody hands while I made out with Wes—is Wes's body.

He's been an advantage when it comes to making it this far, but his knife hasn't suddenly grown fifteen inches in the time it took for Heart Eyes to make his way back up to the mezzanine.

Who's to say he isn't still waving that machete around?

Or what if he's just gearing up? What if he takes it to the next level and goes all *Texas Chainsaw Massacre* on us as soon as we step into view?

The footsteps sound closer and I'm too panicked to try to distinguish if there's one or many, if it's friend or foe. The only thing I can decipher is that there is no rolling purr of a chainsaw idling along with them.

Wes steps away from the partition, pulling me with him, drawing me behind him, his back firm against my chest as he retreats to the side of the room until we're shrouded in darkness. I'm caught between a wall and his well-toned traps. It's clear he's making himself a human shield, and that's not going to do us—me—much good if it is Heart Eyes. I'd end up alone, pinned to a wall by a dead body with nothing but a knife I'd struggle to wrangle off said dead body's wrist.

A shadow spreads across the wall, stretching in from the front of the partition, distorted by the flickering lamps. The exit strategy I thought of when we first entered the room comes to mind: I'm ready to run. I'm ready to drag Wes with me around the other side of the partition, slip out the door as the killer rounds it, and start our cat-and-mouse game all over again.

Wes tenses in front of me as a body finally comes into view. I spy a familiar material over his shoulder, and the relief it isn't pink wool is short-lived when I distinguish the pattern against the shadow-drenched crimson of the walls. Red plaid.

"The fuck?" Stu mutters.

Wes's shoulders drop back down, and when he takes a step forward, I move to his side and stare at the new addition to the room. I can't bring myself to be overjoyed at the sight of the manicured beard or the stunned, gaping mouth in the middle of it, especially when I glance down to see a boning knife gripped in his palm. He drops it down to his side as he stares incredulously between us.

"You're okay?"

That second statement seems a little more appropriate for the situation, but the way he says it, the inflection at the end—he looks at us as if we just performed a flash mob of Michael Jackson's "Thriller" and it *didn't* work to bring a function back to life. He thought we were dead.

A rustle of fabric from the hallway makes us all flinch, but the subsequent whispering voices bring my heart back down from my throat. If there's one thing Heart Eyes has been consistent about, it's maintaining the silent antagonist aspect of the classic slashers. Therefore, voices equal friend.

Or someone who's going to get themselves killed before you.

Wes darts across to the partition as the voices draw closer. Going toward any kind of sound, even if it's obviously some other daters, is a fatality waiting to happen (I know this from personal experience now), but his back is pressed against the wall, and he silently slips around it into the entrance before I can reach for him and pull him back.

I have half a mind to run after him. If not because I'd like to one day—after all this—have the opportunity of a do-over for whatever was about to start before Stu reentered the chat with his stupid, heavy footsteps, then because there is no way in hell I'm going to survive this night with *Stu*, of all people. I've given up following most of the rules of surviving a slasher on Wes's advice and I'm still alive, but teaming up with the Jerk Jock is where I draw the line.

A few breath-holding moments later, Wes comes back into the room with Dani and Jennifer at his heels, and when I shoot a glance across at Stu, I can see the relief settle into his shoulders the same time as mine. I assume I'm not the only one who wasn't happy with potentially being the last ones on each other's dance cards.

Stu pushes off the wall as I swap "I'm happy you're not dead" looks with Dani and Jennifer. "You're okay?" he asks, looking down at them with concern.

It's the same question he asked us, but this time he's inquiring about their well-being rather than inferring they should be deceased by now. I think we can all agree, none of us are okay at this point in the night. The three of them look just as ragged and on edge as Wes and me; there's blood on Stu's hands, bruises on Dani's legs, and Jennifer's knuckles are white around the handle of the first aid kit. It survived the escape from Heart Eyes and I wish it wasn't the only thing that had.

"Is John—"

Jennifer starts the question but doesn't finish it when our eyes meet. I know she already suspected the answer, but her face pales at the unspoken confirmation. She and Dani got away while he stood his ground and bought them time. Exactly what he did for me and Wes.

"What about Laurie?" Jennifer says, and for a second I want to ask Stu why *he* isn't the one posing that question. Then I see the way he's standing closer to Dani, the way she looks up at him with glassy eyes and pink-cheeked gratitude. I guess she doesn't hold the "sending her off into the basement" thing against him despite it ending with the role of her best friend being recast for the rest of the night due to disembowelment.

"Laurie ran away," I say automatically, and that pulls Stu's attention from rubbing the goose bumps on Dani's arms.

His eyes narrow at me when he says, "She *ran* away?"

"We were attacked in the bathroom. She managed to get out while I locked myself in a stall."

I mean, technically, I'm not lying. And if I keep reminding myself that she *did* get out, that all I have to do is keep myself, Wes, and anyone else alive until she sees the plan to the end, then I can see some version of a happy ending to all of this. I can see myself getting to call her an elitist piece of shit again.

"And here I thought you were against splitting up," Stu sneers.

Asshole.

Wes tenses beside me, takes a breath like he's going to shoot a retort that might warrant the same peacocking performance that Stu displayed when we first came upstairs from the basement, but I don't need him to jump to my defense. I may not have what it takes to be a Final Girl, but I am a big girl. And Stu is just a small man.

"You know what? *Fuck you*, Stu, I—"

"You're *such* good friends and you're not looking for her?"

"In the time it took for me and Wes to escape a killer who just ran John through with a machete?"

The words are harsher than I mean them to be, and if my hands weren't covered in blood I'd clap them over my mouth, especially since the statement causes Jennifer and Dani to flinch, letting out matching gasps.

"No, I haven't had the chance," I say. I'm trying to use a calm voice, but Stu rubs me the wrong way. He was hot and cold with my best friend, antagonistic toward Wes, he left his group alone, and I still get the feeling he'd be rude to hospitality staff. "But I know Laurie—better than you. She'll hide. She won't do anything stupid."

When Stu walks toward me, I notice his knife looks more foreboding in his hand than the one resting against Wes's thigh, but maybe that's just because of the person holding it. It's probably due to the way his voice drops low and abrasive when he says, "It's probably good she got as far away from you as she could when you're the one the fucking psycho wants. Isn't that right, Jamie?"

It's clear he's seen my name in the middle of the dance floor at some point, and he doesn't share the same sentiments as my admirer. Even though he said it to try to hurt me, I don't take the bait. If I get out of here tonight there's probably going to be a lot of things I've said or done or didn't do that I'll regret. But doing whatever I can to get my best friend away from danger? Yeah, I'm not going to lose sleep over that.

Although I restrain myself from snapping back, Wes can't stop himself this time. His dark gaze is cold, and the rasp of his voice is sharper than I've heard it all night.

"Keep saying dumb shit, Stu. I dare you."

"Like I'm not saying what we're all thinking."

"What the fuck have *you* done tonight other than put people in danger and then fucking disappear?"

"*She's* the girl who—"

"*Woman*," Jennifer says. I'm not the only one who is shocked that she's jumped to my defense. "She's the woman who's saved multiple people's asses tonight. Including mine. Right?"

She directs that at Dani. Her tone leaves no room for disagreement, and I look at the woman across from me and see a completely different person from the one we found hidden behind a curtain and shaking from fear. Jennifer has gone through some kind of character arc tonight. She seems more akin to a Final Girl than I could be, and it makes me think maybe Heart Eyes should've gotten to know us all a little better before making me the lead of the night.

"Right," Dani agrees, sending an apologetic smile my way, but not making any moves to shift away when Stu retreats to her side. I guess the lumberjack effect hits some people in full force.

"Well, you're really *something*, aren't you?" Stu mutters, and I think we can safely determine he has not been pining over me for the last few hours.

"And you're really an asshole," Wes says before I can express the same sentiment. He turns his stare onto Stu's fist, using his own weapon to point to it. "Where'd you get the knife?"

Stu glares back at Wes before looking down at the boning knife in his hand. The tip has specks of blood on it.

"I got it from Campbell."

CHAPTER 27

"You're not hard to gut at all. You're hard to execute."

—Not *Set It Up*

"*Y*ou found *Campbell*?" I ask incredulously.

Ever since he ran away, I assumed he was either dead or hiding somewhere so obscure it would've become a joke among the horror of tonight. Something rife with dramatic irony where he would've eventually developed the courage to venture back into the club and find some kind of redemption. But then I see the way Dani and Jennifer wilt against the wall and remind myself this isn't that kind of movie.

"Yeah." Stu scoffs, and I don't need him to clarify that he didn't just get it from Campbell; he probably pulled it out of him.

That means another name on the match cards has been figuratively crossed off. I press my palm against the top of my dress and feel the cards crinkle beneath the material, resisting the urge to pull them out and see who is still left.

"He's at the end of that first hallway. The one we ran down earlier," Jennifer says, and I'm reminded of why we bypassed it when Wes and I ran up here.

228 · **SHAILEE THOMPSON**

Retracing your steps rarely leads to anything good.

"He had a whole collection of them, as well as another present for you." Stu points the thin blade in my direction.

"What—"

"Flowers," Dani blurts out, her eyes glazed and exhausted. She props a hand on her forehead as Jennifer fidgets against the wall and adds, "More roses."

They share a look, and I know there's more to the scene that they won't or can't explain. Save for the crude scratching on the bathroom mirror, the romantic gestures have just been getting bigger and bolder. This whole night has been about escalation. Especially if Wes and I are right and Heart Eyes is the one responsible for those murders I saw on the news. He just keeps stepping up his game . . . and I can't even imagine what he has planned for the finale.

But on that note, the knowledge we're closer to the end of this than the beginning when Stu first left the group has me asking, "How have you been avoiding Heart Eyes? It's been hours since we split up."

"Heart Eyes?" Stu spits, and even the others have a range of different reactions. Wes lets out a darkly humored exhale in understanding, Jennifer cringes, and Dani sucks in a short breath.

"His mask. It's pink with hearts where the eyes should be."

Stu mutters something that sounds like "Fucking, psycho, creep ass . . ." before his voice becomes a grumble and I can't distinguish any more words. He points a finger across the room to the back wall, just above the chaise I thought would be an ideal place to grind my body on top of Wes.

"You know how some of the corridors are roped off? I figured it's 'cause they're employee sections." He moves the direction of his finger to point out the door. "There's another one on that side. I took a chance, looked down the last hallway, and found a janitor's closet. It has a lock, a sink, cleaning shit. But there was no phone or anything. I was there for an hour and then figured I'd try to find an exit."

It sounds smart enough, reasonable enough even, but I'm not going to give him credit when at least three people have died while he was allegedly hanging out in a janitor's closet.

He's made it clear there's no love lost (or gained) between us, but I've watched enough Shyamalan movies to know there's always room for a twist. It's highly unlikely Stu's leaving these grotesque declarations of love while continuing to look at me like my very presence conjures up the smell of dog shit beneath his nose. But a good Final Girl doesn't take anyone off the suspect list until the killer is unveiled.

So I say, "We should keep moving. We've been here for a while."

Aside from two jump scares and our group of two becoming five, there's been no sign of Heart Eyes. It's easy to forget what happened downstairs or on the dance floor or down the hallway where Campbell must be when the adrenaline drops and you've gotten used to the tacky feeling of blood on your hands, but I trust the reprieve about as much as I trust a third-act breakup in a nineties rom-com.

It always turns around when you've gotten comfortable with the new norm.

"Should we go to the janitor's closet?" Jennifer asks. "We could clean up, figure out a plan?"

It's a good idea. One I'm about to agree with before Stu suggests we split up again.

"Hold on."

Wes shifts next to me, and when I glance up at him, his eyes are fixed on the back wall. Not quite where Stu was pointing, but higher, in the corner, on a protrusion from the ceiling that's been painted over in the same color as the walls. He strides over to it and takes a closer look. It doesn't resemble the security cameras that have been tampered with. Those are perfect half-spheres—I can see one in the other corner of the room, covered in the same view-obstructing black paint as the others, but this shape looks more like a—

"This building would have a monitored fire alarm system," Wes says as he walks back across the room.

I don't know what that is exactly, but the way he says it is reverent, cautious, like he doesn't want to get too excited about the prospect.

"I'd say most places have smoke detectors, asshole."

Stu's voice makes my shoulders flinch, and this time I make sure he sees my middle finger clearly from across the room.

"It's different from a smoke detector, dumbass," Wes retorts, letting the statement hang in the air before he explains. "*Monitored* fire alarms send a signal to a central station when the smoke alarm is triggered. Emergency services get dispatched, and the building manager gets notified. There should be a manual call point somewhere, but if we can't find it, we just need to set the detectors off."

For the first time since I watched Laurie's ass shimmy through a metal tunnel, hope rears its beautiful head again. If she's still navigating her way through the building, if she's out or—I don't want to think about it, but there's always the possibility—she's hurt and needs us to save her, then what Wes is suggesting could help. There's another way to sound the alarm. Literally.

"If we set off the system, the fire department will be deployed. Since the building is supposed to be empty, they'll send police, too."

I did not know that was a thing. Granted my only experience with fire alarms is when Laurie and I accidentally set ours off by not turning on the exhaust fan over our oven, or in the films I watch, where the building is already a blazing inferno before the firefighters show up. But this . . . this could get us out of here.

"Wes, are you sure?"

I can't allow myself to get too excited at the prospect. As beautiful as hope is at first sight, its effect can fade just as quickly. The same feeling has been ripped away so many times tonight it's hard not to be wary of getting burned.

He nods. "The signal is transmitted through internet and phone lines, and the NFPA—the National Fire Protection Association—requires all systems to have backup—"

"Wait." Stu holds up his free palm, raising the other to point his knife across at Wes, directly at his chest. "How do *you* know all this?"

I feel like that shouldn't really matter right now, but then I catch sight of the guarded looks on not just Stu's face, but on Jennifer's and Dani's faces, too. They haven't moved from their spot a few feet from us, but their bodies lean back from where Wes and I are standing beneath the chandelier. If they aren't afraid—because who can tell the difference between any new kind of fear and the constant terror this evening has imprinted on our faces—then they're wary. That's when I remember they didn't see Heart Eyes while Wes was standing right next to them. They didn't see what we saw, what *I* saw.

Wes reads the room as easily as I do. His gaze flicks toward the knife in Stu's hand and I watch the moment it dawns on him that if Stu doesn't like whatever answer he gives, they're evenly matched. He needs to convince them he isn't a threat.

My instinct is to jump to his defense, especially since he's trying to get us the hell out of here. But then there's a fleeting moment where I think my own words—*a good Final Girl doesn't take anyone off the suspect list until the killer is unveiled*—might come back and bite me in the ass.

It doesn't stick around for long, though. I'm still 100 percent certain I would not eye fuck a killer.

"I know because—" His tongue darts out to wet his lips, and when he finally says it, admits it, the relief doesn't set in like I thought it would, but some things start to make a lot more sense.

"'Cause I'm a cop."

CHAPTER 28

"Kill me. Kill me as if it were the last time."

—Not *Casablanca*

"**Y**ou're a *cop*?"

The look of pissed-off confusion is the only expression I've seen on Stu's smug face that seems appropriate for the situation. I think this may be the first and only time tonight we are on the same page.

"Detective," Wes says. "I'm investigating a string of recent homicides. That's why I came here tonight."

For the first time, I look at Wes and see a different man from the one who sat across from me during our speed date. For the first time, the things he's said and the things he's done appear in a different light. This whole time I thought he was just one of those people who perform well under pressure. But the way he was able to quickly create a plan, the way he assessed a space for danger, the way he's been holding his weapons all night and holding his shit together . . . He patched up my arm like he'd just completed his first aid training refresher.

That's why I came here tonight.

The admission makes my throat feel thick and scratchy. He's been *working*. Everything tonight has been part of his job. He *She's All That*'d me. But instead of being a fucking bet, I was a fucking *beard*.

What was the point of all those weighted looks and lingering touches and intimate assurances if he was just playing out some under-cover role to catch the killer? The humiliating realization makes heat flare up in my cheeks.

What if what I've been feeling since our eyes locked was one-sided? That thought feeds into a particular flavor of fear. The kind I feel when I'm struggling with my dissertation or getting ready for a date or, recently, trying to think and act like a Final Girl. It's a slippery slope that will lead to hurtful thoughts about self-worth . . . and I don't have the emotional capacity to deal with it.

I'm investigating a string of recent homicides.

"The girls. The five women," I say, and he nods solemnly, his eyes meeting mine, just for a second. Then he turns his stare back to Stu and the knife still aimed at his chest.

There was a reason he brought up the murders. A reason he knew the last name of the most recent victim, Casey. He probably knows all of that "getting to know you" information about her we never got to cover in our ten-minute meet-cute. Things like how many siblings she has, where she works, her likes and dislikes . . . things he doesn't know about me. Things I don't know about him.

Wes doesn't just know the information that would've made up her dating profile. He'd also know what the killer did to her, how the fear of her last moments was etched into her face and captured in the crime scene photos when her body was discovered. And he knew *all* of that before coming tonight.

"Where's your gun?" Jennifer asks, her eyes darting across his body as if he's going to pull out a Glock and say, "Oh, this old thing?"

When he doesn't, she asks about the other items I know aren't hidden in his pockets. "Your badge? A phone?"

"I don't have them."

At least he sounds like he really, really regrets that.

"Then you must have backup."

Dani's optimistic, expectant expression when she says it just makes my stomach tie itself into knots, because this far into the slasher that sense of hope is just an illusion. You might be able to flag down the only car on a remote highway, but no sooner does that happen than the driver takes you right back into the fray. It's that glimmer, the promise of a savior getting ripped away that makes the final act so important.

"Wes?" I ask when he doesn't reply, and the way he won't meet anyone's eye, I know what it means.

On our date—if we can still call it that; maybe it was an interrogation—he said he had time off from work. He said it had only happened recently, and if Casey was the fifth woman to die in such a short period of time, there's only one reason he'd be taking a "break."

Dani still looks like she's waiting for the silver lining to Wes's revelation, so I voice the conclusion I've already come to.

"You're not on the case, are you?"

I watch his jaw clench, his eyes dart to mine. They look apologetic, embarrassed, and then he admits, "Not anymore."

I glance across to Stu, Jennifer, and Dani, and watch as one by one they come to the same conclusion: nobody knows he's here. Nobody is coming.

That glimmer? Extinguished.

That hope? Gone.

We've been running around this building for god knows how long and for a moment, after all the carnage, the thought there may have been something happening on the outside, that the cavalry was coming, was something we all wanted to grasp on to. Now, though? I know if Laurie doesn't manage to get out of those vents we're done for.

"What the fuck, Wes?" Stu hisses, and again I concur.

"All the victims attended singles events around the city before they went missing," Wes says. "I figured the perp was meeting these women at these events, and when I was discussing the theory with my partner in the bullpen, this asshole that works in another unit was listening in, and he—our squads work together sometimes, and we've butted heads before," he explains, and even in the darkness of the room I see color rising in his cheeks. "But this time, he said some things—about the victims—that I felt were inappropriate given the circumstances."

He doesn't elaborate, and that makes me think whatever he's about to say next is going to make him look like either the killer or an idiot. Maybe both.

"And?" I ask.

"I didn't like what he was saying."

My quirked eyebrow is a silent "So?" One that makes him pinch the bridge of his nose and say, "So, I punched him in the face."

Idiot it is.

"I was taken off the case and put on suspension, but when Casey's body was found, I knew the killer would be searching for a new girl already, and I couldn't just do *nothing* whi—"

"So you set up a fucking sting," Stu says, interrupting. "Let it fall to shit, and then sat back as a bunch of people die?"

It sucks that he's saying things that sit and burn on the tip of my tongue.

"It was never a goddamn sting," Wes snaps reactively before taking a breath. I can tell he's doing that three-count thing in his head to calm down. I thought the counting thing was cute, but now it might just be a sign he can't control his impulsivity. The kind of impulsivity

236 · **SHAILEE THOMPSON**

that has led to him being put on leave, going undercover, trying to go head-to-head with a cold-blooded killer . . .

"It *wasn't* a sting," he stresses. "This was one of countless events on tonight. I didn't even know the killer would be here. I thought if I could go to the kind of event he would go to, I could understand how he's been able to do what he's done. I was talking to the guys at cocktail hour to see if there was anything that could inform the perp profile. I was going to talk to the host after the dates, too. I just—I just wanted to get in his head. Figure out his MO. And now I just want to get us all out. Alive."

"Did you know this could happen?" I grit out.

The string that was woven into place inside my chest when we first met feels like it's being sawn through with a blunt knife, but I push away the hurt and ask what everyone has avoided saying outright. "Did you know we were all in danger?"

I need to know for sure. Wes has proven so far that he's not stupid. Hotheaded and impulsive, yes, but he's shown how capable he is with the bare minimum. If he started the night with suspicions that this could happen, that whoever is doing this is the same person responsible for the murders he's investigating, there's no way he'd come in unarmed.

His face turns ashen, and that's answer enough until he adds an emphatic "*No*."

He shifts toward me, and it takes everything in me not to flinch. Still, he stops short. "Jamie . . . *No*. None of the women attended speed dates. They met at Italian cooking classes and painting nights and fucking lock-and-key events. This isn't his MO. He finds some-one and takes them home. One person—one woman. He doesn't slaughter a bunch of people while wearing a mask. He's escalated. And the fact I'm here—the fact *he's* here—any of us are . . . All of this is just by chance."

Chance. A twist of fate. That kind of thing should be reserved for meeting the love of your life, not . . . *this*.

I think back to when we were down in the basement bar. When I crawled out from under the table and saw Wes across the room he was scared, angry, but most of all he was shocked. We all were. But now I think his shock was for a different reason. It was because his role-play materialized and then multiplied in horrifying, unimaginable ways like some critter from an eighties creature feature.

"You have to believe that I—"

"We don't have to believe shit," Stu spits before Wes can start a new appeal, emphasizing his final word with a thrust of his knife into the space between us. The air is so thick with tension I'm surprised it doesn't bleed.

"I'm pretty sure being a cop in this scenario doesn't make you trustworthy, Wes. It doesn't automatically make you the good guy. If anything, it puts you at the top of the fucking list of suspects."

There's a moment where Wes seems like he's going to argue, where he seems like he's going to shoot Stu down like he has before, but then I witness the moment he realizes he can't.

Stu is right yet again. I hate to admit it, but he is.

Maybe in the past it would've been something that would instill hope, but relying on the assumption that being a police officer makes someone safe by default is the kind of thinking that can get you good and dead. Not just in a horror movie. Not just in any movie. Taking on the role of a "safe" person is the way that true evil can conceal itself.

It's as much of a mask as the one Heart Eyes has been wearing tonight.

"I know," Wes finally says, his voice hoarse and tight even when he tries to clear his throat. "I know. So don't trust me because of that. Don't trust me at all, if that's what you want, but the alarm system is a chance for us to get out of here. This is a chance for us to end this."

And that's the carrot dangling in front of us. His idea is one that could get us out. Yeah, he lied, but he was standing right next to me when John was killed. I know he's not Heart Eyes. Even though he's hurt my feelings, that doesn't make him a villain . . . it just puts him in good company with a lot of other guys I've dated.

"What do you need us to do?"

I can't bring much inflection back into my voice. Wes picks up on it and I think sourly that it must be those well-honed investigative skills, but then that soft look is back on his face, now with an added layer of apology, and I'm unable to hold his gaze. I turn my face to the partition as if I'm keeping watch. Out of my periphery, I see him turn back to the others.

"The control panel is usually located at the main entrance, but we would've seen it when we were there . . . You said the roped-off areas are employee sections?"

Stu nods.

"Then we'll probably find it in a utility room down one of those halls. We can send the signal from there, but if not, we'll need to set off the alarms through the smoke detectors. Does anyone have a lighter?"

Everyone shakes their head, and I've never been more disappointed that smoking rates have declined among my generation. If we were in a nineties rom-com, at least half of the people in this room would be chain smokers.

"I have a vape? It's flat, though," Dani says quietly, and she pulls a pretty pink vape bar from inside the fold of her blue dress. A deeply primal part of me has a spark of envy that her dress has pockets, but it's quickly tamped down when Wes fashions the grim line of his mouth into a tight conciliatory smile, shaking his head at her offer.

"We should also go back to the janitor's closet, then," he says. "Get something flammable, a lighter or some matches."

"So we should split up."

I can't stop my eyes from rolling. Stu really is a one-trick pony.

"That didn't work out so great last time," I remind him.

"We're alive, aren't we?"

I'm about to point out three other people from our original group no longer have that luxury when he uses his knife to point between me and Wes.

"You two can stick together. I think the three of us would rather stay away from the *woman* this is all happening for and the guy who's been lying the whole night."

That lands about as well as can be expected, and if glares were daggers, mine would pierce right through Stu's skull.

Dani and Jennifer look apologetic when they finally meet my eye, but they don't say anything to disagree. In the last ten minutes, I've experienced the kind of peer rejection and painful unrequited realizations I thought were reserved for coming-of-age movies with melancholic soundtracks. For the first time since Laurie went through that vent, I wish she were here.

"So you'll go back to the janitor's closet?" I ask. I figure Stu would want to take the safest option, the known path. Since he thinks I'm the catalyst for all this chaos and Wes is a liar, I'm sure he also thinks that makes us more disposable. "We'll try to find the control panel?"

"*We* will go find the control panel," Stu says, using his knifeless hand to gesture to Dani and Jennifer. "If we find it, or a phone or something, we'll sound the alarm. *You* go to the janitor's closet. If you find what you need to start a fire, come back here and set the alarm off. It doesn't matter who does it first as long as we get the fuck out of here. If we can't find what we're looking for, then we meet back in this room and figure something else out."

Dani looks up at Stu like he's pulled a glowing exit sign from his ass that'll lead us out of the massacre, buying the hero-complex shit he's hijacked from Wes. I want to tell her not to get too excited. It won't end well.

Jennifer, at least, is unaffected by Stu's new role. When she glances at me, I flick my eyes toward Stu and shake my head ever so subtly.

Don't trust him.

She returns an almost imperceptible nod in understanding that makes me glad women are far more skilled at interpreting nonverbal communication than men. Her gaze shifts to Wes. He's quiet, tense, admonished by the way I won't meet his eye. Jennifer tips her head, and I pick up a similar message: *be careful*.

I nod, even though being warned about Wes makes my gut twist in dissent.

Stu enjoys Dani's fawning attention too much and it makes him bold. He scoffs after Wes explains how to set off the control panel and offers to go find it himself. He'd let the four of us stick together and go searching for the alarm system alone, if we let him. The idea of Wes by himself still makes my heart lodge in my throat. Even after the lies. Even though my nails have left indents in my palm from how hard I've been trying to push down the anger and the hurt.

Stupid, infuriating hero-complex shit that is definitely *not* still sexy . . . not at all.

Stu shoots down the suggestion. "Just because you say you're a cop and you know about this shit doesn't mean we should trust you. You could just as easily disassemble the alarm."

Wes shakes his head, and I hear a mutter that I think conveys what he'd actually like to disassemble.

"And besides." Stu shrugs, his arrogant stare locked on where I'm standing, my bloody hands looking like a crude pair of gloves made to match my dress. I look like a debutante from hell. "If it turns out you are the killer, well . . . this is your chance to have some more alone time with Jamie, isn't it?"

CHAPTER 29

*"You think I'm gorgeous, you want to kill me . . . You want
to stab me . . . You want to murder me . . ."*

—Not *Miss Congeniality*

I'm silent as we make our way to the janitor's closet, exuding
"don't talk to me if you want to leave here with your balls on
the outside of your body" vibes that Wes seems to respect by staying
just as quiet and tense.

We still walk shoulder to shoulder, my side pressed against his as
we navigate the corridors. Running away from your ally or giving into
the anger just leaves you primed for an attack. I'm so mad I can't recall
any films where that's happened, but still, I know it would be a bad
idea to storm away from Wes and put the kind of distance between
us that would allow a blade to find its mark.

Stu's directions pay off, and when we find the closet, open the
door to see it mercifully empty and the light still on, I move in ahead
of Wes and make a beeline for the sink that comes into view as he
locks the door.

I *need* to get John's blood off me. It's all over my hands and my legs, staining my skin. It feels too sticky and there's something in the way it's mixed with my perfume that makes it smell sweet, so when the tap splutters on and water spills over my hands, I can't help the audible sigh of relief as it turns red. There's a bottle of industrial-grade hand soap on the shelf closest to the sink and I pump it aggressively into my palm. It advertises removing grease and paint and chemicals, but I'm sure if the makers knew it could handle washing away the blood of a guy you were flirting with before he got stabbed in the shoulder they'd add that to the label, too.

"Jamie . . ."

Wes's voice is low, wary, as I scrub at the flakes of dried blood with my nails. There's a metallic tap of his knife landing on one of the shelves, the heavier thud of the flashlight, then he shifts into the space next to me and his hands delve into the water, brushing inadvertently against mine. I don't look up from the pink suds.

Earlier, I'd thought it was interesting, admirable even, how he'd managed to carry all his tools. How he figured out his own system despite the stress of the evening. But he's just been relying on memory. He's just been compensating for his lack of a kit belt all night.

Wes's sigh hits the top of my forehead as the water in the sink turns soapy and then clear. I already know what I'm going to say, but still I let him get his excuses out.

Well, almost.

"I know you're pissed at me right now, and I'm sor—"

"Why didn't you tell me who you are?" I reach across him and grab some of the paper towels stacked beside the sink, dipping them into the water and scrubbing the blood on my legs.

There's a pause before he says, "I did. I just didn't tell you what I do," and that draws my gaze up to his. The incredulous look I give him at least garners the "I know that was a dumb thing to say" expression that crosses his face.

"I didn't want to make myself a target." His voice is low as I look back down, continuing to rub my skin even though the rosy stain of John's blood has disappeared. "I didn't want to make you—*anyone* a target. If I'd known something like this would happen, if I'd known he would escalate like this . . ."

He turns the tap off, the sound of the water dripping from our fingers plinking against the tub. "We just wouldn't *be here*. He's gone entirely off script, I know that's not an excuse. I know it's my job to be prepared. But it's also my job to protect. So, I'll do anything—*anything*, Jamie—to make sure the rest of us get out of here. Because you and I both know he's not gonna stop."

I can't argue with that. I mean, I want to, but as this night plays out, as I look back with hindsight, I know if Wes had told us he was a cop he'd be dead.

Heart Eyes would've made a beeline for him in the basement. He wouldn't have loitered at the end of that hallway. It's a sobering thought. One that takes some of the wind out of my sails, makes me meet his eye, and tempts the tiniest of pulls in my chest.

"I wanted to tell you." His voice drops to a murmur as he passes me more paper towels, and it's nice to see my hands—to see *his* hands—clean and free of blood . . . again. "I nearly did—"

"When?"

It's not like he couldn't have casually dropped it into conversation at any point tonight. "*Hey, Jamie, we're the same kind of crazy. Also, I'm a cop.*"

It just falls right off the tongue.

"*So* many times." He sighs, and being in his space, having that soft rasp close to my ear, there's a good chance the only reason I haven't gripped my rubbed-raw fingers into his collar and pulled his mouth down onto mine is pure stubbornness.

"But . . . Jamie, I didn't come here tonight to—"

"To meet someone," I say, finishing his sentence as I push away from the sink, and move back to the door. Having some distance whips up that hot air again, but it's still conflicted. What I'm actually angry at is hazy. I should be concentrating on escaping a killer who is obsessed with me and the eventual truckload of therapy I'm going to have to go through to process all the carnage I've seen tonight if I survive. Instead, I'm pissed off he lied. I'm pissed off that I'm even hurt in the first place, and then there's the other thing.

"You came here to stop more people from dying, and I know we need to concentrate on the matter at hand, which is *not* adding to that count, but I can't help but be a little pissed that you were pretending on our date."

He squints across at me. "What do you mean 'pretending'?"

The "what makes you happy?" question, the slow smiles, the fact any eye fucking I was doing was consensual and reciprocal.

"It was like you were *trying*."

The drawn-out grazes of his thumb on my arm when he was patching up my cut, the way he slipped into teasing me with Laurie like it was second nature. We would've kissed had Stu been able to pick up his feet while walking.

How has any of that helped his investigation?

Wes pauses, processes, then shakes his head slowly, as if the word itself is foreign to him.

"I definitely wasn't 'trying.'"

He says it without a hint of smugness. He's not even looking at me, but still—

"Oh, *fuck off*. I mean you didn't have to act like it was a real date when it wasn't. I actually li—"

I cut myself off before I can say it, but he is a detective, and the syllable makes him glance up from the floor. He meets my eye, and the intensity I see makes me turn and start sifting through the shelves for anything with a "flammable" logo. If not to set off the alarms, then to set myself on fire.

I've had enough experience with modern dating to know you hold your cards close to your chest until you're all but forced to show them. Flirting, touching—any level of sexual touch—is fine, but admitting emotions and putting words to them that define how you feel about someone?

Borderline psychotic.

"Say what you were going to say."

His voice sounds weighted as it travels across the small space. My hands graze more paper towels, unopened mop heads, jugs of hand soap, and a box of those napkins that were on the bar in the basement. Anything that might keep my hands busy and stop them from shaking.

"No."

"Jamie . . ."

I don't know why that makes me pause. He's probably said my name hundreds of times tonight, but this time it grabs my heart in a chokehold.

I want to tell him.

I want to tell him, but I can't look at him when I do.

"I . . . actually . . . like—" I switch to past tense at the last second. "—*d* you."

The admission hangs in the air, and while the weight of saying it is off my shoulders, the anticipation of his response takes its place. I turn around, slower than when Heart Eyes found me in the bathroom, somehow just as scared, and our eyes meet. He stares.

For a long time.

Then his gaze drops to the door, checking that it's still locked, before he glances up and straightens. The energy shifts. There's a momentary internal struggle where all the annoyance and hurt and frustration I feel tries to fight against the pull I have toward Wes, but it's an uneven match. My anger vanishes like the body of a villain at the end of a slasher. All that's left is eye contact, thick air, blood rising under my cheeks, and liquid warmth stirring up low in my belly.

"Can I say something?"

His voice is barely audible, but it sends something visceral down my spine, something that makes me shuffle on the spot when I nod. He takes a step back, props himself against the shelves four steps away from me, not breaking our eye contact for a second.

If we were in a rom-com, this is where he'd confess how he feels, or maybe he'd just do away with the whole speech, say "fuck it," and cross the room to kiss me. I wouldn't mind either option. I wouldn't mind anything that would progress the plot. Anything, until he throws his hands up in the air and grits out, "I fucking forgot."

Jesus, did he hit his head in the last five seconds?

"What you were about to say?" I ask incredulously.

"No. I forgot why I was here, tonight."

I frown. Point to the door. "To catch the kil—"

"For an hour, I was able to keep an eye on what was happening in that room, and then I sat down at your table, and I saw you . . . and it was *over*. All I could concentrate on was you—I don't *do* that. I'm trained *not* to do that, but you made me forget why I was here."

Oh. My. God. *It's happening.*

"And then you started talking about murder and—" His scoff is humorless. "I wasn't forgetting anymore, and I also couldn't help but notice that you fit the victim profile. You're *his* type. But the thing is . . ."

He rubs a palm over his forehead in frustration, letting out a sharp exhale before he looks squarely at me and says, "You're *my* type, Jamie. You are one of a kind and just my type."

Oh no. That hits hard. Like a knockout punch. Like the first on-screen kill. Like the first on-screen kiss. Especially when he lets out a deep, helpless sigh and shakes his head.

"Even when I walked away, I still couldn't get you out of my head, and because of that I wasn't watching the room, and I missed who turned that light off. I missed something that could've stopped all of this before it happened."

Pain crosses his face, the kind that comes from knowing something as harmless as a light switch would lead to devastating consequences, and that makes me take a step forward.

"Wes, that is not your f—"

"And now?"

He's so far through his admission that I have no power to stop it. No desire to.

"I can't stop myself from thinking that if this wasn't happening, if this had been a normal night, if that psychotic asshole was terrorizing someone somewhere else ... I would've tried to take you home."

His eyes lock with mine again, and I'm reduced to sweaty palms and heavy breathing. I'd thought eating street food without any repercussions was my best-case scenario, but now that I know it wasn't, that something better was within reach ... I want it.

"I wouldn't have waited until tomorrow to find out if we matched. I would've taken you out for a drink tonight and listened to anything you had to say about any fucking type of film, and I would've wanted to know what you thought."

It plays out across my mind like an eighties montage. Complete with frosted edges and seasonal wardrobe.

"I would've kissed you in the middle of a rant about Ghostface or Dahmer or some Leading Lady, because I wouldn't have been able to help myself, and when I got you home, when I had you laid out on my bed ... *Jamie* ..."

His voice drops even lower. It's an admission I'm not supposed to hear, but I still catch it, and my blood flares up in my veins.

"God, I would've done anything just to hear you scream my name."

The room falls silent again and all I can think is: *Holy shit* . . .

I've heard a lot of romantic speeches. I know all the elements. I've analyzed them at length. And as far as declarations go, that was pretty. Fucking. Spectacular.

Even though I've witnessed someone's throat being slit tonight and discovered it was nothing like the movies. Even though I watched a documentary on the pork industry and knew the process of gutting long before I'd seen it happen in real life. Even though this whole thing is somehow happening because of me—I can't deny that I will replay this moment in my head for the rest of my life. Even if the rest of my life is reduced to a few hours.

That invisible thread that's been woven into my chest since our date has turned into the hook from *I Know What You Did Last Summer*, lodged underneath my rib cage and pulling me toward him. Because this whole time, from the moment he sat down across from me, it's been Wes.

"I would've liked that . . ." I stare at him, his gaze unblinking, dark and bright all at once. Then, so there's no mistake about what part of his speech I'm referring to, I say, "All of it."

He mustn't have been expecting that, because a groan sounds from deep in his chest. His head drops back against the shelf of paper towels, eyes lifting to the ceiling as if he's asking for divine intervention before he meets my stare again and shakes his head.

"Jamie, don't . . ."

I'm about to ask what he doesn't want me to do, what he wants me to stop, but then his eyes dart between mine and he sees something I can't hide. Granted, I'm not trying hard to hide it. He lets out a sigh, and three counts later—

"Fuck it," he mutters, pushing off the shelves and striding toward me. When he's half a step away, he grabs the back of my neck and wrenches me forward.

CHAPTER 30

"Nice boys don't kill like that."
"Oh yes they fucking do."

—Not *Bridget Jones's Diary*

It's exactly like I feared.

He kisses me in a way that makes me forget we're being hunted down by a complete psychopath. He pulls me into his body so tightly the cut on my arm stings as it splits back open, but even then I push closer. The pressure of his mouth against mine blurs whether we've lost ten or eleven people so far. And when he uses his teeth to pull at my bottom lip, I can convince myself we're perfectly safe in this janitor's closet with only one way out and one lock between us and the killer outside.

I grasp the nape of his neck with my fingers when he steps forward and presses my back into the wall. One of his hands drops to my ass, and when he lifts me up I shift my knees out, his thigh sliding between my own. He uses his grip to pull me firmly against it and the pressure is . . . *Oh.* It's good. It's very, *very* good. Well done, Wes.

Pulling my mouth from his, I move my palms around to cup his jaw, keeping his lips a blade's width from mine when I whisper, "I don't think we should—"

"We shouldn't, but—" he murmurs, and when I open my eyes to meet his hooded gaze, it doesn't matter how that sentence is going to end.

"We shouldn't, but—" is all I need to hear.

"We shouldn't, but—" is a very convincing argument.

"I just—" Wes drops his face into my neck, his mouth hovering at my throat, air pulling away from my skin before he releases it with a shudder. The sound makes me tighten my thighs around his and a sharp, satisfying pulse takes me by surprise. It's just a preview, though. A teaser.

"I need to know what you look like when you—" He raises his head again and the look on his face, it's— "If I might di—"

He shakes that thought away. "I need to know—" It's like there are too many ends to that sentence and not enough time for him to figure out which one is going to accurately convey why we're going to do this. So when he can't seem to settle on one, he just breathes out an affected, extended, "*Jamie.*"

I am this close to going against the cardinal rule of horror films and having sex with this man I just met, because after all the debilitating fear, I just want a distraction, a release, an escape.

I just want Wes.

He waits for my answer before trying to kiss me again—another green flag if we get out of this—his eyes locked on my mouth, his breath hitting my face in hot pants. When his gaze lifts to meet mine again, his fingers grazing the back of my neck as his hand unfurls, I find myself nodding, pulling him closer, leaning in to close the distance.

"I want to." I finally understand why so many of those horny teens met their demise to get some action. "Wes, I want you t—"

He pulls my mouth back onto his and this kiss is brutal. So deep and raw and devastating it should be a crime. The dichotomy of the blunt clutch and pull of his teeth on my lip and the deep, soothing sweep of his tongue against my own isn't lost on me, but it is addictive. It's inciting. It causes me to drop my hands to where his shirt is tucked into his pants and pull, ignoring the tacky parts of the material where the bloodstains haven't fully dried. It makes him drag his hand down from my ass to run back up the front of my thigh, brushing up the hem of my dress and disappearing under it to grab my hip bone as I move against him, seeking more pressure, more heat, more of the heart-pounding effect that finally isn't from fear.

Maybe it's the adrenaline, my body trying to counteract the cortisol with a hit of dopamine or oxytocin, but I can't find a good enough reason to stop myself from smoothing my hands underneath his shirt as soon as it's free from his waistband, desperate to feel his skin against my palms if this is the only chance we'll get.

"That's it . . ." Wes says when his mouth disconnects from mine on an upward sweep, his grip tightening and guiding my movements atop his thigh. His voice is deep, breathless, rougher than the first cut of a student film. "That's it, Jamie. Show me what I've got to look forward to."

I rock against him. Arching, rolling, grinding. Over and over, until the heat in my belly competes with the warmth in my cheeks and the flush blooming across my chest. Up, in, down, circle, again. With a pleased grunt, his lips descend onto mine like they don't have anywhere else to be. Like the odds aren't stacked against us. Like we're in an alternate timeline and he has me on his bed in his apartment instead of next to a shelf of cleaning supplies in a windowless room.

I trail my fingers up his abs, his ribs, around to his back. His skin is just as warm as mine, hot against my hands, and it's smooth and hard, and the more of his body I touch the more I want to uncover. Sliding one hand back around to his stomach, I trace my fingers down the trail of hair that starts beneath his belly button, over the cold buckle of his belt, until I palm the front of his pants, right where he's pressing into my thigh.

He stifles a choked groan against my mouth when I work the pressure of my hand against him, but then his lips pause, and for a short, terrifying moment I think he may have heard something or—maybe even worse—he's reconsidering this, reconsidering whether I'm worth any of the trouble we've gotten into tonight. Before I can spiral, he starts to work his mouth against mine again, releasing his grip on my neck and pulling my hand away before I can do anything too skillful.

When he pins it over my head in a swift move, that warmth, the one flowing through my body, melting and pooling all the way down to my core . . . Yeah, it kicks up a notch from that. I pull back just a little, his lips still grazing mine, and glance up to where he's holding my wrist against the wall.

"Wes?" His name falls out of my mouth on a sigh, sliding between our lips, and for a second I think he might rethink restraining my arm. We've taken the risk, but so far I'm the only one reaping the reward. But then he pulls me tighter against him, his thumb starts to circle on top of my hip bone, and my eyelids flutter.

"We don't have much time."

He mutters it so quietly I can't figure out whether he's saying it for my benefit or his. His lips move from mine to press against the thrumming pulse in my neck. The feel of his tongue on my skin makes my breath hitch.

"Christ, I *want* to, Jamie. I want to, but one of us needs to keep our wits." His voice vibrates against my throat, and I nod, agree mindlessly, because my wits are anywhere but here. "But just wait till I get you out of here. Just wait. I'll do so much better than this."

It's a promise. One that draws a shaky exhale from my throat and makes me grip the fingers of my free hand into the muscles of his back because it's already so good. I'm pretty sure he can tell. When his hand slides from my hip to the edge of my underwear, dips between the material and my skin, his fingertips grazing lower until they slide easily, slickly, against me, the heavy exhale near my ear is confirmation enough that he can tell. He can tell and he's pleased about it, too.

My head falls back against the wall as he works his fingers against me. Everything is reduced to feeling—friction, simmering pleasure, and feverish heat. It's not a race, he's not rushing, but there's an urgency to both our movements. It's the only indication of a distant aware-ness of anything outside of this room. He uses his thigh to keep the heel of his hand tight against my clit and it draws a moan from my throat. One that's cut off just as quickly. Not by any self-control on my part. That's long gone. My eyes snap open, my wrist drops limply back to my side, and I lower my gaze to see his palm clamped over my mouth. Oh, *shit* . . .

That's new.

I shouldn't like it. The firm pressure of his fingers gripped into my cheek shouldn't make me moan again. It shouldn't act like a cheat code, unlocking a secret level that leads straight to where he's working his hand against me, and I definitely shouldn't like it when he leans back and says, "Shhh." My heart smacks rapidly beneath my chest as our eyes lock. He has the gall to smirk darkly. "Don't give us away when my hands are too busy to reach for a weapon."

My legs tremble around his, vision blurring from the sensations he's stirring up with the motions of his fingers. He watches my face for how I react to every stroke and flick and press, and through my own haze I can decipher that his gaze is dark, desirous. I'm at his mercy, but there's no place I'd rather be.

"Is this okay?" he asks, and I don't know what he's asking about specifically, but I'm more turned on than I've ever been. Nerve end-ings that have lain dormant pulse, and ache, and prepare for release.

254 · **SHAILEE THOMPSON**

Everything he's doing feels so good, so I nod beneath his palm, sliding both hands underneath his shirt to grip the small of his back and move with him, grateful for the warmth and soft pressure of his fingers against my lips.

He winces when I dig my nails into his skin during a particularly well-directed stroke of his thumb, shaking his head like it reconfigured something in his brain before he doubles down on the way his thumb works against my clit. Two fingers slide into me and curl up on the way back out in a way that makes me shudder. If an ax burst through the door beside me right now, I think I'd be more disappointed than terrified at this point. Especially when Wes drops his mouth to my neck again, lips and tongue and teeth tracing across my skin, tempting more muffled sounds from my lips. Everything that's happening— what he's doing, what *I'm* doing—it's too much and just enough and genre-defying all at once. I want to cry and laugh and scream and give a giant middle finger to that fucking psycho outside because *See? You haven't ruined everything.*

Every now and then Wes lifts his chin to murmur low words in my ear that have me panting into his hand. The most replay-worthy quotes being: "I'm gonna have dreams about you in this dress for a long time. Taking it off you. Having you keep it on like this . . . Really vivid dreams, Jamie."

Which makes it worth every cent of interest it racked up on my credit card.

"God, you're killing me. You're making me so— Just *watching* you. It's taking everything not to just— *Fuck* . . . you're *killing* me."

I know. God, I know from the way I can feel him pressed against my thigh. I hope we can do this again. I really hope I can help him out with that next time.

"I can't wait to learn every little thing about you. I can't wait to hear what you sound like when we're alone without my hand covering your mouth. Although . . ." He lifts his head to look at me after he says that. The knowing tilt at the corner of his mouth akin to throwing kerosene onto an already raging bonfire. "You might like this, huh?"

Yep, I think I might. I think he has the ability to make me like things I've probably never considered.

And just when I think it can't get any better, when I know I'm *this* close, his thumb stops circling. He just presses it against me, hard, consistent, unyielding, and that's the cue. Roll the tape of rockets blasting off, waves crashing, fireworks igniting, atomic bombs exploding.

My back arches as his mouth rakes up my bared throat, and release flares through my body. Sharp and violent. I shake against him, and for the first time tonight it isn't from fear, as tension and terror leave my body in a rush. All I'm left with is his breath on my face, his fingers stroking slowly, softly, between my legs, and the wet warmth of his skin against my mouth as I gasp into his palm. His grip loosens over my mouth to slide around and cup the side of my face, my chest heaving as I drop my head back against the wall. It's like I've had a hand wrapped around my throat the last few hours, loose enough to let me breathe but tight enough to make it an effort, and now I've been pulled from its grip.

"Jamie?"

I open my eyes and everything is blurry. Wes's voice is concerned. He goes to back away from me and I grip my fingers into his waist to stop him.

"Are you okay? Did I—?"

It's then I feel the warm tears drip down my cheeks and they are . . . very out of place, considering I definitely enjoyed what just happened. If Laurie were here, she'd be able to offer some kind of logical explanation. Chalk it up to a physiological reaction in response to external stimulation and then pin me with a wicked smirk as she let the double meaning of her conclusion settle like blood on vinyl. But while Laurie's and my relationship extends beyond normal boundaries, I would draw the line with her being present, let alone providing commentary, on what just happened.

And so I maintain my hold on Wes, nodding as I direct a teary smile up to him and try to get my breathing under control. He keeps me propped against the wall, wiping away streaks of pink on my cheeks—the usual date night mix of tears and blush and blood—as he slips his other hand out of my underwear and slides it across to my hip, down my thigh. His arm wraps around my waist after he pulls the hem back into place.

"Wes . . ." His name comes out of my mouth throaty and raw, but I don't know what I plan on saying. I don't know if my brain has enough oxygen to form sentences.

"Just breathe, baby."

I follow his directions without too much protest. He is the first officer at the scene, after all, but the new term of endearment doesn't go unmissed. If anything, it makes me feel like I might do that ugly laugh-cry-hiccup most Leading Ladies can get away with, but I know I certainly can't.

"This might be—" he says, his lips falling upon mine in a savoring press before he pulls away and shakes his head, "—the best and worst first date I've ever been on."

That pulls the ugly laugh-cry-hiccup from me. When I can feel my legs again, when my breathing evens out, I lift myself off the support of his thigh and straighten on unsteady feet. Wes doesn't let go.

"Well, I don't usually do that on a first da—"

I tense up when the realization hits me. Like a sharp, discordant scrape of a violin when the audience can see the threat before the characters. We're still in the middle of a horror movie. The only thing I know about Wes is that he's a cop who's good with his hands. It was easy to ignore the rules, to reason they don't apply to us in here, when we'd washed the blood away and locked the door, but now they're coming back in full force and reminding me: "I don't know your last name—" The hand around my throat is back. "I don't even kn—"

"Jamie." His palm moves from my cheek to prop against the wall behind me. The shift brings him just a fraction closer and everything behind him blurs like a vignette. I can't see the safety posters, the shelves, the maintenance supplies. All I can see is him.

"Wes Carpenter," he says. That soft, loaded gaze traces across my face and the pressure in my throat loosens, softens like a caress. "Homicide detective. Badge number 21397. Taurus . . . apparently. I have two younger sisters—they're the ones who told me my star sign is important—and if you made me choose between *The Fast and the Furious* and *Miss Congeniality* . . . Bullock would win."

My shoulders melt back down into place, and I can't help but grin. It's personal, ordinary information unrelated to the life-or-death situation outside. He has a life beyond this. *We* have lives beyond this. We could still get back to them.

I take over wiping away the rest of the tears from my face before planting my palms on his chest, one right over his heart. His heartbeat speeds up just a little beneath my hand when I smile up at him and say, "Jamie Prescott, PhD candidate."

He mirrors the curve of my lips and tilts his head down when I lift mine up to kiss him. I lean away but he follows, our mouths lingering against each other as I disclose, "My student number is the one thing I've never been able to memorize. I'm a proud Scorpio. I have an older sister. You might think Laurie is like my sister, but she's more like my wife." When I open my eyes, I catch the corners of his crinkling in amusement.

"That's not going to change no matter who I date," I warn, because he should know all the fine print before deciding if that's how he'd like this to play out.

"And . . . Bullock always comes out on top."

He kisses me once. "We would've covered at least that on our first date."

Twice. "I don't think we can count this as a first date," I say before he sweeps his lips across mine a third time and then begins to untangle himself from our embrace. "More like a shared traumatic experience."

One we need to escape if we ever want to go on a date with more traditional elements like dinner, a movie, small talk, rather than cardio, first aid, and bloodshed. The janitor's closet gave us a reprieve, but as soon as we leave it'll be like pressing play on a paused scene.

Wes's gaze shifts to the side and I follow it, spotting the bottle of hand sanitizer with the red Flammable Liquid sticker that's caught his attention. He looks back at me, determination etched across his face, and if we were in a movie, his shirt would be—at the very least—artfully ripped to reveal the muscles of his torso. It's a real shame it isn't, but my disappointment is short-lived. Especially when he grabs the bottle from the shelf and gets back to searching the room, calling over his shoulder, "Let's get through this night so I can take you on a real date then."

CHAPTER 31

"I can't believe you're gonna let a few little murders keep us apart. It is a detail!"

—Not *Only You*

When starting a fire to escape a masked killer you need three things: a source of heat, some kind of fuel, and a way to contain it so you don't accidentally go full *Carrie* and burn down the building and yourselves in the process. Dying of smoke inhalation or immolation after all we've been through tonight would be a true form of cruel irony.

Once we straighten out our clothing and wipe away the smudged lipstick, we find a lighter, along with a pretty impressive stash of weed, in an unlocked metal box slid to the back of one of the top shelves. It was half hidden behind an empty mop bucket, and after Wes pulls it down, he pockets the lighter and leaves the pot. It's a sound choice. We've broken enough rules tonight, some more willingly than others, but I think trying to escape while being high as shit is where I must draw the line. The effect of the espresso martinis from earlier in the evening has fully worn off and sobriety increases our chances of survival (thank you, rule nine).

I pass Wes a sleeve of paper towels to act as kindling and he shoves them into the bucket before getting to work on fastening the knife back to his wrist.

"Do you see anything that could be used as a weapon?"

"Your hands are getting pretty full," I say as I toss the bottle of hand sanitizer into the bucket.

"For you, Jamie. Just in case . . ."

He doesn't have to finish the sentence, and I don't want him to. It was nice not having to think about living up to the expectations of the Final Girl for a while. It was nice living in a rom-com instead of a slasher, but we need to go back to the real world even though our real world is unbelievable. Once we walk out that door our roles change again, and I've been without a weapon for too long. My luck is bound to run out.

"Right." I spot the broom the same time he does, and before I ask he's slipping the knife off again. "Do you think you can make me another shaft?"

That draws a chuckle from Wes as he picks up the broom and studies it. The mottled veneer of the wood hints to water damage and he tries breaking it with just his hands. There's a promising crack but no clean break, so he moves across to the sink again, glancing back over his shoulder.

"Jamie, now more than ever is not a time to be using that word."

There's a short, satisfying snap and he turns back holding a rod with an intimidatingly sharp point. I know it's not going to be enough to go up against Heart Eyes, but it's enough to keep him at bay for a while if—*when* we come face-to-face.

"Sorry," I say as I reach for the new weapon. "But you were the one who stopped me from—"

His free arm slips around my waist and pulls me into his chest before I can get too detailed about what I would've done had he let me undo his belt buckle.

"From what?" Wes murmurs, and I make sure I hold his stare, take a second to appreciate the bittersweet-chocolate shade and the way it threatens to make me melt. Not for the first time in these cramped quarters do I forget why we're even in here at all. The rom-com effect is hard to resist. Or maybe it's the post-orgasm effect.

"From making that"—I jut my head toward the wall he had me up against—"a little more mutual."

"Like I said." He ducks his head and I'm already tilting my chin up to him without thinking. It's instinct at this point. "Just wait till I get you out of here. It's not going to be quick, or quiet, and it's going to be very mutual."

His lips fall onto mine, the most innocent of pecks to counteract the heady effect of his statement, and then I'm wrapping my fingers around his shaft . . . the broken one in his hand.

"Thank you." I slide the stake out of his grip and survey his handiwork. "This is the nicest thing a man's ever made me."

And that's true. Women don't need flashy presents like intestine hearts and killing sprees; we just want somebody to make the effort. Cleaning a bleeding gash, fashioning a weapon out of a household item. It's simpler. More personal.

Wes lets go of my waist and works at fastening the knife onto his wrist again, shrugging as he says, "I just want to spoil you, Jamie."

I can't help but laugh at that. At his sense of humor. The fact it's still intact. We really are the same kind of crazy. Maybe that's why we've made it this far.

When his knife is firmly gripped in his fist and the flashlight is in his other hand, I pick up the fire-starting bucket, tighten my hold around the rod, and turn to the locked door. A quick glance at him and I know we're thinking the same thing.

Once we step out into the hallway, we're back in the fray, back in the scene. Out of the frying pan, some might say, but this time the fire could save us.

When we navigate our way out of the janitor's closet, we turn left and head for the back of the building instead of going right in the direction of the dance floor. This path leads to a corridor that runs the same length as the one at the front of the club. Each of the five dark and scary hallways end here, and it's the farthest we've ventured into the club all night. Just like the other floors, there aren't any clearly distinguishable exits, no glowing emergency signs, but before I can get riled up about the numerous code violations this building has, I get distracted by the blood.

So. Much. Blood.

We haven't been down this hallway before and it's *everywhere*. On the walls, on the floor, even on the foggy surfaces of the gas lamps, the red blemishes flickering from the dim light source behind the glass. Some of the blood drags across the walls in intermittent patterns of five lines—five fingers—almost indistinguishable from the wallpaper except for the way it glistens in contrast to the matte finish of the wall. It's not even shocking anymore, and I hope it's not a bad sign about my mental state when I muse it isn't any worse than what we've already witnessed tonight.

Still, it's bad enough.

When the marks start to get bigger, heavier, wetter, the hallway becomes darker. The corridor that leads back to the VIP room where we're supposed to meet Stu, Jennifer, and Dani is lit by the glow of two sconce lights, but past that there's only heavy blackness. A click sounds near my hip and then Wes lifts the flashlight, pointing it ahead of us. The light isn't bright enough to fully illuminate the hallway, but from what I can see it's carnage.

Pure carnage.

Whatever happened down here was violent. Brutal. Deadly.

The cold beam of light picks up more bloodstains and a minefield of broken glass and destroyed furniture. That's why, with a shared look, Wes and I forego walking farther into the darkness. We turn down the corridor that leads back to where we'll meet the others, and Stu comes into view immediately, already standing in front of the doorframe.

Alone.

His knife is crossed over his chest, up near his shoulder like he's ready to bring it down at any moment. He's bouncing on his toes, on edge, and when we're a few feet away Wes reaches out to pull me closer to his side. Stu jerks his head across to us, and that's when I spot the blood spray on his face. It makes his beard glisten like he's sprayed it with glitter. He holds his ground, as we do, but his voice still cuts across the distance between us like an accusation.

"Dani's dead."

Shit.

Wes mutters a stronger curse word as Stu turns and points his knife at us, his voice heavy with fury and frustration and . . . God, he's *terrified*.

"We went to look for the control panel. There were only two offices, or rooms, or whatever down that corridor."

His shoulders shake from the anger and adrenaline of someone who doesn't know how to process something real and devastating that makes you consider your own vulnerability. He's acting like we told him to go there, like he didn't send Wes and me away because he thought we were the biggest liabilities in the group. I think back to when I was first talking to Curtis and recognized the kind of fuel that's powering Stu right now. The kind that explodes. The kind that hurts people on the periphery.

I keep my voice steady as I try to remind him, "You were the one who—"

"This whole place is fucked." His voice is getting louder, but I can't tell if we should be worried or not. I don't know if the killer is within earshot or if he's standing right in front of us. "One room wouldn't open. The handle turned but the door wouldn't budge. Then the other room wouldn't lock, so I told the girls to keep watch, but Jennifer said we should all go in together."

I knew she was smart. *Is*. Is smart.

"And?" Wes asks. He stands on the diagonal, turns his head back and forth between Stu and the space behind us, making sure we're covered on all angles. When I glance down, his grip on the flashlight has changed; it's not overhand anymore. It's not the kind of grip you'd use to direct the light. It's the kind of grip you'd use if you wanted to bludgeon someone who has killed half of your most recent acquaintances.

"And I didn't want to have an argument with her," Stu snaps, and I can't stop myself from lifting the rod from my thigh. Just in case he decides to use that knife he's waving wildly in the air. "We all went in, looked around for-fucking-ever. There was nothing. You were wrong."

"Or you were in the wrong room," I say, but Stu is on a roll.

"It was a stupid fucking plan. So we went back to trying to find an exit."

That wasn't what we agreed on. They were supposed to come back here, but I'm not going to mention it when Stu is just getting more and more irate.

"We walked past a room, and he jumped out and fucking—two knives right in her neck. Me and Jennifer, we just ran."

And that's why Wes and I don't drop our weapons. Stu left with two of the group and came back with none. This isn't the first time, either. It's becoming a pattern. A lethal one.

"So where is she?" I ask, maintaining that same measured tone. Calm and controlled, even though both of those words feel unnatural at this point. Like I've never felt them before. It does nothing, though. Stu's glare could cut through skin.

"Do you have a disorder? I just told you, Dani is—"

"Not Dani." And I can tell if Stu wasn't so riled up Wes would add a "dumbass" for good measure before saying, "Jennifer."

Stu looks around like he's only just realized she isn't there, and if Laurie still had some kind of thing for him, this is the moment where the other shoe would have dropped. This would've been the final red flag. The major ick.

"I don't know." He shakes his head, redirecting the knife away from us and behind him. "We ran in opposite directions. I guess I was faster. I hid in another room, I waited and then I . . ." He stops, looks between the knife Wes holds just above his hip and the stake I'm overtly holding out from my chest. "You don't believe me?"

"No," Wes and I say in unison, and Stu looks genuinely shocked at the answer.

"What the hell? Why not?"

"I don't know, Stu, maybe it's the fact people keep going missing around you."

It's out of my mouth before I can stop myself, and as expected, he doesn't like the inference. He takes a step forward until he's right in front of the doorframe of the VIP room. Which is where we need to go to set the detector off. Where we were going to put our plan in place and finally get out of here. And now he's blocking it.

"That's bullshit," he snarls, stabbing the knife in the space between us. It does a lot for emphasizing his point, but not so much for convincing anyone he isn't a psycho. "You know I'm not the killer. And you wanna know why? Because *you're* the reason this is all happening, Jamie, and I'm at the bottom of the fucking list of people who would do shit for you."

He's not wrong. We've been snapping at each other all night, but when the others were around there was a little bit of restraint. Now that it's just him and his two least favorite people, though, he's like a dog gone rabid. Wes goes to move forward, but I grab his sleeve and pull him back because Stu is too far gone. I can see too much of the whites of his eyes, and there's not a single shred of rationality going through that bearded head right now.

"You need to calm down." Wes's tone is low, a warning, but it doesn't stop Stu's head from jerking toward him, his stare sharp and cold.

"Fuck you," he spits. "If anything, *you're* the one who's doing this shit. And if you aren't? Then your hours are fucking numbered, buddy, because once he finds out about you two, *you're* going to be next. So you need to figure out whether her know-it-all fucking snatch is worth dying for."

I flinch. Wes does, too. The silence that follows Stu's statement is deafening, because even among the rage, he's hit on something that we know is true. Or at least *I* know it's true.

It never ends well for the love interest.

Stu's stare drops to where I'm gripping Wes's sleeve before he lets out a cold scoff, his arms opening wide, the boning knife still held firmly in his hand. "But, no, go ahead. If you guys think it's me, then maybe I should jus—"

We don't get to find out what Stu plans to do because before he can enlighten us, there's movement just inside the doorframe. The darkness is pierced by a glint of silver, and then an ax swings down into his skull.

CHAPTER 32

"If for some reason, underneath all that strength and confidence, you still don't trust that you are killable enough, I'm living proof . . . that you're wrong."

—Not *Bros*

*I*t's like watching one of those Hot Lumberjack TikToks where they don't manage to chop the wood all the way through on the first go.

Stu lets out a groan similar to those made by the frustrated, shirtless, bearded men Laurie follows across her socials and drops to his knees. The ax is still lodged in his head, blood pouring onto his plaid shirt and wiping out the white stripes when he falls facedown to the ground.

It's a regular "Here's Johnny" moment, but in lieu of Jack Nicholson peeking through the splintered remains of a door, Heart Eyes practically floats into the hallway to look at his handiwork. The gray oversized dinner jacket he's been wearing all night is stained, drenched in burgundy blood that blends in perfectly with the dark red of the wallpaper. It glistens on the black coveralls, too, like an oil spill, the fabric visible between the V of the jacket as it stretches across his chest. He steps over Stu's back, leans down, and wraps his gloved hand around the throat of the ax. The sound of the blade being jostled out of Stu's skull is loud enough to reach us, and I taste digested espresso martini.

When he finally gets the ax out and straightens, he looks between us, his head tilting down to where I'm holding Wes's arm and can't make myself let go. He looks up and I see those two heart-shaped holes head-on, staring straight at me, and even though I can't distinguish anything but black within them, I know. I know what he must think. So when Wes turns, using his body to push me back the way we came, I yank his shirt and pull him along with me. Because Heart Eyes isn't going to lodge that ax into his Leading Lady. Not yet anyway. But Wes? Wes is his rival. Another obstacle he needs to cut through to get to me. And that's why I make sure my strides are a little shorter than his, let him get ahead of me, as we haul ass out of there.

I don't look back to see if he's following us. Not when my shoulder smacks against the corner of the hallway and not when pain throbs heavily down my arm as I push away from the wall, spying blood that isn't my own on my collarbone. Wes slows down enough to bring his right arm around my back, pulling me into line with him as we head for the darkness and the debris we avoided earlier. It's the only option we have. Even if we were able to make it back to the janitor's closet, there isn't anything there to help us, and that ax will get through a wooden door a lot easier than Stu's skull. The beam of Wes's flashlight illuminates a few feet ahead of us, granting just slightly better visibility than the rest of the club, but even then I still miss the first piece of glass that slices the side of my foot.

"Ah!"

The flashlight moves closer to my side and half of the corridor goes black.

"Jamie? Are y— *Fuck!*"

The dull thud of a body hitting a resisting force sounds next to me and the flashlight jostles, hits the side of the bucket I've got a death grip on, and falls, casting the left side of the corridor in light. Instead of the bloodstained walls I was expecting, a large pile of wood and velvet and a mishmash of other materials and textures spills down the wall from ceiling to floor. Furniture and chairs are stacked almost six feet high against the wall. Wes reaches for the flashlight on the floor, and I use the short break to check that the glass didn't go all the way into my foot. When my fingers come away from smooth, wet, sticky skin, I step back and breathlessly survey the structure in front of us. The way it's been placed doesn't make sense if they were trying to blockade the hallway. They've stacked too many pieces of furniture on one side and left the other clear enough for people to walk through in single file.

"What the fuck?" Wes wheezes, aiming the light directly on the structure. He tries to straighten but lets out a pained breath at the effort and I figure at the very least he's winded himself from the impact with the barricade. Worst-case scenario he's broken a rib.

"Do you think someone tried to block Heart Eyes with this?" I ask, reaching for Wes, sliding the handle of the bucket onto my elbow and latching on to his arm to pull him close. When he winces at the movement, I think we might have the worst-case scenario.

"If they did, I don't think it worked. Are you hurt?"

I whip my head around to the darkness behind us and try to see if there's a figure stalking through it, but I find it empty. That wouldn't be his style. Heart Eyes prefers to strike when we least expect it. The slow walk is just meant to build the fear, build the expectation of what he could do to us. That what he could do next is always worse than the kill before.

"It's nothing." Just blood pouring out of my feet. "Are you okay?"

He nods, even though his eyebrows are still furrowed in pain, cheeks pallid.

"I'm fine; let's go."

We run from the half-made barricade and I try to avoid the parts of the floor that glimmer. After the fifth or sixth piece of glass shreds the skin of my feet, I can almost ignore the shards altogether. It's when the darkness ahead of us dissolves into a warm burgundy glow that I know we're getting to the end of this path. Soon we'll be in the hallway where I hid from Heart Eyes the first time. Back to where he first made his romantic intentions clear. Then I spy something propped up against the end of the hall and I remember what the others had said they'd found down here.

Campbell.

What was the last thing I'd said to him? *Stay in the corner and keep your back to the wall.* I never imagined that that would be the way we'd find him. When we reach him, my feet numb, both arms throbbing, Wes's breath audibly restricted, I can't just run past. The way Heart Eyes has left him demands to be seen. This is the most posed body I've witnessed tonight, and that's how I know it was meant to be another gift.

I'm pretty sure if Laurie, Jennifer, and I had turned left instead of right when we left the VIP room earlier in the night we would have discovered this. Him. Campbell's head droops low onto his chest like he's had too many Kamikazes. The rest of his body is ramrod straight, pinned like a butterfly on display against the wall. And if the sight of the two knives shoved deep into the skin under his collarbones—more under his ribs and throughout his torso—isn't confronting enough, the bouquet of roses braced between his bloody stomach and his tied hands certainly is.

We need to set that fire.

We need to get out of here.

"Come on," Wes urges, and slips the flashlight back into his pocket, his hand encircling my elbow and pulling me back down the hallway. The bucket hits against my thigh as we pass each VIP room, poking our heads in and trying to catch sight of a smoke detector. Just as I'd suspected, the building is grossly lacking in appropriate fire safety, and it's only when we get closer to the mezzanine that we spot one at the edge of the hallway that runs behind the booths. The one where I found Laurie and her cat-covered ass all those years ago. The one Laurie, Jennifer, and I ran down earlier in the night after I saw Heart Eyes for the first time. It's a full-circle moment.

It feels like the final act now. Like we could avoid the face-to-face with the Big Bad once we set off the alarms. Maybe it doesn't have to play out like the movies. Maybe the front of the club will burst open just when we need it, and emergency services actually will get here in time. I won't have to go up against Heart Eyes. I won't need to take on this role he's been determined to put me in since he spotted me tonight, and finally, *finally*, this will be over.

"All right." Wes digs into his pocket for the lighter and I notice the tight, pursed line of his mouth as the move pulls at his injured ribs. "Let's do this."

He's holding it together, but I know he's working on pure adrenaline at this point, so I douse the paper towels with hand sanitizer, leaving one sleeve to act as the go-between for the flame to reach the fuel in the bucket as we stride toward the detector. He flicks the lighter on while we're still moving, before we've made it out to the intersection of the hallways, but the scrape of the spark wheel is drowned out by something else. Soft, quick steps from around the corner, near the mezzanine. They get louder and then—

"Jamie! Wes!"

I drop the bucket and swing the stake over my shoulder like a softball bat. Wes's knife comes up in the same instant and the flame of the lighter extinguishes as his hand reaches for the butt of a gun that isn't holstered at his hip. If this were a horror movie, we'd make the perfect image for the poster, but then my brain processes who is standing in front of us.

"Jennifer," I breathe, dropping the stake back down to my side.

She's still holding the first aid kit, her brown hair tangled in a low bun, finger-combed into a messy, effortless twist that somehow still looks good. She looks like every Final Girl I've ever studied: tense, tired, but radiant with the kind of badass inner glow you can only get from being sick of the killer's shit. And this is another promising development.

There are two of us. Three with Wes. Four, because Laurie is *definitely* outside. Maybe more than four since there's so many of the daters unaccounted for. We've lost so many people, but some of us are still left and we're going to get out of here. Together. It's not going to be just one Final Girl draped exhaustedly over the side of a boat or laughing hysterically in the bed of a pickup truck. And the promise that Heart Eyes's plans are going to fall to shit is the happy ending we all deserve.

"You're okay?" The laugh that falls out of her mouth isn't shocked like Stu's was, it's relieved. "Oh my god. Thank god you're alive. And you found everything to set off the alarms."

I can't even respond. I can't find the words to convey just how relieved I am that she's okay, too. Not when I spot a figure behind her.

"Billie?"

My god, I almost forgot about her. She's been gone for so long and now she's leaning against the railing just like when we first came up to this level. From the way she leans into the rail with her hip, her legs crossed casually at her ankles, I'd think our nights had played out in two very different ways since she left. I glance down and notice the dark stains all over the black material of her pants, the way her chestnut-brown hair is more tousled than before. Maybe not so different then.

"Can't say I'm surprised you're still around," she quips. Her bored stare moves to Wes. "You're a different story, though."

I can tell our time away from each other hasn't made the heart grow fonder, but Wes and I are too exhausted and injured to get offended. We've all spent enough time with Billie tonight to know what she's like.

"Billie said she's found an exit." Jennifer turns back to us as Billie pushes off the rail and moves forward, her steps unhurried.

"You found an *exit*?" I ask, shifting my attention between her slow, nonchalant walk and Jennifer's tense, adrenalized stillness.

"Uh-huh."

I'm struck by the way she seems so unaffected by the prospect of an escape. She looks exactly like she did when she found out five people had died in the time it took her to hide behind a velvet curtain, and I feel like there should be some variation in her reaction to two starkly different scenarios.

"Why are you still here?" I blurt out. She said herself she wasn't going to get slaughtered for anyone. Staying behind and putting herself in danger of coming face-to-face with Heart Eyes seems like a real contradiction to that.

"Because we're in this together, right?"

The sentence is so . . . *not* Billie. I'm shocked.

"Where is it, then?" Wes asks, more focused on the prospect of getting out than Billie apparently having a lobotomy in the time she broke away from the group. "How do we get out?"

"I'll show you," she says lightly. "There's only one way to get out of here."

How does she know that?

"We should still set off the detector, right?" Jennifer says to no one in particular. "To get the police here faster?"

The promise of escape has made her fidgety, and she swings the first aid kit in front of her like it's a cute purse she wants someone to comment on.

"I don't think we want to do that," Billie says as she keeps strolling forward. My eyes are drawn down to where her hand is shoved awkwardly into her pocket, clenched in a fist, and . . . it doesn't look right.

"Why not?" Jennifer asks, her brow quirking up in an exasperated swoop as Billie steps up to her shoulder.

"Because this isn't over yet."

The hairs on the back of my neck stand up like someone's gotten too close and breathed on my skin when her hand darts out of her pocket. There's a second when I know what she's going to do. A second when my breath gets caught in my throat as I try to sound the first syllable of Jennifer's name. But it's a second too late when Billie swipes her fist across Jennifer's neck. There's a glint of silver, a red line that appears on Jennifer's throat, and then every nerve in my body ignites in terror as I watch her bleed.

It's so quick. It's so skilled. Jennifer only has the chance to take one soundless breath before the wound gushes and she collapses to the ground. It brings me right back down to the basement, to Curtis and the matching arc on his neck before he bled out all over the table. Back to the kill that started it all. I've been trying to block it out of my mind the whole night, but now it's right in front of me again. Like a classic flashback.

Wes swears, and all I can do is gape at the woman standing at ease in a slowly growing pool of blood, a switchblade in one hand as the other reaches behind her and pulls a wad of pink material—the woolen mask I've become too familiar with—out of her back pocket and into view.

Billie tilts her head to the side, letting the mask unfurl until those heart-shaped holes are staring straight at me, and for the first time since we met I watch a slow smile spread across her face.

"Is the movie playing out like you thought it would, Jamie?"

CHAPTER 33

"You don't murder someone you can live with, you murder the person you cannot live without."

—Not *P.S. I Love You*

I should've known this was going to happen. It's when you think you're safe that the twist comes.

And what a twist.

Billie. *Billie.* "The night is still young," "It's always the quiet ones" Billie.

Wes shifts in front of me, the hand on his hip reaching back to keep me at bay, but I lean out around his shoulder. I don't want to take my eyes off her. Not after that kind of reveal, not after the skill she's shown severing someone's carotid artery without flinching. Without blinking.

"Billie—"

"Well, if it isn't our resident policeman." There's an unnerving smirk on her face as she discards the mask onto the ground. It soaks up Jennifer's blood, but the dark chuckle that emits from where Billie stands draws my attention away from the way the pink is turning maroon. "Jennifer couldn't wait to tell me. You really kept that on the down-low, didn't you?"

The amused expression on her face doesn't shift as she bends down and pulls at her pants leg, revealing a handle sticking out the top of her boot. She deftly pulls the stained kitchen knife from where it's pressed against her calf and brings it to her side. The switchblade is steady in her other hand, feet planted on the ground, and it's a familiar stance. All she needs is the oversized jacket and the coveralls, a machete instead of a switchblade, and it'd be a remake of what we saw downstairs at the end of the bathroom hallway. The one John ran toward so Wes and I could get away.

"It's not a great first impression to lie on a first date, Wes. How are you supposed to trust someone if they hide who they are right off the bat? Right, Jamie?"

The way she can still speak in a dry, unaffected tone is terrifying. Emotions have been high all night. All of us have gone through a Technicolor spectrum of fear and shock and rage and—okay, maybe not all of us—horniness, but she hasn't. She never did. Even when she left, she was levelheaded in her retreat, but now I realize that kind of calm can only come from knowing you're in control.

"Put the weapons down," Wes says slowly, calmly, but I know it's purely for show. I can hear it in the tightness of his voice and see it in the tension in his shoulders, the tick of the muscle at the back of his jaw.

Billie shakes her head, tiptoeing over Jennifer's body and the pool spreading out around it like she's sidestepping a puddle on the street. The blood seeps out across the carpet and to the vinyl flooring that's closer to the railing, sinking into the former and settling across the latter. It looks like a perfect coat of nail polish.

"You know I'm not going to do that."

The muscles of Wes's back flinch underneath his shirt as she moves, but the knife stays steady in his hand.

"I have to apologize that I'm not dressed the part. I left my little ensemble downstairs, and the coveralls were getting a bit . . . messy after everything. Anyway, I figure we know each other so well by this point that we can do away with the mystery, right? So! What comes next?" She directs that question at me, and not for the first time tonight I feel ill-equipped to be in this situation. She and Wes are more evenly matched. Cop against criminal. Hero against villain. But still, despite her goading, the fact remains: she made me the center of this. I have top billing. So that's why I move to Wes's side before he can stop me, slipping in next to him so we're shoulder to shoulder.

"If we follow your theory, Jamie, Wes is definitely going to die." She winks as she shoots him a sarcastic pout and then points the still-dripping switchblade at me. "And then it'll just be you. The *Final Girl*, right?"

The way she says it, like that isn't the ending she has planned and it's stupid to even think that, makes me study her. She's followed the formula almost to the letter. All night she's been trying to push me into the spotlight, but what I just can't understand is *why* she's the killer, *what's* driven her to do this.

"You're not in love with me."

I don't say it like a question. Even before this, she looked at me like I was something disgusting on the bottom of her shoe. Though that might not be the right descriptor, since she doesn't seem to be concerned by the thick, congealed wine-colored substance lapping at the edges of her boots.

She scoffs. "Maybe you're not a total idiot."

"But this is still about me. That's my name on the dance floor, isn't it?"

I point to it over her shoulder, but she's not dumb enough to follow the gesture. Her little smirk does drop, though. Very quickly.

"You're just a means to an end."

She says it more to herself than to me, and it's . . . it's baffling.

"Then why? Why the flowers and the hearts and the *rose petals*?"

She puffs up when I mention all the little tokens she's been leaving behind all night. Flinches like it's a sore spot. So I keep scratching at the wound. See if I can get her to launch into a motive-reveal monologue that will kill some time and help me figure out if we have a *Single White Female* or a *Scream 4* situation on our hands. Maybe distract her enough so we can get the upper hand.

"Why go to all that effort? Why not just kill me?"

Her gaze sharpens when I ask the final question, her grip visibly tightening on her blades.

"Oh, I'm going to kill you." The matter-of-fact statement is like a noose around my neck, my breathing restricted as quickly as Wes steps in front of me again. "I just can't kill you *yet*. Like I said, it's not over. Not until we see if you can make it to the end. But I'm sure you'll be a disappointment, just like the others, and then I'll be the one."

"The one what?"

"*The One*. The one who h—"

Wes lunges forward before she can finish, the flashlight back in one hand and his knife brandished in the other, but even with his size and skills and reflexes, he's no match for Billie, who's been doing this all night. She's warmed up, and when she swipes the switchblade in front of her, I swear I can hear the slice of his skin and a grunt that hints to a kind of pain much harder to come back from than an accidental graze.

No. *No, no, no.*

Wes drops to his knees, and when Billie charges toward him with the kitchen knife aimed at his chest, the next part happens so quickly I can't even be sure it's real. I'm already moving forward by the time he goes down, holding the stake with two hands, drawing it back over my shoulder, and I just . . . swing. Front heel down, rear elbow in line with shoulder, eyes on point of contact, as if Wes has brought me to a batting cage for our first date and I want to show him how good I was when I played softball in high school.

And the thing is, I *was* really good. I had to be. How else would I convince my parents to let me watch wildly inappropriate horror as a teenager if I didn't maintain a well-rounded lifestyle to prove said films didn't have any impact on my mental health?

Billie looks up at just the right time and the rod makes contact with her nose. It folds beneath the wood, blood bursting from her face like a firework, so much that it coats her skin like a mask.

One that could rival the disguise she's been wearing all night.

The force sends her backward into the puddle of Jennifer's blood. The blades fall out of her hands, both palms come up to clasp her nose, and a scream sounds from somewhere in the middle of the cherry juice stain that is her face. She slips wildly across the puddle, the blood slick against the bottom of her shoes, and then she loses her footing completely, falling back into the guardrail and— I was right about that railing being too low.

She's gone before I can gasp, and the sound of her hitting the floor below is just as foreign as anything I've heard tonight. Heavy and unnatural and followed by a silence that sounds so conclusive, I don't know if I want to check to see where she landed. *How* she landed. I'll have to, though. As soon as I can drag my eyes away from the rod in my hand. It's stained ruby red in contrast to the white of my knuckles, and embedded in the end of the wood is a—yeah, a tooth. I must have caught her mouth on the upward swing.

"Jamie?"

The strain in Wes's voice pulls my gaze from the stake in my hand, and when I turn he's still on the ground. Slumped over. His knife is hanging from his wrist, flashlight on the floor, one hand on his ribs and the other pressed into his chest.

I can't swallow away the tightness in my throat, I can't stop my hands from shaking, but when he doesn't move to get up I make myself rush toward him. I fall to his side, dropping the stake and ignoring the way my knees make the blood seep out of the carpet. My bare foot accidentally touches Jennifer's elbow and I jerk it away.

"Wes—" When I get him to straighten, I see red.

She got him on the other side of his chest from where Dani cut him earlier in the night, slicing right through the material of his shirt and across his pec in a horizontal line that stops above his heart. His shirt is already soaked. It's deeper than the cut he had before, but once the noise in my brain dies down, I can see it's similar to the one on my arm. He could do with some stitches, but a bandage would hold him over until we can get out of here.

He'll live. He'll live, and that's all that matters.

"She was going to stab me," he breathes. I think he's in shock. "She was aiming for my chest and . . . If you hadn't— If you didn't—"

"Hold on." I push away from him, circle around Jennifer and the blood that's settled back into an even untouched pool after Billie's fall, and make myself look down to where she fell. It only takes half a glance for me to know I don't have to follow rule ten—down doesn't mean dead: double tap.

It's a classic Disney villain death if I ever saw one. She landed on top of the bar at the edge of the dance floor, and the way her . . . the way she . . . She's dead. *Dead* dead.

What I can't figure out is how *this* is the end.

Wes is still bleeding out behind me, so I move over to where Jennifer dropped the first aid kit and rip it open, extracting the first roll of gauze my fingers land on. There's no time for touchy-feely disinfectant.

"Open your shirt."

Wes complies with difficulty, and when I tear my eyes away from the gash across his chest, I can tell why. My eyes start to burn. There's mottled bruising along his ribs, other bruises as well, and the bandage on his pec has bled through at some point. He's endured so much damage trying to keep us alive. My fingers start to tremble as I work at winding the bandage around his chest. I try to solve the enigma of Billie being Heart Eyes in an effort not to focus on all his injuries. This whole time I assumed it was a man. I may have momentarily played with the idea that Billie could be the killer earlier in the night, but that was before the brutality I've witnessed. The strength required to pull the ax out of Stu, pin Campbell to the wall, gut the guy at the end of the hall . . . *How* has she managed that all by herself?

"It doesn't make sense," I murmur before tying off the dressing in a crude knot.

"What doesn't make sense?" Wes pants, buttoning up his shirt before I can figure out whether the black pointed lines of the tattoo creeping over his shoulder are connected to the similar-looking ones high on his ribs that peek out under the bottom of the bandage. It's an observation rather than any kind of appreciation at this point; there's no time for being "afraid and horny." Not when there's a growing feeling, a telltale pull warning me this isn't over yet.

"This. *Her*. It just doesn't make sense."

She made it very clear she hated me, so there goes my "anything for love" theory, but still: the roses, the messages, the pure theatricality of every kill. All that effort requires a motivator. A driving force. I've never done anything that would lead to the accidental death of one of Billie's loved ones. I've never so much as stolen a parking spot from someone let alone done anything that would warrant revenge. Everything has been too meticulously planned for her to have been driven by mindless bloodlust. So what reason is left?

"Jamie, we still need to find a way out of he—" Wes tries to stand and immediately looks like he might throw up. "Okay . . ." His eyebrows shoot high up on his forehead as he huffs, "*Fuck* . . . Jamie, could you help m—"

"Sorry. Yeah." I shift back on my heels, push them firmly into the damp carpet as we both work to pull him to his feet. It's a struggle. Wes swears some more until he's upright; then, after some recuperative breathing, he resituates the knife back into his hand.

We could very well be the last ones standing, and I need him armed if my gut feeling is right and this is a false ending. I always feel safe when he's around, and when he's not, that's when—

The thought stops me.

I always feel safe when he's around.

But what about the times when he wasn't? Those times he left the group. When he was doing that hero shit I found so frustrating. That's when Heart Eyes first appeared. Suddenly it clicks. Why Billie being the sole person responsible for tonight doesn't add up.

Because the first time I saw Heart Eyes, when he showed me just what he was capable of by butchering a man at the end of a hallway somewhere deep in the labyrinth behind us, Billie was down in the basement with Wes. She couldn't have done that kill if she was with him the whole time.

She couldn't have done that unless . . .

It's not over, not until we see if you can make it to the end.

"*We.*"

Because there's always—

"Two," I murmur.

# CHAPTER 34

"Murder me, because I'd like to date you."

—Not *The Proposal*

I wasn't wrong. This night has been following the slasher formula perfectly. Sometimes a killer needs someone to help see their plan to fruition. Teamwork makes the dream work.

"You'll be a disappointment, just like the others, and then I'll be the One."

The One. It seems we're back in rom-com territory, because who better to assist a psycho in their murderous love quest than another psycho who wants to prove they're their perfect match?

"Jamie?"

I look up and see Wes a few feet away from me. I've backed away and didn't even know it. My stake is at his feet, and I should grab it, but he's closer. He's armed and he's staring right at me, chest heaving, eyebrow quirked expectantly.

When it's not two bros bonding over a massacre (if we ignore the homoerotic overtones in *Scream*), there's a whole catalog of slashers where a woman tasks a lovelorn suitor with the heavy lifting of their killing spree. It always backfires, of course, and there's some confrontation where the suitor becomes disposable after they've served their purpose. Despite their undying love, they meet a gruesome end . . . like dying on top of a pressed-metal bar.

"There's always two," I say again. Louder, more forceful. Pain spears through one of my fingers. My hands are gripped so tight one of my nails—that have held up well given the circumstances—bends and breaks. They're not the only thing holding on by a thread.

"Billie couldn't have done all of this alone."

And she wouldn't have. Not for me. And it *has* always been about me.

Wes pauses, his face hard as he presses his palm against his ribs again, like he's steeling himself—or is he just upset that his role in this may be revealed too soon? Was that why he attacked Billie? Because she was about to give away the ending?

After a stunted breath he nods. "I agree. That's why we need to—"

"What?"

I can't make my tone soft. I can't revert to the way I usually talk to him. The way I was always tempted to speak quieter to make him lean in because I liked having him in my space. Because having him close made my pulse race and my skin prickle, and—what if I was just misreading all of that? What if I've misread *everything*?

He's breathing heavily now, and I can't tell if it's from his ribs or if it's because I'm uncovering the plot a little too early for his liking. Before he can take this from slasher back to rom-com. There aren't any roses or messages to accompany this latest kill, and that's off-brand.

"We need to stick to the plan and set off the alarms." His voice is raspier than it has been the entire night. He makes sure he looks me right in the eye, doesn't dare to blink, and that should put me at ease, but the effect of "attraction under aversive conditions" has fully dissolved now. We are firmly removed from "afraid and horny" and right on into "blinded by fear."

"We need to set them off to let people know we're here."

"Or so you can draw the others out?" I ask, and watch as comprehension crosses his eyes. He straightens, winces, starts to shake his head even as I take another step away. "So that it can just be you and me? So that we get the right ending?"

When it comes to Wes, I have never not felt safe. Not until now. Not now that I look back on the night with the knowledge there are two killers and realize Wes had the means and the opportunity to commit at least half of these murders. Not when I'm disgusted with myself because I should have known better than to be seduced by some nice words and unbroken eye contact. I know you never trust the love interest. I *know* that.

"Jamie, you're scared. You're not—"

"Do *not* tell me I'm not thinking straight."

He doesn't. Instead, he starts talking to me in that coaxing murmur again, but this time it just makes my stomach twist sharply.

"I'm scared, too."

I haven't known him long enough for my heart to break, but that thread that's been pulling me toward him certainly threatens to snap because it is *so* unfair, cruel even, to use that voice on me right now.

"Jamie, *please*—" My breath stops when he reaches for me, and even when I step back again, I can't force the next inhale down past my throat. I try to recall the way Billie and Wes have interacted all night to see if there was something I missed. Something that will act as clear evidence in determining his innocence or his guilt, but all I can see is that calculated smirk and wink before he ran for her. And the more I think about those facial expressions, the more warped they become in my mind until she may as well have been standing on a London stoop in the snow holding a cardboard sign that says To Me, Wes Is the Perfect Accomplice. When we were first on this mezzanine, when he was patching up my arm and we were discussing our theories, he said the killer was doing this for the One. Billie *just* said that was what she wanted to be.

The singular, perfect, predestined One.

They *both* said it.

"I know so much crazy shit has happened," Wes pants, dropping his hand to his ribs when I don't reach back for him. His shoulders rise and fall with the force of his breaths, and I can't figure out if this is him getting riled up. Is he getting ready to put that knife in my chest if I reject him?

"But you need to trust m—"

"No, I don't." I stare at him as blood rushes between my ears, syncopated with the sound of someone breathing in quick, short, panicked pants. Me. *I'm* the one who's about to hyperventilate, but I also feel kind of removed from it. Removed from all of it. "I don't *need* to trust you."

I don't know what to do. For the first time tonight, I have no idea what the next logical step is. Even when I was being chased and cornered and terrorized, there was always *something* that would come to mind, but now everything is blurred by panic and hurt and shame and . . . What if it *is* him?

Less than an hour ago, he had me pressed against a wall and . . . Oh my *god*. The rules *do* apply. We had something close to sex and now I'm going to die.

"Please, Jamie." He looks at me with this crestfallen face that compels me to move back to him, to consider that maybe this is an overreaction, but I'd rather overreact than end up dead because I assumed a man who kissed me wasn't capable of killing me.

"I just want us to get out of here . . . I don't want anyone else to get hurt."

I'm tempted to retort that if he wants that he should stop hurting people, but I can't make my mouth work. I don't know what to do.

I can't keep standing here. I can't fight him. So that leaves me only one option.

Understanding dawns across his face, panic fills his eyes when he realizes my intention.

"Jamie, don't . . ."

The last time he said that he ended up kissing me three seconds later, but this time I'm running away before he can move toward me. We're in the third act now and alliances mean shit here, even if they're sealed with a kiss, because the thing about being a Final Girl?

They always end up alone.

I don't stop.

Not when I pass the hallway where I first saw Heart Eyes and spy the body still discarded at the end of it, or when the cuts in my feet open up again and make each step unbearable. Not until I find myself in the hallway John must've turned down earlier in the night and see the stairs that brought him back to us on the dance floor. I don't go down them; I don't want to go anywhere near the dance floor, but I have a clear exit if Wes comes looking for me.

The idea he *could* come looking for me—hunt for me—makes the espresso martinis threaten to make a full reappearance. I push myself up against the wall and force myself to breathe. I need a clear head and my full aerobic abilities to figure out how the hell I'm going to end this once and for all.

Because I *am* going to end it. I have to. I can't deny it any longer. The movie only concludes when the lead fully embodies their character arc, when the Leading Lady gets her man, or the Final Girl . . . well, she gets her man, too.

They always do.

But, an insidious voice at the edge of my mind reminds me, *you are not them.*

I'm not the jaded, levelheaded Final Girl and I'm not the plucky, free-spirited Leading Lady.

Right now, I'm just a woman trying to survive the night.

And even before this I've just been trying to survive in a world that wants women to play the role of one of a few outdated archetypes. It's taken a lifetime to learn how to tread the line between "not enough" and "too much," years to memorize what it takes to be a Leading Lady and a Final Girl, and one night to force me to choose whether I'm capable of being either . . .

I really would be one of a kind if I could be both.

One of a kind and just my type.

The sound of Wes's exasperated, awed voice is hard to forget, and I press my palm against my chest as it tightens at the memory. I hear an unnatural crackle and slip my fingers into the neckline to touch paper. The two match cards are still in my bra and I pull them out, trying to make my trembling fingers straighten the sweat-dampened cards without ripping them. I alternate between the one with the male names and the one with the female names to try to figure out who I know is gone and who could still be out somewhere in the club. The familiar names conjure a montage of brutal scenes, an "in memoriam" of who isn't making it out of this club.

Curtis
Drew
Colette
John
Campbell
Dani
Stu

Jennifer
Billie

Then there's the woman we found next to Drew. The guy at the end of the corridor.

Eleven people.

Then there's the "others." The ones I haven't seen since the speed dates, the ones who, I hope, are hiding if they're not the two bodies we found.

Lee, Michael, Jason, Ari, Nia, Niamh, Ellen, and Shelley.

Not to mention the host, the two bartenders, and the coat check attendant. If I get out of here I'll learn their names, I'll commit them all to memory, because they deserve more than being an unnamed victim at the end of the call sheet.

I move past Laurie's name when I catch it under my own on the match card. I can't think about her right now unless it's the mantra I've been repeating over and over since I watched her slide through that vent: she's okay. She's outside. She's getting help and soon we'll be back together relinquishing last cans of sparkling water and arguing over my dissertation.

God, my dissertation. To think that was the biggest concern in my life a few hours ago, and now I'm using those years of research to work my way through a real-life slasher. If I get out of here—*when* I get out of here—I will just write the damn thing. I'm not going to doubt my ability to write about genre theory ever again. That's for damn sure.

Slipping the male date card back on top, I see Wes's name. I brush my thumb across the ink and tears pool at the edges of my eyes when I think of the way he kissed me, touched me. How even after I ran away from him, I can't fully convince myself he's the one who's doing this. I can't even begin to comprehend how stupid it is that I'm crying over a *boy* while there's a killer on the loose. Especially if the boy and the killer are the same damn person. But now that the panic frenzy has passed, now that I've had a moment to breathe and I can push the image of Billie's body splayed across the bar out of my head . . .

I release a breath.

There is a pretty good chance I might've fucked up.

Wes was right next to me when Heart Eyes lodged an ax in Stu's skull and then wrenched it back out. Billie couldn't have physically accomplished that. She definitely wasn't as tall and broad as whoever did.

While the part of me that's been able to recall so many slasher scenes tonight insists I can't fully discount Wes until the killer is unmasked, I can't ignore the feeling in my gut that tells me it's *not* him. Not when my brain brings other images of Wes to the forefront of my mind; pleasant, rose-colored recollections of what he's said and done tonight that makes the hook in my chest pull.

You're my type, Jamie. You're one of a kind and just my type.

What if my complex has led me to believe a man is more likely to murder me than want to be with me?

That's when I know I must be crazy. Because I'm not just afraid he could be the one who's committed all these murders tonight; I'm afraid that if my intuition and my eye-fucking preferences are correct, I might have just messed up my chances at that real date if we get out of here. And right now, I can't tell which would be worse.

So instead, I focus on trying to figure out how many men are still left.

Because I'm certain Billie would only be doing this with a man— *for* a man. That, I would stake my life on. She proved time and again tonight that she wasn't a girl's girl, and she said it herself: after she killed me, *she* was going to be the One.

It's a concept I'm more than familiar with, and when I think about the way Billie called me a means to an end, a disappointment waiting to happen, I know Wes and I were right. Billie thought—the other killer *thinks*—they're in a rom-com. I just don't think Billie was happy with her role.

That makes two of us, I think, but before I can keep feeling sorry for myself, movement at the bottom of the stairs pulls my eyes from the card, draws my heart up into my throat. A shadowy figure blends in with the darkness. An abstract silhouette that wouldn't be out of place in *Lights Out*, and I can't help but think it would be the cherry on top of the never-ending shit sundae of this night if I have to start dealing with a goddamn haunting as well as a killer. The shape moves up the stairs, becomes more human, and I have to stop thinking this shit into existence because as the shadow ascends each step I realize . . .

It's John.

CHAPTER 35

"I wanted to kill you. I wanted to kill you so badly."

—Not *You've Got Mail*

*J*ohn.

Last seen running chest first into who I now suspect was a machete-wielding Billie in a commendable act of self-sacrifice.

I am dumbstruck as he stumbles up the stairs toward me, the neckline of his shirt gaping. The material over his left shoulder, the whole sleeve, has turned cherry red from the wound I'd tried to stanch earlier. Even if he could manage to get the stain out, he'll never be able to wear this shirt again because there's a long slash down the torso.

It's the artful kind of tear I wished I'd seen across Wes's shirt before Billie actually gave him one. The exposed skin beneath reveals John is . . . more than lean. He's strong. Muscular. So much so the word "misleading" comes to mind when I think about how he looked at the beginning of the night. Everything that's happened so far has taken away any desire to be horny in this kind of situation, but I do reconsider the "belongs in a lecture hall" category I placed him in. Especially since I realize after quite a delay that he's *alive*.

He quickens his steps as I gape at him, stopping a safe distance away, always mindful of personal space, and sighs, "Jamie, you're okay."

"John . . . We— I thought—" I thought he was dead. He should be dead.

Even with how pale he is, even with how he winces with any movement of his arm, that crooked smile pulls up the corner of his mouth.

"I thought so, too."

He *should* be dead, though. He ran into a fucking machete. He should be lying in pieces downstairs, but he isn't and it's impossible.

"What— *How . . .*"

He moves closer, his injured arm extending and cupping my face with his palm. There's a swoop and pull in my gut as the divining rod I thought was finely tuned finally kicks in.

Oh . . . Oh, *no.*

"It's okay," John murmurs, his gaze imploring, his hold on my face tightening as he steps into me. *Leans* in. I'm hit with a cloying, semi-familiar smell and it makes my breath catch when I place it, like someone's spilled a cocktail down my back. My body goes rigid against his, heart thumping behind my ribs, blood rushing in the space between my ears.

"It's okay," he says again, wiping his thumbs across my cheeks because tears are falling freely. I hadn't even realized I was crying. His hand is soft and warm against my skin, and the touch makes me aware that I'm not just crying. I'm shaking.

"John, you—"

My brain finally catches up with my body.

"You did this for me," I manage to choke out, scared stiff against the wall. His steel-blue gaze holds my own, eyes crinkled in that entreating stare. He wants to kiss me. I can tell by the way his thumb strokes down my cheek, how his gaze drops to my trembling lips, and I know, to the very core of my being, I do *not* want him to.

"No, Jamie," he says before he captures my lips in a soft, extended sweep that turns into a firmer press.

For the record, nonconsensually kissing a scared, crying woman while doused in corn syrup you used to fake your own death?

Big red flag.

He pulls back, a whisper away from my mouth, and I hope he thinks I'm shaking from unbridled passion rather than the real reason: I'm scared shitless.

Because Billie was right. It *is* always the quiet ones.

His eyes open, crooked smile looking a lot less appealing than it did earlier tonight when he says, "I didn't do it for you. I did it for *us*."

"John," I say, but he's already shaking his head with a moony, lovestruck "look how far we've come" expression on his face. The grip he has on my cheek drops, and I try not to sigh too audibly when he's not touching me anymore.

"Do you believe in fate, Jamie?" he muses, looking at me from under his bangs before he threads his hands through them and stands back to take a good look at me. His eyes trace over me like we've met by chance on the top of the Empire State Building or on the Manhattan Bridge or in the middle of Riverside Park. Not in a deep, dark corner of a trap he set.

I don't know how to answer that. I don't know how to make sense of any of this, so I ask, "Have we—"

He moves forward slightly, eyes alight with that unnerving affection as he waits for me to finish the question.

"Have we *met* before tonight?"

I consider myself to be a person who is pretty aware of their surroundings, and since John *does* fit the look of my usual type—which is very much no longer the case—you'd think I would've noticed him if our paths had crossed before, right?

"In another life, maybe."

Holy shit, man.

"But you *called* to me, Jamie. Tonight. As soon as you walked in and I spotted you from the mezzanine, I just . . . I *knew*."

I think back to when I entered the club with Laurie. I *did* see a silhouette leaning against the railing. But it didn't cross my mind again for the rest of the night. It didn't have much of an impact on me, but for him . . . for him it was *everything*.

"And then when we had our date, I knew we were perfectly matched. We just . . . aligned." He lets out a chuckle. "You don't scare easily."

I'm sure as shit scared now.

"I knew you would appreciate someone like me. I had to be sure, of course. I've been wrong before and it's just ended badly. That's why I knew it had to be different this time. I knew I had to make her see the real me from the very start. I knew she'd be here—*you'd* be here—looking for me, too."

What was it he told me?

I don't take a lot of risks. I plan things out. I stay in my lane.

Well, the five women he murdered before tonight and the count-less bodies he's left strewn across the club would attest to the fact he's pretty comfortable in that lane. "Billie wasn't so sure. She can be kind of negative sometimes, but—"

"Billie." Her name is pulled from my lips before I remember I should be too scared to speak. A flash of her bent body slumping over the bar jump-cuts across my mind, cutting through the fear, and I have to blink it away.

The corner of his mouth quirks up when he mistakes the furrow between my brows for jealousy.

"She's just a friend," he assures me, moving forward so he can tuck a strand of hair behind my ear, and it takes everything in me not to recoil. "I met her at a singles cooking class a few months ago." He scoffs at the memory. "Can you believe she followed me home?"

Yeah, actually, I can. Her psychopathy recognized his psychopathy—like attracts like. And the idea that these two people found each other and worked toward tonight's common goal (even if Billie had a goal of her own) is terrifying.

"She's been helping me ever since. We're kindred spirits more than anything. *Friends*." He stresses the word and then shrugs ruefully. "I mean, sometimes I think she might want more, but—"

"She does." Now that I've said something and he hasn't immediately stabbed me, it's easier to convince my mouth to make sounds. Even if my throat closes around them, even when they tremble on the way out.

Tonight has been about John finding and winning over the One, but Billie already wanted that role. That's the reason the sight of me looked like it left a bitter taste in her mouth. She didn't hate me. She was jealous. She was trying to figure out why the man she wanted was doing all of this for me and why he wouldn't do it for her. That's why I needed to be last, so she could have a chance to show him I wasn't the one he wanted. She was. All he had to do was look at her after the dust had settled and the blood had dried and realize she was there all along. Right under his nose.

I guess for Billie this was a *My Best Friend's Wedding* situation. My best friend's bloodbath, if you will. And I bet she would've used the same kind of lines at the end of the night if she hadn't fallen over the railing.

Choose me. Murder with me. Let me make you happy.

But just like *My Best Friend's Wedding*, it didn't end with her getting the guy, and even after all she's done for him, he hasn't even noticed she's gone.

He doesn't know.

"She *did* want more," I say.

"Oh." He's well versed in how people turn into past tense—he's been the reason they have all night—and there's only a second of surprised comprehension, momentary disappointment, and then it's gone as quickly as it came. He doesn't need friends when he has me.

"Well, you had nothing to worry about. I knew you were what I wanted the first time I saw you."

Like, what? *Four hours* ago?

Did he think the same thing about the other women? How long did it take for him to fall in love with them, realize they were a "mistake"—ones he could easily erase and dispose of—before looking for the next "one"?

"Those women," I say. "The ones before this—"

He shakes his head, moving a palm to his heart as he concedes, "I know I have a history. I'm sure you do, too, but that doesn't matter now that we've found each other."

"But you—they—" I can't comprehend it. He's talking about them like they're failed relationships, like they're exes we can mutually agree to never talk about again, instead of what they really are: innocent women he killed in cold blood, like everyone else who's crossed his path tonight.

"I was wrong about them, Jamie. I was wrong about what I wanted." He moves his palm from his chest to my shoulder and I flinch. He thinks I'm hurt there were others before me, and it makes him double down on the besotted stare. When he brushes his fingers over the strap of my dress, rubbing one of the small panels of sheer material between his thumb and forefinger, I have to grit my teeth to keep from screaming.

"People always show you the best parts of themselves at first, but when things start to get tough, they show you who they really are." I think his version of things getting "tough" in a relationship might be a little different from most other people's.

"They acted like they liked me, but it wasn't real, it wasn't authentic. Not like us."

Oh my god.

"So this time I made a promise to myself." He's not speaking to me anymore. He's speaking at me, captivated by his own delusion, and I use the moment to flick my gaze around the space to see if there's anything that will bring a Final Girl scene to mind. Something that will help me get the fuck away from him.

"I wouldn't just fall for a pretty smile and some common interests."

He's blocking the stairs so that's a no-go.

"I'd make sure that she was good enough for me."

I could shove him down them, but it's too risky. I know how strong he is. Not to mention, he could pull me down with him.

"I'd make sure she was serious about us going the distance."

He steps back and I try not to cry with relief as he . . . *performs* this rationalization in front of me. He's dropped the injured act. There's no limping or favoring one shoulder or cradling his arm anymore. He's gotten through this whole night unscathed while the rest of us are in shambles. If I had that stake I could shove it into his chest, go full *Buffy* on his stalking—

"And, Jamie . . ."

That draws my eyes to his and he's captivated by me again, walking back into my space, *leaning*. The same way he did earlier in the night, but there's no flurry of excitement or giddy anticipation like before. I know him now, and it doesn't matter that I used to think he was cute. Not when I know he's a wolf in Bill Pullman clothing.

"You're beyond what I expected."

Funny, he's beyond what I expected, too. So far beyond reason I know I can't do anything to convince him I didn't want anything he's done tonight. I don't appreciate any of his efforts.

"You did all of this to—"

"To make sure. I thought I could just go about meeting my soul mate by doing what everyone else does, but I'm not like everyone else."

Well, that's for damn sure.

"I know I'm the right man for you, but I had to make sure you were the right woman for *me*. I had to make sure you were—"

"The One," I say, and he takes a deep, delighted breath.

He ducks his head in that self-effacing bow I thought was endearing. He's so proud of me for acing this messed-up test he's put together, but I can't feel too much satisfaction I was right. Not with the sharp, cold, realization that the guy who asked me if I liked scary movies decided to put me right in the middle of one.

"I knew you'd get it." The rueful shake of his head makes me want to throw up. "I knew you would understand."

"I don't." I don't understand at all. I don't see how you go from seeing someone across the room and thinking they're the One to murdering everyone else in it. "All those people—Curtis and—"

"He was a piece of work." He clicks his tongue. "Remember how I told you I plan things out? I always do, Jamie, but as soon as I saw you, I knew you were worth changing the plan for. Curtis was—men like that don't know how to treat women. I know you can hold your own, but when I saw you arguing I saw red. I had to put him in his place. Billie was pissed when I told her I didn't want to wait until the last date." He chuckles like the chain of events that followed are not going to haunt me for the rest of my life, like his whole justification for what he's done isn't completely batshit insane.

"Once she made sure the host wouldn't get in the way, she had to sprint to lock the front door and hide the phones and make sure that girl in the coat check wouldn't stop what was meant to happen. You can't fight fate."

But according to him you can manufacture it, because everything that has happened has been by his design. There is nothing predestined about this.

"I knew if we just had this time together, if I showed you who I am and showed you what I would do for you, that you'd see I'm the man for you. You deserve to be pursued, you know? You deserve to be shown that you are wanted, that someone—that *I*—will do whatever it takes so you know nothing can come between us. And I deserve someone who will fight to the end, someone who will fight to be with me."

When I don't say anything, when I can't, he says, "Look, I know it's been a long night, but we can get that drink now, okay? We can—"

I'm shaking my head before I can catch myself. It's a pure, primal reaction to the disgust that flows through me when he suggests we can just go clink glasses after this. He thinks people will ask us how we got together and we'll say, "Well, it's a funny story . . ." But my body's decided it's reached its limit of being in the presence of a delusional, bloodthirsty *murderer*. I press my back into the wall, ignore how the movement causes the cuts and bruises on my arms to throb, and cast a quick glance to the only exit option I have. The one that rarely leads to anything good. Back the way I came.

"Jamie?"

He sounds worried. Which is ironic, considering he's the biggest threat I've ever faced and he has me cornered. But I don't think he sees it that way. He thinks this is intimate. It has all the markers of a clandestine meeting between two lovers rather than what it actually is: he's a predator, and I'm his prey. So I use that to my advantage, swallow the fear, look up at him with wide eyes, and go into Leading Lady mode.

"This is a lot to process. No one's ever—" I cut myself off, letting out a shaky breath that sounds like I'm overwhelmed by emotion.

Really, I just want to even out my breathing before I try to make a run for it. "I think I just need a little space."

He steps back immediately—he is a gentleman after all—and directs an indulgent smile at me when I straighten off the wall and brace my feet in the plush carpet. It's like he was prepared for a rebuttal. He knows during the first big speech the girl will always try to argue that we're too different or our families won't approve or society won't allow it, and that's why he starts his second appeal.

"Jamie, I can tell you've been hurt before, and you feel like you have to hold back, but I'm *not* like those other guys."

Oh my *god*, this is why you need more than a ten-minute date with someone to know they aren't absolutely insane.

"I'm all in for this. For us. You belong to me."

That captures my attention.

"You—you wrote that in the card. You left it in the room after you . . ." *Gutted another human.*

The memory makes him smile, like I'm recalling a quirk from a first date that's going to star in our "how we met" anecdote. "The Police. 'Every Breath You Take.'"

Oh. Of course. It's a certified stalker anthem.

"We thought it was Taylor Swift."

It's not a very pertinent comment, but it's out of my mouth before I can stop it, and it just makes his smile turn placating as he moves closer to kiss me again.

"I admit, I don't listen to too much of her music, but I will for you. There's no limit to what I'll do for you, Jamie. You're my dream come true."

He wants to end his romantic musings on just the right note before the film fades to black. I've been in this kind of situation before. In this very club, in fact. Backed up against a wall by a guy who thinks persistence makes the heart grow fonder, and if it were as simple as that, I'd do exactly what I would've done back then and shove him out of my face. Choose violence. But I have no weapon to be violent with. Even if John didn't have the advantage of being, you know, a *murderer*, he is physically larger and stronger that I am. He could go mano a mano with any of the Big Bads, and even if I try to push him away, I don't think he'd budge. I can't go on the attack yet, not when the only reason I'm standing here now is because he thinks I'm going to stop playing hard to get and give into my feelings. So I wait until his eyes are fully closed, his eyelashes splayed against his skin, his defenses are down, and then, for what might be the thousandth time tonight, I run.

CHAPTER 36

*"What I really want to do with my life—what I want to do
for a living—is I want to murder your daughter. I'm good
at it."*

—Not *Say Anything*

I don't look back.

John calls after me. His confusion and concern are palpable
in the echo of my name, but it just propels me down the corridor.
My muscles scream out in protest, every inhale is sharp and piercing,
but I push past it and just run. A body splices into sight again when I
pass the hallway where I first spotted John in that mask. It's become
a permanent fixture, a landmark to determine my location, and I start
to head for the janitor's closet. It's the only room I know of that has a
lock and I might just be fine with living out the rest of my hours there.

When I sprint past the open air above the dance floor, I catch a
glimpse of a slumped figure near the corner of the railing before it's
replaced by red walls and a deeper feeling of regret.

Jennifer.

She liked John, too. So I guess I can't kick myself too much for buying into his nice-guy routine. She had all the necessary qualities to be both a Leading Lady and a Final Girl, but he'd already made his choice based on a few seconds of long-distance, partially obstructed, badly lit observation. And clearly he made the wrong choice.

I know I should switch back into Final Girl mode and try to find a weapon rather than a hiding spot. I should wear my pain and trauma like a Harry Winston necklace at a "Frost Yourself" gala and place myself on the middle of the dance floor for a final showdown. But I'm all out of Leading Lady optimism and resilience. Everything hurts, and everything sucks, and if tonight were a film I'd give it zero stars.

I'm so done with this drawn-out narrative, the exhausted escape options, the ridiculous stakes that have been set, and the reveal that doesn't have the same kind of entertainment value when it's someone you know. Someone you once thought you could—

I almost run past the closet as I try to avoid spiraling down that dangerous, shame-ridden path. I have to reach back for the handle of the door like it's a hand reaching out of the water and I promised I'd never let go. It turns easily, but when the shadows at the end of the hallway start to shift I release my grip. Not out of fear. The shadows extend and bend in reaction to a light source, and when the shards of darkness turn gray, lighten, and a clear beam of light splays across the carpet, I run down the hallway toward it.

My muscles still throb. My breath still feels serrated in my throat, but the promise of what—*who*—is holding that flashlight pulls in my chest and overshadows it all when I turn the corner and see him. See Wes.

We both freeze. He blinks. I blink. The sound of my relieved sigh blends perfectly with his, and then I collide with his chest, forgetting about his injured ribs and his fresh cuts until he grunts in pain. Wes doesn't let me go, though. He wraps his arms around me, pulls me in tighter, and it's my turn to hiss from the ache that resonates through my body, but there's no way in hell I'm moving away. Not when the feel of his cheek pressing to my temple and the pressure of his knife's handle at my back is the safest I've felt since coming face-to-face with John.

Wes starts pulling me back the way he came before I can even think of the right words to convey how sorry I am for thinking he was Heart Eyes. I ran away from him when he was injured, innocent, and if I thought word vomiting about murder in the final minutes of our date was bad, that was much, much worse.

"I found them," he says before I can apologize, heading for the darkness we've been doing everything to avoid.

"Found who?"

"The others. There's six of them."

The other names on the match cards. The people unaccounted for and presumed dead based on the trend of the evening.

"Alive?"

Because, given how the night has played out, I have to clarify.

"Alive. Remember how Stu said he couldn't get into one of the rooms?"

We pass the broken sconces, and he tips the flashlight down to the ground to aid our steps through the minefield of glass. I still catch the lift of his shoulder, the grimace when the action pulls at his ribs, before he says, "I had a hunch."

That's not even the most impressive thing.

"And they let you in?"

I turn my focus back to the carpet and tiptoe around the shards. My feet are so numb now it's not like I can feel if I get cut anyway. I used to think my feet looked like a massacre at the end of a long night of dancing at Cravin'. Now I know I wasn't even close.

"I can be persuasive."

I can't argue with that. Ten minutes alone in a closet and I threw everything I'd ever learned from horror movies out the window.

"The control panel was in there," he says. "But it's been tampered with. One of the guys—you remember Lee?"

Yes, I do. I was gonna wingman for him with Nia, the woman who gave a mini plant tutorial at cocktail hour. I was looking forward to it before all of this. Knowing that Lee and Nia have been stuck in a room together this whole time is a promising development. That kind of forced proximity can really help you bond.

"Lee tried to set off the control panel hours ago and it didn't work," Wes says. "Not all of the video cameras were damaged, either. The one above the dance floor is still there."

So Wes found survivors, a hiding spot John hadn't discovered the whole night, and he decided to go for a stroll along the corridors. Has he learned nothing from our time together?

"Wes . . . *what* are you doing out here then? Why didn't you stay there?"

That makes him stop short, and he shoots me a look like it's obvious. He shakes his head, eyes locked on mine, and already I'm stepping into him. Because as soon as I realized he wasn't responsible for killing half the people we met tonight, that thread in my chest snapped right back into being a steel hook.

"I was looking for you. I needed to make sure you were o—"

I cut him off with a swift pull of his head down to mine and cover his mouth with my own, trying not to cry from relief when he slots his arm at the back of my neck, pulls me in, and kisses me back. It's quick, though, the best reconciliation we can hope for given the circumstances. When we part, it's habit to look around to make sure no one can sneak up and stab one of us. When there's no movement at either end of the hall, I move my hands from his neck to his chest. The bulk of the bandage underneath brings a hard lump into my throat.

"I'm sorry. I'm so, *so* sorry, Wes. I was—"

"Hey." He uses the arm around my neck to pull me into his side and starts walking, dropping a kiss against my temple. "It's gonna take a lot more than that to get rid of me, Jamie."

That makes me scoff.

"Really?"

"You'd probably be able to convince me to go back into that closet even if *you* were the killer."

And that changes the whole tone of the conversation because the killer is still a nameless, faceless, unknown suspect to him.

"It's John."

Wes stops, a few feet away from the pile of furniture he barreled into last time, and even with the flashlight directed on the floor, I can see the look of confusion on his face.

"But he . . ." There's a second of doubt, and then he catches up. "He wasn't actually hurt, was he?"

I'd like to think it's because my tutelage has led him to expect the unexpected, but it's probably more to do with his occupation, his experience with how you can't underestimate people who would do something as heinous as taking a life in the name of love.

"He was just playing the part . . ."

His body tenses next to mine when he realizes there's only one way I can know for sure, there's only one thing that would bring that much conviction into my voice.

"Jamie—"

"We ran into each other."

"*Fuck* . . . Are you okay?" He shifts the flashlight over my body like I've just told him I've got three stab wounds in my back. All his efforts achieve is a nice view of my tits.

No, I'm not okay. Not really. "Yeah."

"Jamie, I'm—I'm sorry." He goes to brush his hand through his hair, almost scalping himself before he realizes he's still holding the knife and jerks it away, drops it to his side. After a second of silent reflection, his gaze meets mine and he just looks . . . sympathetic.

"I know you— He— I know you and him—"

He can't say it, but we both know if the first part of the night was a reality TV show, he and John would've been standing side by side while I decided whom to give my rose to.

"Wes?"

I reach out and curl my fingers around his wrist, trail my thumb down his skin, and hope he also knows—

He had me at *Miss Congeniality*.

"We should probably go back to where the others are hiding. I bet you're not his favorite person right now."

John will be getting ready for the next grand gesture, and he won't appreciate that I'm here reconciling with his competition. Not after he's been doing the serial killer version of shouting his love for me from the rooftops. The image of a pink woolen head reciting poetry on the roof of this godforsaken building is a weird image to conjure up, but it's quickly pushed out when a foggy memory intrudes and turns the red walls around us back to Cravin' black. My head jerks toward the mountain of wrecked furniture ahead of us because I remember this hallway. I remember *what* is up here.

For the first time, hope isn't dragged away as quickly as the other times we thought we found a way to escape. It holds on. Digs its nails in. It's not just *We* could *get out of here*. The modality has ramped up. Now it's *We* can *get out of here*.

In the movies, dark and scary means death, not salvation. That's why the lights were smashed, furniture was scattered, and the walls were marked. John and Billie were trying to make it look like the kind of place where you'd meet your end, not the kind of place where you'd find your escape.

They used the rules against us.

"Wes?" I pull him over to the structure, make him raise the flash-light until I can see the top of the furniture pile. He directs the light between some curved chaise legs, and shadows flare out behind it, which means there's *space* behind it.

"Remember how we thought somebody had tried to barricade the hallway? What if they were trying to hide a door instead?"

The night I made out with vape guy, we went up to the smoking section on the roof. I ended up leaving him there when he started trying to sell me cryptocurrency, but still. There was a door, a stair-case, one that led to fresh air and the night sky, and a fire escape that always had security stationed near the access point to stop someone from drunkenly attempting to scale the building. And we ran past it earlier tonight. Wes ran *into* it. The impact is painted in black and blue across his ribs.

I shift my gaze back down from the top of the barricade and find Wes staring at me, his eyes alight with understanding and his chest heaving in anticipation.

"Where does it lead to?"

"The roof."

"And there's a—"

"Fire escape. Yeah."

His face splits into a grin and it's just as stunning as the first time I saw it in the basement bar a few hours ago. Just like when we were down there, I can't help but grin back.

"I could kiss you right now."

He could, and I would let him, but there are more important things we need to be concentrating on. Like getting out of here so he can kiss me without fear of having a meat cleaver lodged in his face.

"Hold that thought. We're gonna need some help."

We don't know how long Billie and John worked on this blockade, and the two of us deconstructing it without causing an avalanche is going to be hard in itself, let alone with Wes's injuries. Even though I know he'd still try to clear out the space and cause even more damage to himself in the process, there's strength and safety in numbers. So we head back to the survivors' hideout, scanning the hall and speaking in hushed, rushed murmurs as we figure out a plan to finally draw the curtain on this night.

"Once we get on the roof, we search for the fire escape on the side of the building," Wes says, and I'm already thinking about what happens after that. I hope it'll play out the way I want. I hope, when we make it up onto the roof, the sky is awash with alternating flashes of red and blue, and when I look down to the street a willowy, waifish figure wrapped in a foil blanket will be waiting to give me a handshake in lieu of a hug.

"Laurie should've gotten out through the air vents by now, so—"

"Wait." Wes's head whips around to stare at me as we hurry down the hall, and the only way I can describe the look on his face is . . . delighted comprehension. I don't care that I've only known him for a few hours—I might actually have to marry this man.

"She *McClane*'d her way out?"

CHAPTER 37

"So, what happens after he climbs up and stabs her?"
"She stabs him right back."

—Not *Pretty Woman*

"**W**ho's to say John isn't going to cut us down as soon as we try to clear the stuff blocking the door?" Lee asks, and it's a fair question. Safety first and all that.

Wes performed a coded knock that sounded suspiciously like the bass line of Queen's "Another One Bites the Dust" when we made it to their hideout. After we heard something heavy being dragged—which I soon discovered was a tipped-over filing cabinet—the door opened to reveal all six of the missing people who escaped up the stairs at the beginning of the night. Scared and exhausted and covered in blood. Just like us. Except they all still had their name tags stuck to their chests.

"We've been here this long, and it's saved us. I think we just need to hold out a little longer," Lee says. He's standing close to Nia, their bodies angled in toward each other in the same way I find myself standing when I'm next to Wes, and it makes me smile. I can't help it. I'm a romantic at heart. Though maybe Lee would be more willing to assist in our escape if my wingman services were still on the table.

"It's only a matter of time before he finds us here," one of the women says. When I look down at her name tag I spy the name Ellen. She's standing closest to the monitor that displays the video camera footage of the club. I imagine the screen is usually a grid showing the main areas of the three levels, but the squares are all blacked out except the center image—black-and-white footage of the dance floor. It's grainy, but I can make out the heart in the middle of it, a prone figure draped over the bar in the top corner. The dull light of the screen shines against Ellen's face, the underlighting making her look of concern even more pronounced.

"Wes said he has an ax *and* a machete?" She directs that question to me, and I nod.

John wasn't armed when he caught me in the corner, but he's been pulling weapons out of thin air all night, using his never-ending stash of deadly blades. There's a good chance he just put the latest in a safe place to maintain the romantic atmosphere he was going for.

Ellen sucks in a breath. "All we've got is one knife between eight people."

I can tell this conversation is one that's been had a lot by this group. I can't even hold it against them—not after everything that's happened, and not after their current strategy has led them into the final act when so many others haven't made the cut. John made sure of that. He's directed this whole night to ensure nothing would come between us. He cast everyone in a role and all of them are disposable. And that's when it hits me. *They* are all disposable . . . but I'm not. Not yet.

Billie said as much.

I just can't kill you yet, but I'm sure you'll be a disappointment, just like the others.

The others. The victims before this. The ones who failed the test.

I had to make sure you were the right woman for me.

I've been putting this whole night into the context of a slasher, using my knowledge of the formula to try to stay safe, stay alive, and make it to the end, but we're not *just* in a slasher. Like Wes said, this is a fucked-up rom-com. And rom-coms aren't about playing it safe. They're about taking risks. They're about going big or going home. That's what John's been doing. I was right when I said the murders are just a means to an end. A way of getting closer to his happy ending. That's why he's been leaving all the roses and tokens of affection. Why he delivered his little speech when he had me cornered. He's been playing out a different movie than the rest of us, and that's why it hasn't ended yet. Because his fantasy isn't complete.

All night I've been wanting to avoid the final showdown between the Final Girl and the Big Bad, but rom-coms don't end that way. I've been concentrating so much on not wanting to be the Final Girl I keep forgetting about what else he wants me to be.

The Leading Lady.

The One.

Taking on that role when I was stuck with him in the hallway, even just for a moment, seemed to work in my favor. It was like he thought we were the only two people in the club. The only two people in the world. So what if I did it again?

What if I make him feel like it's just us?

Interrupting the murmured back-and-forth that's started up between the group, I say, "What if I can guarantee he won't go any-where near the roof?" and the room falls silent. It's a bold claim, but I've studied enough movies to know it'll work.

When no one answers at first, the six hiding survivors share a look that speaks to the fact that spending the last few hours locked in a room together is the best bonding exercise there is. Then Nia shrugs and says, "Then, we'd—"

"*Jamie.*" Wes's voice cuts into whatever Nia was going to say on behalf of the group, and I try to keep my self-assured smile for the benefit of the other people in the room. The ones who don't know that while Wes may look calm, the tone of his voice is anything but.

I think it's a good sign for our future relationship that I can pick up on it so well, and that's why I'm still smiling when I tilt my head up and see Wes's arched brow.

"Yes?"

"Can I have a word?"

We move to the other side of the room, the weight of the others' stares heavy as Wes leans down and pins me with an unimpressed look. I think it's another good sign for our future relationship that he knows what I'm planning. Not so much that he shoots it down immediately.

"I'm telling you now, as both a police officer and a man who wants to date you—you *cannot* go up against an armed assailant. You're a civilian."

"I'm the Final Girl," I whisper. "And the Leading Lady. *And* the all-around expert on this shit."

"Jamie, there is no way—"

"You can't clear the barricade by yourself." I gesture to how he's pressing a palm to his ribs, his jaw tense with pain, but even then he just lets out a restricted, frustrated breath and shakes his head as I keep listing reasons. They come to mind so easily now that I know what I have to do. "They are scared shitless. You're the only one who can get them out, and I can buy you the time you need. I'll go down to the dance floor. I'll do something to draw him there and distract him while you clear the barricade and go up to the roof. You'll be able to see when he's there from the video, and then you can all get out of here. He won't come after you if he has me—"

"*Jamie—*"

"*Wes . . .*" I've already told him Leading Ladies are assertive and independent. We're not like ingenues who need to be saved. My mind is made up.

"This whole night, he hasn't tried to hurt me." The one deviation was when Billie came after me in the bathroom. I'm sure of it. I'm also sure the "J" etched into the mirror was not meant for me. Not in the way I thought. She was staking her claim.

"He just wants me. He wants me to play the part, and he's not going to stop until he gets what he wants. If you're going to get to the roof, you need him to be distracted, and you know better than anyone else I can be a distraction."

He lets out a humorless breath but shakes his head. His lips pull into a petulant line, so I hit him with the final point. Sometimes you need to make a person eat their own words to understand yours.

"You said you would do anything to make sure as many people got out as possible. I'm the 'anything' Wes."

He knows I'm right. I can tell by the way his mouth sets firmer into that thin, grim line, and the way he won't meet my eye as I wait for a rebuttal. He knows John is going to come looking for us again. He knows he can save these people before John decides they are obstacles in the way of winning my heart. Just like I know he's going to do it even if he doesn't like that it leaves me alone. He lets out a weighted sigh, glancing over at the others before he takes hold of my arm and turns us until my back is against the wall. When he's firmly in my space, looking down at me with that loaded stare, I know I've won.

"This hero-complex shit really does get old," he mutters.

"Is it a turnoff?"

"Yeah, it is." He nods, gesturing between our bloodstained chests. "I'm rethinking this whole thing between us now."

He's lying, and that's why I grin. "Noted."

When his face turns serious, I say, "He won't hurt me. Not if I play along."

He lifts his stare above my head, eyes narrowing as they dart back and forth, and I watch him try to figure out the plan in his head—how he can be in two places at once, get the survivors out and stay with me—but every time he plays it out and it doesn't end right, the furrow between his eyebrows gets deeper.

"I'll come back for you," he says finally, his dark stare dropping down to meet mine, and I have to tamp down my smile because it's the *most* cliché thing to say at a time like this.

"As soon as we reach the exit, as soon as they're up on the roof, I'll come back. Set the detectors off to make sure an alert gets out, and then I'll come back for you and—"

"Stop."

I hold up a palm, direct my most serious expression at him, and when it looks like he thinks I'm going to deliver some deep, heartfelt parting words, I sigh.

"You're coming on really strong."

After an extended startled silence he laughs, followed by an exhausted, incredulous scoff, and I have to bite down on my own smile.

"What . . . *the fuck*, Jamie?" He shakes his head, but the way he looks at me, the way his eyes shine . . .

"We've only just met, and I'm not really looking for anything long term right now," I say gravely, trying not to break character when his gaze doesn't falter and he lifts his palm to my face. When John did it, I was apprehensive, then terrified. But when Wes traces the peak of my cheekbone with his thumb, slides his fingers into my hair, and cups the back of my head, it just feels right. I lean into his touch, step into his body, until we're nose to nose, and he murmurs, "I'm gonna fall in love with you, aren't I?"

God, I hope so.

I hope we make it out and go on that date and do things that don't include makeshift weapons and debilitating fear. I hope what happened tonight doesn't change us so much that we're no longer the people who sat down at my table a few hours ago, locked eyes, and had an inkling things were going to be different once we walked out of this building. Even if it had been a normal night with zero percent chance of murder, I still think this evening was going to be life changing for me, because I'm pretty sure Wes is my "Oh, it's *you*" person. I'm pretty sure I'm his, too. And I need us to make it through tonight so I can find out if I'm right.

That's why I rise onto my bare, bruised, bleeding tiptoes and press my lips against his until he kisses me back. I count to three before I pull away, and he's right: it really does work.

It doesn't take long to get the others on board with the plan. I'd like to think it's due to my Leading Lady optimism, but it could also be the collective desperation to get the fuck out of this hellhole. Either way, I make sure I keep a composed, confident expression on my face as Jason and Michael shift the filing cabinet away from the door, allowing myself one more look at Wes's grim expression before I open the door just wide enough to slip outside.

Only when I'm alone in the hallway and hear the filing cabinet being slid back in front of the door do I let myself have the briefest moment of doubt. A real sense of imposter syndrome hits me like a blood spatter because I never asked for this. I never asked to be the lead in John's romance, or the villain in Billie's. But now that I'm in it, now that I've been cast in this role, I have a real chance of controlling the ending to all of this.

I'm done worrying about whether I'm too much or not enough.

I'm done trying to figure out whether I can be a Final Girl or a Leading Lady.

But most important, I'm done playing hard to get.

Because if John wants me so badly . . .

He can have me.

 **CHAPTER 38**

"I'm also just a girl, standing in front of a boy,
asking him not to murder her."

—Not *Notting Hill*

𝓘'm standing in the middle of the dance floor like Josie Geller on the pitcher's mound in *Never Been Kissed*. Well, not exactly in the middle. I can't stand directly under the disco ball because that's where the intestines are, but I'm close enough that I'm visible from every angle of the mezzanine. It means I have a good vantage point while I wait barefoot, bloody, holding John's flowers to my chest.

I picked up the bouquet from Campbell before I went down to the dance floor, calling out John's name as I descended from the mezzanine with roses in hand and Campbell's blood on my hands, because I need this to look the way John wants it to. I need him to see me waiting with these large red blooms like they mean something to me. I need him to realize that I came back for him and I'm ready to play the role he cast me in. If this is going to play out like he wants it to, then everything has to be perfect.

It's almost silent on this level. There's only the faint sound of blood dripping onto the floor from where Billie is slumped over the bar behind me. It's slow, soft, so much like water droplets falling into a puddle that I start when the speakers crackle to life. The plucking of a banjo sings out across the room. I flinch at the first note, but then I recognize the song, and—

Ahhh, *shit.*

"We were both . . ."

I never should've told him I like Taylor Swift.

I close my eyes just like the lyrics suggest, but instead of a flashback to a balcony I'm granted the muted darkness of my eyelids. It's a bit bold of him to assume I'm a *Fearless* girl, when some questions about the topic would have revealed that I'm a *1989* stan, but a classic is a classic. On a sigh, I open my eyes again, pressing my lips together to fight the urge to sing along. I may never be able to listen to it in the same way again after tonight, but "Love Story" is still a great choice when you're trying to woo someone.

Fragments of silver light catch my eye, and I glance up as the disco ball starts to spin. It catches the reflections of the blue and white lights that suddenly shoot out from the corners of the ceiling and rains them down onto the room. Down onto the guts in the middle of it. Down onto the body behind me.

A patch of darkness shifts on the mezzanine level right above me, and I see John walk forward, grip the railing, and look down at me with a soft smile. Our roles are reversed—he's Juliet on the balcony and I'm Romeo. I see what he was doing with the song now, but it's hard not to think about the ending of the original story.

"You came back," John calls out over the music. "I thought I'd scared you off."

My eyes drop to where his ankles are crossed. His shoes were black at the beginning of the night and now they're completely burgundy. The coveralls didn't do much covering with that part of his outfit, and I want to kick myself for not noticing the little details like I should have. Like I always do when it's a movie. If I had just *looked down*, then—

"I shouldn't have run away," I say as he uncrosses his ankles and trails the railing, heading for the stairs on my right side. I lift my gaze back up to him, to the soft, imploring stare I thought was cute earlier in the evening. I'd thought so many things about him were "cute," but all of it was just a mask. More so than the one that's been mussing up his hair all night. He doesn't say anything while he's moving into his next position and it's a short reprieve. One that lets me try to get my breathing under control as my hands sweat around the bouquet of roses. At least I think it's sweat; I'm holding it so tight it could be blood.

I count each second it takes for him to get down from the mezzanine. Fashion my face into something neutral. Something that doesn't look desperate, because it's crazy how much I want him to walk faster. To be closer. I *need* him to be closer. It's almost like a pull of attraction . . . almost.

He doesn't hurry, though. When he comes back into view he pauses and leans against the edge of a booth. He's foregone the coveralls and jacket for this date. His hands are in his pockets, and while I can spy his pink mask sticking out of one of them, the absence of any visible weapons tells me he's come here as John rather than Heart Eyes. That doesn't put my mind at ease, though.

"You don't have to run away from me, Jamie."

He means it, too. I can tell from the forlorn way he shakes his head before he pushes off the booth and gestures between us. "You don't have to run away from this."

Funny, because that's exactly what my amygdala is screaming at me to do.

"I know." I nod jerkily as he starts to edge around the dance floor. "Love Story" is still playing in the background, jagged diamonds of light still showering across the space. It has all the elements of a rom-com ending, but I need him to be closer if we're going to do this right. If this is going to end the way it's supposed to.

"I know that now."

I don't break our stare. I don't look away in case he reads into it and interprets it as disinterest, and when he pauses in front of another booth and gets this faraway look on his face, I can predict what comes next.

There's always some reciprocity within a rom-com grand gesture. He told me how he felt but I haven't given my reply. That could've worked against me, if it weren't for the fact that the first attempt to confess your feelings usually doesn't work in a rom-com. You overhear a conversation out of context and mistakenly think they don't feel the same away. They fall asleep before they hear you and you lose your nerve. Their flight has already taken off, even after the mad cab chase . . .

If it were real life, you'd have to deal with it.

But in rom-coms you always get a second chance, and this is his.

"Jamie . . ." He takes a step toward the dance floor, his head tilted, hand to his heart.

"I love you. I loved you the moment I saw you. I've been looking for you for so long and I thought I must've been dreaming when you walked in here tonight, but . . . it's you. I knew it was you. And everything that's happened, it's all because we're meant to be together. Call it fate, or destiny, or *serendipity* . . ."

He chuckles, like he hasn't orchestrated this entire night. Like he didn't choose this club as his setting, Billie as his sidekick, me as his love interest, all so he could direct his warped idea of romance. So he could manufacture something as elusive and essential and enduring as love.

"You were meant to be mine. Nothing was going to stop that

because you're the one. You are perfect for me . . ." He pauses for effect, or maybe it's so when he reaches the edge of the dance floor he can time it with the music when he says, "This is our love story. All you have to do is say yes."

Doesn't listen to much of her music, my ass. But I'll give it to him. The delivery is good, though he gets zero points for originality. I've heard all the things he's said before, from other nonassuming, floppy-haired, misty-eyed men. I've soaked them up and dreamed of being on the receiving end of these kinds of declarations, but it just doesn't have the intended effect when you've witnessed the person saying it split someone's head open with an ax.

"Jamie?" he says, and when I meet his gaze, he nods. That little crooked smile twists the corner of his mouth. He's done his speech and now he wants my response. He's the Leading Man, after all, and I'm supposed to respond accordingly.

"I . . ."

When I open my mouth, the words refuse to come out. I can't make myself shape out the consonants and vowels without wanting to throw up. It's one thing to look the part, another to act it, and the thing with these admissions of love is that they are requited. The audience knows the two leads feel the same way about each other. John said himself that the other women—his victims—had said they loved him, and he could tell it wasn't true. What if they all got to this part? What if *this* is the final test that everyone fails?

The silence extends, and I see his smile falter. My window to keep the scene running smoothly is closing. There's a split-second difference between a pause for effect and one that kills the mood. The stakes are even higher when the mood isn't the only thing that could get killed.

I can't say the words he wants to hear and make him believe them, but I'm still determined for this to end the way I know it has to. I can play my role, but it has to be one of my choosing, not his. Because I'm not something that falls neatly into a category on Netflix . . . I'm one of a kind.

I still need him to come closer for the scene to play out the way I want it to, and if I can't compel him to come toward me I have only one other option.

I have to provoke him instead.

"I kissed Wes."

His face drops. He looks genuinely hurt, but before the social conditioning can kick in and I feel too bad, he shakes it off. One foot finds its way onto the dance floor.

"You made a mistake."

Even with the understanding look back on his face, he's not asking. He's telling me. His eyebrows are furrowed in confusion, but he's ready to forgive me. I'm his dream girl, after all.

"Twice— No. Three times . . . Maybe more."

I wait until it seems like he's fully processed that, and when he looks like he's ready to reason it away, when both of his feet are on vinyl instead of carpet, I say, "Oh, and I fucked him in the janitor's closet."

And *that* is the plot twist he did not see coming. His face loses its swoony, infatuated expression as if I've slapped it off. When he takes another step forward, it's longer, quicker than the others, and I have to stop myself from taking one back.

He needs a little more time to mull over that bit of information, head tilted like he must have heard me wrong. ". . . You what?"

The hypocrisy is out of this world. His body count doesn't matter, but suddenly mine does?

"I thought you were dead," I say, as he pauses. I think he's trying to recalculate the fantasy, reconcile what I've told him with how he wanted the story to play out and still come up with a happily ever after.

"Well then, I guess—"

"But I would've done it anyway."

He is so stoic. We're well into "Love Story"—the drum really kicks in at this point and the beat resounds throughout the club, so it's more the fact he's closer, he looks somber, that makes it feel like the volume drops.

"Why would you do that?"

Without his mask—not the pink, bloodstained one hanging out of his pocket, but the nice-guy one he wore when we met—it isn't hard to imagine him fileting strangers for the better part of the night. Without the head tilt and reluctant smile and imploring eyes, he's . . . scary. Terrifying.

"Honestly?" I release a heavy sigh over the roses and the moment of faux contemplation draws him closer. "After everything that happened tonight, I just needed a distraction. And Wes, well . . ." I let the pause extend, let John fill in the blanks and watch as his shoulders rise before I say, "He delivered."

He shakes his head, disheartened, disappointed. I'm just like the five other women who didn't make the cut. Five beautiful, vibrant, innocent women who didn't love him back, so he had to take everything away from them. And that thought steels me, because they didn't deserve it—I don't deserve it. *None of us* deserve that.

"Everything I did, I did for you."

He takes another step forward. My hands tighten around the stems and the divots of the removed thorns press into my fingers.

"I would've been happy with just the roses."

I nick my thumb on something sharp, something cold, something unyielding among the dying stems, but I ignore it as he exhales a heavy breath and looks back up at me, determination cutting across the hurt.

Our love story isn't over yet.

"Say you're sorry."

I blink innocently up at him as he takes the penultimate step. Maybe this whole time he's really wanted the doe-eyed dream girl. I can give him that. Especially if it draws him closer. I just need him to take *one* more step toward me.

"For what?"

"For— For—what you did."

This isn't playing out like he planned, and it flusters him. The shards of light from the disco ball skim across his face, and I spot the color rising underneath his skin.

"What did I d—"

"You *fucked* him!"

His roar cuts right over the music. He's so angry, so disgusted with me that I can see his teeth. They're white, straight, a fantastic example of dental work, but he bares them like fangs. It makes sense why he only smiles with a closed mouth. I would've known he was a serial killer in the first five minutes of our date if he'd grinned at me. I'm glad I learned that about him before things got too serious between us.

I click my tongue, narrowing my eyes in thought when I say, "I think it's more accurate if we say *he* fucked *me*."

And as if on cue it starts raining.

It's like the perfect end to a rom-com, but instead of pattering around us it sprays out in random arcs across the room, and instead of thunder we've got a persistent out-of-time alarm bell that cuts into "Love Story" intermittently.

It's an instant reminder that while I've been down here, the others have been working at clearing the door to the roof. Many hands must make light work, but I can't be too happy about that because it means Wes might be on his way to us right now. There's no way John is going to gracefully bow out when he sees who stole the show from him.

"Jamie—" John's chest is heaving. Even as the cry of the alarm builds, you'd think he would notice, but he's too far in the love bubble. He's too deep in his own delusion.

"Jamie, you're *my* dream girl."

He really believes it. So much so he still wants to give me a chance. He still wants me to turn around and say I'm sorry, I love him, it *was* a mistake and he's the only one for me. So when I look up at him, release one of my hands from the bouquet, and grip his shoulder, he sees what he wants to see. He misinterprets my pity for regret, manages to twist his lips into one more soft, crooked smile, and takes a final step until we're standing chest to chest.

In the theater elective I took in my first year of college they had a name for this, when the actors are so close to each other the audience knows there are only two possible outcomes:

Kiss or kill.

"Oh, John . . . No." I shake my head slowly, tightening my hold on his shoulder, tightening my grip on the handle tucked between the stems. "No, I'm not."

I shove the roses into his chest, buds first, and his eyes go wide as the blade glides right up underneath his ribs. I've heard the telling wet thud many times tonight, but it's the first time I've been on the other side of it, and the action feels just as foreign as I thought. It's like nothing I've ever imagined, but when I pull the knife out and the crimson rose petals burst across his chest, it looks exactly like I pictured it.

We've got the wrong Taylor Swift song playing—we should be listening to "Red." Because when the rose petals fall away from his shirt and scatter on the floor around us, that's what spreads across his chest.

She's All That red, *Funny Face* red, Cher Horowitz reluctantly lying on the ground in Amy Heckerling's incomparable classic, *Clueless*, because "*This is an Alaïa!*" red.

The stems peel away from the knife as he staggers back and falls to the ground, but I just step over them. Because a good Leading Lady always goes after her man, and a good Final Girl knows that one hit, one shot, one *cut*, is never enough.

So among the wail of the alarm, the pounding of water, and Taylor singing about Romeo falling to his knees, I drop to mine, pull John into an embrace, and give him the ending he deserves.

# CHAPTER 39

"*You kill thousands of people and none of them really touch you. And then you murder one person and your life is changed . . . forever.*"

—Not *Love & Other Drugs*

Whatever playlist John chose must be set to shuffle.

As soon as the final strum of the mandolin fades out, and after a brief moment of silence—where all I can hear is the patter of water hitting the dance floor and thick, unnatural sounds coming from beneath me—a quicker, tighter pluck of an electric guitar sounds. And just like that it's the end of one era, and the start of another.

The knife is slick and warm in my hand, and I drop it into the growing puddle of diluted blood, peeling off a rose petal that's stuck on my forearm and letting it fall as I push to my feet.

I don't know how much time passes before John stops moving. All I know is that when he does the muscles in my right arm burn from exertion and I'm panting as I look down at him, lying still, and leaking on what is objectively, as Taylor points out over the speakers, the cold, hard ground.

330 · **SHAILEE THOMPSON**

Water is still pouring down around us, the music and fire alarm battling with each other. The disco ball keeps stubbornly spinning overhead, casting a reflective haze of silver and red across the space.

If this were a movie, it would fade to black at this point, or we'd cut to a scene months later where the characters have adapted to a new normal, but I'm not granted that luxury. When I step away from John's dead body, I still have to see him there in front of me. I have to feel the effects of what I've done in my body and see it on my hands. I know I did what I had to do. I know that whether it happened tonight or tomorrow or weeks later, I wouldn't have survived John's brand of love. And though I can't muster guilt just yet for what I've done, there isn't a stirring sense of triumph, either. Perhaps we've got the wrong soundtrack or the wrong lighting, but I can't help but think that this would look so much better in the movies.

The realization is interrupted by noises louder than the heavy bass drum that plays over the speakers. I'm still running on fight-or-flight mode and I've kind of used up all my fight on John. So when a crack—so loud I think it might be my own ribs breaking open from the panicked beat of my heart—rings out from the front of the club, I bolt over to a booth on the streetside wall and push myself up against the red curtains.

A mass of people barrel into the building, spreading and searching for the horror that has drawn them here. The most disturbing preview of what they'll find throughout the club is right there in the middle of the dance floor. John's body is the tip of a carnage triangle that spreads out over to the bar and trails into one of the booths. Maybe it's because I blend in with the velvet drapery, or because the sight of John and Billie and Colette has a stronger pull, but the police and paramedics run right past me, until the path to the door, the path to outside, is clear. Flashing red and blue lights seep into the entryway and hit the walls, a cold breeze filtering in with them, and after that initial rush of police and medics pushes through the club, splitting across the three levels, I just . . .

Walk out.

It's a completely anticlimactic exit, and the scene I step out to—the lights, the vehicles, the cordoned-off areas, the army of people scurrying between them, the reporters and cameras that are visible even though they stand on the edge of it all . . .

You'd think we were on a film set or something.

There are barricades up in the middle of the street, tents erected, emergency services everywhere. The consistent frenetic energy outside is such a stark contrast to the stop-start reactiveness I had to adapt to while inside the club that it all melds together into an overwhelming cacophony.

"Ma'am?"

The voice sounds muffled and echoey even though it comes from a navy-clad figure who appears at my shoulder when I step out of the entrance. I ignore him. First, because any sentence that starts with "Ma'am" is not one I want to hear, but mostly because I'm investing all my concentration into trying to make my feet move so I can walk out onto the sidewalk.

That's what this whole night has been about, right? Getting outside.

Even though it's still dark—I lost track of time hours ago, but it has to be early morning by now—this is my "dawn break" moment. This is the "walking out of the ashes" scene that forms the end of every slasher, and even after everything tonight, even though I want to leave, it's hard to take that final step.

There have been so many things to be scared of tonight, but every time I faced a fear, I survived. I may not have been the perfect Leading Lady, or the perfect Final Girl, but whatever I am is enough to make it out of this. Every choice I made led to me standing where I am.

Alive.

Yeah, there were some close calls. Yeah, I'm going to have some scars, but I'm still in control of this narrative. And that's why I will my stupid, sore feet to move.

"Ma'am, we're going to get somebody to check you over and then we need to ask you some questions."

A hand wraps around my arm before I can follow through with my plan. When another lands between my shoulder blades, pushing me forward, I start to panic. Distantly, I know the police officer is trying to guide me away from the building, but I've just had an affirming epiphany—I'm literally about to walk onto the street by myself, not to mention the last man who touched me killed more than two handfuls of people tonight. I jerk away from his grip, but that just makes his hold switch from guiding to restraining and I'm wishing I hadn't left that knife on the dance floor.

Then I hear it. A voice.

"Jamie?"

I freeze, planting my feet firmly against the cold cement as the officer tries again to pull me away from the club entrance. The familiarity of the voice drags my thoughts far away from stabbing a well-meaning member of New York's finest, and I search through the moving bodies and the bright lights to find the source of my name.

"Jamie! *Jamie!*"

I shove away from the hands that have become more insistent now that I'm fighting against them while the shrieks continue to sound out from the other side of a barricade. Her cries sound exactly as they did when she was going into that vent, but this time they're laced with hysterical relief. And when I spot her, when I see Laurie, it's exactly as I imagined. Right down to the silver foil blanket.

She pushes away from a paramedic and starts running toward me. Another cop appears at my other side and takes hold of my arm. I'm sure they're both just trying to lead me over to medical attention, but since they're stopping me from getting to Laurie, I struggle harder. Thrashing in their arms like I wanted to do when John kissed me on the mezzanine, I yell, "*Laurie!*"

It's only when another voice, this one feminine and assertive, commands, "Let her go before she hurts herself," that the grip around me loosens and I'm able to wrestle out of their hold and head straight for her.

"Laurie!" I cry out again. My feet are stinging from the cold and the grit of the road, but I can barely feel it, not when she darts around a police barricade, almost barreling over another paramedic as she sprints toward me. Her arm is outstretched—I assume to give me that handshake—but when she reaches me she doesn't shake my hand. She uses that outstretched, dirty palm to grab my shoulder and wrench me forward. My nose lands in the center of her chest, and for a second I wonder how we graduated from handshakes to motorboating in the space of a few traumatic hours. But then her arms wrap around me, her cheek drops, she presses her head hard to the side of mine, and I realize—she's hugging me.

She feels greasy and grimy, and she smells like shit, but she's *hugging* me. And it's hands down the best hug I have ever experienced in my life.

I manage to extract my head from her chest and look up at her, tears streaming down her face, her arms so tight around my shoulders that my wound has opened up *again*. Her black silk jumpsuit is shredded, her dark, previously straightened hair has returned to its natural wavy texture, her face is blotchy and tearstained.

And she's okay.

I wrap my arms around her slim waist, initially trying to keep the blood on my hands from touching the fabric before giving in and clenching my fingers into it, since neither of us are ever going to wear these outfits again. When my grip just makes her pull me closer, I direct a watery smile up at her.

"Hey, baby girl."

She lets out a laugh-cry-hiccup and it works. For someone who doesn't like rom-coms, she sure is a master at it.

"Hey, yourself."

"You've got something coming out of your eyes," I say, and she lifts a palm to wipe at the telltale signs of her human emotions.

"God, I must be due for my period or something."

She isn't. Our cycles synced up years ago and her—our—period isn't due for another two weeks. I indulge the lie, though.

"That must be it."

"I—" She stares down at me for a long moment, her eyes tracing over my face, and just when I think she's going to point out that my winged eyeliner is completely fucked, her breath comes out in a shudder.

"I am just so happy you're alive."

"I'm so happy you have a body like a bendy straw." Even though I'm 100 percent not joking, she lets out another laugh-cry-hiccup before her expression turns serious again.

"Jamie, I . . ." she says. "You could have—"

"I didn't." I shake my head, resting it on her shoulder. I'm getting the most out of this hug while I've got it.

"But I just—" She blows out a breath, and I know what's coming. I've been on the receiving end of a few declarations tonight—I think I can recognize the signs by now. But when I look up and she locks her eyes with mine, I know this might be the first time such a declaration brings me to tears, too.

"I just need you to know. If you don't already, that you—you and me, we're like—you're—"

She can't say it. I think the hug has really taken it out of her, but just like when we were in that bathroom, I know what she wants to say. I know how she feels because it's how I feel. I can even put it into words. She's—

"You're my favorite," she blurts out, and I can't stop the unquestionably ugly sob that tears out of me. The big, fat tears that fall. It's not like those big rom-com declarations. It is short, simple, straight to the point. But it's *so* Laurie, and that's what makes it perfect.

"Oh my god, that's such a relief," I groan, dropping my head into her shoulder again as she pulls me in tighter. "'Cause you're my favorite, too. Like, it really is a tragedy we're both straight."

A gust of amused air hits the top of my head and we both fall silent. Still. For the first time tonight, I feel calm. I feel genuinely safe. The kind of safe you feel when you're with someone you can be your completely authentic self with. The kind of safe you only get with your best friend.

"I love you, baby girl," I say, still not expecting to hear her say it back.

And when she responds with, "Yeah, I know . . . And for the record, next time I'm shoving *your* ass into the vent," it's the only answer I need.

"Ms. Prescott?"

I lift my gaze from the folding table that's been set up in one of the tents. A medic has been working on my injuries while I wait to be questioned and we've both been silent as she's patched up my feet and removed the bandage from my arm to properly treat and suture the wound. The police didn't let my reunion with Laurie last for too long. After another minute of hugging, where I could feel Laurie starting to get twitchy beneath my arms, a group of officers and medics broke us up. I was led into the entrance of a tent that now frames an older woman with short gray hair and a stern, thin-lipped expression.

"My name is Captain Strode," she says as she walks toward the empty chair on the other side of the table, and I recognize her voice. She's the one who told the officers to let me go so I could reach Laurie. And while my ability to trust has been beaten within an inch of its life tonight, the gesture does work in her favor. "I have a few questions for you."

"Police captains don't usually conduct interviews with witnesses."

It's out of my mouth before I can stop it. A fact I know from a Reddit trawl after a break from slashers and rom-coms led to a *Brooklyn Nine-Nine* marathon. It's probably not the most unbelievable part of the evening, but she doesn't get offended by the comment. The side of her mouth just twitches.

"No, we don't. But this is an exceptional case."

"Exceptional" really isn't the word I'd use, but to each their own.

"I need you to help me understand what happened tonight," she says as an officer strides through the tent and places a stack of folders in front of her. The corner of a photo slides out and the glimpse of blond hair and rose petals makes me avert my eyes. At least they've already started connecting the dots.

"We will be gathering other witness statements, and we will be pulling as much security footage as possible, but from what your friend Ms. Hamilton has already told us, I think we'll be able to have better insight based on what you have to say."

Right. This is the part of the movie that always cuts to the credits. The audience doesn't want to sit around for the fallout once they know the Final Girl escaped. They don't want to see how the Leading Lady and her man get on with their day after they've kissed, and the camera has pulled back to focus on the city skyline.

"I'll tell you as much as I can," I say, wincing as the medic finishes off the stitch and the pull of the thread isn't fully dulled by the anesthetic. When she replaces my silver blanket over my shoulders and exits the tent, I launch into the key plot points that underscore what happened in the club, leading with the spoilers: I stabbed John. I did it because he was one of two killers with an astoundingly misplaced motive. When I point to the folders and say, "John all but admitted that he was responsible for those murders, and earlier in the night Wes and I thought—" Captain Strode's dark gray eyes flick up from the folders to meet mine.

"Detective Carpenter?"

It's kind of weird to hear the title, but I'm quick to move on from it when I realize I haven't seen him yet. I haven't seen him since I left him in that room with the other survivors. I assumed everything went well on his end, but who's to say he was actually successful? Who's to say there wasn't a *third* killer waiting in the wings? Some kind of murderous triad . . . My *god*.

The panic in my voice grates against my ears when I ask, "Do you know if he— Is he—"

There's yelling outside. An angry, desperate voice melds with quieter, pacifying ones before a gravelly statement cuts through the racket.

"Where is she?"

The agitated rasp draws my eyes away from the captain and I look outside just in time to see Wes stride into view. His profile is visible through the opening of the tent, soaked and chest heaving like a Regency-era love interest, like the whole reason he wore that shirt tonight was so it would look as good as it does ripped and wet and stained with blood.

"Jamie!" he bellows, and I don't think this is the first time he's yelled it.

Captain Strode winces at the sound, her tone irritated when she yells back, "She's in here, Carpenter."

He freezes, turns, and spots the captain, but it isn't until he looks beyond her and our eyes meet that he walks over, shrugging off the two officers determined to stay by his side. When he's inside the tent he takes in the whole scene, dark eyes darting between the two of us before they land back on Captain Strode, and the look of recognition, the immediate change in his posture, the way she knew his name . . .

I don't think she's just a captain, I think she's *his*—

"Captain," he says faintly, attempting to straighten even more. All he achieves is a pained grunt for his efforts.

"Detective," she says coolly, one eyebrow arched in exasperation. "While you're Marlon Brandoing out there"—Ooh, I think I like her—"I'm trying to get to the bottom of the shit show that happened tonight so I can figure out a way to get both of you out of an even bigger shit show. Maybe even get you back to work sooner so you can return to your favorite pastime of annoying the crap out of me." Her other eyebrow joins the raised one as she adds, "So, can you shut the hell up?"

The directive makes his head dip and . . . yeah, I might love this woman, actually.

"Yes, ma'am. I'm sorry. I just—"

"What?"

He swallows. His eyes shift away from hers and lock with mine, and I have to fight the urge to shove my chair back and throw myself into his arms. It looks like it's taking all of his effort not to do the same thing when he swallows again—I swear I can see him counting down from three in his head—and then says evenly, "I had to know she was okay."

"Why's that, Carpenter?"

"Because . . ."

He doesn't finish, just gestures at me like that's answer enough, and stares at me with that look. I think if I could step outside of myself and watch the scene, I'd be able to see a mirror image of it on my own face. The "you had me at hello," "I wrote you 365 letters," "I wanted it to be you" look.

I drop my gaze to take all of him in. This is the first time I've seen him away from the club. Away from the red lighting or heavy fluorescents or the darkness of the hallways, and without all that . . .

He's still Wes.

"Huh . . ." Captain Strode says, and when I hazard a glance at her, I see the puzzled realization cross her face. "Oh . . . well, that's . . . interesting. Certainly explains the performance outside."

"Ma'am, I—"

She cuts him off. "Ms. Prescott, would you like some coffee?" she says, pushing up from the table and taking the folders with her. "You're gonna need it and so am I. Even though he's on leave, I'm sure Detective Carpenter here can hold things down while I'm gone for five minutes. With two officers stationed outside and listening in, of course." She turns her attention back to Wes. "Then I want you to go see a medic and stop bleeding all over my tent."

He ducks his head again, but I catch the quirk of his lips as this five-foot-five woman manages to look down her nose at a man who towers over her.

"Yes, ma'am, I will, thank you."

"And while your instincts have proven to be impeccable, Carpenter, your ability to get into hot water leaves a lot to be desired . . . something we'll need to fix when you return to work."

She goes to move past him but pauses. Even though her voice is low, I still catch her say, "When I saw your name on that door list . . ." She reaches up, placing her palm on his shoulder. "You had me scared for a second there. I'm glad you're okay, Wes."

He offers her a thin smile, then after squeezing his shoulder, she walks out of the tent. As soon as she's gone, he closes the distance between us, one hand holding his ribs as he walks. I think maybe we should delay our reunion so he can go see a paramedic, but then he slides his palms underneath my jaw as I rise from the chair, and I could cry because there was always a chance I wouldn't get to feel it again. His hands on me, the heat of his body close to mine, the "you complete me" look in his eyes. Timing is everything when it comes to slashers and rom-coms, and if he'd been quicker unblocking the roof access and coming down to the dance floor, if John saw him before I—

This all could've ended so differently.

He doesn't kiss me, he just stares down at me like he's thinking the same thing, like he is well aware of the alternate ending. His thumbs trail across my cheekbones, his pulse beating strongly against my fingertips when I curl my hands around his wrists, and for a moment, I'm unsure of how we pick up from where we left off. Where we left off was with me on the way to meet a killer.

"Did you get them out?" I ask, going with the safest opener, and when he nods before pressing his forehead to mine, I really have to will the tears away. At this point I should be all cried out, but there seems to be a bottomless supply when it comes to surviving a slasher.

"They're okay. They're all okay."

Him being here confirms it, but hearing the words still prompts a relieved sigh from deep in my chest.

"Is Laurie okay?" he asks.

My heart melts at the concern in his voice for my friend. For my girl.

"Yeah, she is. They're talking to her now."

He pulls back, his expression serious as he pushes my hair from my face and trails his palms back down to cradle my jaw.

"There's gonna be a lot of that. It's gonna be a long road from here, Jamie. They're going to question all of us over and over again. Make us recount everything that happened. It doesn't get tied up neatly like in the movies, you know?"

I'm getting an idea. In a perfect world I'd wash away the remnants of this evening and come back stronger, wiser, and maybe a little more jaded but still intact. But he's right—it's not like the movies. There are consequences and repercussions and widespread aftermath to what happened tonight.

"I heard you—they told me . . ." His voice is quiet, soft, and he doesn't need to continue for me to know what they told him. I was very forthcoming with what exactly a Final Girl does at the end of the movie. But theory and reality are two different things, and maybe this—what I did to John—is the turnoff of all turnoffs. Maybe this is the thing that stops us before we even had a chance to start. But before I can say anything, Wes beats me to it.

"So, you know how you said you weren't looking for anything long term?" he asks, tilting my chin up so I can see the reassuring look in his eyes that puts any uncertainty at ease.

Wes is made of stronger stuff than that.

So am I, it turns out.

"Yeah?"

"That's a real deal-breaker for me, Jamie Prescott."

I nod, moving my hands down to grip the remains of his shirt—mindful of his ribs—to pull him closer.

"Well, *Detective Carpenter* . . ." He closes his eyes when I murmur it, shaking his head and whispering a little "*fuck*" that would make me smile if I wasn't tired and torn up inside. I wait until his eyes open again to say, "I'm willing to make an exception when it comes to the long-term thing."

"Yeah?"

"Yeah. Not to spoil the ending . . ."

I have the opportunity to chicken out here. I have the chance to downplay this thing between us, to keep my expectations low so I don't get disappointed. But of all the risks I've taken tonight, I know—

without having to refer to some movie scene for comparison—this one will pay off.

"... but I think I'm gonna fall in love with you, too."

If this was a rom-com, he would laugh, but everything is too real and too raw right now. Instead, he breathes in through his nose and exhales sharply, his hands tightening on my jaw before he pulls my mouth firmly onto his and kisses me like his life depends on it.

EPILOGUE

"Whatever you do . . . don't fall in love."

—Not *A Nightmare on Elm Street*

EIGHT MONTHS LATER

here's movement outside of the bathroom. Not like someone is creeping around or trying to hide themselves, but normal apartment sounds. A door shutting. Keys hitting a counter. Shoes tumbling onto the floor. That still doesn't stop me from freezing under the showerhead and listening more intently to the noises. If someone is stupid enough to break into my apartment, I feel positive, confident, in my ability to handle it.

Don't they know who I am?

The footfalls sound closer to the bathroom door, and though I figure it's most likely just Laurie coming back for something she forgot, I don't return to washing my hair just yet. Our new apartment is like Fort Knox, and you'd have to be crazy to try and break in. We moved after what happened and our new place is bigger, more secure, easier to escape if you know how. Not that that's a necessity for us. We were in more danger in a public place than we ever were in our shitty little apartment with its paper-thin walls and laughable water pressure. Not like our new shower, which pelts down consistently warm torrents of water as I listen for movement outside of the door.

I'm not going to call out "Hello?"

I'm still not a fucking idiot.

In the last eight months I've gone to *a lot* of therapy, determined to make the most of the life I walked away with after that night. My therapist is very proud of me, and really, that's the whole point of therapy, isn't it? To pay a stranger hundreds of dollars so they can show you how to deal with your demons and then tell you you're doing a good job at it. And after all the sessions and exercises and strategies and support people, I feel okay. It helps to avoid any of the more misogynistic, blamey-sounding news articles and reels about what happened, too. No, "John"—not his real name as it turns out—didn't need the love of a good woman to stop him from doing what he did. He needed to be under the care of a good medical professional.

It's the knocks that bring my shoulders back down from around my ears. Our agreed-upon code is the melody of the "fa fa fa fa" part of the Talking Heads song "Psycho Killer." The door opens, and instead of a polite greeting, there are more footsteps and then the shower curtain wrenches open *Psycho* style.

I blink. He blinks. And then Wes steps into the shower, giving me a quicker version of the once-over he knows makes me lose joint control before he grasps my chin, his mouth covering mine as he pushes me back under the spray.

He's obsessed with me.

Not "murdering ten people" kind of obsessed. More like "walking into the shower fully clothed to make out with me" obsessed.

Which is pretty fortunate, since I'm obsessed with him, too.

And that's why I wrap my arms around his neck and kiss him back. I kiss him until the material of his shirt gets slick and heavy under my hands. When I lean back, cast my eyes down his face and watch the way the water trails over his cheeks and his lips, I smile. Because even after the fallout, even though real life doesn't get tied up neatly like a ninety-minute feature film, there are still some perks to being on the other side of that night, and one of them is seeing him relaxed and happy and not covered in blood.

"Welcome back."

He's been away for a week, conducting training at some precincts in Chicago. Quite possibly the longest amount of time we've been apart since we walked out of the club, covered in blood and sweat and grime and that *stupid* fucking glitter.

"It's good to be home." He grins, taking a step back and starting to peel his clothes off. Something he should've done outside of the shower.

"I thought I was picking you up this afternoon."

"I got an earlier flight." His voice is muffled beneath the soaked fabric of his shirt as he pulls it over his head. "Where's my sister wife?"

I grin. Wes moved in with us when we left our tiny Bed-Stuy apartment a few months ago. It might seem like a big step to take so early in the relationship, but I feel like once you've lived through a massacre with a person, you're allowed to jump a milestone or two. He has slid into our lives so easily, effortlessly, that depending on the day, I both love and hate that I get ganged up on by my two favorite people every time I come home.

"Laurie's on location," I say, and reach for my conditioner.

She began development on the documentary a month ago. It'll be a while before they actually get into production, but it's her way of healing. Going back to the scene where it happened, recording and documenting every event and eyewitness statement.

She asked if I wanted to go back sometime and I refused.

I know every level, every corner, every hiding spot of that club, and I don't think seeing it in the light of day is going to give me any kind of closure. I don't think knowing exactly how John and Billie were able to cancel the cleaners and get into the club that morning to set up the entire space like they were preparing for a surprise party instead of a massacre is going to make me feel better about surviving their efforts. Knowing that they killed the security guy and left him in the alley before checking in, or that John was able to murder the two bartenders and still manage to fashion a look of fear onto his face when the lights came back on, hasn't achieved anything other than unhelpful replays of a night that I can't change. My therapist agrees. You don't go back. You don't go back to the shitty, bland ex. You don't run back up the stairs if the killer is in the house.

I don't judge Laurie for wanting to find order in something so senseless. Her story played out differently than mine that night. While I had a front-row seat to the action—high-definition images, surround sound—she had darkness and dead ends and the debilitating unknown.

So if she has to go back to find a way forward, then I'll support her every step of the way, but I know what happened and the roles I had to play. I know when the years pass and interest dies down and other, more gruesome events play out and take the spotlight away from what John and Billie did, I'll need things other than what happened that cold Tuesday night in November to define my identity.

And that's why I won't go back.

When Wes is more appropriately undressed for the shower, he reaches up to grab the body wash, his hand hovering dangerously close to my nice, expensive bottle until I smack at it, and he settles for his three-in-one instead. I pause in rinsing the conditioner out of my hair to watch him soap himself up. It's . . . compelling. The best thing I've seen all week.

"Have you got a class today?"

Funny how fast you can finish a dissertation when you need a distraction from the outside world. Also funny how you become more employable after a highly publicized bloodbath. It's not genre theory just yet, though. Somebody is going to have to die for me to teach that. But I'm now teaching, in a college, and getting paid for it. Introduction to Film Studies. While it's a smaller class for the summer semester, it's my trial run for the larger lectures in the fall. I've come to terms with the fact that while some people come to my class because of my newfound notoriety, at least they stay because I'm actually good at my job.

"No class today. It's my day off." I go back to rinsing my hair because there is no way that slow, extended glide of his palm across his abs is *not* on purpose. When I glance up, the amused glint in his eye says it all. *Eye fucker.*

"Awesome. Are we finally going to do this *Poltergeist/Ghost* double feature you're always talking about?" He grabs my hips and shifts us around to rinse himself off, but when he doesn't let go, I take that as an invitation to move in and lap the water that pools in his clavicle. I dig my index finger into the tip of his tattoo and trace the abstract tangled vines and spiked leaves back over his shoulder, down his back, around his ribs, until I hit the untouched pane of skin over his heart. He threatens to extend the tattoo and add my face there every time I try to convince him to finish watching *The Conjuring*—poor guy couldn't make it past the clapping scene—but thankfully the space is still bare. Reversing the direction of my finger, I work around the detail of the ink by memory. I'm very familiar with it now.

I'm very familiar with all of him. I've traded minutes of surface information for months of getting to know him and what he's like outside of a terrible traumatic situation, and I was right. If things had been different that night, I think we still would've made it here. Together.

His head tilts down from the spray, his lips pressing against my forehead before he lays his cheek against my temple and slides his hands around to smooth across the small of my back . . . It's all so very nice.

"I'm movied out for the week." I say, and he stills, his back stiffens.

"Who are you and what are you doing in my shower? I mean, you're gorgeous, you look great naked, but—" He pushes me away, still holding my hips when he growls, "You are *not* my girlfriend. Get off me."

Despite his words, he pulls me straight back into his chest and I'm laughing into his mouth. When I'm able to stop, when I realize I haven't had him in my space for the last week, that months ago there was always a chance he wouldn't have made it out, the hook in my chest, the one that feels permanent now, pulls. The scar across his chest is just below my eye level and I graze my fingers over the pink line cutting across the hair and tanned skin.

"I missed you," I say.

He dips his forehead down to press against mine, and our noses touch as he murmurs into the minimal space between our lips. "I missed you, too."

His hands lift to grip my jaw, and when I look up into his eyes, he nods once, brings me back to the present. We're here, now, planning out our day because there's no danger and no threat, the credits already rolled on that part of our lives, and we've decided not to stay behind in the theater afterward.

"Maybe we just stay in here for a while," I say. He kisses around the words my mouth makes, and it takes all my concentration not to lose my train of thought. "And then let some cool barista butcher your name on your coffee order."

"Sounds good to me."

I have the feeling I could've suggested watching paint dry or streaming the latest documentary about Nepalese goatherds Laurie wants us to watch with her new boyfriend—he wants to be the next Edgar Wright, of all things, so we get on great—and he would've said the same thing.

"Hey, Wes?"

Other things are starting to draw his attention. Like my breasts, my belly button, my . . . *Mmm*. I pull his hands up to my waist, but it must be the water that makes them slip down again.

"Mm-hmm?" he says distractedly, winding an arm around my back and drawing me under the showerhead.

I lean back to ask, "What makes you happy?"

He hits me with that smile. The one that, whether in the middle of a murder scene or the middle of my shower, still makes it feel like the blood in my veins is running hot.

"I would've thought that's kind of obvious, Jamie."

He knows what I'm doing. It's a thing we do. We do things other than run from psychotic killers now. Things like farmer's markets, and driving each other to the airport, and shared showers, and asking questions I already know the answer to because he tells me all the time.

His lips come down onto mine when he asks, "What makes you happy?"

He already knows the answer because it just so happens, *I* tell him all the time. We have a lot in common. And I've heard that's a very strong foundation for a successful relationship. That and surviving a killing spree. That's a pretty solid foundation, too.

"I would've thought that was obvious, too," I say, biting my lip to stop smiling. When he lifts a hand from my waist to hold up three fingers in front of my face, it pulls my mouth into a full-blown grin.

It's disgusting how in love I am with this man.

And to think I once thought—in my defense, for like two minutes, tops—he could've orchestrated a slaughter fest that gave me a whole new appreciation for cardio training.

He folds one finger down.

Three.

His arm tightens around my waist, so we're belly to belly.

Two.

My arms loop around his neck and we're chest to chest. There are only two possible outcomes in a position like this, but when it comes to Wes only one comes to mind.

One.

His eyes close just before mine, but his smile is a perfect match for where my lips are curved up against his.

"You."

"You."

After that we stop talking for a while. Our dialogue replaced by a soundtrack of water echoing off tiles, breaths hitching, and the indulgent sounds of two people who've had the opportunity to learn each other's preferences and the luxury to play them out because there isn't a killer on the other side of the locked door.

And that's good. It's the promise of the good, that there are still good things to be had, that helps heal the scars that lie deeper than the ones tracing across our skin.

Sometimes it's not all shower sex and sharing breakfast and holding hands while you wait for your coffee order ("Wentz?") to get called out. Sometimes I do find myself dragged back into the darkness, the survivor's guilt, the trauma, the anguish, the fear. It happens to Wes. Laurie, too. But most of the time we're able to pull ourselves out, and if we have a hard time doing that, just like that night, we take it in turns to help each other, support each other, remind each other we survived. And not by chance or destiny or fate—despite what John may have wanted to believe—but because of the choices we made. Even when you know the formula, you still have to decide how the story is going to play out. You have to decide how you want the movie to end. You have to decide what role you're going to take in it. Because Final Girls and Leading Ladies aren't born. They're made. They're a culmination of their choices.

And in the end I chose to be both.

ACKNOWLEDGMENTS

My first thank-you will always go to my number one fan and perpetual "first eyes" on all my work, Ryanna. It's no exaggeration when I say you are the reason why this, and any story I write, has made it into the world. Your encouragement, support, and real-time commentary gives me life. Not to mention you gifted me the legendary phrase "dusty-ass piece of coal" in its original context. Thanks for grinning and bearing through all the parts of this book that made you squeamish (the romantic parts).

Thank you to my former work wife and the woman who ignited my passion for horror movies. It was a real gamble watching *Creep* to start off our friendship, Melody, but *good god* did it pay off. There'd be no Jamie and Laurie without you and me. Love you (even if I'm the one who initiates most of the hugs).

Thank you to my incredible agent, Hana El Niwairi, for taking a chance on my voice and believing in my ideas no matter how unhinged. In hindsight, pitching a slasher rom-com at eight a.m. on a Tuesday morning from the other side of the world was quite a bold move on my part, but you saw the vision immediately and have championed it ever since. I'm gonna keep writing these weird female main characters for you (though they might be the only kind I can write).

The incredible Anthea Bariamis, Molly Gregory, Molly Crawford, Rosie Outred, Matt Attanasio, Faren Bachelis, Christine Masters, and everyone at Simon & Schuster, Atria Books Australia, Gallery Books, and Simon & Schuster UK who had a hand in bringing this book to life—this very well could have been B-grade schlock if not for you all. Thank you for poking at the plot holes, affirming all the Easter eggs, and loving these characters as much as I do. Thank you to Tonia Composto for the incredible map. My initial sketches probably would've been more helpful if they'd been drawn on a bloody napkin, but you've brought the insanity of Serendipity to life.

You don't write a book with a friendship like Jamie and Laurie's without some real-life inspo, so here's a quick roll call of some incredible women who have been invested in this book since its infancy: Gemma, I'll never be able to articulate how much you keep me sane and seen. Your belief and support make me feel like I could go up against any and all Big Bads. Jenna, my OG roommate and the first person I told all of my story ideas to (even if they put you to sleep when we were teenagers). You're my good luck charm, and your emotional investment in my fictional people knows no bounds. Rachelle, another one of the early eyes on this work and a champion of . . . literally anything I say I want to do. Not to go all Josh Groban on you, but you raise me up, and I can't love you enough for it.

Thank you to Queensland Writers Centre. A very, very (like *very*) early sample of chapter 1 was read aloud anonymously at GenreCon in 2024, and the opportunity and response was the kick in the ass I needed to get this story out into the world. Not to mention all of your incredible programs and opportunities for emerging writers.

To my friends and family. I'm so lucky to say there are *a lot* of you, and you've all supported me in numerous ways. I can't thank you enough.

And finally, to you. Yes, you. Reading the acknowledgments, huh? You probably stay back at the theater to watch all the credits, too, dontcha? You curious little cretin. Anyway, I probably shouldn't have called you a cretin in what is likely our first interaction, but I want to thank you for taking a chance on this book—for taking a chance on me. While it may be incredibly bloody, this story was written out of so much love. That's not to say it was easy, but these pages are full of many things that bring me joy: films, female friendships, eye fucking, Bill Pullman. As well as a few things that I don't love so much and wanted to take a literary machete to. I hope you enjoyed Jamie's story, and I hope you come back for more.

ABOUT THE AUTHOR

SHAILEE THOMPSON is a writer and educator based in Brisbane, Australia. She's always had a penchant for women with smart mouths, soft hearts, and strong wills going up against extraordinary odds. *How to Kill a Guy in Ten Dates* is her debut novel. Find her on Instagram @ShaileeWrites.